Praise for So

'Instantly gripping, this n̶o̶
from first to last … I s̶i̶m̶p̶l̶y̶ ̶c̶o̶u̶l̶d̶ ̶n̶o̶t̶ ̶s̶t̶o̶p̶
reading. Exceptional storytelling, full of heart,
wisdom and passion. Unmissable'
Antonia Hodgson

'A wondrous, captivating novel … with depth, beguiling
characters, and an enthralling, racing story,
A Map of the Damage is a triumph'
Kate Mayfield

'*A Map of the Damage* is a gripping mystery with
a passionate Victorian love story at its centre …
Sophia Tobin's masterful storytelling kept me hooked
throughout, and her vibrant characters and beautifully
rendered historical settings made this a real
pleasure to read'
Sophie Hardach

'Sophia Tobin uses her beguiling creation, the
Mirrormakers' Club … to unite a vivid cast of
characters from two eras. All are engaged in trying to
solve a mystery that – with wonderful ingenuity on the
part of the author – will finally be fully
revealed only to the reader'
Miranda France

Sophia Tobin was raised in Kent. She has studied History and History of Art, and worked for a Bond Street antique dealer for six years, specializing in silver and jewellery. She currently works in a library and archive. Inspired by her research into a real eighteenth-century silversmith, Tobin began to write *The Silversmith's Wife*, which was shortlisted for the Lucy Cavendish College Fiction Prize. It was published by Simon & Schuster in 2014. Her second novel, *The Widow's Confession*, was published in 2015, and her third, *The Vanishing*, in 2017.

By the same author:

The Silversmith's Wife
The Widow's Confession
The Vanishing

A
Map
of the
Damage

Sophia
Tobin

**SIMON &
SCHUSTER**

London · New York · Sydney · Toronto · New Delhi

A CBS COMPANY

First published in Great Britain by Simon & Schuster UK Ltd, 2019
A CBS COMPANY

This paperback edition published 2020

1 3 5 7 9 10 8 6 4 2

Simon & Schuster UK Ltd
1st Floor
222 Gray's Inn Road
London WC1X 8HB

Simon & Schuster Australia, Sydney
Simon & Schuster India, New Delhi

www.simonandschuster.co.uk
www.simonandschuster.com.au
www.simonandschuster.co.in

A CIP catalogue record for this book
is available from the British Library

Paperback ISBN: 978-1-4711-5166-8
eBook ISBN: 978-1-4711-5167-5
Audio ISBN: 978-1-4711-9413-9

Typeset in the UK by M Rules
Printed and bound in Great Britain by CPI Group (UK) Ltd, Croydon, CR0 4YY

MIX
Paper from
responsible sources
FSC® C020471

To Miss Kilmartin and Dr Hume

CHAPTER ONE

1940

Her destination was the Mirrormakers' Club, but she did not know it. Her feet guided her through the two-hour walk to the City of London, that maze of streets which sat behind ancient walls in the heart of the wider city. She walked through the autumn leaves that were gathering in the gutters, a chill deeply bedded into her bones, feeling pushed by some superior force like a chess piece. 'I have somewhere I must be,' she had told the rescue party. And then she had walked away. From their questions, from their care, and from the ruins.

At the sight of it, she felt a thrill of recognition: a hit, like a shot of whisky entering the blood. The Club looked like a small palace, faced with pale Portland stone, classically symmetrical, with six columns demarcating its central section, unadorned wings on either side, and carved trophies above the five tall windows on the piano nobile. Seeing out its first century, it could not have been accused of lacking grandeur. But now, its windows were blacked out, a single pane broken in a first-storey sash window, third from the left. She stood there, in a shaft of autumn sunlight that transformed the pavement from grey to gold, and glanced at her wristwatch. The glass over the dial was cracked, the hands frozen at half past six.

She walked up the front steps to the wooden doors which were twice her height, and pressed her fingertip against the ivory button of the doorbell for a long moment. Its aggressive trill made her flinch.

She waited, the wind stirring up dust and leaves on the narrow street behind her, and raising a single sheet of newspaper. The air felt thick with ash blown in on the autumn breeze, the scent of the newly bombed city.

She heard no approaching footsteps, so when the door was opened she jumped: a stocky middle-aged woman stood there, dressed in a pinafore over a mauve day dress, her hair tied up in a scarf. She had bright blue eyes, the same blue as the sky above them. She frowned.

'Hello?' she said. 'You weren't meant to be working today. You said you had something to do.'

The girl stirred with surprise. 'I'm so sorry,' she said. 'The thing is, I don't seem to be able to remember my name.'

The woman led her visitor through the panelled Entrance Hall, up the York stone steps and into the great Stair Hall, onwards to a small green door leading to the basement. When she reached the door, she realized the girl was not behind her. She turned, to see her looking around the space, as though she had never seen it before. Her face was tipped up to the light, and she turned a full circle to take in the walls clad in coloured marble, the columns topped by carvings of City of London dragons, the gilded chequerboard dome high above them in the great quiet space.

'It's so beautiful,' she said.

'Come on, now,' the woman said, gruffly but kindly. With a sudden instinct, she went back, and took the girl's hand, as though she were a child. She had never touched her before. The girl did not resist: her hand closed tightly around the other woman's.

'I'm Peggy,' the woman said. 'You knew me as Mrs Holliday.' But she saw no recognition in her colleague's face.

In the basement kitchen, Peggy made tea, and dropped a saccharin tablet into the girl's cup. 'A strong, sweet cup of tea will put things right,' she said. She watched as the girl took off her gloves, opened her handbag, and rooted through, producing a buff-coloured ration book. She opened it and read the contents. 'My name is Olivia Baker,' she said. It was a question as much as a statement.

'That's right.'

'Will you call me Livy, though?' said Olivia Baker. 'I would – prefer it. I have no memory of a surname or prefix but – I do remember Livy.'

The woman cleared her throat. 'Well – yes, if you wish.

SOPHIA TOBIN

I am used to calling you Miss Baker – but I can get used to it. I'm the housekeeper here. Do you know where we are?'

Another firm shake of the head.

'The Mirrormakers' Club in the City of London. It's a private members' club. You work here. You were a secretary here before the war, briefly. And now – well, there's a handful of us here.' She said the names carefully, slowly. 'Me; my husband, Bill; Miss Hardaker; the fire parties. You help Miss Hardaker with filing and correspondence. The other staff have been evacuated. It's just us in this grand old place. Quite something to have it to ourselves. It seems to have a life of its own, noises and all kinds of things.' She hazarded a smile before something else dawned on her worried face. 'You do remember there's a war?'

'Yes.' Livy blinked, eyes glassy. A strange film of calm lay over her face; it made Peggy feel rather cold. Without asking, she added another saccharin tablet to the tea, and stirred it vigorously before Livy could raise the cup to her lips. 'It's shock, that's all. Everything will come back to you. You said there was a bomb?'

'Yes.'

'What do you remember?'

Livy swallowed and considered what to say.

> I remember a concertinaed stack of
>   rubble and wood,
> and a fragment of red satin, fluttering,
> which looked like the belt of a dressing gown.

4

'I don't remember much. Only the last few hours,' she said. 'They asked my name. The rescue party. I was standing in front of a house that had been destroyed. My house, I think. They kept asking me my name. But I just said I had to get somewhere. I knew I had to start walking, somehow.'

'They didn't try to take you to hospital?'

'No. The doctor wanted to look me over. I said no.'

'Well,' said Peggy. She had run out of words.

'What on earth is going on?' said Miss Hardaker in an unforgiving tone. She had happened upon Peggy and her husband, Bill, standing over the sleeping Livy. Livy had closed her eyes immediately after her last mouthful of tea, lulled by the sudden warmth.

Peggy explained as best she could, but the others were incredulous. Sympathy would not be expended today. It took a certain amount of energy which could not be spared; it was an unnatural thing for both of them. Unlike Peggy, who felt sympathy as easily as she breathed. 'One does hear of such things,' said Miss Hardaker. 'But she always seemed so sensible.'

'I'm not sure that has anything to do with it,' said Peggy. 'I wish I knew who her folks are. At least I could telephone someone.'

'I always thought she was too high and mighty for her own good,' announced Bill.

'She might wake and remember everything this very moment,' said Miss Hardaker testily. And she put down the armful of papers she had been carrying, and clapped her hands.

Livy started awake, and stared at them all. Gently, Peggy began to introduce everyone.

'There's work to be done,' interrupted Miss Hardaker. Sleepily, Livy looked at her. This woman knew her place in the world. She, at this moment, did not.

'What would you like me to do?' she said.

'Can you remember how to type?' said Miss Hardaker.

'I think so.'

'Thank heavens,' said Miss Hardaker, with a sideways glance at Peggy and Bill which indicated that she did not believe in this memory loss thing at all.

Livy followed the woman up the basement stairs, out of the green door, and came face to face with a Victorian portrait which she had somehow missed on her journey down.

'Who is this?' she said.

'Look at the plate.'

Livy did. It was inscribed *Woman and Looking Glass*. The woman's white shoulders and neck were exposed by the cut of her black velvet dress. Behind her, on a shelf, there was the looking glass of the title; and over her other shoulder, a window, with distant hills and trees, lit by the same soft light that glanced off the glossy dark ringlets which cascaded down each side of her face. The woman was rich, it was clear: although her shoulders and neck were left unadorned, there was a large diamond pinned to her bodice, blazing against the black of her dress.

'Are you looking at the stone?' said Miss Hardaker as Livy stood, barely an inch from the painting. 'So vulgar. Don't you remember it?'

'No.'

'You should. You saw it every day.'

The woman in the portrait stood in part defence, part openness. One arm crossed over the waist, the hand hidden beneath the opposing arm; the right hand resting on the back of a chair, casual but a little forced, as though someone had moved her into that position. It was her face: heavy-lidded eyes, with a tinge of amusement, and of challenge, which was so intriguing. The steady, unrelenting gaze, the beginnings of a smile, but slight, as though she were waiting for someone to speak. Before Livy's eyes, it seemed to scintillate. Her focus flicked between the face and the diamond. It was as though the painter had caught something of the lady's soul, and frozen the viewer in eternal battle between her eyes and the jewel.

She reached out to touch it.

'Miss Baker!'

Livy turned. And whatever Miss Hardaker saw in her face, it made the stern woman take a step back.

After an afternoon of typing, Livy slept and slept as the others listened to the wireless. When the siren went, it was Peggy who gently woke Livy, and led her into the bomb shelter section of the vault, and Miss Hardaker who finally shut the metal-clad doors as Bill went up to the roof.

'Sleepy-head,' said Peggy with a smile, as Livy yawned.

'I suppose you did work relatively hard,' said Miss Hardaker, but in a tone that indicated it was a reprimand rather than a compliment.

'I hope I'm useful,' said Livy. 'My head feels as though it is stuffed full of cotton wool.'

'If you're fishing for a compliment, Miss Baker, none will be forthcoming,' said Miss Hardaker. She was rifling through a small knitted bag she had brought into the shelter. After a moment she turned, and came towards Livy, a small stack of clothes in her arms. 'I have a friend in the WVS,' she said. 'She runs a clothes centre on Milk Street. When you had your tea break this afternoon, I went to see her.'

Livy unfolded a grey skirt and grey jumper, several slips, some underwear, a pair of slacks, a blouse and a bright fuchsia day dress. The colour was so bright it made her eyes sting.

'You'll need *something* to wear,' said Miss Hardaker. 'And I thought that little dress rather glamorous. Just in case you get any exciting invitations at some point.' She gazed at her own hands, as though they were of sudden interest.

The kindness of the gesture overwhelmed Livy. She stared at the two women, as Peggy calmly unpacked her knitting, and Miss Hardaker inspected her nails. 'I don't know what to say,' Livy said.

'Then say nothing at all,' said Miss Hardaker brightly.

'Thank you,' said Livy, and she placed her warm hand over Miss Hardaker's cool one.

Miss Hardaker stifled a smile. 'Who needs diamonds when there are such beautiful colours in the world?' she said. 'You will put the black-clad woman in that portrait to shame.' She gave a little sigh. 'That's enough for now. I would like to disappear into my book.'

But she had no chance. Bill came and said they were short of watchers on the roof, and Miss Hardaker got to her feet readily, and said it would be good for Livy to come with her.

'Surely not,' said Peggy, putting her needles down. 'Look at her.'

'I'm happy to go,' said Livy, in an expressionless voice. 'Really.'

'Very good, Miss Baker,' said Miss Hardaker.

'Why is it called *Woman and Looking Glass*?' said Livy, as they trudged up the stairs, more stairs, and emerged onto the roof. 'Surely she should be described as a lady, at that time?'

'Still worrying at it?' said Miss Hardaker archly. 'One of the members is a relative of the person. A Mr Whitewood.' She paused at the name, and an expression flickered across her face which Livy couldn't quite identify. 'I could write and ask, if you wished me to. Now, watch.'

Livy was still possessed by that deep tiredness which stifled any fear in its wadding, but she listened carefully as Miss Hardaker explained how to use the sand and shovel to put out incendiaries, a dustbin lid in one of her white, red-tipped hands. She carried it as Livy imagined an ancient warrior would have done a shield: aggressively, as much a symbol of courage as an implement of protection.

Afterwards they stood in the shelter of the dome's rafters, the dull drone of planes high above them. So possessed was she with dwelling on her questions about the painting, Livy hardly noticed when Miss Hardaker went out across the roof.

'There's one here. Miss Baker. Come quickly!'

Livy was too slow. She picked up the bucket of sand, but stumbled over the raised step to the dome and fell hard. Embarrassed, she scrambled up.

'Come *on*!' And Miss Hardaker looked up at Livy. Livy saw the glitter of her eyes in the half-darkness. She moved towards her, wary of missing her step in the darkness.

Two seconds more and she would have reached her. But with a blunt puff of energy, dull, inconsequential, almost trivial, she saw the dustbin lid blown backwards and into Miss Hardaker's face, as though subverting the rules of gravity.

And then cool, controlled Miss Hardaker was screaming words which made no sense, and her face was covered with blood.

Livy felt the warm trickle of liquid on her own face, but no pain, and did not know if it was her blood or Miss Hardaker's as she landed on her knees beside the prone woman. Behind her, she heard the shouts of the other firewatchers as she gathered her colleague in her arms, and lifted her.

'I'm sorry,' said Livy. And she had the sense that she was not just apologizing to Miss Hardaker, but to some other person that she had wronged. 'I'm so sorry.'

A medic came, quicker than she thought possible, and someone lifted Livy up and out of the way, his hands beneath her arms. 'She should never have brought you up here,' she heard someone say, and she realized it was Bill.

As they tended to Miss Hardaker, bent over her, their dark backs edged with light, Livy walked away, shivering. The coldness of the morning had returned. She shook her head. Stared at a speck on a roof a little way away: the tiniest speck, which fizzed into life, blazing white, suddenly. *Was it some kind of flare?* she thought. *Was it a bomb?* Unaccountably it reminded her of the diamond in the portrait, against the black velvet of the woman's dress: a hard, adamantine brightness, too elemental to be ignored.

She stepped towards it, towards the edge of the roof. Looked down the length of the building from that high, dizzying viewpoint. And then she felt a hand on her shoulder, and turned.

'Don't even think about it,' said Bill.

CHAPTER TWO

1940

Entrance Hall, the Mirrormakers' Club

Peggy was standing in the doorway of the Mirrormakers' Club with a broom in her hand, staring out onto the street, when a small balcony on a nearby building collapsed. She watched as the masonry crumbled and fell, scattering a small group of rescue workers. The building had been the offices of Smith and Fisher, a firm of solicitors. Before the war, she thought, she would have run screaming into the street. Now she simply waited for it to finish, and began her sweeping again.

The morning light bathed her tired eyes. These were the Blitz mornings: waking to the relief of survival, framed by sadness and exhaustion. She heard soft footsteps approaching from behind, and wondered if it was a person, or if she would turn and find the Entrance Hall empty. It didn't frighten her; one got used to causeless things, living in the Club. A slammed door here, a distant set of footsteps there. Although somehow it had felt worse since Miss Hardaker's departure. In her sudden absence, Peggy had often wondered if she would appear one day, as if nothing had happened. Sometimes, she simply forgot. No one knew where she had gone. When Peggy had telephoned the hospital on behalf of the Club, she was told Miss Hardaker had discharged herself. Her resignation had been sent to the director in Suffolk.

She felt a hand on her shoulder, and turned her head. It was Livy, standing behind her, as though she were sheltering from the daylight.

'It was a parachute landmine, that one we really felt last night,' Peggy said. 'Windows blown in on the front side. A man from the council has already been in, looking around, early on. Bill let him in. I was waiting to see if anyone turned up to work over there and offer them a cup of tea.'

Livy nodded. She remembered that sickening procession of detonations which had made her curl forwards and cover her ears with her hands. So close, she could feel the detonations in the tissues of her body. She had dropped her chin to her chest, and waited. *My bomb*, she thought, as the dust had rained down from the gaps between the bricks in the vaulted basement bomb shelter. But she had been wrong.

'I just checked upstairs,' she said, as Peggy waved to some of the rescue workers. 'The News Room has its whole ceiling down. I don't think we should go in there anymore. The Red

Parlour is less bad, but it looks – shredded. And *Sir John Blake* has been damaged in the Committee Room.'

Peggy glanced at her, and saw the tightness of her expression. The uneven scar from the night on the roof which had slowly healed shone pale, but was only noticeable if you looked for it. 'Young skin heals better than old,' she said, and brushed Livy's face gently with her fingers. Livy was no longer a colleague, but a child to be taken care of, an innocent to be protected.

'I told Bill to move the paintings weeks ago,' Livy said.

'Have you ever known Bill do something because you tell him to?' said Peggy, watching her face, seeing her try to bury her anger. 'Besides, he's tired now. He didn't really believe that bombs would fall on London. They kept us waiting a long time. And now, there's always something else to do. He doesn't feel for these things like you do, sweetheart. And the director hasn't told him to put them away.'

She observed Livy carefully. There was a certain wariness to the girl's expression today: she looked out at the street as though a missile might fly from it at any moment.

'Sweetheart?' she said.

'I'll go and make some tea if the water's back on,' said Livy, pulling the sleeves of her grey jumper over her hands.

Peggy glanced out at the men on the street. 'Six cups should do it,' she said.

Livy nodded and went quickly, soft steps over the marble, her bobbing stride saturated with nervous energy.

Peggy went back to her work. She was sweeping the last of

the debris from the front steps when a young man appeared before her so suddenly that it made her gasp in a way the falling masonry had not.

'I'm so sorry,' he smiled. 'I didn't mean to startle you.' At first sight, he looked dreadfully tired, and rather dishevelled, but his smile was pure. He wore a long winter coat and had thick, tousled hair which he brushed away from his forehead with a closed hand.

'Not at all, how I can help?' Aware that she had adopted her formal tone, the one Bill called her telephone voice, Peggy paused to pat the scarf on her head.

'I saw someone upstairs, at the window,' he said. 'Is there someone up there?' Now she saw the strain on his face. As his smile died, the shadows beneath his eyes came to the fore.

'Miss Baker was up there a minute ago,' said Peggy.

She saw him take a breath. 'Olivia Baker?'

'Yes.' She looked at him with new interest.

'Thank goodness. I thought I'd seen a ghost.'

He was still standing, but she saw that something in him had buckled. An almost imperceptible movement. 'Would you like to sit down?'

He shook his head. Peggy wondered about extracting information without prying or taking liberties. 'You know Livy well?'

Another breath. She saw the sharpness of his glance. 'She's known as Livy?'

'Yes – that is, she asked us to call her that.' Peggy thought carefully for a moment. She felt the heat rising in her face. 'I should warn you – Mr—'

'Taylor. Christian Taylor. Forgive me, I should have said. I'm with the LCC. Architect's department.'

'Not at all. I'm Mrs Holliday, the housekeeper here. I was saying – I should warn you that Miss Baker – Livy – well, she doesn't remember anything.' She coloured at the baldness of her tone. 'There was a bomb, a couple of months ago, and she found her way here, but she remembers nothing from before.'

'Nothing at all?'

'That's what she says. I have no reason to doubt her. How do you know her?'

In the basement vaults, Livy filled the kettle, and worried about the man she had seen from the window.

When she had gone upstairs, she could hardly bear to look at the rooms. The quality of the light ahead of her, falling from the Committee Room door, had been too bright, and she had sensed even before she stepped around the corner that the floor-to-ceiling windows of the room had been blown in. Sure enough, when she faced the room she saw the shafts of light falling over the dark mahogany furniture, and small pieces of glass stood upright, embedded in the leather upholstery of the committee table. On the far side of the room she could see the sparkle of glass, obscenely pretty, glistening in the cheek of *Sir John Blake*, a portrait painted in 1752.

She had gone to the window, and looked out, trying to escape the devastation behind her. As with the building, she could not remember a single thing about the pre-war view from this room. Everything further back than the day her house had been bombed was still suspended somewhere inaccessible in her mind. She remembered her favourite film stars, her favourite colour, her favourite food. The wider parameters of her life were still in place. But when she tried to picture her own personal past it had a pale, watery quality, as though she were on the bottom of the sea and looking up, trying to work out what was beyond.

No, not everything: almost everything. There was a small, rapidly dissolving island of memory. A job she once had. It must have been years ago. And she remembered that she was happy. She had a few fleeting scenes, a few faces. Her typing letters. A group of young men, laughing. Her, sitting at a typewriter, trying not to laugh too, because she had been listening.

She had a vision of a man, his back to her, in a tweed jacket, sitting at a desk, writing, in the yellow circle of light cast by an anglepoise lamp.

These scenes were fleeting, barely known, like something she had dreamt, which was beginning to dissolve, while the present was pin-sharp, vivid. A little too bright for her eyes, like the light from blown windows.

As she stood staring down from the Committee Room window, the rescue party surveyed the rubble where the offices had been. One of them scratched the top of his helmet in puzzlement, as though it was his head. Then, a jolt. A familiar face. A young man, in a coat that had seen better days, hatless, his dark blonde hair thick and untidy. He was talking to another man, looking over the building, a notebook in his hand, taking in each detail of the exterior with care, as one would assess a person for injury. As she stared at him, his eyes met hers.

One of the men in the architect's office.

She had stepped back immediately, and let the drape flutter down, screening the glassless window. When, after a few moments, she peered cautiously around the edge of the window frame, he had gone.

The kettle began to whistle, and Livy piled pale green cups and saucers onto the tray. She made the tea, and rationed out milk into the cups. Then she carried the loaded tray up the basement stairs and across the Stair Hall. Ahead of her, the double doorway into that slice of darkness which was the Entrance Hall. She had wondered why it was so dark; thought that, perhaps, the Club's architect had an eye for drama – dark panelling, and a doorway into the light and coloured marble of the Stair Hall, so that it sent the mind spinning like a top.

She stopped in the doorway of the Entrance Hall and stared at them. Peggy and the man. They turned at the same moment, alerted by the sound of rattling china. She wanted to run away, but it really was not practical: a whole tray of teacups, after all, sat in her arms, barring her from anything but a messy escape.

'Livy,' he said.

Peggy came up the small flight of steps and took the tray

from her. 'It's all right, love. I explained that something happened, that you might not remember him.'

'I don't want to speak to him,' Livy whispered. She focused on Peggy's blue eyes; on not looking at the man who stood a few yards away.

'Do you remember him?'

'No. That is, not really. But. I just don't want to.'

Peggy put the tray down on the floor. 'He's a very nice young man. He says you worked together in the architect's department at the LCC. Speak to him, love. It won't do any harm. It might even help. I'll go and see who wants tea out there.'

As Peggy went past the man, with a smile and downcast eyes, Livy looked towards him. He stood there patiently, perfectly still. Livy folded her arms, and came down the few steps towards him.

'Hello.' Her voice sounded younger than she was, and uncertain.

He smiled. 'Hello. I saw you at the window. For a minute, you know, I didn't quite believe it was you. And such a strange coincidence. I told you once how much I love this building.'

She frowned, felt a pin-sharp pain in the centre of her brow. 'I'm sorry. I don't remember that. I've not been well.'

'Mrs Holliday mentioned that. Do you remember me?'

'Not really. You were in my office, that's all. I'm ever so sorry.'

'Please, don't apologize.' He seemed so calm, but she

19

sensed his struggle in the way he looked at her, almost unblinking. 'Pleased to meet you again. My name is Christian Taylor.'

She nodded. 'What's your business here today?'

He spoke slowly. 'I am from the architect's department of the LCC, Statutory Branch. The department maps the bombing. I don't usually come out to sites. Reports come in from the ARP wardens, and from our damage recorders, and we take note of them on the damage maps. I heard this morning there was a hit on the Mirrormakers' Club, and I wanted to see it: they phoned through that it would be a Category B.'

'Which means?'

'So badly damaged that demolition is necessary.'

She felt a dull flash of alarm. 'They've got it wrong then, haven't they?'

He smiled briefly. 'Of course. Don't worry at all, Miss Baker. It is, still, Miss Baker, isn't it?'

'Yes.' She gave a grim little laugh. 'As far as I know.'

He nodded, and swallowed hard. 'I've spoken to my colleague outside. He has looked around this morning, and it's clearly a Category C(a). Seriously damaged, capable of repair, still usable.' He smiled. Then he glanced down at his notebook. 'Not the official record,' he said. 'Just my personal notes.'

He held his notebook half-tipped towards her. She nodded towards it. 'What did you write in there?'

He caught the flash of interest in her eyes, the merest chink of it, and it lit something in his own. He held the notebook out to her, without a moment's hesitation. He even turned it around, so that she could read it without any difficulty.

'You might not remember,' he said. 'You were the only person in the typing pool who could read my handwriting. And as this isn't an official record, I can show you.'

Windows out on the west side. Some signs of damage within.

They said the building was destroyed, or as near as, but it is not. The walls still stand, and the roof.

And, like a miracle, she is in it. Nothing she is in could be described as destroyed. Unless I have imagined her. Another ghost in a mind already crowded with them.

She looked up at him. Whatever had lain between them was wiped from her memory, but his gaze was alive with it, and her fear of the unknown opened up beneath her, as though she stood on the edge of the Club's roof again, looking down from a great height. She sensed too, instinctively, the sense of loss in him. 'I'm sorry,' she said.

He saw the fear in her eyes. 'Don't worry,' he said. 'We needn't talk about any of it. I'm just glad to see you, that's all, Livy.'

He took the notebook back, brushed it off with the sleeve of his coat as though it had an imaginary covering of dust, closed it and put it into his inside coat pocket. As he did so, she noticed that he kept his left hand closed, and drawn

21

within his sleeve. She looked at it, and his gaze followed hers.

'I signed up, would you believe,' he said, his expression hardening. 'Army. I was in a reserved occupation, but I persuaded them. Second week of training, blew two of my fingers off. Daresay I could have gone back in afterwards but they didn't want me. Thought I was a commie. Worried about socialists having guns these days.'

She looked down, her arms wrapped around her waist.

'I'm sorry,' he said. 'Talking too much. I keep forgetting. That you don't know me. Do you really not know me?'

And he reached out to touch her arm.

She stepped back several paces. Against the panelled wall of the Entrance Hall. The dark panelling, which smelt of old varnish and centuries of city smoke. And she turned her head to it, so that she did not have to look into his face. The oaky, old smell was strangely reassuring. She put one hand to the wood: felt its smooth, syrupy texture. Too many layers of varnish, she thought. 'Please,' she said, her face turned away. 'Please make sure they don't think it's unfit to live in.'

He stared at her, astonished. 'I promise,' he said.

'Can I offer you a cup of tea, Mr Taylor?' Peggy had come back in, her face glowing with curiosity. 'Have you offered him a cup, Livy?'

Christian turned to Peggy. It seemed to her as though a light had gone out in his eyes. 'No, but thank you ever so much,' he said. 'I must be going.'

'I'm sure you'd be very welcome to come back,' piped up Peggy. 'Wouldn't he, Livy?'

Livy said nothing, her face still turned to the panelling.

'That's very kind of you,' Christian said. 'I firewatch at St Paul's one night a week, so I'm often in the neighbourhood, and may look in one day if that's agreeable. Well, goodbye – Mrs Holliday.'

'Peggy.'

'Peggy. And Miss Baker.' He turned, gave a mock bow in Livy's direction, his gaze no longer on her face, but on the grey York stone floor. 'Goodbye. I hope you start to feel better soon.'

'Thank you.'

'And if, for any reason, we don't meet again – life these days is unpredictable, after all,' they both looked up at the same time, and their eyes met briefly, 'have a good war.'

Christian Taylor walked down the front steps, and had a brief conversation with his colleague before bidding him goodbye. He walked smoothly, his back straight, his head up. It was only after he had turned the corner into the narrow side street on the north side of the building that his pace slowed until he stopped. He put one hand to the cool grey stone of the Club, and rested his forehead there. Then he drove his fist into the wall, so hard that when he looked down at his abraded knuckles, scraped and bleeding, he could see the pattern of the stone's texture there.

CHAPTER THREE

1940

Redlands

'Must you go?'

Jonathan Whitewood signalled to the head gardener to linger in the topiary, out of sight, like an actor in a farce.

'I must.' He tried to smile, but managed only a conciliatory grimace, like a man squinting into the sun.

His wife proffered her powdered cheek, accepted his goodbye kiss, and forced a smile. A faint mist of exhaustion seemed to hang over her eyes.

'You are a wonder, darling,' he said, and he meant it. Her stance was always elegant, even in her wellington boots. Cool and limber; perfectly made-up, her short hair tightly curled. Still, Jonathan knew that this look was now a matter of decision and immense effort rather than a simple expression of who she was. Every day he thought about what a toll it must be on her, to see the house crawling with people, to hear the sound of wheels over potholes as cars and ambulances motored up and down the drive. It had always been such a quiet place, their estate, cut into a Hertfordshire hillside.

'There's no need to dig up the rose beds,' he said. 'We have the entire Redlands estate to grow vegetables for the war effort.'

She gave a determined smile: an expression which translated as *I insist*.

'You can go to Emma if things get too much here,' he said. A cousin in Scotland.

'They won't,' she said. 'But don't stay in London too long.' It was a phrase of love, of longing, that she had used throughout their marriage when he left for business, and it now had the quality of a custom. To omit it would be to admit that something was terribly wrong.

Things would get better, he thought, if they could just be left alone: him, her, a nurse for her bad days. But not here. He had handed the keys over to the government without rancour; it was his duty. He could not resent that, even with the trouble it had caused over the past year and a half, a timeless present, as his wife wilted like a rose out of water.

'Darling,' Stevie had said, when they knew war was inevitable. 'Could you use your influence? Can you make sure we are a school?'

He had been smoking a cigar when she said it; drinking whisky over ice. He wondered if, in that moment, a fragment of ice had taken the wrong route from his throat, and entered his heart. In the following months, as he witnessed her disappointment, he gained clarity, and he realized that it had always been this moment, every evening, that she chose to bring forwards her most risky thoughts, to woo him with the background music of her voice. Only now he saw it, tracing his wife's influence with the precision of an archaeologist brushing mud away from fragments of the past.

He felt like a fool. He was an intelligent man, but he had always thought that Stevie's every utterance proceeded naturally from the moment. He could not bear to think she had been calculating, even for the purposes of good. More than that, he could not tolerate the idea that his autonomy, something so precious to him, had been shaped by her thousand suggestions over the last twenty years. That he was, unwittingly, the product of her plans and wishes. Poor Stevie. For the first time in their long marriage, she had misjudged him, and drawn back the curtains on the subtle, well-tended mechanisms, so that he heard the click of the clockwork behind their relationship.

Yes, he could have used his influence. He had friends and acquaintances from school and university dotted about the government. Yes, he could have made sure their house was converted into a school rather than being used for other purposes. But he couldn't bear the thought of Redlands crawling with children; of how it would throw their own childlessness into relief. *Can't you leave it alone?* he had wanted to say to her, despite never having been a man prone to melodrama.

Can't you understand that the children, even if they delight you for a day or two, will be a torment to us?

Not that a single child of theirs had been born; even those formed only from hope, a day or two of delay, had never really had long enough to spark into even imaginary life. But he knew that a houseful of children would conjure the spirits of what-might-have-been out of the house's hitherto protective air. He could exist with the vacancy but not with the embodiment, by proxy, of possibilities.

So instead of a school, at the outbreak of war Redlands was adapted to become Number Eighteen General Hospital, London Region. Lines of beds occupied the ballroom, the suites of salons. His grandfather's smoking room became an office, while, perversely, the doctors and nurses smoked in the breakfast room; and the billiard room doubled as a linen store.

Jonathan and Stevie occupied a suite of rooms in the west wing. Their favourite things went into storage, chiefly the paintings, for they were closest to Jonathan's heart: old masters and family portraits. Stevie arranged for her favourites to go too – the family collection of gold boxes and vertu. Extravagant Dutch still lifes, gauzy French landscapes and outraged, imperious ancestors now peered out of the darkness of some underground room, alongside locked metal cases of tissue-wrapped hardstone carvings and enamelled snuffboxes. But there was not enough time or space to send everything, so most of the furnishings stayed, shunted to the sides of rooms and passageways. He had stopped going into the dining room when he saw metal bedsteads pushed up against the seventeenth-century tapestries.

His sudden protectiveness towards the house unnerved him. Redlands had been remodelled by his great-grandfather Ashton Kinsburg, and he had always viewed it as a kind of gorgeous monstrosity. He made jokes about it at dinner parties. He called it a money pit of the worst kind, with its leaking roof and impractical bathroom arrangements. In the early years of their marriage, lying warm against Stevie in the depths of the night, he had murmured to her that he was sorry that they had to live there at all. If he hadn't been the eldest son, she could have had a townhouse in Chelsea, fitted out in the most modern taste. He could not remember how she had replied, but thought now, rather meanly, that whatever she had said would have been perfect and well-judged. Perhaps she had laughed, and turned, and kissed him. Perhaps she had said nothing at all, drifting gently and silently into sleep.

The anger that had grown in him over the months had surprised him. He had struggled to contain it; it felt rather like trying to hold a thunderstorm in one's chest. He hoped he did not let it show to Stevie, although he was aware that he occasionally called her Stephanie. In the past, he had never used her full name unless in anger. He still felt it now, walking away from her in the garden, and he supposed she felt it in return. Only now, he felt that his anger was a feint, a gateway for other, darker things.

He went into the hallway of the house, which was, as usual, bustling with people. A doctor talked intensely to a nurse beneath the coats of arms – not necessarily about medical matters, he suspected – and he saw a tracery of cobwebs swinging from the ceiling like an abandoned trapeze line. Two men in uniform discussed administrative concerns. One of them leaned against a liver-coloured marble console table, his arm a hair's breadth away from an ormolu girandole, its sockets empty of candles and its crystal pendants swinging in the breeze from the door.

'Mind that,' said Jonathan sharply.

'Yes, sir,' said the man. Jonathan's rank from the last war was always respected.

Before he reached beneath the table and extracted his suitcase, Jonathan straightened the girandole himself, and saw the two men glance at each other. The stupid thing was, he'd never liked it. 'Perhaps someone will break it,' he'd joked, before they came. But now, it seemed incredibly precious, its familiarity conferred on it the status of a relic. For hadn't he walked past it at eight as he now did at eight-and-forty? No one understood the tenderness he felt for the damned thing suddenly, in this moment; he didn't even understand it. He wondered if he was going insane. He nodded at the men, and walked briskly out.

The air outside the house was the only normal thing: sharp with the advance of winter, the November bareness of it brewing, its scent insistent, complex, a mixture of autumn decay and approaching ice. He breathed it deeply as he walked towards the stable-block, where one of his old retainers had prepared the tub trap and pony – no need for petrol.

He thought of the lines of desks in the smoking room. His great-grandfather's ridiculous smoking room in the bachelor's wing, fitted out in some fantastic Victorian approximation of the Gothic, so intensely strange that it had given Jonathan nightmares as a child. He disliked that room. But what he disliked even more was to see its character cancelled out by lines of desks, its purpose disregarded and overlooked. Unacknowledged, not even worth a dinner-party joke, now. It had been a man's life. Yes, they were involved in more serious things now, in a lethal battle. But did it mean that every hope and dream from the past had to be ignored, erased by indifference? 'I'm afraid so, darling,' Stevie had said. 'It is, really, a monstrous folly of a room. You know that.' Jonathan had looked at her, and seen a stranger.

He patted his breast pocket, felt the package tucked there, too large for the pocket but too precious to leave anywhere else. It was the source, in his mind, of the sudden changing of the quality of his anger, from engagement to estrangement. He felt separated from Stevie, from his own home, and he could not un-feel this estrangement no matter how much he turned it over in his logical mind; like a faulty engine, it stuck each time he turned the key. The gemstone in his pocket had let him down and it was this, he thought, lighting a cigarette, which was clouding everything. It felt more like a death-fall than a missed step.

'Sir,' said Jones. He had loaded Jonathan's suitcase onto the trap, and now stood at the pony's head. Jonathan climbed up without help; it was he who held out a hand to the old man, and helped his servant to scramble up. 'You have too much work with the others gone, don't you?' Jonathan said, speaking quickly, with a nervous tension his companion immediately picked up on. Highly strung, thought the old retainer, that was the Kinsburg blood, uncountered by the Whitewood solidity.

'I'll manage, sir,' he said.

'Of course, life isn't perfect,' said Jonathan.

Jones exhaled softly, a sigh by other means.

Jonathan smoked on, ticked off the years as the pony moved slowly forwards. Unlike so many others he had survived the Great War unscathed, protected by luck, a shock of adrenaline and the innocence of youth. There had been disappointments in business, and despite much investment he had never rid Redlands of the persistent smell of drains. And his brother's brats would inherit everything, if there was anything left to inherit after the war. But these cumulative sadnesses were as nothing to the strange coldness which had overcome him since he had extracted the Kinsburg Diamond from its bank vault. It was as though his warm emotions – his affection for Stevie, his exasperated fondness for the old house – had been cut off, cleanly, like turning off a tap. All that was left was a sterile, empty feeling, and an exquisite sensitivity to the pain and wickedness of the world; a protectiveness towards the swinging, cloudy pendants of the girandole which would soon be destroyed, he had no doubt. It seemed he had no agency in anything; he could neither protect the girandole, nor Stevie, nor the house. So it was not worth feeling anything like the old allegiances and affections.

'Nice bright day,' said Jones. Jonathan looked around, full of amazement that the man should say such a thing. At the trees, nearly all bare; the birdsong; the clopping of the pony's hooves as it circled the house and emerged into the front courtyard. He could observe each element objectively and agree that it was a beautiful day. But he could not feel it; not even the brightness of the winter sun as it broke through the clouds.

'We'll get through all this, you know,' said Jonathan, and Jones was left wondering whether his master had gone and lost his mind completely, as he seemed to be having a completely different conversation in his head.

The visit to London would allow him to take arms against his disappointment. The Kinsburg Diamond had been his insurance policy, and the key to everything: to fixing the house, to fixing Stevie, to shoring them up. And now, it had let him down. Its mythical value was precisely that: a myth, an aberration, a betrayal. He had left the safe-deposit building as calm – outwardly – as he had entered it, shaking the hand of the valuer and hailing himself a taxi; but only because he was a gentleman.

'How long will you stay in London, sir?' said Jones.

Jonathan flicked the cigarette stub wilfully into the hedgerow, and a pair of startled sparrows flew out, a pale brown, dull as his thoughts. 'As long as it takes to settle my business matters,' he said. *As long as it takes for me to feel as though I can begin anew, back here, and call it my home again.*

As they entered the Long Drive he turned back, certain he would see Stevie in the doorway of the house. She always saw him off, not waving of course – she never did that, for her mother had told her it was bad manners to stand waggling your hand like a shopgirl – but she always stood and watched him go, her slight, elegant form pale in the dark shape of the doorway, watching until he was out of sight.

She was not there, and he felt the slight fall in the centre of his torso. Had he been his normal, gentle self he would have thought: of course, she is tired, she must still be in the garden, or maybe she has gone to lie down. But he was not usual, or gentle; he was disappointed, and bitter, and unfair. Instead, as he turned back to look ahead, and touched his breast pocket again, he thought: *damn you, then.*

CHAPTER FOUR

1940

STAIR HALL, THE MIRRORMAKERS' CLUB

A visitor to the Mirrormakers' Club on the late afternoon of a November day might have seen what they thought to be a wraith. The grand central staircase of white marble, which split at the first landing into two, looked forlorn in the emptiness, as though it awaited guests in crinolines and tailcoats. The left branch of the staircase led to the north landing, from which could be accessed the large Dining Hall, Miss Hardaker's office, known as the Hide, the Committee Room and Red Parlour. The right branch led to the south landing, which presented another entrance to the other end of the Dining Hall, and the News Room, before the ring met in the Red Parlour, but these had been rendered inaccessible by bomb damage. A slim figure, dressed in a grey jumper and darker grey woollen skirt, was seated on a step on the right branch, and was staring up at the central dome above the staircase, which was decorated mesmerizingly in tapering black and white checks. Either side of the dome, demi-lunes with ornamental grating let in the light, but the large chandelier, shrouded in white sheets, would have done well to be lit, to bring the panels of green, pink and white marble on the Stair Hall walls to life. What light there was caught fleetingly on the woman's hair and in her eyes. She was examining the place, sensing it, as though, even in the blackout, she might be able to find her way by touch. It had become her daily habit, to know the place well, as though it were a code that needed to be deciphered. It was home; it was everything.

The wraith was Livy.

The sound of the doorbell interrupted her, the hard-edged trill echoing through the near-empty building. Up to the dome above the staircase, and back again, halting her in her place.

A robust knocking at the door.

She walked towards the darkness of the Entrance Hall slowly.

'I say, hello?' A man's voice. 'Is that you, Bill?'

Livy came to the door, stood on her tiptoes and looked through the peephole. A man stood there, smartly dressed, with a large case in his hand, and carrying his gas mask in a brown leather box, its long strap over his right shoulder. He was older, late forties at least, and despite his height and broad shoulders had a rather hungry look to him: defined cheekbones, pale green eyes, and thick black hair. The face was handsome, perfect by some buried classical equation, and this beauty overrode his tiredness. He looked rather like a faded matinee idol.

But the face inspired faint dread in Livy as she paused behind the peephole. Another stranger, and perhaps one that knew her.

'I know someone's there,' he said.

She turned the key in the door, and opened it a crack.

Their eyes met, and she saw him take a breath. 'Well,' he said. 'Hello there. I didn't expect to see you. I thought all the staff were let go apart from Mr and Mrs Holliday.'

'No,' she said. She did not open the door any wider.

'Don't you recognize me?' Beneath his detached tone she heard the affront in his voice. 'I am on the committee.'

'Of course,' she said, feeling the energy drain out of her. 'Good afternoon, sir. Please come in.'

She opened the door widely and he passed her. 'Find a place for this, will you?' He handed her his hat and coat and mounted the steps to the entrance of the Stair Hall. 'Where to?' He looked at her, was perplexed by her silence. Finally, his irritation broke through properly. *Where are Mr and Mrs Holliday?'*

'If you'll take a seat here, sir, I'll find them.' She pointed towards one of the large, architect-designed chairs which sat beside the staircase, domesticating the vast interior.

Walking behind him, she felt the weight of his beautiful

36

coat, a grey Chesterfield ripe with the mixed scent of cigars and cologne.

She fetched Peggy, who greeted him with reverence. 'Oh, Mr Whitewood!' she said, hurrying towards him. The note of gladness in her voice was caught in the acoustic of the marble-clad hall. 'We didn't know you were coming, sir. Would you like a cup of tea? A poached egg and some buttered toast?' Livy glanced at her. They were only supposed to have one egg per person per week.

'Only,' he spread out one hand, '*only* if it's not any trouble, Mrs Holliday. I'll be staying for a few days, perhaps even weeks, so I'll register for temporary rations. I don't want you to be short of anything.'

'Or you might wish to eat in restaurants,' said Livy. The moment the words were out of her mouth, she realized how rude they sounded.

Peggy ignored her. 'Very good, Mr Whitewood: a poached egg it is. Where would you like to take your tea?'

'I'll take it here with you, if you'll permit me, Peggy, and,' one hand out, to indicate Livy's presence, 'this young lady.'

'Miss Baker, sir,' Peggy said, her eyes widening. 'You remember Miss Baker?'

He nodded. 'I do, I do. But I don't remember why she is here now.'

Livy did nothing; despite Mrs Holliday's pleading look, as though to say 'smile at him', she stood there silently. Already, she sensed the shift in the room: this man had power, and he was therefore a threat. In the midst of his energy she felt her own sense of self, which she had gradually started to accumulate over the past few weeks, guttering like a candle flame in a strong breeze.

'Miss Baker had a direct hit on her lodgings two months ago, sir. She's registered for war work now but until she goes, she's helping us, especially when we give tea and supper to the firewatchers. And in the day she's working in the Document Room, trying to organize things with the archive. The director and the manager both know, and signed it off. Miss Hardaker was meant to put things in order before the war but it never quite happened.'

'Ah,' he said in a regretful, slightly patronizing tone. 'The venerable Miss Hardaker. Do you know, I once caught her piling documents into the furnace?'

'Oh, goodness,' Peggy half-laughed fearfully.

Livy took her chance, watching Peggy tiptoe off to make toast. 'The archive *is* rather patchy. Finding things is rather a matter of luck than anything else,' she said.

A frown briefly crossed the visitor's face but then he smiled cordially, attempting to make a connection. 'I might have need of your expertise,' he said. 'I am here to visit friends, but also to look for some papers which have a connection with my family. We've been members of the Mirrormakers' Club for generations. Looking-glass-makers' Club, perhaps I should say. It's not quite the thing to say mirror these days, but as our greatest poets used it, why not? "And in her hand she held a mirror bright".'

Livy nodded, flushing that she did not know the reference.

Peggy had explained to her that the Mirrormakers' Club was known more formally as the Mirrormakers' and City Club. The original founders had been well-connected traders in small mirrors, cabinets and glass, who had loosened ties with their livery company and decided to form a club for convivial company, the first in the City of London. Its members now included any City gentleman who knew the right person through blood or business, but the name had been kept. Members were elected by ballot.

'I can't remember seeing anything related to the Whitewoods,' she said. 'But I'll gladly look for you.'

'That's not the name,' he said. 'I'm researching my mother's side of the family, the Kinsburgs. And I can look myself, if you just point me in the right direction.'

'I'll do my best,' she said.

They sat in awkward silence, until Peggy came bustling out with the poached egg and toast on a tray.

'Sorry not to have a newspaper for you, sir,' she said. 'We do take *The Times*, thin as it is these days, but Mr Holliday's done something with it.' She tried to keep the irritation out of her voice and failed.

He tucked into the food with gusto. 'Will it be the Blue Room I am in, tonight?' he said between mouthfuls. 'I assume no one else is staying here?' The guest rooms were on the top floor of the building, along with the flat the Hollidays had in peacetime.

'Oh, Mr Whitewood,' Mrs Holliday said. 'We don't stay up there now. It's closed up. Of course, I check things, and

39

keep the rooms aired, but it is far safer to stay down in the basement shelter, what with night after night of the bombing. It would be unwise to sleep up there.'

He swallowed a mouthful of toast. 'That's rather overdoing it, don't you think? After all, we should carry on as usual, shouldn't we?'

Livy watched him. It seemed to her that he really rather wanted to sleep in the Blue Room now, solely because Peggy had told him that he couldn't. She could see the tiredness on the housekeeper's face as she worked out how to pacify him, and it angered her.

'You'd do best to listen to Peggy's advice, sir,' she said. 'The upper rooms are closed off for a reason.'

He put down his knife and fork. 'I'll sleep in the Blue Room,' he said.

'Very good, sir,' said Peggy, with something like sadness in her voice.

Staring at his face, Livy thought of the portrait *Woman and Looking Glass*. There was something about the line of his face, something about the way the shadows fell on it, which reminded her of the painted face she returned to again and again. Bill had assured her that the painting was safe in its current position: 'it'll only be damaged if the whole building comes down' was his reassuring phrase, but after every long night of bombing it was the first thing Livy checked, and the anxiety was growing within her.

Jonathan ate on in silence, and the others sat quietly with him. Darkness was falling, the early darkness of an autumn evening with the lights kept off. The Stair Hall seemed to contract in the fading light, the coloured marble walls fading into shadow, and as the light dwindled the occupants finally left it and went into the basement.

Mr Whitewood was looking with curiosity around the basement vaults that had been adapted as their living quarters when they heard the wail of the air-raid sirens.

Bill came running down the stairs. 'Planes!' he called. 'I'll put the electricity off.' Then he saw Mr Whitewood. His hand went to his tieless throat. Livy felt a sudden pang of affection for him, entwined with pity. A sudden reminder of the old life had left him exposed, dressed in his overall with his collar button undone. 'Sir,' Bill said.

It was then Livy remembered *Woman and Looking Glass*, and the tension she felt tipped over some invisible line. In that moment, it became simply unbearable. She rose suddenly from her chair.

'What is it, dear?' Peggy had paused in the middle of the washing-up, her face kind, softened like someone regarding a startled animal.

Livy stared at her. '*Woman and Looking Glass*,' she said.

'We said to you, dear, it's perfectly safe where it is. There's no glass near it. What's this sudden fret? You've been fine about it for weeks.'

'I'll just get it,' Livy said.

'What's all this?' Whitewood extinguished his cigarette. 'Did you mention *Woman and Looking Glass*? Presumably it was sent to safe keeping with the treasury?'

41

Livy glanced at him. 'No, it's upstairs in the hall. I have to get it.'

The first distant thud shook the ground beneath their feet.

'Not now. Tomorrow.' Mrs Holliday turned away to stow the plate. 'We need to go into the shelter and shut the doors. Quickly.' She glanced at their guest. 'She is suffering from shock, sir, she has these sudden fits about things.'

'It can be moved tomorrow,' Whitewood said firmly. 'I understand your concern, so we'll do it first thing. I really can't think why it wasn't sent to Sussex with everything else. Don't go,' he said as she moved across the room. 'Can't you hear them?'

But with exasperation Livy shook off their words. 'I'm going to get it.' She went past Bill and out towards the stairs.

Whitewood watched her go. Then he looked at Mrs Holliday. 'Is she quite right in the head?' he said. He unclenched his hand, and put his cigarette lighter down on the table with a clatter, harder than he'd intended to.

Livy's eyes adjusted quickly to the darkness of the Stair Hall. As she came out of the green door from the basement she could see reasonably well in the gloom of the vast space. Searchlights, or bomber's moon, she was not sure.

The first detonation took her to her knees on the stone floor and she curled up like a netsuke. Just for a moment; just as she waited to see if the building would fall down on her head. The sound was so vast that she assumed they had taken a direct hit; the noise in the room was inseparable from the noise in her head. She covered her ears but it was there, nonetheless. She thought how the reinforced basement shelter had protected them, all these nights.

Then there was a brief space between noises and she got to her feet, her legs as unsteady as a calf's. Why did she think of that? Sickly, she was made of marrow. More light – our lights or theirs, she wondered. The retort of ack-ack guns into the sky. She was on her feet again. The moonlight shone in from the demi-lune of grating beneath the dome. It cast sharp ornamental shadows of the grillwork, black tendrils cutting through the white gaze of the moon. She put her hand out and touched the column of a lamp as she passed, unlit of course in the blackout, but the moonlight glanced off its ormolu frame.

She stumbled towards the painting. But then something made her turn and look behind her; a shadow moving out of the shadows. It was Whitewood, running towards her, his hands up as though he wished to push her forwards. She remembered his slow, careful walk from the front door; the way he held his cigarette; the sardonic turn of his mouth. She had not thought him capable of moving at this speed. His mouth was moving but she could not hear his words.

The room was filled with the sound of planes, of bombs, of war: the roar of it, the scream of it.

She landed against the far wall, Whitewood behind her. She felt his hands on her shoulders pulling her around the corner and pushing her forwards against the wall. The press of the cold marble against her face. His body was over hers, his arms either side against her shoulders, holding her still.

She was not trembling and she was glad of it in that moment; almost proud. She turned her face amid the roar of the bombers. She saw the chandelier, suspended from a metal chain below the dome, the Victorian crystal shrouded by white sheets. The demi-lune glass blew in; a flying piece of debris sheered the metal chain and the chandelier fell. It bounced off the first flight of steps and lurched onto the floor with hideous momentum. As it hit the stone it exploded, glass flying through the gaps in its shroud. And in that moment Whitewood raised his hands and covered the sides of her face with them. He pressed her against the wall. She felt the warmth of his breath in her hair, noted it, as though from a distance. She closed her eyes.

It seemed like hours that they stood there, until the bombers moved away, until the bombs were distant thunder; a brief respite until the next wave came. His grip on her loosened, and then he released her and stepped away; one step. She turned and looked at him, feeling the grind of broken glass under her heels. His face was black, white and grey in the moonlight.

'Can you hear?' he said, or that was what she thought he said, because she could just see his lips moving; her head was ringing. She shook her head, as though coming up from water and trying to clear her ears of it. He put his hands to her shoulders again, a gesture of reassurance.

She was trembling now, but her legs felt strong again. She stared at him, his face white in the moonlight, saying words which she could not hear. And she felt the vast emptiness within her, as wide and without foothold as the space of the Stair Hall, filled with immense and flickering violence.

She took hold of his face and she kissed him. Without looking into his eyes. Without knowing why. Reaching out as she had for the wall, for something solid, for something which could be touched which would not hurt her. His clean-shaven face was surprisingly soft, the smell of him the smell of cigars and the slight mustiness of unwashed wool.

He froze under her touch for a moment, and then his lips parted beneath hers. As he pushed her back against the cold marble, his hand covered the back of her head, cradling her skull against the stone.

CHAPTER FIVE

1940

Basement Vaults, the Mirrormakers' Club

It was morning, but you could not tell, in the basement vaults. All of it was the same white-painted brick, which raised the light level from dull to slightly less than dull. As Livy folded tea towels for Peggy, she wondered if she had dreamt the night before. It seemed so unreal in this greyed-out, prosaic light.

Peggy was talking about their guest. 'I don't mind it, of course, as long as he registers for temporary rations. He'll be wanting bacon and eggs, no doubt, and things are different now. Bill already gets through the sugar ration so quickly I'm using saccharin tablets. I can't offer Mr Whitewood the food he used to get, I can't.' She said it as though repetition would erase the unthinking servitude of a lifetime.

As though she were frightened that she might, unwittingly, offer Jonathan Whitewood everything. After the night before, Livy understood it completely: his stillness drew things from one.

It had been a passionate kiss, with nothing held back. The length of Whitewood's body against hers. And then she had pushed him away, and they had stood apart from each other in the blue darkness. They had gone down the stairs to the basement side by side, him holding up his cigarette lighter, the flame dancing. Once, she had briefly lost her footing, put out her hands like a dancer trying to keep her balance, and his hand had flashed out and caught hers, held her fingertips, just for a moment, to keep her steady.

'The painting,' she said.

'Tomorrow,' he said.

In the bomb shelter with Bill and Peggy, they had kept wide of each other like repelling magnets. At the next lull, he went out, saying that he wanted to go up to the Blue Room. They had let him go.

'I hope he'll be reasonable.' Peggy was still fretting.

Livy put her hand out. 'I think he's coming down.'

She had sensed him, the hairs standing up on the back of her neck. And he entered the room silently, fully dressed in a grey double-breasted suit and red silk tie, a crease in his shirt, which ran like a scar from the left point of his collar down to where it tucked into his trousers. If he had his valet with him, Livy thought, that would have been pressed out.

'I thought you might show me the Document Room, Miss

Baker,' he said, once he had been served his tea, from old leaves, like everyone else.

Livy unlocked the section of the vaults where the archives had been put to protect them from the bombing. Jonathan followed her in, and the weighted door closed on its own behind them. Like the other basement rooms, the room was vaulted in white-painted brick. Before the war, grey metal shelves had been installed, awkwardly, for they were too tall for the vaulting, and stood away from the walls. There was a small desk with an anglepoise lamp, a chair, and a set of library steps by it.

'This strange underground life you have down here,' he said. Looking around the harshly lit room, with the smell of dust and paper in the air, so different from the red and gold and coloured marbles above.

'I rather love it,' she said. She walked along the shelves, one hand glancing off lines of buff-coloured boxes, their sides labelled in black ink in Miss Hardaker's neat, spiky handwriting. She had gathered from Peggy that before the war, the boxes had lived on the first floor, on wooden shelves in the Hide, a room where Miss Hardaker had smoked, and taken telephone calls, and typed. Despite the two large windows that let the best of the city light into the room, it was dark, the light absorbed by the shelves of archive boxes. Here, under harsh electric light, they seemed less mysterious.

'Where is the copy of *Utopia* by More?' said Whitewood, running his finger along a box, and finding a thin layer of already-settled dust. 'It used to live on the shelves in the News Room. I thought I might read it one evening.'

'The valuable books went to Sussex, with the financial records,' Livy said. 'And just as well, because the News Room was destroyed a few weeks ago in a raid. We don't go near it now.'

He turned away, saying nothing. His glacial serenity seemed rather arrogant to Livy. It was as though, with one kiss, he had used up a brief spark of attraction, and cast her aside, like a dead match. She was sure that men of his type kissed whomever they wanted, whenever they wanted, and that one was meant to be grateful.

'If you tell me what you are looking for, it might be easier.' She kept the 'sir' out of it. Its lack floated in the air between them, surprisingly noticeable.

Jonathan stared at her, aware of the faint scent of her perfume – lily of the valley. It reminded him of the hothouses at Redlands. It made him feel heady, slightly drunk.

But he knew his face wore its habitual mask of coolness: that she would not sense his agitation. He remembered how cold and distant his father had been, and thought how ridiculous it was that such chilliness should be handed down in the blood, but how often he had made use of that innate iciness of manner. Even when he smiled, he knew, it had the quality of winter about it. Only with action could he convince someone that he lived and breathed as they did.

'I'm looking for traces of two of my ancestors, by the name of Kinsburg. Ashton and Charlotte,' he said.

SOPHIA TOBIN

'I've seen the Kinsburg arms in the window of the Dining Hall,' said Livy.

'Yes, well, you would. Ashton Kinsburg, my great-grandfather, largely financed the building of this Club, and served on the committee that approved its design. He was descended from one of the great glass families, and he wanted to make this building proof of his wealth and taste.' He leaned against the table, and attempted to smile. 'It's rather important,' he said.

She watched the cigarette lighter turn in his hand, noticed the tension in the movement. Whatever this thing was, he wanted to know it very badly.

'Where would you like me to start?' she said. 'Do you have a date? And is there anything particular you are looking for?'

He considered her for a moment. Then, from his pocket, he took a folded piece of paper. 'That,' he said, 'is an extract of a letter from my grandmother Isabel, Ashton's daughter, written forty years ago. Forgive my poor handwriting: I copied it out.'

Livy opened the piece of paper, and stared at the lines scrawled in pencil:

You must understand, our lives were ordinary, until the building of the Mirrormakers' Club. It was during the business of the building that everything changed, and by 1841 the happy, golden summers I had known as a child at Redlands had come to an end.

'Redlands?' she said.

He looked down. 'Our family estate.'

'And you're looking for anything to do with Ashton and Charlotte?'

'Anything at all.' He said it too quickly.

She nodded. 'I'll begin down here, with the files on the building of the Mirrormakers' Club. I'll check upstairs too, in the Hide. Miss Hardaker was much more familiar with things than me, and it wouldn't surprise me if she'd started to compile an index or hand list.'

'And you will be thorough?' It was the first uncertainty she had seen on his face.

'Utterly vigilant, I promise,' she said. 'I rather like the idea of solving a mystery – it is a mystery, isn't it?'

He looked sharply at her. 'Yes.' He tried to smile. 'As you like *Woman and Looking Glass* so much, you should know. It's about her.'

'What do you mean?'

'The woman in the painting. According to family legend, she's Charlotte Kinsburg, my great-grandmother.'

'I'm sorry?'

He smiled. 'Now you're interested.'

'Well, of course I am! But – why is her name not on the frame?'

He shook his head. 'I'm not sure. Why are *you* so attached to the painting?'

She considered it. 'It's hard to explain,' she said. 'She seems – present. There's a vividness to her.'

'I know,' he said. 'It's as though she might come to life at any moment, as though she is itching to get out of the position she is standing in.'

They laughed in unison, but when silence fell again, she felt his eyes upon her.

'Miss Baker,' he said. 'What was it about? Last night?' He looked at her face: so pale, almost bloodless. Beautiful, but as though glazed by something, separating her from the world. Like him: her touch had shown her to be more, but now, he felt as though she hardly existed, her presence a shadow.

Her lips tightened. 'I don't know. Does one have to explain everything?'

'Not at all. I was just curious why an apparently respectable young woman would make a play for a married man old enough to be her father.'

A hit, he thought: she looked stricken. 'Make a play? I wouldn't call it that. And why did you kiss me back?'

He looked at her, eye to eye.

'Because I wanted to. I haven't done something completely selfish in a long time.'

For a moment she forgot to breathe. The way he looked at her took her back to the precise moment when he had put his hand around the back of her head, his mouth against hers. A sudden brightness in the Stair Hall, real or imagined, she could hardly tell, so that for a moment the colours of the marble sang, as vivid as the face in the painting. 'Perhaps we could forget it.'

'Perhaps.'

'So, Charlotte and Ashton Kinsburg are who I am looking for.' She wrote their names down on a pad. 'You must have things to do,' she said. 'Why not leave me to make a first pass at things? Lunch is always at half past twelve on the dot, and Mrs Holliday has been cooking a casserole in a straw box since last night. I have some housekeeping to do, then will look for things here, and check Miss Hardaker's room. As soon as I stumble on something I will show it to you.'

'I consider myself dismissed,' he said. He cleared his throat. 'Thank you. And in exchange, after lunch, shall I move *Woman and Looking Glass*?'

'Yes, please,' she said. Her gaze was already fixed on the lines of boxes on the shelves.

CHAPTER SIX

1940

Livy sang as she cleaned the vast expanse of red carpet on the north landing of the Stair Hall. She sang over the clunk-whine of the carpet cleaner and the sound of men working on the other landing: Bill and his mates, patching up the broken demi-lune, robbing the coloured marble walls of more winter light. It occurred to her, startled by the novelty of the feeling, that she was happy. After Jonathan had left her in the basement room, she had pulled out seven boxes of archives on the subject of the Club's construction, and they waited for her downstairs while she completed her duties.

Her thoughts kept returning to the portrait. *Charlotte*, she thought. *Her name is Charlotte.*

She paused on the threshold of the Dining Hall. The

54

entrance was just a few steps from the top of the stairs. There was a clock at the entrance, and Bill wound it every week. It was a head taller than her and an original feature of the Club, the case of carved mahogany around a large dial of faded white, with a glass panel set in its front, so that one could watch the stately swing of the pendulum. The swish and sigh of it, the stateliness of it, the emphasis, seemed to slow time itself. It gave each moment its weight. Turned time, which hurried by so often, into something one could watch, hear and measure. She stood, transfixed by it, and the happiness settled, a warmth in the pit of her stomach.

'Hello.'

The handle of the carpet cleaner left her hand and landed on the floor as she turned. Christian Taylor stood on the top stair, the light behind him. Suddenly the sound of hammering from Bill and his mates filled the air.

Livy looked at the carpet cleaner. Christian hurried to it, and picked it up. 'I'm sorry. I didn't mean to startle you.'

'Why are you here?'

'I said I might come by,' he said.

'But that was weeks ago. I thought you'd forgotten.'

He looked at the hat in his right hand: he was smarter today, wearing a single-breasted dark blue suit. 'It's been a fortnight, actually. I wasn't sure I would come back again. Sometimes it's best to let things lie. But I found I couldn't.'

Livy stared at him wordlessly.

'Mrs Holliday said I could come up. I said I liked the building, and she said you would show it to me.' She still hadn't taken the carpet cleaner from him, and he leaned it gingerly up against the wall. 'But if you really want me to go, I will.'

'Not at all.' She turned away from him, pushing her hair behind her ears. 'We can have a quick look around, if you really wish to. This is the Dining Hall. You'll hardly see anything,' she said. 'The light is dull as ditchwater in here. We can't waste the electricity.'

She did not hear him behind her, as she led him in: across a margin of sprung boards, on to the carpeted section. But she sensed his step behind her.

She was right: the vast room was dull in the half-light. Although one side had four large windows, decorated with coats of arms in stained glass, the presence of buildings across the narrow street outside – for the City street plan was still medieval in its dimensions – blocked the sunlight from entering. The palest dove-coloured light fell through the windows, was transformed, fluttered, and gone, absorbed by the colour and the density of the room.

Livy turned, and saw Christian gazing up at the ceiling. High above their heads, it was coffered, with elaborate neo-classical motifs executed in red, blue and gold leaf, glinting a dull orange in the light. The gold leaf revealed only the ghost of the details, a hint of what was there. Christian narrowed his eyes, trying to make them out.

'Early Victorian,' Livy said.

He glanced at her. 'Yes. Classical motifs.' He looked at the metal carcasses of the two central chandeliers, their lustres dismantled. The four corner chandeliers were intact, their glittering glass shrouded in makeshift sheeting. 'They should be taken down, surely? And the windows boarded?'

'I've said the same.'

He walked up to one wall and examined the cornicing, decorated in gold leaf, separating a section of green marble from a section of mustard-coloured marble. But Livy sensed that this interest only allowed him to concentrate his peripheral senses on the room as a whole. That even as he gazed at the details, he was containing his excitement at the whole of the room.

'They must have had trouble getting all the marble here,' she said.

'It's not all marble.'

'I'm sorry?'

He smiled. 'It's not all marble. Some of it is. But these sections are scagliola. Painted to appear as marble.'

She came close to him, inspected it in the half-light. 'It looks real.'

'You will hardly be able to tell – not with craftsmen of this calibre. But I promise you, it's an imitation. Not everything here is what it seems.'

She looked at him. She sensed her importance to him: absorbed it wordlessly from his look. She felt suddenly that she did not want to look at him for another moment, and turned away, her breath catching in her throat, close to panicking.

'It's all right.' He was behind her. 'Please, don't be upset.' He began to talk, and she had the feeling he was filling up the silence, allowing her to gather herself, raising his voice in the great room, following her across the carpeted floor at a safe distance. 'This building is different from the architect's others. Every building has its language, its vocabulary. But there is a departure between this room and the next – I've read about it – this room is neoclassical, the Committee Room is baroque, the Red Parlour is rococo. The ground plan may be neo-Renaissance, symmetrical, but up here – he's doing the equivalent of mixing his metaphors. It seems – a little disordered. Rather strange.'

She had regained her voice. 'You really do know a lot about this place.'

'Less than I'd like to. Will you let me come back and sketch the rooms?'

'It really isn't my decision.'

'Whose, then?'

'Either the director, the ceremonial head of the Club, who is holed up in a country house somewhere. Or the manager, who runs things from day to day – he is in Sussex, at present. You could write to him there. Or you could ask the man who is staying here at the moment – he is a member of the committee, and I suppose he could authorize you. But, like the army, I don't think he likes socialists.' She tried for a smile.

He smiled in return, and it dissolved the worry on his face. 'Perhaps I won't mention it. What's his name?'

'Jonathan Whitewood.'

She saw his face change; she was not sure how. 'Did you say Whitewood? Does he own a house called Redlands?'

'Yes! Do you know him?'

'Not really.' He gave a dry smile. 'Well, thank you – for letting me look. I've wanted for years to come here. To see these rooms.' He looked around. 'Henry Dale-Collingwood really threw everything at this place.' He saw the questioning look on her face. 'The architect. I'm sorry, I didn't say – it's him I've been thinking of, standing here. I almost feel as though he is standing beside me, pointing out the details: he was that kind of man, I think. He completed the building almost a hundred years ago: 1841.'

Livy thought of Charlotte and Ashton Kinsburg, and that they must have known him. 'What kind of man was he?'

'A well-connected, nineteenth-century gentleman architect,' said Christian. 'Not particularly well-known, now, but I've always rather liked him. He liked scale, and drama, but most importantly he had an eye for detail – an obsession with it, in fact. There is a small archive of his papers and drawings at RIBA, and I looked at them when I was a student. I got the sense he was rather an exacting man, not altogether easy. Incredibly hard on his craftsmen and builders, if they did not reach his high standards. And he wouldn't have liked me at all, being a member of the lower orders – he spent his weekends at country houses, living it up with various patrons. I have a certain fondness for him, I don't know why.'

'I suppose you like his buildings more than him.'

'I don't know that I do really like them.' He smiled. 'They're mostly quite conventional, apart from this one.

Besides, I'm a little more modern now. I want to focus on the future, and that's encouraged in the architect's department.'

'Why aren't you there right now?'

'Because I've been at St Paul's all night and I wanted to see you.'

He was perfectly still; not fidgeting with his hat, not looking away from her. He looked straight into her eyes. Like Jonathan, his stare was direct: but his eyes were dark, and his gaze seemed freighted with emotion rather than cool assessment.

'You should probably go.'

'They'll give me leeway just this once.'

Livy glanced at the empty minstrels' gallery at the far end of the hall, its gold-leafed balustrade holding back the shadows beyond. She thought of Charlotte, and of the men who were just names to her. 'I'm doing some research on the Club in the archive,' she said. 'There will be documents and minutes about the process of its design and execution. I could tell you about them, if you come back one afternoon. I'm sure Peggy is dying to give you tea.'

She saw the relief on his face. 'I'd like that very much.'

'I've grown fond of this place. I don't remember it, before the war. I don't remember what I thought of it. But now, it's my home. I feel safe here.'

'And yet you've applied to join the Land Army?'

She looked sharply at him.

'Peggy told me,' he said.

'It's my duty. Not that it's any of your business.'

'Fresh starts are overrated.'

'And yet I seem to have been gifted one,' she said. As she turned to walk away she saw Jonathan, standing in the doorway. He was smoking a cigarette.

'I'm sorry to interrupt,' he said. 'I came to tell you that I've moved *Woman and Looking Glass*. Do you need any assistance here?'

'Not at all,' she said. 'Mr Whitewood, may I introduce you to Mr Christian Taylor? Mr Taylor works for the London County Council, as . . .' She glanced at Christian, floundering and blushing.

'An assistant architect,' said Christian, walking towards Jonathan, and holding out his hand. 'Pleased to meet you.'

Whitewood did not advance, and only reluctantly, eventually, shook Christian's hand. When Livy looked at Christian, she saw an unknowable expression on his face.

'Mr Taylor knows a lot about the building,' said Livy. 'The architect was a Henry Dale-Collingwood.'

'And this is one of his most famous creations,' continued Christian.

'My ancestor financed the building of this Club,' said Jonathan. 'He was involved deeply in its design, as far as I understand, along with a very involved committee.'

'But Dale-Collingwood had such a strong personality,' said Christian. 'He's written all over this place. Committee or no committee.'

There was a kind of challenge in the words. At length,

Whitewood nodded in Christian's direction, but spoke to Livy. 'Lunch is almost ready, Miss Baker.'

'Of course. Good day, Mr Taylor. If you wouldn't mind seeing yourself out.'

As she walked away, she heard Christian clear his throat and say her name. And she could not help herself. She turned towards him instinctively.

'I forgot to tell you,' he said. 'I meant to point it out. The infinity of mirrors in this room. Have you noticed it before? The mirrors on the facing walls are placed directly opposite each other, so when you look in them, the rooms seem to go on for ever. Look, Livy, won't you? When you get a moment. And then ask Bill to wrap the mirrors, so they aren't broken in the bombing.'

She nodded, and followed Whitewood from the room.

Christian waited for a few moments, then walked out, and watched Livy and Jonathan descend the stairs. Then he silently continued onwards, along the landing, to the north anteroom. To his right, there was the Committee Room, in the baroque style which he had read about; to his left, the Red Parlour. He stood on the threshold of it, and settled his hat back on his head as he looked at the bomb damage. It was as though some malign energy had entered the room and shredded it, peeling away plaster and gilding, leaving only wood and the stripped muscle and bone of the room. There were piles of plaster-whitened wood and gilding on the floor. One window was completely free of glass, its white drapes blowing in the breeze. Only the marble fireplace remained undamaged. Through a far door, he glimpsed a bombed-out room, its ceiling down.

It was ruined, he thought, as he was: and he thought again of Livy, as she had been. Over the last two weeks the same memory had stirred in him, unwanted, like an old injury making itself known in a cold winter: the line of her naked back in the moonlight, her eyes wide and open to him, drinking the sight of him in. And then he thought of her as she was now: anxious, desolate, watchful. Perhaps lost to him for ever. Her beauty sharpening as her flesh melted away. For they were both changed, irrevocably.

As he blinked his stinging eyes clean, he looked around the destroyed Red Parlour. He could make out enough of the decoration and its proportion to imagine what it must have been. And he was surprised to realize, with a slow-dawning knowledge, that it wasn't just familiar because he had read about it. He had seen this room before.

CHAPTER SEVEN

1940

BASEMENT VAULTS, THE MIRRORMAKERS' CLUB

Livy excused herself from coffee after lunch, leaving Peggy, Bill and Jonathan at the table. She wanted to find the Kinsburgs; to be alone with her task. Seated at the desk in the Document Room, she turned to the first box, labelled: 'Club: building of'. It was an archive box of stiff buff-coloured card, its structure secured with heavy metal staples. It was discoloured, as though it had spent its life absorbing London's smoke, and its years of neglect gave it a faintly reproachful air.

She opened the box. On the top was a paper folder, labelled 'Invoices, 1839'. Sure enough, it contained a pile an inch thick of workmen's bills: for plasterwork, carving, and all the allied trades required to create the building. Livy closed the folder, and lifted it out carefully. Beneath it, and on top of another folder, there was a small notebook, the smooth ivory-coloured leather of its cover showing signs of age and some decay. Livy picked it up and opened it.

Henry Dale-Collingwood. Architect and surveyor.
The Mirrormakers' Club. 1839.

She thought of Christian. She turned a page. There was a sketch of an acanthus leaf, made in pencil, alongside an ink drawing of a cornucopia. She turned another page, and frowned at similar drawings: almost the same, but not quite. Repetition with the smallest details changed. *Just small designs,* she thought. Material which would delight Christian, but which would mean nothing to Whitewood. She turned to the end of the notebook, and slipped a folded piece of paper out of the back. Unfolding it, she wondered who had last read its contents.

Gentlemen, I beg leave to submit to you some designs
for the Red Parlour, to be executed in the richest style
of finish ... although a slight departure from what was
originally discussed.

Livy turned back to the first page and began to read.

She assumed the scrawled note next to a column's capital was by the architect. *The scagliola to match the colour of blue supplied in my paper sample. To match it* <u>*exactly*</u>. She frowned and turned the page. Dale-Collingwood had begun the draft of a letter there.

The colour of the scagliola does <u>not</u> match the sample. It does not answer. It must be remade and I will <u>not countenance</u> delay or argument. I did not wish it to be in imitation of verde antico: that was part of the old scheme, and this is <u>new</u>.

She frowned. Christian had been right: demanding was the word.

It was the same with the plasterers, it was the same with the flowers. The flowers must <u>match exactly</u>, must match my drawing, in every detail.

She wondered whether the letter had ever been sent: saw then lines, the writing less tidy, the ink fading at the end of each sentence.

It is the same in everything. Nothing can match it. Always I ask for it, always I put down what it must be. <u>Nothing can match it.</u>

Livy sat back in her chair. She turned another page: saw drawings of a bunch of flowers, annotated for colour, gilding and type. Turned another page: a drawing of a chaise longue. No mention of the Kinsburgs, no shadows of other people: only the architect's relentless attention to detail.

Then, she saw what at first sight was a doodle; swirls of ink. But as her eyes focused on it she saw that it was a cypher, two letters intertwined in a design.

She felt her heart give a little jump in her chest. It was the same feeling she had felt in that moment in the Stair Hall, kissing Jonathan, when a sudden brightness had lifted the room into colour. *CK for Charlotte Kinsburg*, she thought. But she could see no mention of the full name. She turned one page, then another, but there was no name. Initials were too small a clue to go on.

Instead there was a heading. *Committee meeting, 22 September 1839*. Beneath it, a list of items to be addressed.

Impatiently, she turned a chunk of pages, and another bill fell out. This one for a safe. The architect's scrawl across it: *more precautions! not just one lock*. Livy closed the book.

She got up, turned the lights out, and went out of the basement room and up the stairs. Crossed the Stair Hall, up the staircase, taking the left branch. Straight ahead, past the entrance to the Dining Hall on her right, and down a short passage into the Hide. The doorknob, polished brass, turned with a slight squeak.

The room that had been Miss Hardaker's Hide was in

darkness. The windows were covered with blackout material. Livy pulled a small corner back, and light fell across the desk. The room was not big; the walls were covered with empty mahogany shelves, which had once held the archives, and these looked mournful to Livy. She avoided the sight, sat down at the desk, and started to go through the drawers. Astonishingly, the top drawer was full of unlabelled keys, all, it seemed, of different vintages; Livy stared at them, then shut the drawer.

It was the bottom drawer, the last she checked in, which finally yielded something. Piles of files, not orderly at all. Livy opened the top one, saw the typewritten list, entitled 'Index'. She took it out and closed the drawer, replaced the blackout, and went out of the door, through the same passage, and onto the landing, emerging with the large doors to the Dining Hall on her left. The vast double doors had been closed when she had passed them before, but now one was open. Frowning, she went to close it.

She was drawn into the room by the sense that there was someone there. Someone, or something; that she moved through a room shot through with presence. But the room was as she had left it: the same dull light, bathing its details in shadow, the gold leaf darkened to ochre. She walked across the small margin of sprung boards, and when she stepped onto the carpet the light changed in the room; changed so that she blinked, and looked again. Some trick of the light – a few clear shafts penetrated the stained glass, and were not lost, so that the glass pendants of the corner chandeliers, beneath their sheeting, seemed to glow briefly between the gaps. A pale orange light, as one sees in the last moments from the setting sun, or – she thought, and could not check it – from a city on fire. In that moment, she looked straight ahead, and realized that she was facing the mirror at the far end; she was central to the reflection, and she could see the mirror behind her, and in that brief breath of light, she saw the reflections repeating, on and on, into an infinity, as Christian had said, so that it drew an exclamation from her.

The light dissolved, a cloud across the sun, and in a moment, it was as it had been – only she saw a figure, the edge of a figure, just leaving, behind her; she saw a figure in the reflection of the mirror. And she thought she knew who it was.

'Mr Taylor?' she called as she turned, thinking he must have stayed to look around more, and that he was wrong to linger so. Christian, she sensed, would have come back at her call, but nobody came.

She started to walk towards that door, thinking it could be one of the firewatchers, the 'Index' folder flapping in her hand. She came out onto the landing, but nobody was there. Then she saw Whitewood, striding up the stairs to her left; and she gasped.

'Were you just in the Dining Hall, behind me?' she said.

'What? No.'

'Has anyone passed you?'

'No.'

69

Livy walked swiftly on into the north anteroom, then the Committee Room. 'Mr Taylor?' she called, though she knew he would not be hiding anywhere. She didn't see the way Jonathan's face changed as she said the name.

Livy stood, looking between the Committee Room and the ruined Red Parlour. 'There was someone here,' she said. 'I know there was.' And she did not say the other name which came into her mind; the hurried, agitated handwriting.

Henry.

She jumped when Jonathan put his hands on her shoulders. He turned her around and looked into her shining eyes, as he brushed one hand against her pale face. One sheaf of her dark hair had fallen free from its pins.

'He's gone for now,' he said. 'This – Christian.'

'It's not that.' She looked around her. The feeling of presence, that sense of another person, thickened the air.

'I am worried about you. Over coffee, Peggy mentioned – your home. The shock may not be over yet. These things can overtake you. I know something about that. From the first war.'

She frowned. Sensed the pressure building behind her eyes: the swell of her blood, loud as the sea. Her sight seemed to pulsate with it, the rhythm of uncontainable agitation. And she walked past him and towards the staircase.

'I should have told you,' he called after her. 'Miss Baker. Our mystery. I am looking for a diamond.'

She turned sharply and stared at him, on the top stair.

He came to her and pulled her back from the top. 'You're too close to the edge,' he said. 'You might fall.'

She shook his hands from her shoulders. 'I don't care. What does the Mirrormakers' Club have to do with a diamond?'

He looked flushed and a little ashamed; only now did his steady gaze falter. They had talked of family, of a beauty in a portrait, but not of money. She remembered the turn of the cigarette lighter in his hand; that barely contained agitation. 'Charlotte is wearing it in her portrait,' he said.

'I remember,' she said. 'It's that specific diamond?'

'Yes,' he said. 'It's an heirloom. I was left it – or thought I was. But I've been told the stone I have is a fake, and is worth nothing at all. The real diamond is somewhere else. The real diamond is, I think, somewhere in this building.'

She stared at him for a long moment. 'And you want me to find it for you?' she said.

She remembered how he had reached out for her, in the Stair Hall. His apparent coolness; his attempts to smile and be jovial. He had needed her for something. He had needed her to be on his side.

'Miss Baker?'

For a moment, she turned, and teetered on the edge of the top stair. Stared down the length of those steps to the half landing. They were steep, and marble, and it was not as if she hadn't thought about it before: their seductive height.

She moved forwards.

'Livy!'

But she did not look back at him. And she did not jump. There were things she wanted to know; a mystery she wanted to solve. She ran down the marble staircase as fast as she could.

Jonathan paused for a moment, cursing under his breath, and then he followed her.

At the top of the stairs, the doors to the Dining Hall remained open, a perfect rectangle. And had Livy and Jonathan been there, they would have seen it: a bright glow, as though all at once three hundred and thirty-six candles, set in their glass sconces and surrounded by glass lustres, flared into life in the chandeliers, briefly, before the half-darkness fell again.

CHAPTER EIGHT

1838

It was the violence of it. The slow-moving emptiness of the moment of the accident, and the scream of the horse. The jolt threw Charlotte Kinsburg from her seat, cracking her head against the side of the carriage before she fell back again. They were in the busy heart of the City, close to the Bank of England and the fire-ravaged site of the Royal Exchange, but in this instant they were in their own private moment of catastrophe, of noise-framed slow-moving silence.

After the accident, a stunned moment of shock.

Charlotte reached out, hardly seeing. A hand met hers: her husband's. She stared at him, saw and heard him saying her name, but for a moment she was beyond reach.

'Are you hurt?' she heard at last, insistence in his tone.

'No,' she said. He squeezed her hand, and released it.

Then she heard the horse whinny: but it was high,

heart-piercing, a cry of pain and bewilderment. Their brougham was being pulled by one of her favourites, Gilbey. She put her hand on the door. Ashton put his hand out to bar her from it. He reached down and picked up his hat. 'It's a wonder we didn't go over completely,' he said, his face white. Charlotte touched his arm.

'No,' he said. 'Stay here.'

She sank back, obedient. But a moment after he had gone, she realized that she could not stay there for another moment, so she scrambled after him down onto the street. As her feet touched the ground she became aware of the hum of her nerves. It had been raining a quarter of an hour before, and the road and buildings were damp, grey beneath a suddenly blue sky, the road with patches of slickness. Already, people were gathering.

Their coachman was with the horse, and Gilbey was on his knees, cut free from the harness and traces, his neck turning at an unnatural angle, a pinkish foam at his mouth. Charlotte knew he would rise if he could, and wondered if he had broken his leg. She went towards him, and the horse's eye rolled at her.

'Madam,' said the coachman warningly.

Charlotte knew the horse meant her no harm; he lifted his head, as though to smell her palm, as he did on the occasions she had visited the stables to feed him a carrot. She sank down beside him and put her hand on his neck, heedless of the damp and dung-slicked cobbles.

'You were going too fast,' shouted a man who had climbed down from a cart.

Their coachman was not about to back down. 'You spooked him! You caused this!'

Already crowds were gathering and cabs and buggies and carriages were queuing up; already there were people leaning out of carriage windows, annoyed that the traffic on Cornhill was not moving. There was one sin in the City of London, and one sin only: to neglect commerce. The people on the busy, transient streets were unused to pausing for anything. As Charlotte sat in the road beside Gilbey, she saw Ashton speaking to a short, stocky gentleman who had climbed down from a nearby hackney. Their coachman continued to argue with the other driver; violent words were being spoken, and now Ashton was joining them, strong-voiced and imperious. And still Gilbey writhed on the ground. She murmured his name. He thrashed, and the foam from his mouth flicked onto her white dress.

'Help him, please?' she cried, and the stocky man who Ashton had greeted the moment before came towards her, taking off his overcoat as he did so in the sharp air. His face was darkened with stubble, and she saw his face as shapes of light and shadow as he leaned over her. 'Do I have the honour of addressing Mrs Kinsburg?' he said, encircling her with the coat. 'Please, it is cold.'

He put his hand out to help her stand, watched her accept the coat and wrap it more firmly around her shoulders. He assessed her face with concern. 'You will have a fine bruise on your forehead,' he said.

Charlotte stared at the seeping pink stain on her dress,

where her horse's blood-flecked foam had landed on her, and the dark patches of ordure-coloured dampness from the road. 'I have Gilbey's blood on my dress,' she said.

'Please, come away. He will be taken care of, I promise you,' he said.

He steered her away from the accident, close to the buildings. 'There is only one thing to be done,' she said dully. She was rigid with the sheer effort of self-possession. She felt something trickle down her forehead, warm as a teardrop.

The man took out a white handkerchief, and dabbed at her head. 'A little blood,' he said, and she saw that he was poised to catch her if she should faint.

'Who are you?' she said.

He folded the blood-stained portion of the handkerchief closed. 'Henry Dale-Collingwood at your service, if you will forgive me for making my own introduction,' he said. 'I know your husband. I was on my way to the same meeting.'

The machinery of the City was churning. Somehow, the crowd had conjured a man with a gun out of the alleys of the nearby streets. *Of course*, Charlotte thought, there were always slaughterhouses near. As the man loaded, Ashton approached, satisfied by concluding the disagreement soundly; blame had been apportioned, and damages would be paid; but he had to stay to see things were done properly. As the gun was pointed at Gilbey's head, he stood close to Charlotte, took her face in his hands, and turned her head so that she was not able to see the prone horse. She submitted to his touch; a decision, a habit, the easiest course, aware of the

76

stillness and silence of the other man as he stood behind her. A gunshot rang out, but the city gave not a moment's pause. Charlotte compressed her lips tightly, and kept her unshed sobs inside, pushing her emotion down.

'My dear,' said Ashton.

She said nothing.

'Charlotte.' He released her face. 'Will you go with Mr Dale-Collingwood? He is to be at the same meeting as I, at the Club site.'

'But I was to visit Mrs Anderson.'

Her husband glanced at the other man. 'You are not well. Not at all. This evening I will arrange for your usual doctor to call.'

'Of course,' she said dully.

He glanced down, compressed his lips. 'Your dress is ruined. You should not have gone to the horse.'

'But you know me,' Charlotte said suddenly, and she felt Dale-Collingwood flinch at the sarcasm in her voice. 'What a dramatic moment. Do you not think, Mr Kinsburg? A carriage accident in the heart of the City!'

Her husband looked at her steadily, and she could see the annoyance beneath his cool gaze. Their old battle; the exposed nerve she could not help but touch. After a moment, he took her gloved hand, and gave it to Dale-Collingwood, a faint apology in the gesture. 'I would be most obliged.'

'It would be my honour,' the man said.

Ashton bowed and went back to the melee.

*

Charlotte and Dale-Collingwood walked silently down Cheapside, carving their way through the pedestrians, some of whom were heading cheerfully towards the scene of the accident.

'Londoners rather enjoy this kind of thing,' said Dale-Collingwood grimly. 'They see it as part of the spectacle.'

'I suppose the more blood there is on the road, the better it is.'

'I am sorry. Let us not talk of this.'

She shook her head.

'Do you come to London often?' said Dale-Collingwood.

'No. I am used to being quiet at our house in the country. I loved London when I was a girl, but now,' he saw her turn, and look after a man who had pushed through the crowds, and was running with urgency, 'every time I come here, it is – so—'

'Busy?'

'In a way. One only has to enter the city to feel the weight of people's lives – the unrelenting noise of it all. Sadness and happiness in such close quarter – lives clashing – coming together and then parting again – like lines of soldiers in a battle.'

Her hand was on his arm. He put his own gloved hand over it for a brief moment. She felt it as a kindness.

'Why are you going to the meeting?' she said eventually, trying to return to conventions. 'Are you a member of the committee?'

'No,' he said, with a slight bow of his head, as though

making obeisance, even though they were in motion, and the effect was slightly comical. 'I am the architect. So, in effect, your husband is one of my employers.' His mouth twitched a little, in a half-smile. It was then she noticed something.

'Where is your hat?'

'Ah,' he said. 'I was hoping you wouldn't notice, Mrs Kinsburg. And I fear the committee will notice now too. I left my hat in the cab when I got out to assist. And while I was assisting, the cabman left with it.'

She looked at his bare head, his dark curls, then realized she was wearing his coat. 'You must take your coat back,' she said, 'it is cold.'

'No, no, not at all, and you will do me the kindness of keeping that on. We are nearly at the site, and there is a tolerable lodge set up there for us to hold our meetings, and the housekeeper will make you some strong tea.' He cleared his throat. 'You have had a shock, you must rest, and I am charged with ensuring that.'

They turned the corner, and though they must have seemed conventional, a lady resting her hand on a man's arm, it felt to Charlotte as though they were clinging to each other. Unlike Ashton, he did not seek to put distance between them. Warmth seemed to radiate from him, and it seemed, strangely, as though he were porous to her, and everything was fluid, thoughts and feelings moving between them without border.

The gap in the road startled her. 'What happened to the old building?' she said.

'We took it down brick by brick,' he said. 'And sold the contents, not three weeks ago, on the site. Almost every chair.'

'How strange to think of it. It seemed so permanent.'

'In fact it was quite an unsteady building,' he said. 'Too many gaps, and the wind whistling through.'

As he looked at the building site she saw the strange combination of tenderness and ambition in his eyes.

'It will be all-consuming, building this? How will you leave it when it is finished?'

A bright, handsome smile broke his intensity. 'Perhaps I won't. I will lurk in the vaults, below ground, and come out at night to look at my creation.'

She gave a delighted laugh, and then there was silence.

'I have strong nerves, as a rule,' she said eventually. 'It was just the horse. I love my horses.'

'Yes,' he said sadly. 'So I gather.'

'And he will be angry that my dress is ruined. He says I invite drama.'

He looked at her, puzzled, and his kind, steady stare unlocked her grief.

He said nothing as her eyes filled with tears. But he did not turn away from her, or show any kind of embarrassment. They stopped for a moment. He turned to shelter her from curious passers-by as she wiped her tears away. Then they began to walk again.

'None of us look for troubles,' he said quietly, as the lodge came into view. 'They come readily enough. And out of nowhere.'

He led her into the lodge; settled her on a chair near the fire, still draped in his coat, and asked for tea to be brought. Already, other gentlemen were arriving for the meeting, clad in heavy coats, gloves and hats, talking about the rain. He went and greeted one or two, and then he returned to her, ostensibly to check that the tea was to her satisfaction. She tried to apologize, but he silenced her with one direct look. They looked at each other, and it seemed to her that they were in perfect accord.

'Thank you for being kind,' she said.

'Why would I be anything else?'

She bit her lip, to stifle the bitter smile that came to her. He took her silence for something softer.

'It is strange,' he said. 'May I tell you a secret?'

She nodded.

'I was nervous, coming here today. The committee do not give me an easy ride of it, Mrs Kinsburg. But you have banished all my nerves. You have made me my – usual – self. Vehement, stubborn, overconfident.'

'I cannot believe it.'

'Do. I am all of those things. I forgot myself – I felt self-doubt – but you – you have trusted me, and you have been honest. Just your presence has jolted me awake.'

She did not know what to say. She looked at the cup and saucer in her hands.

'Do not,' he said, 'do not, blame yourself for anything that has happened today.'

She looked up, and into his eyes. It was inexplicable,

perfect, wondrous: his expression, his kindness, the roughness of the stubble on his face, his dark untidy curls, the scent of him caught in the coat around her shoulders. All at once he seemed strange and yet intimately familiar. She felt an overwhelming wave of happiness: intoxicating, dangerous and – yes, how Ashton would dislike that – dramatic. This moment must be enough to sustain her.

'If you would do me the favour of forgetting everything I have said to you,' she said.

His face changed; she saw it then, his stubbornness.

'I will do you any favour I can, Mrs Kinsburg,' he said. 'But I am afraid that is quite impossible.'

CHAPTER NINE

1940

THE CITY OF LONDON

The sunshine was bright to Jonathan's eyes, after the days inside in the cool purple light of the Club. The sunlight made him feel saved, and lost, all at the same time. Sitting in the basement vaults the night before, as the bombing shook the Club to its foundations, he had allowed himself to hope that a mistake had been made, and that the diamond was real. When he woke, his hope was gone; like drunkenness he had slept it off. It was the rollercoaster of it. Because as he began to think again, so it revived.

As he came down the front steps of the Club, putting his hat on his head, he decided he would keep asking the question, until the right answer was given. He had known a man like that, before the war: a man from university, who had risen from the working classes. Bullish persistence had seemed, then, a regretful quality to Jonathan; rather vulgar, rather unnecessary. Either one cleared the hurdle at first leap, or not at all. But now, only now, he felt the need for it.

The bombing had changed the City of London. He wandered, bewildered, towards High Holborn. Past collapsed buildings, torn-up roads, exposed pipes and 'Danger' signs. Some buildings were still whole and standing, some were precarious. He passed drifts of rubble; quiet people, hurrying on, taking refuge in silence that answered as courage. There was a strange subdued diligence in the air: no wailing, or crying; these things were superfluous. There was the occasional shout: an instruction, a joke, a request for tea. A bus turned, re-routed, and Jonathan caught sight of the passengers, their calm faces at the window. After the first shock, no one needed a door hanging off its hinges, or a person out of their wits.

As he walked on, Jonathan felt his optimism pall. Not because of the ruins he saw; he was, at least, still alive. He felt a secret exhilaration at that. No, his fall in mood was because he thought he might reach the café and find it gone, wiped clean off the face of the earth. And if that café was gone, he had no idea how to find his contact. He could make enquiries in Hatton Garden – but. The thought tired him so that, traversing a cracked pavement, broken upwards as though the force had come from beneath the earth, he wondered if he might not lie down and rest, here, on the broken ground.

He took another step, and thought of Livy at the Club,

looking through the boxed archives, something she had been doing assiduously over the last day or two. She was quiet, but efficient: she had a job to do, she said, and she would do it. 'A mystery,' she said. 'I always liked solving those.' Her foot tapping against the floor. Tap-tap-tap, as steady as a clock, keeping time. She might dislike him, he thought, but she wanted to know where the diamond was, just as he did.

He had watched her. Sitting quietly at her basement desk – a broken table, one leg supported by an old book which had bomb damage. Lifting the lid of a box, and laying it flat, interior facing up. Picking up the first letter and unfolding it carefully with her reverent hands. The way her face stilled, and opened, to the musty papers. She had small hands, pale and dramatically veined, and unlacquered fingernails. So different from her predecessor, he thought: the red-nailed Miss Hardaker. He had kissed her once, too, years ago. Reached out and taken hold of her as, he thought, he had the right to do.

As Livy leaned forwards, the waves of her brown hair fell forwards too, leaving the back of her neck exposed. He had watched her a good long time, and she had not lit a cigarette, or spoken, or done anything other than read the letter in front of her, written by a long-dead architect who she had never met. He hoped that, one day, someone might read his letters with such reverence.

'He is agitated,' she said. 'Henry. He feels his orders are not being met.'

Jonathan had not told her where he was going today, and

85

felt slightly ashamed, as though he were violating some kind of pact which he had not been aware of forming.

Let the diamond be real, he thought, *and I will tell her everything.*

Let the diamond be real, he thought, *and I will never touch her again. I will be the faithful husband I have never yet been.*

He passed a man, dressed like him in overcoat and trilby hat, hollow-cheeked, and pale-haired, his lips forming silent words as he passed. The man tripped and fell into Jonathan; Jonathan supported him.

'I say, forgive me.' A strange, ghastly smile filtered over the man's face. A difficult politeness, in the midst of desolation.

'Are you all right?' said Whitewood, bluff, reassuring. A kindness to be strong, and to pretend the other man was strong too. This was how wars were fought, and griefs were borne.

'I am. Thank you.'

They parted then, two London strangers. And as he walked, past a knot of heavy rescue workers and police and firemen, looking at the heap of rubble which had until last night been a building, Jonathan felt in his pocket. The stone was still there. It was precious to him. He was ashamed at how precious, in the midst of the ruin of human lives.

Mrs Cohen's café on the corner of Greville Street and Leather Lane had miraculously survived the night, and Jonathan could see Mr Moscow sitting at his usual table, like a woollen-clad miracle. There was a slight problem at the door, when Jonathan could not remember the code word he had been given. The man at the door was immovable, and Jonathan knew there was no way he could bluff or bluster his way through. He was not respected here. If anything, his voice counted against him, but to pretend to be anything other than who he was seemed ridiculous. Luckily, Mr Moscow caught sight of him through the haze of cigarette smoke, and sent one of his sons to tell the gatekeeper to let him in.

This was the only place Jonathan could remember feeling self-conscious in. The air was dense with smoke, the warmth of steam and bodies, and the noise of conversations being conducted in many different languages. As he walked towards the steady-eyed old man, sitting at his table with his cup of tea, he felt a flush move up his neck and into his face.

Jonathan pulled out a chair opposite him. 'May I?' He glanced to the right. The table next to theirs was home to an intense chess game, but the two players had stopped and were looking at the stranger.

Mr Moscow's elder son, who sat next to his father, nodded. The younger son had gone to talk to an acquaintance. Mr Moscow himself, his face as lined as an Ordnance Survey map, with his ravines and extravagant pores, kept his unblinking dark gaze on Jonathan for as long as he could, beyond the bounds of civility. Then he took a sip of his tea.

'Nice to see you, Mr Whitewood,' he said. His cigarette lay smoking in the metal ashtray with its broad rim, cut in with semi-circles. There were no paper packages containing gemstones on the table, just a small cloth pouch containing, Jonathan knew, the tools of his trade.

Jonathan found himself focusing on his own discomfort. He was beginning to sweat in the oil-drenched smoky air. He felt almost anaemic sitting opposite this old man, who was possessed, he was sure, with a powerful spirit. A kind of animation that Jonathan could only dream of. He marvelled at Moscow; the man carried only the smallest notebook, where he made notes of diamond deals. The notebook was not out today. Jonathan wondered how the war had affected his trade.

'What do you want?' Mr Moscow's son now.

Jonathan cleared his throat. 'I'm sorry, I should have said. Mr Moscow, you will remember, perhaps, the meeting we had before.'

'Of course. I remember everything.'

'Pa.' The elder son tutted.

'I do.' This was a statement of fact, it seemed.

Jonathan persevered. 'You may remember that I had a diamond in my family.'

'Yes, a most unusual case.' The old man waved his hand. 'What of it?'

Jonathan took out his package and put it on the table. It was not wrapped in paper, as diamonds usually were; he realized now he should have done that. It was simply swaddled in a clean handkerchief.

'You walked here?' Mr Moscow looked alarmed. 'If it is what you told me, you are a reckless man.' It was clearly not a compliment.

'I've been told it's not a diamond,' said Jonathan, thinking: Emmet the valuer, bloody Emmet, with the tips of his moustache waxed, saying *I am very sorry to tell you, sir, that it doesn't seem to be a diamond*. Now, it seemed stupid to have believed him. 'I'm still sure it is. But I know you will be able to confirm it.'

'I see.' Moscow's lips twitched with amusement. Still, he did not unwrap the stone; just left it lying on the waxy red and white checked tablecloth, alongside a ketchup stain. Just to emphasize his nonchalance, he sipped his tea.

'Before I look at it, shall we be clear?' he said. 'If it is a diamond – if, if, if, I spend my life on ifs, Mr Whitewood—'

'As we all do, these days,' said Jonathan, and couldn't keep his tone clear of bitterness.

'If it is a diamond,' said Moscow – no room for sentimentality, his rather disappointed gaze seemed to indicate – 'if you wish to sell it – which you do, otherwise why come here? – then I wish to have first refusal.'

Jonathan opened his hands, palms up. 'But of course,' he said.

And with that settled, the diamond dealer took his loupe from the cloth pouch, and began to unwrap the stone.

CHAPTER TEN

1838

Henry Dale-Collingwood returned to his West End club at six. It was dusk in the city, and the lamps were lit, but he did not glance to his left or right as he ran up the steps and into the lobby, handing his coat and hat to the attendant. Normally on such an evening he would have enjoyed sitting at the window of the library, his chair pulled discreetly to one side, watching the traffic on Pall Mall, cabs running people to the theatre, to dinner, to indiscretions. London by gaslight fascinated him, and especially when watched from a warm room with a good fire. But not tonight. Although his body was full of strength and energy, his mind was tired. He took a table for two in the dining room, asked for a drink, and declined to order dinner just yet.

He sensed the head waiter's bewilderment, and knew that in changing his routine he had caused an astonishment close to offence. So it was with relief on all sides when his friend Peregrine arrived in the dining room. The waiter brightened, obviously hoping that this sprightly young gentleman would set things back on the right track. And he was correct. 'Duck, spinach and a baked apple should set us to rights,' Peregrine said, having briskly consulted the menu, 'and a full claret-jug, if you please.'

Henry silently sat back in his chair, content for everything to be done, his mind still full of the day's events. When the wine was brought he toasted his friend, hoping that it would restore him to conviviality, but it did not.

'I saw a horse shot today,' he said.

Peregrine choked on his mouthful of wine. 'That's a nice way to begin our evening together, I must say,' he said, once he had recovered himself.

Henry smiled. 'I apologize.'

'What if there had been ladies present?'

'Here?'

'Well, yes, point well made, but – we are meant to be gentlemen, aren't we? And I am sure that is not the correct way for a gentleman to begin polite conversation.' His own shakiness about his social standing made Peregrine fastidious. It had the reverse effect to his intention: it flagged his lack of confidence.

'Your perception of yourself as not quite a gentleman yet really bothers you much more than it does anyone else,' said Henry. They had met at the Royal Academy drawing schools. Both sixteen years old; both with more determination than the sum of the others' in the room put together. It could have alienated them, and yet from the first day, they had formed a bond.

Peregrine swallowed another mouthful of wine to fortify himself. 'That's because you've got a duke buried somewhere in your lineage, but I haven't. A speck of dirt on my collar or cuffs and I feel I am on the defence. Horse shootings are not on the list of civilized topics for conversation. And why did you see a horse shot, for God's sake? It should be a gentleman's privilege to avoid such things.'

'There was a carriage accident.'

Peregrine made an indiscriminate noise of disgust. 'There is enough trouble in this world without discussing it over dinner.'

Dinner was served. Henry turned the conversation to Peregrine's current preoccupation. He was designing a townhouse for a wealthy patron who had bought a house in the West End and razed the site. The style had been dictated by the owner. 'It really is too much sometimes. I shall name this a new style: Ultra-gothic. Could we fit in another arch, Mr Brownlow? Another arch? There are already two thousand pointed arches in that place. I dream of arches, and of arches within arches. But the interior – he gives me all the freedom I wish for, I suppose because he is not married yet, and so there is no special darling for him to please. And as a result, I am obsessed with the interiors. I care more about the coat-hooks than I do the capstones.'

Henry listened with amusement to his friend, laughing

when he was meant to, and sympathizing too. They both ate quickly. And it was only when Peregrine ate his last mouthful of baked apple, and put his spoon down with a hearty clunk, that he turned from his building project to something else.

'There's something the matter,' he said, wiping his mouth on the starched napkin. 'Is it the horse? I suppose if you *must* talk about it.'

He clearly expected his friend to laugh, but Henry only smiled gently and, staring at the tablecloth, put his own spoon down.

'It's not the horse,' Henry said. 'Just a difficult day. Tomorrow, I will be better and brighter – you picked a bad evening to dine with me, that's all, and I apologize for my lack of good humour.'

'In that case, I insist I dine with you again tomorrow,' said Peregrine.

'Agreed, and heartily,' said Henry. 'Mirrormakers' is playing on my mind. Some of the internal arrangements to the service rooms – may I show you the plan? It is in my room.'

'Gladly,' said Peregrine. 'As long as we can smoke a cigar there. I've stolen two of my fathers'. I know, I know, it's a poor thing for a man of two-and-thirty to do, but no matter what I buy, he always gets better. And a man shouldn't be made to feel inferior by his father's cigars.'

They went upstairs together, greeting some of the other members on the way. Henry had a suite: a bedroom, a dressing room and a small sitting room. The lamps were all lit, but the room was still in that low, grainy light which, Henry thought, sometimes was called cosy, and sometimes melancholy. He went to his desk in the dressing room and heard Peregrine exclaim. Returning, he saw a familiar female who had shocked his friend by skittering out from behind one of the heavy curtains, where she now and then stowed herself.

'Good evening, Foi,' said Henry. 'You're not meant to be in the rooms at this time of night, are you?' He spent most of his time with Foi stating the obvious.

The maid curtseyed low in his direction and gave him a knowing smile. 'Just thought I'd check that all was in order in your room, sir,' she said. 'You know I always make sure you have the best. And there was a letter for you.'

He took it from her with good humour. 'Off you go,' he said, and she left with another smile.

'Is she a whore?' said Peregrine, after the door had closed, rather more loudly than he should have done, and evidently in the hope that the departing Foi would hear him.

Henry broke open the letter with rough hands. 'She's harmless enough. But she shouldn't be around here at night. I'm honourable, of course, but the others . . .'

'I have no idea why she's following you around. You're so ugly, especially when one compares you to me – and I'm here often enough. I'm surprised she's never – er – approached me.'

'Perhaps she's never happened upon you in the right circumstances. I'm sure that's all which is keeping her from storming you.'

'And what's her dreadful name?'

'I have no idea. Everyone calls her Foi. Why do you want to know? Are you planning to propose to her?'

Peregrine pulled a face; Henry well knew that he was planning to marry up, and his intensity had already won him admirers from the groups of pale, young, pious ladies he wooed at Southwark Cathedral each Sunday with his downcast looks alone.

'God damn it.' Henry closed the letter and fought the urge to crumple it up.

'Henry?'

'Another letter from the committee of the Mirrormakers' Club. It's always the same: courteous to my face, then half an hour after every site visit they sit down and write out what they so sweetly describe as "their concerns" as if I don't know my own business. I've built railway stations, for God's sake!'

'Technically, you've built one railway station.'

'And they don't think I can manage their wretched little building.'

Peregrine put his hand on Henry's arm. 'My dear chap, this is not a wretched little building. This is a jewel, at the heart of the City of London: the same City from which you draw most of your clients. You're in sight of St Paul's and dealing with the type of people you always deal with. Did you think it would go without a wrinkle?'

Henry put the letter down. 'No.'

'And are you letting your clerks take the correct burden of the work, or are you, as usual, trying to do everything yourself? Normally I wouldn't object. I know how you are, but—'

'But what, Perry? Do you think I cannot manage it?'

'Don't be ridiculous. If Her Majesty asked you to rebuild Buckingham Palace you could manage it. What I am trying to say is: normally, you would laugh at this kind of thing. It's simply what we have to deal with, isn't it, Henry? But tonight you don't seem to be thriving on it. And dinner wasn't so bad that it should put the night in your eyes so completely.'

Henry sat down in one of the faded leather easy chairs. 'It has been a long winter,' he said.

Perry sighed. 'I know. And your parents, and Kitty.'

Henry nodded, suddenly unable to speak. His parents, and his beloved sister, all swept from life by an infection, while he was building a civic hall in Birmingham. On his return he had stood in the empty doorway of the family home in Russell Square, listening for them. He knew they were not there, but he almost – almost – thought he could hear them.

'What is it like, being in the house?'

'I'm staying here at present. I am not quite ready – to take ownership of it.'

His friend accepted this in silence.

'The truth is, I have not been thinking of it,' said Henry. 'Work is distracting me, that is a good thing. Or it was. But now – these men. Always questioning, always presuming to know things. I have a hundred things to think of already; from stone samples to scagliola. I have a long list of things to attend to tomorrow morning alone. And now I will spend time trying to write a polite answer to these wretched men who know nothing of architecture and simply want to have their say, for the sake of having their say. Showing off.'

'Maybe they do know things – just not the same things you know.'

'I met one of them, at the accident today. Ashton Kinsburg. He's a rising man, with a lot of money in the build. Quiet, before, generally supportive. I knew about him, of course I did – we'd nodded to each other at dinners – and he's rich as Croesus, Perry. He has just finished remodelling his estate in Hertfordshire, Redlands.'

'Good lord! Of course. I knew I'd heard the name.'

'I should say so. How much did those alterations cost? It was a Queen Anne house, correct? And now, according to reports, it covers twice the area and has the interior of a French chateau – a fucking French chateau in an English shell. The dissonance, when one walks in! All the man can talk about is gold leaf. And today: he speaks up. This letter is written and signed by him. I cannot move, in this room, for his opinions.'

Peregrine frowned at his vehemence. 'Well, knock him down a peg or two. Did you not see it coming? Was he quiet today, or had he found his voice?'

'God damn him, he had found it. But I would not bring him down.'

'Why not, just a little? It's your site, and you have been commissioned to build it. You're a gentleman, like him.'

Henry snorted. 'Not quite. I don't own a glass factory. I

could have needled him a dozen times, but first: it is not my style, and second: his wife was sitting nearby, with her dead horse's blood on her dress, the poor creature.' He looked at his wine glass. 'The wine's gone. Where's Foi when I actually bloody need her?'

Peregrine folded his hands in his lap; his stillness showed attention to the strange tenderness on Henry's face at the mention of a woman. 'Much as I always hesitate to say so, I think the dearth of wine might be a good thing in this case. Just for a minute or two. This is not like you. This Mrs Kinsburg. What was she like? Did *she* speak up?'

Henry frowned. 'What? No, of course not. She was by the fire, trying to recover her spirits. I took her from the accident, trembling like a child that thinks it will be kicked – Kinsburg showed her hardly any kindness. She listened to the meeting, of course she did: I saw her eyes from across the room, watching us, trying to catch what we were saying. She seems a woman of sense. I would have welcomed her opinion.'

'I see.'

The coolness of Peregrine's voice halted Henry's feverish annoyance.

'What is it?' he said.

Peregrine looked at his hands. 'We came up here to see a plan,' he said. 'Would you care to show it to me? You mentioned the service rooms – the position of a scullery?'

'Not until you tell me what's set your mouth as prim as a governess's.'

Peregrine sighed. 'I don't intend to meddle in your affairs, but this Mrs Kinsburg. Beautiful face, yes? Lovely eyes?'

'She is a perfectly ordinary woman, whatever revolting direction you are going in.'

'Ordinary sounds like a lie. And remember, Henry, I can tell when you are lying. My friend, you are raw at the moment. No, do not laugh – that is the word. If you prefer, you are – susceptible. If this Mrs Kinsburg and her pale and downcast face is causing your poor temper, you should cut it off right now. I mean it.'

Henry stared at him. 'I'll get the plan.'

'Good chap.'

Henry went back to his desk. Unusually, the wine had gone to his head; he felt drunker than he had in years, and he was a two- or three-bottle man normally. He fumbled angrily through the drawer of his desk. He wanted to erase the day; to live it again, taking another route to the Mirrormakers' Club site, a route which did not involve carriage accidents, or dead horses, or another man's wife.

He had felt an attachment to her immediately, and he had reasoned that it had been the way they had been thrown together, in the aftermath of the crash: a sudden intimacy, which would fade. He had driven away from the meeting having barely nodded goodbye to her.

But nothing had faded. This evening, sitting at the table as Peregrine talked, he wanted to speak to Charlotte Kinsburg. He remembered the way she had watched the meeting at the lodge, her gaze bright and curious, now and then the hint of a smile on her face, despite the trial she had just been through. He wanted to ask her what questions she wanted answered: to tell her that she could ask him question after question. That he would tell her what she wanted to know; as long as she also spoke of herself.

'Henry.' It was Peregrine. He came to his friend's side. 'Can you not find it?'

'You're talking rubbish, Perry,' said Henry roughly, but he did not look at his friend. 'About the lady. I have no – intentions.'

'I'm sure,' said Peregrine, patting him on the shoulder. 'You're nothing but honourable, as the disappointed Foi knows. I'll come for dinner tomorrow, and we can look at the plan then. Let's go downstairs and have a brandy. And one of my father's cigars. Yes?'

He paused, looking over Henry's shoulder. 'What's that?'

'The lighting plan for the Dining Hall.'

Perry whistled. 'Six chandeliers. That's a lot of glass. Imagine the potential for breakage.'

Henry sighed, and smiled at him bravely. 'I think of little else,' he said.

CHAPTER ELEVEN

1838

Charlotte leaned close to the chessboard, as her husband pushed a knight towards her. She did not hear a single sound of the city night. London was banished; they were behind their high walls, their ornamental gates.

'Thank you for asking me to play,' she said. 'I thought you did not wish me to.' He had never really liked the idea of her plotting, or game-playing, she was sure: he never really wished her to think more than sixty seconds ahead.

A little half-smile warmed his face. 'An occasional game, with your husband, is not unproper,' he said. 'The London house looks well, does it not?'

'Very fine,' she replied.

It is a terrible place, she thought, everything white and gold and blue and red, imagined into life by Ashton. He was a man of definites.

He toppled her king, with satisfaction.

The chess game finished, they retired separately, her London maid – new, and taciturn – assisting her swiftly before retiring. Charlotte was sitting on her bed, listening to the tick of the clock, when his knock surprised her. She had assumed he would leave her to sleep, as the doctor had seen her. He was a fastidious man.

She called his name, and when he opened the door she saw hesitation in him, a rare thing. He was still dressed. He held a box in his hands. It was covered in brown leather bordered with ornate gold tooling.

'My dear?' she said, watching him, paused on the threshold, as though he were gathering his words. His eyes glittered; she had sensed his excitement about something throughout the evening, had thought his meeting with the architect must have pleased him.

'I have something for you. From Hamptons. I meant today to be – a happier occasion. But you seem recovered. So – here.' He handed it to her.

She took the box and opened it. There, on a bed of navy blue velvet, lay the largest diamond she had ever seen, cut into an asymmetrical pear shape.

She looked at her husband wordlessly.

'*Le Fantôme*,' he said, like a child who has opened a Christmas present. 'Nearly thirty-five carats.' He could not help himself; he took the box from her hands, and she saw then that the delight in his eyes had been caused by the diamond and his possession of it, and all that that possession said about him.

He was telling her its provenance. He spoke of a ship-wreck, of royal houses, of private collections, of an unbroken whispered thread of history that this strangely cut diamond had. Named for the inclusion deep inside the stone, which had seemed so mysterious to its first owners, this was no modern gem. This thing had to be known, decoded, and treasured. And now it was theirs.

Charlotte smiled brightly. 'It will be a wonderful addition to your collection,' she said, watching the light from the diamond on his face. She could not help but think of its provenance with misgiving, of the generations holding it and then handing it on as something burning with history.

He looked up at her. 'I will have it set in a tiara for you. It will be part of our family jewels. It will show what I have achieved. Redlands, our children, my growing influence in the City. I can see you in your green dress, or your red dress, with that diamond in your hair. You will seem a queen to those around you.'

'I cannot possibly keep the diamond in my jewel box,' said Charlotte.

'Of course not! It shall go into a safe. But you are pleased, aren't you? This diamond is for you. This diamond is for you.' He sought a better reaction, she knew, from repetition. What should she do? Burst into tears? Feign joy and sink to her knees with audible prayers of thanksgiving? 'I am so grateful, dear Ashton,' she said, as strongly as she could, and yet all she could think was: *I would give anything for my horse to still be alive. I would give this diamond to*

*Hamptons, and this dress and this room, and this house
which is not a home.*

They climbed into opposite sides of the cold bed. She
sensed she had disappointed him in some unnameable way,
but that he was puzzled rather than angry. Their coupling
was brief, almost chaste, and silent. They did not look at each
other directly.

'Are you looking forward to going home tomorrow?' he
said afterwards, rolling away from her.

'Of course,' she said. 'I am like an old lady these days,
only happy in my own little salon, with my own occupations.'

He kissed her on the cheek and climbed out of the bed.
'You are still young, my love. I cannot imagine you ever
being old. I will let you sleep. It has been a difficult day. I
will take this.' He closed the diamond into its box; it had lain
beside the bed throughout.

She watched him go, and the sound of his footsteps faded
immediately, so that it were as though he had never been
there at all, except for the disordered bed, and the slight
soreness he had left behind.

It was not difficult to get older, she found. She rather welcomed the idea of fading, and of her husband losing interest
in her. What was difficult was remembering what it had felt
like to be young: the sense of endless possibility, and the
certainty of future happiness. Mr Dale-Collingwood had
reminded her of the romantic dreams of her youth. She lay on
her back, looking at the ceiling as her candle burned down.
She remembered his kindness, the way he had guided her

away from the scene of the accident. The instant sympathy which had seemed to connect them. Then she put it aside, and blew out her candle.

She had not lied to Ashton. She had been glad to leave Redlands to come to London, and now she was glad to leave London for Redlands. As a young woman she had hated leave-takings and goodbyes, but as a married woman she thirsted for them. Every time she travelled she courted the possibility of change. Then she would arrive and – smiling, greeting the servants, ordering the dinner, choosing a gown to wear – realize that everything was the same as it had been, as it would be, for ever and ever, amen.

The next morning, Charlotte left the scent of her perfume in the rooms of the London house. She had smothered herself with oil of lily of the valley: the flower that symbolized the return of happiness. Her pride had not failed her yet. She would be fragrant, leaving a sweetness that would take hours to fade as the staff shut up the house again, threw dust sheets over the furniture, and mocked her and her husband. These things, people remembered.

My mistress was a bitch, a trial, a whore, but she always smelt sweet.

The air was cold. A fresh pair of horses, and their travelling coach. The footman opened the carriage door, and she took her husband's hand and jumped up the steps. She always took his hand with an exaggerated flourish, because she knew his love of a graceful gesture. Today, she saw

SOPHIA TOBIN

from his dark expression that his mood had turned, and that she had irritated him. But her own husband was too powerful to be pitied. *Even Henry Dale-Collingwood*, she thought, *is indentured into service, like me.* Perhaps that answered why they had that strange kinship. The coach set off.

'What did you do with your gown?' Ashton said. He had been watching her expression, and she felt guilt pass over her face like a shadow.

She looked at the window, its blank black surface, shielded by a blind. 'Which gown?'

A small sigh. 'The one I sent to Paris for. The one you got the horse's blood on. The one you knelt in the road in.' She heard the rhythm of building annoyance.

'It was ruined. I left it with Sarah.'

'I see. So one of our London maids will be dressed in the finest day gown our Parisian dressmaker had to offer.'

'It would have been impossible to get the blood out of it.' At least in her mind, she would have always seen it there, the seeping stain. 'I have said sorry.'

'Yes, you have said sorry.' He leaned forwards, balancing his weight on his silver-topped cane. 'But I'm not sure you truly appreciate what you have done.'

She sat silently; it was impossible to interrupt at this point. The mismatch of their emotions, of their respective reactions to every situation, had been so charming and playful in their courtship, but marriage had rendered it dreadful.

'Is this about the diamond?' she said, in a low voice. 'It is very beautiful, Ashton. If I did not show my feelings enough, it is only because I was tired.'

His eyes flashed at her. 'It is about your ingratitude, but not about the diamond. I went to a great deal of trouble to order that gown. I ordered it, knowing you would suit it, knowing that you liked it, having shown you the fashion plates. The care I took over it, Charlotte. Imagining that you would be delighted to wear it; that you would take care of it.'

'I was very grateful for the gown, and for the other gowns you ordered with it. I still am. I did take care of it. I did not mean to soil it. The whole matter was very unpleasant for me.'

'You point out I bought you a lot of gowns, as if that lessens the offence. Don't play that game with me. And please remember that the whole matter was very unpleasant for me too. In the midst of all the difficulties, you were another worry added to my list of worries, because of your indelicate behaviour.'

She tried not to let any expression cross her face.

'Don't do that!'

Her tone even, her face still. 'Do what?'

'Make your face small and tight and pinched like that.'

She closed her eyes. It was impossible; if her face showed her annoyance, it would provoke him; blank, it provoked him. The only possible defence was stillness, and silence. She must play dead, she must fake utter submission. Each beat that passed was hopeful, each moment when no words broke from him. But she would not weep.

'You have been very ungrateful,' he said eventually.

She kept her eyes closed. She knew now he would leave it, but that her own battle was not over. For now, in the sudden rush of relief, she would have to suppress the breaking wave of her own anger. When she opened her eyes, her husband was dozing, and she could not help but imagine satisfaction in the line of his mouth.

They made good time. The hours passed quickly in silence and reverie; in the late afternoon they were on the Long Drive, the straight, tree-lined avenue which led to the façade of Redlands. Charlotte knew it by the perfection of the surface and the straightness of the road.

'Home,' said Ashton. She saw the contentment in his face. She smiled slightly, enough to show agreement. She had lived here for the nine years of their marriage. Thanks to the endless repetition of the house's routine, her memory tricked her into thinking it had gone quickly. And it was home, because here she had had her children. As always she glanced at the distant spire in a clump of trees, the parish church where her first child, Loveday, now rested. The twins, Isabel and Thomas, still lived.

How Redlands filled the sight. The central symmetrical body of the house had been added to with two long wings. Its windows glittered in the afternoon sunshine. She had seen it at its best on her first visit: in the midst of a ripe English summer, its lines softened by the green of abundant shrubs and trees, her eyes drawn by the blue of a cloudless midsummer sky. Intoxicating, it had seemed like a magical place. No other arrival had ever matched that first one.

The staff lined up to greet them. Charlotte smiled blandly, nodded, murmured, her hand on Ashton's arm. Her own maid, Katie, was not in the receiving line: she would be upstairs, waiting, with lavender water.

The wood-panelled stone hallway was cool. Already she heard the sound of their son coming, the distant running footsteps in a strange rhythm, for he was galloping like a knight on a horse. He and his sister had rattled around this vast house for days. She would have to wait for him to reach them. Her son, with his large eyes, and his silken hair, and his plump cheeks. He was his father's boy, and even as a baby he had looked at her with that uncomprehending, expressionless stillness that she could not fathom.

'Papa!' He stopped himself at the top of the first staircase – for there were many at Redlands. 'Mama.' His nurse caught up with him. Beneath an arch with a coat of arms above, he stood, their little prince.

'My dear,' Charlotte said. 'Where is your sister?'

'Miss Isabel is resting, ma'am,' said the nurse. 'She is a little tired today. No cause for alarm.'

'Are you sure?'

'I am.'

'I will visit her later.'

'My sister is a weakling.'

'Hush now, dear.'

'Come here,' said Ashton, holding out a hand. Thomas came down to them, slowly now, and in the manner of a little

Cavalier, which he had been practising, she could tell. He babbled of swords, and of his tutor, and of his nurse being naughty to him. Charlotte touched his hair: soft, clean, and as golden as hers was dark.

'I must change,' she murmured. He made a slight move towards her, and she found herself dipping to kiss his head. He did not smell of her; he did not smell of her daughters; he was, still, a little foreign object. 'You look very fine in your new suit.'

'You look very fine too,' he said. His chin rested on her shoulder. It was enough.

She rose, and Ashton put his hand out to her. She took it, and kissed it, in a swell of tenderness which had seemed unimaginable hours before. Such was the shifting kaleidoscope of her marriage, for her feelings towards her husband were not constant – they changed with the light and the hour. She left Ashton talking to their son and his nurse, and climbed the stairs softly. She saw the shadow of a servant at the turn of one flight, and she took another, pretending she had not seen them. Past the eyes of a dozen Kinsburg ancestors, made rich by glass; past a wall of arms and armour; through a corridor where the Dutch still lifes hung, to her suite of rooms, where her maid, Katie, greeted her. Charlotte embraced her, enquired after her, and finally sat down with a sigh.

'I'll wear the green dress,' she said.

'Best not be late to tea,' said Katie. 'Mr Lemaire has been working flat out.' And she smirked.

Charlotte groaned. Barbara, the wife of Ashton's brother Nicholas, largely expressed difficult emotions through the medium of patisserie, and had engaged a French specialist, Mr Lemaire, to execute it. The scale of the cakes she ordered for tea was proportional to her rage each day. They were cakes of garish colours, iced elaborately, stuffed with cream, sixteen-layered, mirror-glazed. Cakes that had to be attacked rather than eaten. Barbara rarely ate a slice herself, instead forcing portions on those around her.

Charlotte went to the window as Katie brought the gown she had asked for. She looked out at the perfectly manicured gardens of Redlands, with their topiary and fountains, and always a gardener, so perfectly dressed, carefully and quietly tending to something. She had looked at this view every day of her marriage. In the past it had chilled her; its perfection had a certain power over her. But now, all of a sudden, the columns of light and shadow falling through the pruned trees on the horizon were no longer about order and confinement; they were simply beautiful.

'You seem well, madam,' murmured Katie.

Charlotte looked at her and wondered if everyone could see the hope in her eyes when she thought of Henry. She did not have to see him again, but he had changed everything. She felt that beyond the window, the sun had been released from a covering of clouds, and was filling the room with an intense golden light. Some kind of new beginning had been made.

She felt the density of the feeling between her and Henry

as they sat in the lodge, comrades and friends. She was filled with it, as the golden light warmed her.

She smiled at Katie. 'I have been calm too long,' she said. Her maid shrugged, used to her strangeness.

CHAPTER TWELVE

1940

In the Committee Room the light poured in through the broken windows, left unboarded by Bill. Way above Livy's head, the gilded cornicing depicted cherubs with plump and babyish faces, horses racing across the countryside, and stylized trees. The light bounced off the gilded highlights. This side of the building got good light, and its furnishings, although lavish, were also businesslike: the long committee table and leather upholstered chairs imparted a briskness which was comforting to Livy. She found a section of the table which was not studded with glass, and put her small pile of boxes there. She was tired of the vaults, and wanted to come up into the light. She was also tired of her emotions. Despite her disappointment at Jonathan, she felt drawn to

113

him. She always knew when he was watching her, as she read through the archives. Felt his eyes; sensed him. And the kiss had lingered in her mind.

The smoke and dust from a hundred bombed buildings hung in the air of the empty City streets. Thick and noxious, the kind of air that stuck its nails into the back of your throat, so that you felt the scrape of it there hours later. And yet, standing at the glassless window of the Committee Room, Livy thought she sensed the freshness of the winter, a hint of the irrepressible life of the city.

Earlier that morning, she had sat with the painting in its basement vault where Jonathan had placed it, wrapped in sheeting. On the floor, leaning on one hand, her legs folded behind her. Not memorizing any details, just interrogating Charlotte's vivid face on that flat surface. *Who are you looking at?* she said. *Who are you focusing on, just past my shoulder? Ashton? Henry? Some other person I know nothing of, lingering in the corners of your life?* She thought if she looked long enough, Charlotte might give her some answers. That the vivid face might speak, glowing with the light from beyond the window, Redlands behind her. Charlotte's face: self-assured, almost mocking. Slightly impatient. But silent. Charlotte's expression seemed to change with the colour of Livy's own thoughts. Today, she had seen a slightly rebellious look in those eyes.

Livy realized that she had equated Ashton with Jonathan. Ashton was so absent from the things she had read, that this vacancy had simply been filled by his great-grandson, with his black hair and his green eyes. Jonathan had lingered around her these past days, and his silence was harder for her to bear than if he had spoken. It was silence that drew things from her, that made her want to fill it with words, and questions. She had worked on, reading through the boxes, sensing him always nearby, as though he were waiting for something. The scent of him intoxicated her – she both longed for and dreaded the touch of his hand on the back of her neck.

Sitting at the Committee Room table, Livy turned another letter. Henry Dale-Collingwood's writing was variable: sometimes so neat that it seemed like a formal exercise, sometimes so scrawled and on the borders of indecipherable that it seemed to tell of agitation. Her connection to him, set in motion by Christian, had strengthened over the days. He repeated phrases, phrases so formal and impenetrable that she was sure he was hiding behind them. Surely a man could not be so pompous?

> *I send respectful thanks to the committee for their valuable and enriching insights . . .*
> *I beg leave to inform the committee . . .*
> *I ask the committee's permission to . . .*
> *If the committee will forgive me, I will take the liberty of . . .*

Occasionally, she thought she heard him clearly: a weary sarcasm in the elaborate phrasing. But she could not be sure.

She glanced at the clock on the mantelpiece. She had been reading, she thought, for a minimum of an hour and a half, and all of the letters so far had been by the architect. They were full of politeness and brusque, gentlemanly vocabulary. Nothing personal at all. Miss Hardaker's 'Index' had not helped. She had focused on financial matters, rather than individuals. The only thing to do was to keep reading.

The next letter was in different handwriting, and Livy's heart rate spiked when she saw the name at the bottom: *Ashton Kinsburg.*

She leaned back in her chair, and breathed out. Then she scanned the letter, and the result was deflation. She had found the first mention of the name Jonathan had been looking for, and it was the dullest letter she had ever seen, referring to the proposed proportions of a room. It was written in a hard, firm, large character, which she did not like. The writing was ugly. And there was an insistence to it, even when he obscured reprimands. *That matter we spoke of; I would be grateful if you could give it your attention as soon as possible.*

She turned it over, to the address side. There, she saw a drawing, in slightly lighter ink – the ink Dale-Collingwood's last letter had been written in. He had drawn a face: a creepy, funny little face, like a green man, tendrils proceeding out from it. Beneath it, he had written '*taceo*'. Livy did not understand the Latin, but she found that she was smiling. She lay the doodled side of paper alongside one of Henry's more formal letters; there was no mistake, it was his ink, and his hand.

'I say, Henry,' she said. 'There you are.'

A thought occurred to her, and she sifted back through one of the other boxes looking for a typewritten list she had seen earlier. She assumed that it had been typed by Miss Hardaker, who had evidently been through these boxes: she saw the traces of her, such as, in pencil, a date written out beneath a scrappily written ink version, clarifying it for future researchers, or perhaps even just herself.

The typed list was headed: 'Works of art displayed in the Mirrormakers' Club on its opening in 1841, taken from the committee minutes'.

Livy ran her eyes down the list, all three pages of it: and then again, frowning.

There was no trace of *Woman and Looking Glass*, or any other title like it; no trace of a painting called *Mrs Charlotte Kinsburg*.

She put the list back. So Henry hadn't known this painting. It must have been acquired for the Club later in its history.

'You're a sight for sore eyes.'

Her heart jumped, and she looked up to see Christian. 'Why on earth do you come tiptoeing in?' she said. 'Can't you announce yourself? You're forever making me jump.' And she began to laugh, unexpectedly.

He laughed in return. 'Can't help it.' He stood there, hat in hand, and the same old reverse magnetism kept them apart: her wariness, his caution. 'I just thought I'd stop by,' he said. 'I'm meant to be having lunch with a pal at Fishmongers' Hall.'

As she looked at his watchful face, she found herself wanting to confide in him, and the strange mixture of closeness and alienation troubled her. Her feeling towards Jonathan was a simple desire. But for Jonathan she felt none of the familiarity she had with Christian: as though she could yield every thought to him without any effort.

'As you're here, you might as well make yourself useful.' She patted the chair next to her. He came to it eagerly, drawing it out and sitting down.

'Are these the archives you mentioned to me?' he said.

'Yes. Do you know what *taceo* means?' She pointed at the letter where Henry Dale-Collingwood had written it.

He frowned and thought for a moment, his lips moving as he ran through the options. 'If my schoolboy Latin answers, I think it means "I keep silent",' he said. 'What's the context?'

'I hardly know. He's written it on a letter from Ashton Kinsburg, one of the patrons who funded the building of the Club. But it's clearly a private note to himself. Like a doodle.'

'What are you looking for?'

'It's a kind of mystery, which Mr Whitewood wants me to solve.'

'You always did love a mystery. Agatha Christie, if I recall.'

A part of her slotted into place: of course she had. She blinked, and considered it. 'Not that kind,' she said. 'Not a death. It's a diamond, actually. What Mr Whitewood is looking for.'

'How bizarre.' Christian glanced at her then back to the

archive material. He was running his eyes over the letters. 'These are a goldmine, architecturally speaking. Can I sit here, with you, and read them?'

She felt the blush run its way across her face. 'One day, perhaps. But Mr Whitewood might not like it.'

'I'm sure. Does he think I'm a threat to him?'

'In what way?'

He kept his eyes on the letters, turning one in his hand, as though he were reading it. 'He wants you, Livy. That much is clear.'

Her stomach muscles tightened. 'Don't be ridiculous.'

He put the letter down, abandoning the attempt to read it, and looked into her eyes. His were a clear brown, and his expression was tinged with sadness, but without any of the reticence she had seen in him before. He almost looked angry. 'Of course he does. You're beautiful, innocent and vulnerable. Just his type, I'd have thought.'

She got up from the table: he put his hand out to take her wrist but withdrew before touching her. 'I'm sorry. Have I upset you? I apologize. I didn't mean to. Please, sit down.' He looked down at her wrist. 'Your watch is broken.'

'Yes.' She put her hand to it. She didn't know why she continued to wear the cracked watch. She could not bring herself to take it off.

'I know someone who can fix that,' he said.

'It's perfectly fine. You'd best go. I'm meant to be mopping the backstairs.' She was. She had already spent far too much time 'going through the old papers', as Peggy called it.

SOPHIA TOBIN

'Can I come with you? You never finished that tour you promised me.'

'I don't think I promised you anything.'

He looked away sharply. 'Touché.'

She felt sorry at the look on his face. 'It's not that exciting. The backstairs are just the servants' stairs: stone flights of steps. And they get muddy, because the firewatchers use them. On the ground floor, there is a ring of service rooms, which run around the perimeter of the building, against the larger rooms, but hidden mainly by the Stair Hall and its marble walls. Much smaller than the grand rooms, and not that interesting.'

His eyes sparked. 'But coming from the servant class myself, I would like to see them, very much.'

She sighed, trying and failing to stop the smile that came to her face. 'Oh, come on, then. I suppose we might trip over the diamond in the dark.'

She had left the mop and bucket behind one of the Committee Room doors. She led the way, him dawdling behind, pausing on the upper landing of the Stair Hall. She couldn't blame him: with its colour and grandeur, its scale, it was an intoxicating room. He was looking up and around, trying to absorb every detail of the place, she could tell. As she reached the door to the backstairs, by the door to the Hide, she put the bucket down.

The door was rattling in its frame. For a moment, she wondered who had opened another door in the ring of rooms, or if air was flooding in from a bombed and broken window downstairs, setting up a kind of current which was making the door shake. The shaking became more and more violent, the slight margin of room for rattling in the wooden frame somehow making it more concentrated, more horrible.

But then, the doorknob turned. It turned as though there were someone on the other side, trying to open a locked door. The doorknob turned and reverted again and again, and Livy could sense the pressure on the other side, the pushing. She did not know why; it sent a sick chill around her heart.

She glanced to her left. Christian was still on the north landing, looking up at the dome. She went to him. He turned and read something on her face. 'What is it?'

'Come here.' She led him back to the door. In those few moments, those few steps, everything had fallen silent and still. It was just a door.

She glanced at him. 'I think it might be locked. It was shaking, as though someone were on the other side.' She didn't want to touch it.

Christian reached forwards, and turned the doorknob. Gently, it unclicked and opened, smoothly and easily. He pushed the door, stepped back and Livy took a step forwards, flipped the light switch on, and looked down the turning staircase. There was no one there, no sound or sign that anyone had been there.

'I must have been mistaken,' said Livy.

'Old buildings,' said Christian, 'all have a ghost or two.'

CHAPTER THIRTEEN

1940

<small>SERVANTS' STAIRCASE, THE MIRRORMAKERS' CLUB</small>

Livy and Christian set off down the empty back staircase, and every step echoed. Here there were no carpets to soften the noise of everyday life, and the shape and materials of the long staircase made the acoustics harsh and ugly. The door slammed behind them, the noise reverberating off the stone. Christian put down the mop and bucket on the first turning step. The steps were of lead-coloured grey stone, their centres smoothed by a century of comings and goings.

'I'll just show you the other rooms quickly,' she said. 'Then you must leave me to mop the stairs.'

'I'll mop them for you, if you like.'

'I'm perfectly capable. But thank you.'

Livy put her hand to the smooth surface of the wooden

bannister: the stair spindles were metal arabesques. Designed by Henry, she had no doubt: in fact, she was sure she had seen a sketch for them in pencil, in one of the notebooks. Christian was half a step behind her. She stopped; he stopped. As the sound of their footsteps faded into silence, she felt the sense of him behind her.

'There's a bathroom to the right, the firewatchers fill their buckets there sometimes,' she said. 'But the other service rooms are shut off. The blackout is left up, permanently.'

'I don't mind the darkness if you don't,' he said.

At the bottom of the stairs, she turned to the left to lead him into the shut-off rooms, and stopped. She felt a sudden obstruction there. She didn't want to step forwards, into the rooms which had been closed off. These past weeks, she had kept to a few places: the vaults, the Stair Hall, the other public rooms. Not the darkness. And it was Christian who was making her step forwards, into the shadows. For a moment she thought about turning back, about telling him to go, that he could not make her do it.

'Livy?' he said, behind her.

She stepped forwards.

The ghost of the light from the staircase helped them find their way into the dust-sheeted rooms, thick blackout material over the vast windows. Strange forms loomed out at them: dust-sheeted desks and chairs.

'This was a scullery,' Livy said. 'In 1841. And the next room was a small dining room for the director. But they're both offices now.'

Christian squinted in the gloom. 'Not much ornament here.'

'And no gold leaf.' They said it in unison, and glanced at
each other. She saw his smile in the shadows.

'Can you make it out?' she said. 'These offices are painted
in a certain shade of institutional green. Not 1841 original,
I'm sure.'

'But the windows are large, and beautiful.'

She stood back, and let him absorb what he could in the
low light. When he turned and smiled, she smiled back.

'Did you see on your way in downstairs,' she said, 'one of the
slabs of pink marble in the Stair Hall has cracked, and a corner
has come away. It's just bricks beneath, you know – London
stock bricks and mortar, lined with marble panels an inch thick.'

'It doesn't surprise me,' he said, his hands in his pockets.
'I told you this place isn't entirely what it seems.'

'I think it's rather beautiful, the damage,' said Livy,
remembering the distaste on Jonathan's and Bill's faces when
they'd seen it. 'It's sad the piece of marble has broken, but to
see the underside of the building – its humility, in a way – it
rather makes me love it more.'

'Yes,' he said, 'I quite agree. I want to get into the bones
of things. See what other people cannot. It's why I love architecture: seeing beneath. I try and remember that, when I'm
feeling tired and bitter.'

She saw the trace of it in his face: the curl of his lip. She
knew it must mask some deeper, darker distress. Still, that
strange openness she felt with him spurred her on.

'What is it like? Seeing how the landscape changes every night?'

Christian thought of the bomb recorder's notebook: a slim burgundy Carlton cash book, ruled up to account for other things. Dates, locations, everything as dry and precise as possible.

Approximate damage: unsafe until shored up
Rescue service operations: searching for casualties
Casualties: 2m/2f (walking). Succeeded in recovering
the body of a female

He closed his eyes for a moment, and thought of the right thing to say. 'When I mark a house as still usable, it's a kind of triumph. There may be cracks in it, a window out, but it's still standing. It's still a home. When you see a map, and the street is coloured in black . . .' He shook his head. 'I pretend it's not real. One must put a wall up. I can't imagine – I used to enjoy using my imagination. Before the war. It was what I did the most, daydreaming. But now, I actively suppress it. It seems to me it's a quality that is no longer helpful. Everything I see – I try to forget it.'

'What do you do to forget it?'

He took another step towards her, and she could see the shine of his eyes in the darkness. 'I think about you, sitting on a picnic blanket with me in Hyde Park, before the war.'

She stood there: frozen. There was a foot between them. He did not advance; he did not touch her.

125

'Do you want me to tell you, what it was like?' he said.

She said nothing.

'You were curious about everything,' he said. 'You had ambition. You wore your hair,' his eyes moved over her face, 'much shorter. In a bob. Pinned. A plain, dark suit. Sensible shoes. You didn't want to be beautiful. You wanted to be taken seriously.'

She had the sense he was getting closer to her, and yet he had not moved.

'But your smile,' he said. 'The first time I saw you. It was your smile, which halted me in the office doorway. The world was fine as it was, before you. That is, I thought it was. But when you came into it, you made it brighter. You made it come alive, Livy. Alive in a way it had never been before. Vivid.'

The room had narrowed. The space felt unfamiliar, unsafe. Her and him, in the darkness. She turned away from him, putting her hand out to the wall to steady herself. She felt torn between wanting to run away and wanting to know more; she hardly knew whether she wanted him to come closer to her. But all around her she was edged with a thin line of terror. Surely he must see it, she thought? Surely it must halo me, bright white in the darkness? Everything crackled with it.

'Livy,' he said.

'If we keep on walking this way, we'll come to the Entrance Hall,' she said briskly. 'At the end of the corridor, that door opens onto it. As I said, the service rooms form a ring around the public rooms. It's symmetrical, and logical.'

She turned and walked on, hearing his footsteps behind her. After a moment, he caught at her hand, and the movement was enough to turn her to face him. He took hold of her shoulders. She felt the burning heat of his hands through her blouse.

'Do you remember?' he said. He drew close to her, and she knew then that he wanted to kiss her, but that something was stopping him. 'You must remember.'

She read it in his eyes: *I won't, unless you know who I am.*

She put her hands on his chest. For a moment they stood there, cocooned in this kind of strange embrace. But the space between them felt uncrossable, and her hands curled into fists.

'No,' she said. 'I don't remember.'

He let her go then, absolutely, as though relinquishing her. Let her go, and stepped away from her.

Livy felt tears in her eyes and she did not know why. She had not cried once since the day of the bombing: she had felt frozen, suspended in aspic. But now the feeling that rose in her was terrifying. She wanted very much, in that moment, to die. Just as she had for a moment on the top step of the staircase, after Jonathan had told her about the diamond. And it was a kind of crime, she knew, to feel that way, when so many other people were dying with no choice in the matter.

'I must go,' she said flatly. 'I have things to do. The diamond.' She wanted to be back in the Committee Room, reading the letters written by Henry, searching for the woman in the painting. Working out mysteries and puzzles. Burying herself in someone else's past. She turned, and began to walk swiftly towards the door which led to the Entrance Hall.

'One more thing.' Christian raised his voice. 'You are a strong person. Warm, kind. Not fragile, not anxious, not broken. You will recover. You *are* strong. Livy?'

But she had gone through the door, and he heard it bang shut behind her.

CHAPTER FOURTEEN

1838

The candles were lit, but the *salon bleu* at Redlands lay in deep gloom as the clock struck ten. Supper had been eaten and cleared; now the inhabitants of the room sought their own occupations. Charlotte took up her sewing, then let it sit in her lap, as she thought of her daughter Isabel. She had visited her before dinner, kissed her warm forehead, and received assurances that the little girl was getting better. And yet, the child seemed so far away – Charlotte feared that she might slip from this world, ungraspable and silent, in her upper-floor nursery. This fear, which continually followed her, gained strength every time her child was ill. She had been hopeful during Loveday's illness, and it was a mistake she chose not to repeat.

Tea had been a trial. Nicholas had been absent, and Barbara had ordered so much cake that even Ashton had murmured disapproval. Barbara had stood, poised over Charlotte, golden-eyed and unflinching.

'Do eat, Ce-Ce,' she had said.

Charlotte had tasted the end of her fork. 'Divine, Be-Be.'

Nicholas had not surfaced for dinner and could not be found in his room. This was not unusual: he seemed to resent the inflexible routines of the house, and occasionally removed himself from its machinery. Now, as they all sat in the salon, they heard the oak front door slam, and the unmistakable tread of Nicholas, accompanied by the softer footsteps of a servant who was no doubt gathering Nicholas's coat and hat as he hurtled through the house. In her chair, Barbara ruffled herself like a bird preparing for confrontation.

'What a charming scene!' cried Nicholas as he entered, waving away the servant as he handed him the last of his outdoor clothing. Ashton looked up, and then returned his eyes to his book.

'Where have you been?' said Barbara.

'I had business to transact in the village.' An answer which drew blank looks from everyone there, but said with the definite intention not to be questioned. 'Good day to you, dear sister.' With a careless gesture, he took Charlotte's hand and kissed it. She smiled at him. Her brother-in-law's sarcastic, easy manner was one of her few delights.

'Nicholas has bought another watch at auction,' said his wife. 'Won't you show darling Charlotte your new toy?' She named a Swiss master jeweller, and Charlotte heard her husband's breath catch. He rose and went to the fireplace.

Barbara gave the final garnish to her words. 'It doesn't work, of course.'

'It should be seen to in London,' said Nicholas, turning his lazy smile on Ashton and Charlotte both. 'I'll take it to the Hamptons on Bond Street when I am next there.'

'Which will be soon, won't it, my dear?' said Barbara. 'One carriage rolls in and another leaves. Ce-Ce and Ashton had a carriage accident, Nicholas, by the way – yes, London can be a dangerous place. Still, it seems I am the only person who is content to stay here at Redlands.'

'You may go to London whenever you wish,' said Ashton, turning one of the ornaments on the mantelpiece. 'And we are unharmed, Nick – in case you were worried.'

Barbara said nothing, but Charlotte noticed how she watched them, almost hungrily. Barbara had been married a year when Charlotte had arrived, and though they had been friendly at first, it had clearly pained Barbara to watch Charlotte fall pregnant and bear children. Barbara had no children of her own, and now Charlotte knew that her sister-in-law disliked, perhaps even hated, her. She did not resent it. She recognized that Barbara was swept away in a storm tide of something that was quite beyond her control. Whenever she prayed, Charlotte always included Barbara; she knew that her sister-in-law suffered the most of all of them, and deserved the most mercy.

'How was the business at the Mirrormakers' Club?' said Nicholas, who had finally lost interest in his watch.

'Interesting,' said Ashton. 'The site is clear. That old

commercial building is gone. Strange, it always seemed about to topple, and yet when it came to it, it was hard to bring down – like digging out the roots of the honeysuckle.'

'And Dale-Collingwood?'

'Well enough, though we will have to keep him in line. But he is just as we thought: intense, focused on the work, despite that dreadful bereavement he suffered last year. In short, he is just what is needed. I'm surprised you're taking an interest in it.'

'Why? I'm a member, even if I'm not on the committee.'

'Yes,' said Ashton carefully. 'But you've never cared to involve yourself in its affairs.'

Nicholas shrugged. 'Dale-Collingwood seems like a decent fellow. I've heard he's close to a lot of artists. Interesting chap; I might call on the site one day.'

'If you do, kindly don't try and engage him as some kind of art dealer. Aren't there enough people up and down Bond Street taking your money? Or should I say my money?'

Nicholas fixed him with suddenly cold eyes. His look reminded Charlotte that he and Ashton were brothers, when they often seemed so different. 'That's a filthy thing to say.'

Barbara had taken one of her tiny dogs into her arms and was feeding it a dainty.

'My dears,' Charlotte said softly. Everyone returned to their occupations: Charlotte to sewing, Ashton to his book, and Nick to inspecting his new watch. Only Barbara remained agitated, so that the dog jumped down despite her attempts to keep it in her arms.

'I think I will retire for the night,' she said. Nick did not look up. She came to Charlotte and kissed her on the cheek. 'Do not sit so close to the fire, Ce-Ce; you will ruin your complexion. You haven't sewn much at all; whereas I have almost finished the cover for the table in my boudoir.'

Charlotte accepted the kiss. She watched her sister-in-law traverse the long room until she was finally swallowed up in the darkness at the far end. Then she caught Ashton's eye and, in accordance with his look, moved her chair back from the fire. She put down the piece of ornamental sewing she had been pretending to work on, for it was now too dark to see it properly.

'Shall I ask for more candles to be brought?' said Ashton softly. He was a man of focused attention, he was a man who understood motivations, and this was something she had once loved about him. Now, his watchfulness irritated her a little. *Leave me some space that you do not enter*, she thought. She did not know whether he sought to increase her comfort, or to remind her that she was being watched.

'No, thank you,' she said. 'I am a little tired of it. It would be best if I continue in the daylight. Are you not looking at pieces from the collection tonight?' It was his custom to bring a piece or two into the salon of an evening: a box, a clock, a medieval reliquary or a mineral sample. Ashton bought the rarest treasures he could find, garnered from dealers in London, Europe and America. He would sit at the Louis XVI desk in the corner, surrounded by candles, and look at them with his various magnifying glasses, making notes. His was a great mind, she knew, aswarm with context and history, with a dozen languages, for during the day he balanced riding and business with reading and contemplation of his many pieces. She knew he missed his treasure while they were away, and thought he would have eagerly come down with a whole tray full of beloved objects to examine.

But instead, he shook his head. 'There is time enough for that tomorrow,' he said, and she saw that his hand stole to his pocket, as though in search of something.

Nick looked up from his watch suddenly. 'Where is Barbara?'

Charlotte smiled. 'She has been gone these five minutes, dear.'

Her brother-in-law cursed, and went without ceremony. Alone for the first time that evening, Charlotte and Ashton looked at each other.

'I am tired,' Charlotte said, rising and adjusting her silken skirts. She knew her husband loved her to dress in the colours of the Renaissance enamels he collected: the uncompromising greens and blues and reds rather than the softer tones favoured by the current fashions. Tonight she had made a real effort to please him, her dark hair smooth as lacquer, her jewels carefully chosen, and he looked at her appreciatively. 'I will wish you a good night.'

'May I come to you tonight?' he said, as formally as if he were offering her tea.

She felt a slow sinking, but inclined her head. 'Will you put the lights out first?'

Each night, Ashton toured the ground floor of the house with Sam, the under-butler, who was so burly that he could take on ten housebreakers. Ashton watched Sam secure the doors by the light of a candle, as the other servants swiftly put out the candles and the house was gradually bathed in darkness.

It was a large house, and it took time, so Charlotte did not hurry to undress. Katie helped her, pulling out the fifty or so pins they had used to coiffure her hair, and brushing it out down the length of her back a hundred times. They did not speak to each other. It was only when a creak was heard outside the main door to Charlotte's room that Katie caught her eye. Ashton shifted there, making himself known. Katie hurried to the servant's door, which led to a dark passage that threaded its way unobtrusively through the house, and went out, closing the door in the panelling softly behind her. Charlotte had no idea whether Katie ever lingered there. Perhaps that was why Ashton disliked the girl: the sense that he had felt her eyes on him in intimate moments, the suspicion that she watched in the night.

It was only once that door closed, that Ashton knocked.

'Come in,' called Charlotte, rising and turning, and he came, candle still in one hand, unbuttoning his waistcoat with the other. It surprised her, that he had dismissed his valet and not prepared for bed in his room. He took off his jacket and draped it over her dressing-table stool. But then he reached into the pocket and drew out a box.

'The diamond?' she said with surprise.

'You looked so beautiful this evening,' he said. 'You pleased me.'

She settled beside him, a foot or so from him, and saw the hesitant delight in his eyes, not truly believing that she had caused it.

'I was interested to hear you talk of the Mirrormakers' Club,' she said. 'I can see why you are so fascinated by it. What shall it look like, when it is finished?'

He frowned, smilingly. 'Look like? It is of a classical model. Grand reception rooms, splendid detail. I may supply a painting or two – the ones I am tired of. That group of men giving a toast, the one my father bought. The Club will need some older pieces to give it gravitas.'

'And the architect of the Club?' she said, trying to return the conversation to Henry. 'He seemed rather young.'

'He looks younger than he is. He is in his early thirties. And exactly the right sort: from a good kind of background, but with a father in commerce, so aware of reality. Trained at the Royal Academy schools; travelled in Europe. A thorough grounding in the classical.'

'And you said he had suffered a bereavement,' she said. 'Was it so terrible?'

He frowned in earnest this time. 'What? Oh – yes. His parents and sister, taken all at once. His only family.' He undid his cravat. 'Let us not talk of such things.'

'Yes. I'm sorry.'

He stroked her hair. 'I did not think we would get on so well again, so soon, after yesterday,' he said. 'And yet, you have a way, Charlotte, when you are so delicate, so absolutely right and proper, caring about your dress and your deportment, you can convert me just like that to loving you again.'

She caught his smile from him, as one would catch a ball in a game, and did her best to throw it back. 'I'm glad I know how to please you,' she said.

'Lie down,' he said.

Obediently, she lay back against the pillows. He leaned over her, and swept his hands through her dark hair, spreading it over the white linen. Then he placed the diamond, nestled it in her hair, above her forehead. She saw the shine of it in his eyes as he stared at her: saw the sense of desire there, balanced by the comfort of possession, the hint of sadness that he could not sit like this for hours, simply looking at her.

He kissed her then. Watched her a little longer, before he put away the diamond, carefully, with gentle hands, before he returned to her, and kissed her again, and again, and she submitted. His breath, even; his eyes, fixed ahead. He did not seem to wish to look at her. He never had, in such moments as these. He had the thought of her as he wished her to be fixed in mind. It was that which moved him to desire.

Once, she moved, only slightly, but enough to make Ashton pause.

'Do not forget yourself,' he whispered.

Nine years before, their wedding day had been the grandest of affairs. They had only met a handful of times, but they were well-matched in looks. Ashton was one of three suitors. She had chosen him, she preferred to think, because of his great mind, although these days she was not sure – perhaps it had been the money, the enchanted world of Redlands. She was not sure she knew that bride, or what had been in her mind. The die had been cast, and she went forwards without further thought. True, during their courtship, she had noted in a place beyond knowing that he seemed to mimic enjoyment in her company, and sometimes looked faintly pained when she laughed. But they had each played their roles well, and the marriage was declared a love-match by all who saw them.

At the wedding breakfast she had displeased him by taking a second glass of champagne. She was silenced by the coldness of his gaze. Without knowing it, she had angered him. Her dear, sensitive husband. She had excused herself, with her bridesmaid, and walked quietly out, a smile drawn tight across her face. They walked the length of Redlands, through salon after salon, and when the noise of the guests had faded to silence, she stopped, and held on to a mantelpiece without a word, staring at the sightless eyes of a Kinsburg ancestor in a portrait above the fireplace.

Her wedding night had steadied her disquiet – it was short, and painful of course, as it had to be, but warmed by his gentleness afterwards, when he dried her tears, and said 'there, there', and held her in his arms with such warmth and kindness. No, it was in the week that followed that she truly realized who her husband was, in the act of love. Beneath his careful, sightless thrusting, she had felt a flicker of pleasure, and instinctively arched her back, and murmured. He stopped his movement. He looked down at her with that same look he had had in his eye when he saw that second glass: a mixture of disappointment and disgust.

'Do not forget yourself.'

How strange it was, to feel both loved, and undesired. From that moment, her study had been how to prevent that look of disappointment from entering his eyes, both for his sake, and for her own. She had always been quick at her lessons, even if those lessons had never amounted to much. But she supposed it was lying beneath him that the seeds of her rebellion had been sown. She had thought, in their marriage bed, that closeness would be possible. She had seen a look which, now and then, passed between married couples of her acquaintance, a look of warmth, of secrets, and of something accessible only to them. But there was no such rapport between her and Ashton. Only their strange, repetitive routines, which she sensed gave him comfort. They did well in public; they could catch each other's eye at the right moment and smile, when the eyes of the room were on them. They both had an instinct for performance.

Charlotte kept her eyes on her husband's coat, lying on the chair, and thought of the diamond, as his breath grew ragged. He finished; collapsed half onto her, just for a moment. She reached up, and curved her hand around the back of his neck. Their faces lay close to each other for a moment, shadows between their profiles. Then he pushed himself up, and sat there for a moment, before he kissed her goodnight and left, carrying the diamond in his still-trembling hands.

CHAPTER FIFTEEN

1940

ENTRANCE HALL, THE MIRRORMAKERS' CLUB

When Christian emerged into the dark, panelled Entrance Hall, Livy was nowhere to be seen. Bill was standing with his hands on his hips, staring at a large oil painting of a group of Georgian men raising a toast. which hung behind the reception desk. He looked over his shoulder at Christian.

'I'm not going to ask,' he said. 'She's run off that way like a greyhound out of a trap.'

Christian sighed, and put his hat on. 'I'd best be off then. Good to see you, Mr Holliday.'

'Hang on there. I need your help. This here masterpiece or whatever you want to call it is the last of the paintings on the walls and we're going to get it down.' His breath whistled through his nose. 'It's been giving me the heebie-jeebies.

We're going to wrap it up in some of my old sheets and stow it downstairs.'

'Is this for Livy's sake?' Christian said.

'No, for mine,' said Bill. 'Come and stand below it while I get up.' He stood on a box. Christian did as he was told.

'Hold on, ready yourself,' said Bill. 'One, two, three.' With a grunt he lifted the painting off its hook, and Christian took the weight of it, feeling his muscles come to life. His war work had strengthened him; he was no longer just a desk man, and he felt an obscure pride at it. Bill came down the steps and took the other corner of the painting. Together they eased it to the ground.

'Why does it give you the heebie-jeebies?' said Christian, looking at the pained expression on Bill's face as he gazed at the painting.

Bill gave a little shudder. 'The other night, I was late locking the doors before the raid. Bloody thing was shaking. Thought it was going to come off the wall,' he said.

'The bombing causes vibrations, I suppose,' said Christian.

Bill rolled his eyes. 'If that's what you want to think,' he said. He watched Christian tilt his head and look at the painting. He didn't want to bring the words out, but it had frightened him.

He had stood there, shining his torch up, seeking some explanation for the violence of it. As though something beneath the bottom length of the painting was pushing it up, levering it up, and releasing it with a crash. Unseen hands. At that moment, no bombs had been falling. 'It's a queer place,' he said. 'Someone's been unhappy here, at some point. Apart from us, that is.' He sneezed heartily into his handkerchief.

'Livy will be glad you're moving it, anyway,' Christian said. He couldn't help but glance towards the Stair Hall, to see if she was there; but she was not. 'I'm sure it's out of kindness to her, even if you don't say so.'

'You go on believing the best of people if you wish,' muttered Bill. 'If you'd give me a hand now, though.'

It was dirty work. The painting had hung there unmolested by a duster for decades. Still, they shifted it into storage, and as Christian came out into the lobby, brushing dust disconsolately from his coat, he saw Jonathan Whitewood walk through the front door. When Jonathan caught sight of him his face tightened with irritation.

'Good day, Mr Whitewood,' said Christian.

'You here again,' said Jonathan.

'I've been helping Mr Holliday move a painting.'

Jonathan nodded as though the conversation had finished, but as he turned away Christian said his name. He looked back.

Christian smiled. 'When Livy introduced us, you didn't remember me, did you?'

'Should I?'

'I was wounded during army training. I was sent to Number Eighteen General Hospital, London Region.'

'I see.' Jonathan took the cigarette lighter from his pocket and turned it in his hand. 'I can hardly be expected to remember every injured soldier who was brought to my house.'

'I suppose not. Do give my regards to Mrs Whitewood, please. She was kind to us. Visited, even put flowers in the wards.' His words won a long look from Whitewood and Christian saw guilt there. Out of sight, within his sleeve, his injured left hand clenched tight.

'It is in my wife's nature to be kind,' said Jonathan.

'But not in yours?'

Jonathan's expression hardened. 'Young man, I'm really not sure why you are here. As a member of the committee of this Club—'

'I'm from the LCC. I have a perfect right to be here, to inspect bomb damage. If the government asks whether the building can be used for the homeless, then my department will be asked to advise on its state.'

'My dear boy,' said Whitewood, 'I should think bringing the homeless to stay here would be a route to their certain deaths. We are catching it pretty hard here at the moment. Mrs Holliday doesn't even like us to go upstairs at night.'

'There is a large shelter downstairs,' said Christian. 'We shall see how things pan out.'

'I should think we shall,' said Whitewood, and Christian couldn't help but think the man was mocking him. 'I think it's a ghastly idea.'

'Ghastly idea or not, it is not up to you,' said Christian.

'We'll see about that.'

'It must be strange for you, not being the one in charge,' said

Christian, trying to lower his voice in volume at least. 'But you may as well get used to it. The world you knew is already gone.'

Whitewood smiled darkly. 'Is it? A trifle melodramatic, aren't you? You forget, I lived through a war before.'

'Redlands is a beautiful place,' said Christian. 'The Mirrormakers' Club has an echo of it, doesn't it? I've noticed the similarities. But surely you see, they were built for another world. This place still has some life. But the air is different at Redlands – rarefied. It's a museum. It has no connection with the way real people live their lives.'

'I suppose you think I'm not a real person,' said Jonathan. He took out a cigarette and lit it; he did not offer Christian one.

'It's not what I meant,' said Christian. 'But if you're asking whether I think you live in the real world? No, I don't. You live in a beautiful dream. And it's dissolving. Merit will be the thing that distinguishes society's leaders when we win this war. But we will lose other things too – places like Redlands. Trying to hold on to them is futile.'

'God almighty,' snapped Whitewood. He raised his voice. 'Bill?'

'Have me thrown out, will you? As a member of the lower orders?' said Christian, in a low voice. 'Consider what you're doing. With Livy.'

'Who on earth do you think you're talking to?'

'I know who you are. I don't think *you* do, but I'm asking you to try and see how your behaviour affects people.' He paused, tried to gather his thoughts. 'You're the shadow that stands in the way of love. I don't think you know what love is.

I think you see people as objects, as things which are either convenient or inconvenient to you. Especially women.'

The words felt like a knife turning. Jonathan heard the catch in his own voice when he spoke. 'You don't know me.'

'I saw enough, when I was at Redlands.'

'You *don't* know me.'

'Leave Livy alone. At least, in that way.'

Bill's slow plodding feet could be heard, moving slightly quicker than usual. When he arrived on the scene, he looked backwards and forwards between the two fuming men.

'This' – it was clear Jonathan could not remember Christian's name – 'person is leaving, Bill.'

'Anything else you'd like to say?' Christian said loudly, as though it were a public declaration. He waited for Jonathan to ban him from coming back, for him to use the terms a man of his generation might dredge up: filthy anarchist, communist. But Jonathan only turned away and walked through the door to the Stair Hall. Bill, obviously perplexed, looked at Christian as they heard Jonathan's footsteps fade.

'I suppose I'd better go,' said Christian, as cheerily as he could, though his voice shook a little.

Bill held open the front door with ceremony. 'We'll be seeing you then,' he said. And Christian saw what he thought was a slight smile beginning in his rheumy eyes.

Jonathan was breathing heavily as he pushed his way through the green door and began the descent into the vaults. He heard the sound of the wireless drifting up to him; Livy and Peggy must be having tea, and listening. Perhaps to a cooking show, about how to make the most of vegetable tops and bones.

He had telephoned Stevie on the way home, stopping in a small café where he drank a pale cup of tea and summoned his courage. Her voice, low and throaty on the line. He heard the disappointment in it; in the way her voice stayed even, as though she were keeping herself on a tight rein.

What do you mean, the diamond is a fake?

You must look through the family papers, Stephanie. Look through. Is there anything there relating to the diamond? To Charlotte, to Ashton Kinsburg? You must do this for me. I had a brief look before I came to London, but I didn't really believe it at the time, I was furious, and I might have missed something.

That solicitor's letter is the only thing, from your grand- mother. It outlined the provenance, didn't it? Said it had been stored at the Club before it went into the safe deposit?

Yes, but the real diamond is not in the safe deposit. And I can't find it here. We need more information.

It doesn't matter, Jonathan. Just come home. Why do we need the diamond, anyway? Forget it.

You must look through the papers, Stevie. Stevie?

I'm tired, Jonathan. These strange obsessions you get. It takes a certain courage to be married to a man like you, and I'm running low on it.

Stevie?

I must go now. You know they don't like us to hold the line.

*

146

As he walked down the stairs, he drew hard on his cigarette, but the smoke caught him in his throat, and he began to cough. When he reached the vaults, Peggy was sitting on the edge of her seat, turned, and waiting for him. Livy sat with her feet curled up beneath her on one of the large Club chairs, one arm propped on the chair arm, supporting her chin.

'Hello,' he said. He went to her, and pulled the stone from his pocket, no longer wrapped in anything. 'Hold your hand out.' He dropped the sparkling thing into her obediently open palm. She looked down at it, then up at him.

'Take it,' he said. 'It's yours.' She stared at him in astonishment.

'It's so beautiful,' said Peggy, getting to her feet. 'It can't be real, surely?'

'Quite right,' he said. 'But the real one is somewhere in the world.' A beautiful dream, he thought. Had a man ever woken wanting a dream to be real as much as he did?

CHAPTER SIXTEEN

1940

Roof Leads, the Mirrormakers' Club

That night, one of the firewatchers didn't show, and Bill went onto the roof to help the others. He spent a good proportion of the night smoking cigarettes, standing in the doorway of the dome, sometimes bowing his head against a nearby explosion, his hands always trembling. He felt he was always a little too slow with the sand or the pump, a little hesitant with the shovel. He could not bear to look up at the sky, at the searchlights and terrible droning planes. When the sky flashed white, he closed his eyes.

He thought of Christian, helping him get the painting down; of the wounded hand he had glimpsed, and how the young man had pulled his sleeve over it. He thought of the wounds he had received in the first war, of how he felt them sometimes spring into life. A ghost pain which chased its way around his body and his mind. Had he seen that picture move off the wall? He hardly knew. Only that his imagination was sometimes as vivid as reality. As it was for all them, he thought: all of them had some other version of a life running in the background, behind their eyes.

Once, he picked up an incendiary with a shovel, and flicked it hard and strong, almost straight up into the air, and he heard the shouts of the watchers; watched it curve high in the air, all the time the vision of Livy's scar in his mind: of the sight of her cut and bleeding face, the blood a deep red on her pale skin; and of poor Miss Hardaker, the skin bubbling, her eyes open in agony, her hand a red scraping of burnt skin.

The sizzling bomb rose in the air. Then it fell, not straight down, but just past the roof of the building, onto the narrow lane below, landing on the street, catching and bursting into flames.

One of the watchers, a laconic man called Louie Robinson, poured water from the edge of the roof onto it. A waterfall, scattering in the air, but enough, just enough, to dampen it.

He handed the bucket to Bill. 'Go and fill it up again, mate.'

'Sorry about that.' Bill rarely apologized; he felt it, as he said it now.

'None of us perfect.'

Bill nodded in agreement, and did as he was told.

In the shelter, behind blast-proof doors, Peggy knitted on her camp bed. Jonathan and Livy sat on cushions on the

floor, a chessboard between them. Jonathan had found it in
one of the member's rooms on the top floor, a ghost room
covered with dust, the drinks bottles and glasses still there,
one pane of the window smashed. He had been wander-
ing around, half-dazed, and was happy to find it. He had
brought the box down, set it down, dusted it off and lined
up the pieces.

'White or black?' he said.

'Black,' Livy said. An explosion shook the ground, and
dislodged more dust from the vaulted ceiling. It sometimes
felt as though the building were being destroyed grain by
grain, each night crumbling a little more. Livy looked up at
the ceiling. 'Poor Henry,' she murmured. Then she looked
over and saw Peggy, her needles still, her head forwards,
chin resting on her chest. She rose quickly, silently, and
went to her.

Peggy was deeply asleep. Livy took the knitting from her
hands and, at Peggy's stirring, gently supported her into a
lying position. Peggy murmured, but did not open her eyes.
Livy knelt by her until she slept properly, stroking her hair.

'I hope you haven't cheated,' she said softly to Jonathan
when she returned to the game.

He smiled at her and she looked away. In that shadowed
room, the board before him, his hair a little ruffled and his
jacket cast aside, the ghost of his handsomeness had risen in
his face. His beauty was like a thorn she kept catching herself
on. He looked worried this evening, and the contrast between
his arrogance and his vulnerability magnetized her to him.

She pushed a piece softly across the board as they discussed what she had read in the archive that day.

'Dale-Collingwood was greatly concerned with safe specifications,' she said. 'There were several. There was one built into the back of the fixed cabinets in the News Room. I mentioned it to Peggy, but she'd never heard of that one – the others, yes; before the war Miss Hardaker used to have to cash everything up.'

'A hidden safe?' he said. 'I'll have to look.' He pushed his king over with his index finger, in sudden surrender.

She watched in alarm as he got to his feet. 'You can't go up there now,' she said. 'The News Room is dangerous enough as it is – it's half-destroyed.'

'It really doesn't matter,' he said as he shrugged his jacket on. She saw the look on his face: a hard recklessness. They had been talking quietly, calmly, almost as friends. Now, the air had shifted and changed.

She got up. 'I'm coming with you,' she said.

They went up through the building side by side, Jonathan pointing the torch at the floor, so that no stray scrap of light would escape from the Club's blacked-out silhouette. They walked through the Stair Hall and up the stairs. The demi-lunes were boarded up now, but light seeped through the seams of the boards like smoke. The air smelt metallic, like the moment on a hot day before a storm breaks. Soon, the air would thicken with the black smoke from many fires.

They took the right branch of the staircase for once,

ignoring the door to the back of the Dining Hall on the left at the top of the stairs. The News Room ran the length of the building from the end of the Dining Hall to the front, in parallel with the Hide and Committee Room on the opposite side of the building, then an anteroom attached it to the shredded Red Parlour, which you walked through to reach the other side of the Club, and the Committee Room. This side of the first floor had been left alone since a bomb had blown a hole in the top corner of the News Room. A pile of tangled wood represented a makeshift barrier put there by Bill. They climbed over it easily enough.

Jonathan pulled at the door to the News Room. The door grated on the floor. Something was out of joint, the structure shifted by the bomb shock. He forced it open.

'Turn the torch off,' said Livy.

They stood looking at the turmoil of the room. The ceiling was down, as it was in the Red Parlour, but the difference here was that on one side of the room there was a large hole, open to the night. The damage joined with a window, which had lost both its blackout and its panes. They stared together out at the flickering sky, at the red and yellow light: fire and starlight. Searchlights scraped the sky. Water poured down past the hole, and for a moment it was as though they stood behind a waterfall, watching light refract through the water, the glimpses of the blue darkness beyond.

'It's the firewatchers,' said Jonathan. 'They're keeping the building damp so that it doesn't catch.'

'The safe was over there according to Henry's notes,' said

Livy. 'Not behind the bar, but in the back of the cupboard where the older papers were stored. I'll go.'

Before he could stop her she left his side, scrambling over heaps of debris. He put his hand out, but he said nothing. He watched her go. A nearby explosion shook the room, and he saw in the strange waterlogged light the dust rise like ghosts from the ground. It filled the air, stinging his eyes. He had let her go into this room, putting herself at risk. He couldn't see her for a moment – what was that shape in the corner, in the darkness? Was it her? He knew he should go himself in the direction she had gone, should try to find her, and yet he did not. He stayed there, in relative safety, clinging to the jamb of the door, his eyes filling with grit and water.

Then he saw her, her head edged with light, as she climbed over something – was it a table? Covered in plaster and wood. She reached him. He put his hands to her waist, pulled her to him.

'I've got a hundred splinters,' she said into his ear. 'But there's nothing in there. The safe is open, and it is empty.'

They sat together in the doorway of the News Room, each propped up against one side, opposite each other, listening to the scream and sail of bombs, distant and close.

'We should go downstairs,' he said to her.

'I want to stay here for a while,' she said. 'Go down there if you want.'

He put his hand on her knee. She turned her head as another

stream of water passed the gap where the window had once been. Stared at the glittering fall of light through water.

'How do you know that Ashton didn't simply buy a fake diamond?' Livy said.

He shook his head. 'Impossible. Ashton would never have bought a fake for Charlotte. He was a clever man. It wasn't just a gift for her, it was part of his collection, and his collection meant everything to him.'

'More than his wife?'

Jonathan glanced away. 'These things cannot be compared. With the documentation for the diamond, the invoice and suchlike, there was a letter from my great-grandfather's solicitor. He seemed to indicate that the diamond was kept in the Club for a period. In the past we had dismissed it as a temporary thing – after all, we thought we had the diamond in the safe deposit – but now, that letter takes on more significance. Especially when you pair it with the idea that this building was linked to the family's unhappiness in some way, as my grandmother hinted.'

'What were they like?' she said. 'Charlotte and Ashton? Henry, I feel I know. But I can't grasp them, somehow.'

'I know most about Ashton,' he said. 'He was a difficult man, I think. A patriarch. But life was about duty for him – I have some sympathy with that.' He paused. 'He bent things into the shapes he wanted: Redlands, his children. That was his right, his prerogative. My grandmother – his daughter – once said she never had a word of kindness from him after she was out of the nursery. That he considered her a burden to be got rid of. She only spoke about him once – a little too much wine at dinner. My father hustled her away. Exposing family secrets, he said, and everyone laughed. If I had to describe Ashton, from all that I heard, I would say: he was a collector of things; he had to control things; and he were a kind of genius, completely single-minded. He made the family business yield more than anyone before or since. And Redlands is utterly his.'

'What is Redlands like?' Livy thought of the landscape in the portrait, just glimpsed behind Charlotte: green hills and trees, lit by the softest light imaginable.

She saw the twinge of pain in his face: homesickness, she thought. 'The estate itself is beautiful. Although I suppose I am biased. Acres and acres of parkland, a very beautiful coppice. Ashton had the house remodelled and it's rather strange inside, a mixture of styles. I'm so close to it, I hardly see it: it's just home to me.'

'And Charlotte?' she said.

'She was beautiful, as you know. That's her chief characteristic as far as I'm concerned. The daughter of a wealthy man. Had three children with Ashton, two that lived to adulthood, and one that died. I don't know anything else, or even if she had any part in designing Redlands – so strange.' Jonathan paused. 'I didn't realize there was such a gap in the record, in what I know of her, until I started talking.'

'A child that died.' Her face had stilled. He tapped her knee, and she blinked and looked at him. 'There are gaps here, too,' she said. 'I came across a letter today. It was from

Ashton, asking Henry Dale-Collingwood to stay at Redlands. Perfectly conventional. But at the bottom of the page a fragment is cut out. Not cleanly – the person who cut it has left the margins there, and simply cut out a section. The end of the letter. Editing the record, Miss Hardaker would say.'

Jonathan thought of red lips, and red nails, and looked at the floor with a sigh. He moved his hand up Livy's knee, beneath her dress, to her thigh. She sat there, as though he were doing nothing at all. He leaned forwards, drawing her to him with his other hand, and kissed her hard on the lips. She yielded, but without the passion he had expected. When he drew away from her, her face was blank, her eyes cool. It sent a shiver through him.

'Not quite the same as the other night,' he said, trying not to sound harsh, and failing.

A ghost of a smile flitted across her face. 'I didn't promise to be here at your beck and call,' she said.

'Not when Mr Taylor calls so frequently,' he said. 'Are you hedging your bets, Miss Baker?'

He saw the line of her mouth harden. 'I wouldn't bet on you if my life depended on it,' she said. To him, in that moment, she did look like Miss Hardaker. She looked like almost every other woman he had known before. Apart from Stevie.

As he was thinking, she leaned towards him, and kissed him again. Her choice, this time. As the kiss lengthened she felt her heart begin to beat hard. A drumming in her chest, the heat rising in her cold blood, she felt intoxicated, as though she were drunk.

But even in the midst of their embrace that frozen part of her mind was analysing, analysing. He was utterly strange to her: and what she felt was thrilling but not dangerous, in that it was not of the soul – it was simply of the body. She knew, absolutely, by the way he responded to her, that with him she could surrender absolutely to pleasure. In the morning there would be nothing but his cool stare and the turning of the cigarette lighter in his hand. There was none of the loaded familiarity that lay between her and Christian: the tenderness in his gaze, a kindness which seemed to lead to all kinds of complications. In the moment when she had stood with Christian, in the darkness of the shut-off rooms, she knew that had he kissed her he would have set in motion something infinitely more dangerous than lust. His expectation was a burden that she could not carry.

A nearby explosion broke them from each other. They each sat back against the door frame. Livy turned from him, and caught her breath.

'Tell me more about the diamond.'

She saw the vulnerability in his eyes as he looked up at the ceiling. 'It is called *Le Fantôme* – the Ghost Diamond. Pear-shaped. Thirty-five carats.'

'Why was it called the Ghost?'

'An inclusion in it meant that there was a kind of an illusion, a little flicker in the heart of it, which gave it its name. Ashton gave it to Charlotte. We know that: we have an invoice from a London jeweller. After that, it was known as the Kinsburg Diamond.'

'I thought stones had one name, and that was it.'

'He was a determined man. If he wanted it to be called something else, he had only to wish it.'

'Ah, I see it.' She looked askance at him. 'The family resemblance.'

Jonathan clasped his hands together, and rested them on her knees. There was nothing sexual about the way he did it; that mood, it seemed, had passed. It was an admission of something, and it moved her in a way his kiss never could. 'I need the diamond,' he whispered to her. 'Not just for my sake, but for Redlands, and for my wife. I know it's here somewhere.'

Livy nodded, her eyes bright, pressed her hands to the floor, and rose to her feet. 'We'll find it,' she said. 'Don't worry.'

She held her hand out to him, and he took it.

CHAPTER SEVENTEEN

1839

Henry received the note at just past seven on the clock, pushed noisily under his door by an enthusiastic Foi, who hummed loudly to herself as she did so. Henry found himself tiptoeing to the door, sure that she was there and waiting for an excuse to speak to him. As he leaned over to pick up the note, he heard the unmistakable sound of her heavy-footing it back down the corridor and realized he was holding his breath. He smiled, and only stopped when he opened the note and read who it was from.

Ashton Kinsburg was to pay an impromptu visit to the building site that morning, and he hoped that Mr Dale-Collingwood would join him for dinner.

Henry said every curse that his memory held. Not only had he fought long and hard to clear his mind of Mrs Kinsburg, but also to calm the annoyance he felt at her husband's interference in the project, for Ashton's letter outlining various concerns had been followed by almost identical letters from other committee members, clearly incited by him. Henry itched to write to Kinsburg and tell him that he, Henry, was not open for business. The plans had been approved long ago, the foundations were being dug, the walls would soon be raised, and no consultation was required. Although, if Kinsburg wished, Henry would be happy to consult him in due course about the colour of the drapes.

Another option was to invoke the gentleman clause. Showing offence at the interference. Brandishing the long-forgotten duke in his background. It was hardly possible that they would have him taken from the building site – hardly possible, but just. And it did matter to him. A building such as this, which would surely stand, unshaken, for centuries; a kind of palace that he was building. A tribute to all the architects that had gone before him, particularly the masters of the Renaissance; an equation of balance and symmetry which would hold as the disorder of time crumbled his bones. But above all, his own monument, *or*, he thought, *perhaps it will be the railway station which is my monument.*

He laughed, and rubbed his prickling eyes. He was slightly pained by his own vanity. He had long been a relaxed man, with an eye for detail. Now detail was all that he saw, his mind thronged with detail upon detail from joins in wood to the shape of a clock hand. Mrs Kinsburg's appearance in his life had been a moment's distraction; a shadow across the sun. Now he was in the full glare of the committee's attention, and working for his life and his place in eternity. This was what he told himself.

A knock at the door brought one of the manservants with water and a fresh shirt. Henry washed, was shaved, and dressed, and he did not eat breakfast. He went out into the London streets in a daze, and walked for half an hour before he thought of hailing a cab. 'My head is full of marble samples,' he said to his clerk of works, Brokes, when he arrived, and the man laughed awkwardly, trying to keep in favour with him.

The pattern of the new Club lay before him, men swarming over the site, horses departing every moment with carts full of rubble and London clay. Under bright blue skies the small patch of the City of London was alive with effort and labour. Henry went to the lodge, and was brought tea, 'strong, please', was all he said, and he took the chair that Charlotte had taken weeks before, drawing up his small table before it. He unfurled scrolls of paper and looked upon the decorative scheme he had worked on the night before, that of the Dining Hall. Mirrors would be key in such a building, of course, for the Mirrormakers' Club depended on seeing the glory of glass. He carefully considered his designs for coffering, the neoclassical motifs, the amount of gold leaf that would be required.

His mind was so engrossed in the drawing, and in considering each implication of each detail of the design, that he noticed nothing else around him, save occasionally the cup of cooling tea beside him, which he drank, and then another, brought to him by an indulgent housekeeper who interpreted the wave of his hand. It had always been so, ever since he was a boy: the intellectual focus of drawing and designing, of calculating, took him outside of time, making the clock hands move faster than anything else.

'Mr Dale-Collingwood, sir.' It was one of the foremen on the site, his cap in his hand. 'Mr Brokes said you should come quick. We've found something that you'd like, he said.'

The man seemed resolute and cheerful, so Henry came without agitation, save the slight irritation of leaving his drawing. He and the man walked the lines of the footprint until they came to the south-east corner of the building, where Mr Brokes stood, looking down, surrounded by a group of labourers who had downed tools. They were standing on the edge of the outline of the building, Henry noted in the back of his mind: one day, this would be the moat, a passage running the perimeter of the basement, protecting it from damp.

'What's this?' said Henry, and followed Brokes's pointing hand. One of the labourers down in the pit lifted a large stone chunk in his burly arms. They had scraped the dirt off it, and one of them had tenderly poured a bucket of water over it, so it was damp. On the face of the stone Henry could just make out the figure of a woman, decisively carved, of evident antiquity.

Mr Brokes, who Henry knew was an antiquarian of sorts, gave a laugh of astonished joy. 'It's Roman, I'd say, Mr Dale-Collingwood. Likely something to do with a local deity. Harry here found it when he was digging.'

'And hauled it out like a lump of rubbish,' said the

labourer, putting it down with more tenderness than he'd evidently recovered it with. 'Is it worth any money?'

'Not to you,' said Brokes. Henry had to admire the man for asking, and felt in his pocket for some coins to slip him later. Not in sight of the other men, otherwise they'd be turning up at the lodge every five minutes with shards of pottery and clay pipes. London had lived many lives; she gave up her layers of stories to those who laboured for them. The men who recovered her occasional treasures deserved something for their effort.

'We can keep it in the building when it is up,' said Henry. 'For now, Harry, take it to the lodge, will you? And I will arrange for it to be stored somewhere.' He gave the man a meaningful look as he passed, hoping that it signalled to him he would have payment for his trouble. 'And don't drop it. She's survived this long, and we don't want her haunting the place if we break her altar.'

There was a hallooing from near the road. In that moment, Henry loved his workforce, troublesome as they sometimes were, for they had that habit of signalling like a pack of hounds. He always knew when something was afoot on the site. He turned to see Ashton Kinsburg picking his way over the earth, his eyes fixed on his boots.

'Mr Kinsburg,' boomed Henry, as loudly and authoritatively as he could. 'Pray, don't come any further, sir. We can speak in the lodge. The site is dangerous.'

Kinsburg stopped and looked at him, frowning. 'I think I can find my way well enough,' he called.

Henry shrugged and turned away, knowing that he was rude to do so but unable to feel sorry or careful about it. He was aware of tension in Mr Brokes, who had sweat breaking out on his face even in the chill morning air. He had taken off his hat and was looking between Henry and Kinsburg.

Ashton arrived and was given an account of what had been discovered by the now uncomfortable Mr Brokes, as Henry stood, focusing on a distant point, attempting to radiate superiority and efficiency. Eventually Brokes excused himself at a nod from Henry, who eventually made himself look at Ashton. As always, he found the rich man's visage as smooth as an egg at first sight; but at second, in the daylight, he saw the vertical lines in his forehead, indicating a constant frowner. Grey eyes, a high forehead, topped by a luxuriant spruce of black hair. Henry fought the urge to touch his own curly, slightly thinning thatch; a gentleman had no business having such luxuriant hair, he thought, almost like a lady's. And today Ashton had the habit of running his right hand through it repeatedly. He had never seen him do that before.

'Are you satisfied with the site?' said Henry brusquely, but his words were lost on a gust of wind and he had to repeat them.

Ashton looked around, taking his time before replying. 'Yes. It looks very orderly. Are you running to time?'

'As much as possible. Perfection never quite runs to time,' said Henry. 'The marble samples provided by the quarries in Belgium and Italy are not quite as I wished them. The alabaster from Staffordshire is exactly what I wanted, however. And I have secured excellent craftsmen for the scagliola.'

'I can see your design now: those audacious pinks, yellows and deep greens,' said Ashton, with a smile.

Henry said nothing, annoyed that Ashton could remember so clearly elements of the design of the Stair Hall. He must have committed the design to memory.

'I am working on interior sketches of the Dining Hall,' Henry said, just for something to say. 'If you remember, the committee asked for small adjustments.'

'May I see them?'

'They are not ready for inspection yet. And they are in the lodge.'

'I was planning to take tea in the lodge. Just informally, perhaps you can show me.'

They went without another word, Henry hoping that the dinner invitation had been forgotten, but he suspected that Ashton Kinsburg was the kind of man who forgot nothing. Henry rambled on about the Dining Hall interior, not showing the drawing, and trying to be as inexact as possible. They were drinking their last mouthfuls of tea before Ashton spoke.

'You haven't replied to my dinner invitation,' he said. 'It would just be a brief dinner. My London house is not open at present; my wife is in the country.'

Henry tried not to exhale with relief. 'The invitation slipped my mind, I am sorry to say. I am so engaged with the details of the building. And I must decline, due to a prior engagement. Forgive me, I hope my absence this time will be remedied at some point in the future.'

'You should come and stay with us at Redlands. I have done much to it; you would hardly recognize it as the house of my fathers. Two new wings. I'd be interested in your opinion of it.'

'I have no opinion on domestic architecture. Civic buildings are what concern me these days.'

'No opinion?' Ashton gave a short, rather surprising, high peal of laughter. 'I have never met a man of taste and knowledge who had no opinion, Mr Dale-Collingwood. If you think to be polite, do not mind it – I can take a frank opinion.'

Henry said nothing, sure only that Kinsburg would not wish for his frank opinion about anything.

'You do not like me, do you, sir?' said Ashton. Henry felt his heart thunder to life in his chest, at the danger of it. All at once the site outside, so busy and productive under the blue and cloudless sky, seemed at threat. He could find no answer and was clearing his throat when Ashton continued.

'But I like you, very much indeed. And whatever wrong impression of me you have, I am determined to clear my name of it. You simply do not know me yet, and if I am reserved – well, that is a reserve of a gentleman who is most often concerned in business. But this is not business, Mr Dale-Collingwood; this is pleasure. And as I like you, I am determined you will like me.'

'I have never said . . .' Henry trailed off. He had dealt with awkward situations before – relaxed, with valour – but this was different. It was unnerving.

Ashton tutted under his breath, as though addressing a

166

spaniel dancing at his feet, and all at once Henry saw him in his house, with acres of grounds and a plethora of dogs and possessions and paintings and gilt, and a wife. The man had everything, even the freedom to come here and interrogate him, and he could not be older than two-and-thirty.

'Come now,' said Ashton. He was trying to be soothing but it did not come off well to Henry's ear. 'I am a friend to you, sir. We are all in awe of you, and of your accomplishments. You are just as much of an artist as your painter friends, but also an engineer, a technician. There is no honour I would not lay at your feet. But you are tired.' He sought Henry's gaze, until at last Henry had to give it to him. 'You are tired. Where is the affable fellow I met last March, so relaxed that he would unroll his plans on a table without ceremony and with confidence?' He paused. 'I have heard of your losses. You do not have to be at this site every day. You may come and visit us at Redlands. There is no luxury that we do not have.'

His face was just inches from Henry's; his eyes grey and unblinking, cold and yet filled with a kind of concern that Henry had never seen before.

'I will think on it,' said Henry gruffly.

Ashton seemed satisfied, and their conversation returned to normal matters, the younger man showing such a cool distance that Henry half-wondered if he had dreamt Ashton's intensity. Mr Kinsburg left soon after.

When Ashton wrote, giving possible dates for his visit to Redlands, Henry tried to ignore it. So often, he told

Peregrine, obligations evaporated when one merely ignored them. But Ashton persevered. He did not pay another site visit, but he wrote each week. Brief letters, barely covering even one half of the folded page, which he sent sealed. His black writing slanting, large, jointed like insects' legs. *That matter we spoke of; I would be grateful if you could give it your attention as soon as possible.*

'I say, old chap,' said Peregrine. 'Do you think he *loves* you?' Only Peregrine could say things like that.

The pile of letters built up in Henry's office, for he took them there rather than leave them around his room at his club. It was business correspondence, after all. Peregrine cautioned him – hardly necessary, for Henry knew the danger of angering a patron. But he kept distant, and continued with the work. Heavy rain had delayed the digging. None of the committee came to London. With satisfaction, Henry worked on, unencumbered.

Then, the letter which tipped him into decision came. On a Tuesday morning, with a sigh, Henry pierced Ashton's latest letter savagely with his letter knife. His eyes ran over the phrases, neat and polite, asking him when he would come to Redlands. Then, beneath it, another hand. So different from his: lighter strokes, looping forms showing a hand that had long been disciplined but in which individual character was struggling to break out.

My husband begs me add a few words here, to tell you how much we wish to see you here at Redlands.

*It would be a great favour to both of us if you would
come here, and give your thoughts on my husband's
works. Yours etc, Charlotte Kinsburg.*

He put the letter down. He felt his tiredness engulf him. He
kept it at bay so often, and yet his grief always seemed to be
waiting for him. In this moment, he dearly longed to be able
to speak to his father and seek his advice.

He made a flying visit to Peregrine's nearly completed
ultra-Gothic folly, and showed him the letter. 'He solicits her
to his cause now,' he said. 'Will you come with me?'

Peregrine read it in the shadow of the pointed porch while
Henry studied it. *Arches within arches.*

'Do you think he forced her to write it?' said Peregrine,
only half-jokingly, for there was sorrow in his face. 'You look
awful, by the way. You have been shutting yourself away with
your difficulties.'

'I am quite well. He may blame her if we do not go. It is
simply the matter of ordering a carriage, if you will let me
know when it is convenient for you.'

'Oh, Henry,' said Peregrine. 'Very well. But if we go, when
we return, you must open the Russell Square house. These
things cannot be put off for ever.'

'Very well,' said Henry. 'Life has to begin again,
I suppose.'

CHAPTER EIGHTEEN

1839

'I believe you're enjoying this,' Peregrine said, as they rattled down the lanes of Hertfordshire. Dressed splendidly,
wearing a waistcoat depicting knights on horseback – having
embraced the Gothic nature of his latest project – he was
nevertheless looking carriage-sick, rather than valiant. 'And
why did Kinsburg insist on providing the carriage and driver
from the George? Does he not know you are a gentleman
too? I swear you could have provided us with a cleaner ride.'

'He insisted that he would convey us this last part of the
journey, at a time of his choosing,' said Henry. 'And it seems
fine to me, but I travel better than you, perhaps. If it helps,
once we're on his land the road should be in perfect order.
I'm sorry to put you through this. I could have come alone. I
believe I've overblown the whole thing.'

When he'd fixed on a date, Henry had felt a sharp stab of

despair, which dulled into calmness over the next few days. He would see Mrs Kinsburg again. And it was highly likely that she would disappoint him. The mild romantic infatuations of youth had often left him untouched within a short time, for he was good at seeing things in the round. Prettiness faded, he knew that, and he told himself that, beneath sweetness, often other things lay. The sudden rush of feeling, of connection, that had occurred on the day of the accident would be revealed as a temporary, fleeting thing, as human and as intangible as a trick of the light. No one to blame, he thought soothingly, least of all her. And yet, he put his hand in his pocket, and it closed over the fragment of letter he had cut from Ashton's: a small piece of this woman, something she had touched.

'It's best that I'm here,' Peregrine said, with a dry glance in Henry's direction. 'Is this land all his? Kinsburg's? I haven't seen any gold glinting in the distance yet.'

'It's all on the inside,' said Henry, with a brief smile. He felt fully in control of himself; and he had arranged himself so that every line of his body seemed to tell of relaxation. But beneath it all, it were as though he had drunk a glass or two too much of champagne and might behave unpredictably. Only he was aware of it, and he knew that he did not betray himself by the slightest movement as they traversed the deep, hollowed-out lanes beneath trees, the acres of neatly cultivated land. He thought of the house awaiting him in Russell Square, under dust sheets and empty of life. It was an absence, rather than a presence, in his life, and he dreaded returning to it. 'I wish every day could be so picturesque as this,' he said. 'Look at that sky: perfect, blue, cloudless. And these fields.' He touched the sketchbook in his pocket. 'If we weren't moving, I'd try and draw it.'

'You'd be bored in no time,' said Peregrine. 'Besides, these people have no need for buildings. There is but one in this vicinity. You and I would have to fight over the yearly alterations. Oh, look at you. Don't go all misty-eyed over the idea of a simple life. You came from that, remember? And you ran from it, to the city, as fast as you could.'

'Perhaps I should not have. Been . . .'

'What? A country clergyman? I don't think so. A school-master? Or perhaps you would have found a home in business, with your connections. Don't even toy with the idea, Henry. You and I both know you love your work. Creating balance, and worth, and harmony, and you are doing the job that the good Lord put you on earth to do, so don't start getting sentimental at one glance of a haystack.'

Before long, they were approaching Redlands, and were at the lodge house. And then, carefully, but definitely, the driver pulled them up. After a moment or two, Henry leaned out of the window.

'What's amiss?'

The driver turned and touched his hat. 'Begging your pardon, Mr Dale-Collingwood. Mr Kinsburg asked that we arrive at four, or as near to as we can. I had measured the distance from the inn to here, and done a run more than once, but I'm a bit ahead of myself today. My watch here tells me so.'

Henry settled back into the carriage with a mystified frown at Peregrine, who had heard it all.

'What kind of man is so pernickety about time?' snapped Peregrine. 'It's bad manners, is it not, to keep us waiting this far from the house? I'd bet he's on the roof leads with his telescope.'

'He likes to control things,' murmured Henry. 'That is all, I suppose. He has taken it a little far, rather.' And he inspected his fingernails.

They sat there for a while, the horses shifting gently, and a soft breeze of early summer moving through the trees. Henry looked at his pocket watch. 'We should be on our way soon, Perry,' he said.

And, as if at his words, their horses – two finely matched chestnuts – set their hooves upon the surface of the two-mile drive, moving at a brisk trot down that road, the trees evenly spaced either side, so that now the carriage fell into sunshine, and now into shadow.

'I am unwell,' Charlotte said. 'Dearest Ashton, I am unwell.' She bit her lip: the 'dearest' had been too much.

'Our visitors will be here soon,' he said.

'I know they will, and I know that it is my duty to ensure their comfort,' she said. 'If you would but let me rest during tea? I can then be fresh for dinner. Barbara would like to be the hostess at tea, you know that. She has arranged some of her very best dainties.'

His expression was impenetrable. 'What has tired you so much?'

She sprung on this hope. 'It is the planning. Mrs Alton has been wonderful, and the staff most obliging, but I have felt the need to create our very best menus, as you asked for, and it has taken much study, and much thought over ordering of provisions, and stocking the ice house. I have supervised the selection of the flowers, and arranged them myself: thirty arrangements. And I have overseen every detail, from the bringing out of the first service and the polishing of the silver, and the arrangements of the tables, and the seating plan.' As she spoke, she saw his expression fade and sour. Her husband did not care for problems.

'Enough,' he said. 'You have over-tired yourself for two visitors? Arranging the flowers, when you simply could have left instructions? I do not understand it.'

Charlotte put her hands behind her. For the last arrangement she had removed her hot hands from her gloves, and they were speckled with a small number of thorn pricks. Ashton saw the gesture, reached around and pulled her hand out, and inspected it. A deep sigh escaped him, a signifier of his misery.

'Cover them,' he said. 'Charlotte, you are the mistress here, and you have been for some years now, which makes this even more mystifying. Pray, behave as though you are worthy of the role. If you have injured yourself with over-exertion, it is no fault of mine. You must appear to greet our guests. It would spoil the whole effect if not. They will be here very soon.' The shadow of displeasure aged his young face. He could not look at her, but she could sense that he was actively trying not to be harsh. 'Go and check that Thomas is ready,' he said. She nodded, pressed a kiss to his warm cheek, and went.

Charlotte's son was looking out of the window when his mother arrived. Isabel sat nearby, playing with her dolls, ignored by her brother. She was judged too weak to attend this weekend, with her usual feverish aches and pains, but Charlotte knew that, although Ashton did not wish his little girl to be ill, it hardly mattered to him whether she attended: his son and heir was the central concern. Charlotte touched her daughter's hair, and they exchanged a smile. But it were as though Isabel knew why Charlotte was here: she looked towards her brother, standing at the window. He had not turned at his mother's approach. He was dressed as a miniature version of the master, in trousers and a waistcoat and jacket to match his father's. Charlotte couldn't help but remember that, when she had met Ashton, she had noticed that he was fully aware of what kind of power his wealth and good looks gave him. He had transmitted the same deep confidence, bordering on arrogance, to their tiny son.

Charlotte felt a dull storm cloud around her, the vapour of nausea, so it was with effort that she approached Thomas, and smoothed out his jacket. She crouched to adjust it around his neck, her dress spreading out around her, pale cream with richly embroidered flowers and leaves.

'Do not dirty your gown, Mama,' said Thomas, a little

frown on his face. He took her hand and played with it absently. 'Nurse told me about my sister Loveday,' he said.

Charlotte rose, and as she did so the floor seemed to tilt; a strange dizziness came to her. She winced with it, as the nurse came forwards, full of excuses. 'He asked about Miss Loveday, madam. It was not I who told him of her.'

Thomas was tugging on his mother's hand. 'Do not worry, Mama, do not worry.' Charlotte looked back at him. 'For surely, I am as good as my sister? As a son I am better than both Loveday and Isabel.' His twin did not even murmur or look up.

He gave her the sweetest smile. Charlotte disengaged herself from his hands and stepped backwards. 'All of you are precious to me. Let us not speak of it. Are you ready to receive our visitors?'

The boy had frowned again, deeply this time, and his bottom lip stuck out. 'You are not being tender to me. You have not told me I am better than my sisters. You tell me now.'

She looked at him.

'Or I will tell Papa.'

She gazed at him: her son. Remembered the days of the twins' births. Pain that had hummed around her body like clouds of flies in the August afternoon.

'Mama?'

Charlotte adjusted the fingerless lace mittens she had selected from her room on the journey up through Redlands to the nursery. She pressed one hand to her face now: smelt the trace of lavender. She looked down at her son and smiled.

He spoke again. 'Papa is best to me. Papa buys me things. My sword, my pony, my globes.'

His nurse decided to intervene. 'And yet Mama oversees your food and your clothes. Mama orders you the fire that keeps you warm in the evenings. And your favourite pudding.'

He looked a little troubled now. He took Charlotte's hand again, and pulled her a step or two to the window. From a distance, a black carriage trundled across the horizon. 'Look,' he said, suddenly excited. 'They will be here very soon.'

Charlotte stared at the carriage. 'Yes, my dear.'

He frowned again. 'I have been watching for them all afternoon, and now that you have distracted me, they have come. You have ruined it.'

'If you are not a constant watcher, Thomas, that is hardly my fault,' said Charlotte, and immediately felt guilty at her sharpness. She put her hands on his shoulders, and gently moved them up a little. 'Stand up straight when you meet them.' He shook her hands off him. This movement of rejection shook her, and she leaned forwards and embraced him. But his little body was stiff in her arms and when she took his face in her hands she saw there only his sullenness, the anticipation of speaking ill of her. She kissed him on the forehead. 'Say whatever you wish to your father,' she said. 'But hurry down now. We must greet the visitors.'

'What a monstrosity,' murmured Peregrine, as the carriage pulled up.

SOPHIA TOBIN

'Oh, come now,' said Henry, as the door was opened and the steps let down. 'It is not as bad as all that. He's just added an extra half a mile of frontage onto it.'

And here was Ashton, dressed more flamboyantly than Henry expected, in a vivid yellow waistcoat beneath his black frock coat. He seized Henry's hand and shook it, half-bowing as he did so, and this burst of almost youthful enthusiasm drew Henry up. But Ashton was now greeting Peregrine, and then leading both men towards the grand entrance of the house, where his son stood, shifting on his feet with excitement.

'My son and heir, Master Thomas Kinsburg,' cried Ashton, throwing out his arm and directing the men there. Henry glanced at Peregrine; he felt foolish paying obeisance to a child, but both men managed encouraging remarks for the small boy, who had clearly been primed by his father and prattled on about his home surely being the greatest building in England. Henry bit his lip and did not dare glance at Peregrine during the course of this, but was glad when, after several minutes, the child was taken off by his nurse, and his father returned to his normal manner of disengaged archness.

And then there was Mrs Kinsburg.

She had stood back, a pale shape in the vast, dark doorway. One might have mistaken her for a servant, with her preference for the shadows; or had he spent too long poring over plans, and straining his sight? But when she came forwards, Henry saw what an astonishing production she was: the hair, plaited intricately and lying in loops over her ears, a band of

178

the finest lace over the top. Her dress was cream-coloured, adorned with pink roses and green leaves, the many layers of stiff petticoats beneath making her skirt an exaggerated dome. She wore fingerless lace mittens. Her face was free of artificiality; the slight line of pink at her cheekbones was from where she had pinched them. At Ashton's direction, she came forwards, and she brought the scent of lily of the valley with her. She did not look directly at them: never once did her eyes meet Henry's, and he was glad of it.

It seemed to Henry that he and Charlotte were frozen for a moment in a tableau: her curtsey and his bow. It was clear that Peregrine and Ashton saw nothing. But he felt – she felt – it, though neither of them signalled to the other. The grey stone of Redlands; the shimmering green of the hills beyond them; a sky so blue it was unearthly. And, just for Henry and Charlotte, the opening shaft of light, as everything suddenly became bright. He had seen it in paintings, felt it pierce his heart. Chiaroscuro: a shaft of light through shadow.

CHAPTER NINETEEN

1839

The front hall of Redlands was unremarkable enough: stone, wood, coats of arms. But instead of woodsmoke, dogs and soot, the scent of flowers filled the air, creating a sense of intensity and expectation.

'We will be taking tea in the *salon de printemps*,' said Ashton. He ushered them through a series of smaller older rooms towards one of the new wings.

'Do you mind if I take drawings throughout the weekend?' said Henry suddenly. He felt for the sketchbook in his pocket, sensing Peregrine's eyes on him. 'I don't want to forget what I have seen.'

Ashton's face showed at first astonishment and then gratification. The relief of a person who had expected to display and demonstrate to extract approval, but who had been handed its gift immediately. 'Of course,' he said. 'That is – I did not think – you approve, then?'

'Yes,' said Henry with a brief nod. There was no flattery in his tone; he sounded tired. Ashton blinked, perplexed; the approval had not come in the form he wanted.

'My friend is rather eccentric in these things,' said Peregrine hurriedly. 'Drawing, always drawing. Let us go in to tea, Henry.'

The *salon de printemps* did not receive its guests: it erupted upon them. Its decorations and furnishings were all in the rococo style: curves and scrolls and shells and flowers. A frenzy of gold leaf and vivid green silk. There were a number of small ornate tables dotted around the room, and at least six servants at Henry's count stood formally at several points of the perimeter. At the sight of the guests, a vast silver teapot was brought, together with tea-making apparatus and tiny porcelain cups and saucers in Sèvres Rose Pompadour. Immense ornamental cakes were placed around the room on the many small tables. Henry found himself tended to by Charlotte's sister-in-law, who was disconcertingly known as Madam Barbara to differentiate her from Charlotte, the other Mrs Kinsburg. He chose a slice of multi-layered sponge cake and watched as the lady sawed through it with an admirable mixture of delicacy and brutality.

'How marvellous,' he said, when she eventually presented it to him. Several feet away Peregrine was tackling an immense construction of choux pastry. Staring at the severe black and white stripes on his own piece of cake, Henry rather envied him. He tackled the cake with speed, imagining that it would be best to get it over with. The sugary cream and icing made him feel slightly giddy.

As they ate, Ashton spoke of the formal gardens. Henry nodded, and tried to take in what his host was saying, although his words faded from his mind almost instantly. He sat there for some time, his plate empty in his hand, as Ashton questioned him about his architectural education and travels in Europe. As he continued to talk, Charlotte came and gently removed the plate from Henry's hand, passing it to a servant. There was a moment when Ashton took a forkful of cake into his mouth, affording a pause in his questions.

'Do you like this room, Mr Dale-Collingwood?' said Charlotte, in a low voice.

Henry glanced up at her. 'It's very pleasant.'

She smiled. 'It is known as the *salon de printemps*,' she said softly. 'But I always refer to it as the very-very green salon – we have many salons, of different colours. And we do not yet have the correct colour of Sèvres to complement this one.' He saw the dry humour sparkle in her eyes. But before he could say anything she moved off to speak to Peregrine, and Ashton continued. In the far corner of the room, their tea discarded, Barbara and Nicholas seemed to be having a disagreement, mainly conducted in furious whispers.

Peregrine rose with an air of selfless sacrifice. 'I say, Kinsburg,' he said, rather more grandly than anyone would have wished. 'Did I see various coats of arms carved out of plaster and painted in the entrance hall? I'm rather interested in heraldry.'

Ashton's face twitched in irritation. 'That's an old part of the building, I've done nothing to it – my ancestors would recognize it.' He seemed sorry at the thought. 'But if you are interested, let me show you, of course.' He rose with perfect good manners, and went out with Peregrine.

In that vast room, with the sunlight pouring in, yet instantly interrupted by the green walls and drapes, Henry sipped his tiny cup of tea and felt parched. He felt the eyes of the many servants on him, but it was Charlotte who approached him, and filled the teacup using the heavy silver teapot. A swiftly approaching maid offered him milk and then departed again.

'Thank you.' He smiled up at Charlotte. She was not looking at him, but turned and carried the teapot back to its tray.

'A pleasure,' she said. Then, glancing at Barbara and Nicholas, 'Do forgive them. My brother-in-law will depart for London soon and his wife is not happy about it.'

'I can't imagine why anyone would wish to leave here,' he said, taking a sip of tea, and relying on standard politeness.

'Really?'

They looked at each other. The instant familiarity astonished him; caught his breath.

'Perhaps I can,' he said, and drank the lukewarm contents of the cup in one go. He glanced at the others, saw they were not observed. He could not help but soften; her very presence uncoiled something in him, both energizing and comforting.

He glanced at her dress and coiffure. 'You look very different from the day I first met you. Is this the real Mrs Kinsburg?'

She touched her hair. 'This is all illusion. Sugar water and pins. You have already truly met me.'

'Have I?'

'Yes.' She rose, held her hand out for the cup, and with her other hand touched his wrist briefly with her bare fingertips. They were cold, and it felt almost like a sting: the shock of connection, which left an impression on his skin, a buzzing site of activity.

He felt the touch, the impression of it. It was as piercing as grief, and he felt it as an exact parallel. He felt the pressure build behind his eyes. She put the cup on one of the tables, then returned to him. 'Are you well?' she said softly.

'Yes.'

'You look almost afraid.'

He replied to himself as much as to her. 'I am.'

She sat down in the nearest chair, her dress's many layers gathering, sighing and crunching together. How strange and beautiful she looked, he thought, her back perfectly straight, every detail correct. But her eyes were the same – the same troubled eyes that he had looked at in the lodge at the Mirrormakers' Club. Yet here – there was something about the restraint, the slight sense of all that lay beneath – here at Redlands, she had a certain power. She was not the fragile creature he had raised from the road in the City of London. She rather frightened him.

In the rooms beyond he heard Peregrine and Ashton

talking – Peregrine talking rather too much. He knew he should go and support his friend, take himself away from this situation and its simmering tension. Instead, he drew his sketchbook and pencil from his pocket, and said, loudly:

'Will you permit me to draw this room, Mrs Kinsburg?'

She tilted her head slightly, a question. 'Of course.'

Barbara did not cease in the low drawn-out reprimand she was giving Nicholas. As he made a show of shifting in his seat, Henry leaned towards Charlotte.

'Go and stand by the window. Think of your favourite things.'

'If my husband discovers that you have drawn me—'

'He will not discover it. Go.' He smiled. 'It is the only thing that will help me recover my spirits.'

'Then I must obey.'

She rose, fluffed out her dress, and then walked to the window and looked out. He looked at the brightness of her profile in the summer sun, and set to drawing her. No details of hair or dress, only that profile, only the strange pools of light and shadow. He did it quickly, the pencil darting over the page, suggesting things rather than the linear drawing of his architecture. He enjoyed breaking from precision. Then, when he felt he had captured her – her life and her light – he slowed down, and began to draw what surrounded her. He had been truthful when he said he would draw the room – he captured the c- and s-swirls; the stylized shells and flowers. So different from his beloved Mirrormakers' Club, which he still was imagining into life, with its classical precision.

He did not notice that Barbara and Nicholas had stopped arguing. First, he heard the swish of Barbara's dress: she moved with an assassin's swiftness.

'What are you drawing, Mr Dale-Collingwood?'

He had not been prepared; he moved to cover it. He supposed, now that he looked at her, that she was dressed as elaborately as Charlotte.

'Is it a secret?' That tone – the tone of a bully on the hunt, a kind of glee and cruelty all mixed together.

He rose to his feet, slapping the sketchbook shut as he did so, smiled and bowed as he rolled it and put it into his capacious pocket.

'Madam Barbara. I asked Mr Kinsburg if I might draw his rooms – and I must say, you are correct, my working sketches are a secret. I am a proud man. I will work up watercolours of these rooms and send them to you as a gift.' She looked at him uncertainly; she knew that to go further would be a failure of manners. 'They will be jewel-like in their beauty,' he continued. 'But allow me my sketches.'

'Stop toying with our guest, Be-be,' said Nicholas, taking his watch out and checking it. 'Don't let her bother you, my dear Dale-Collingwood. I would like to talk to you about art later.'

'It would be a pleasure.'

Barbara glared at her husband.

Henry glanced at Charlotte, still standing at the window.

'I will just,' he said hesitantly, and could not find the words. 'Just go and see if they need me.'

'I'm amazed they have been there so long,' said Charlotte in a carrying voice, without turning to look at him. 'My husband is very happy we bear arms, of course, but it usually bores him terribly to talk about that kind of thing. He is more interested in beautiful things.'

'Thank you so much for the tea,' Henry said, in the perfect volume to carry. 'And the cake, Madam Barbara. I shall dream about it.'

He left the room with a benevolent smile. He found his friend dominating the conversation and Ashton frowning. He smiled and nodded as Ashton and Peregrine conversed, but he heard nothing of what they said. At the corner of his eye he kept the doorway within sight, so that he would know if Charlotte or one of the others came to join them. But when the conversation of heraldic charges petered out, and they returned to the salon, everyone had gone. Family and servants alike had seemingly departed through other doors, either the formal far one which led on to further rooms, or through secret servants' doors in the walls. The many cakes had been taken, and the tea apparatus cleared, and only one servant stood watch, a footman, with the ticking of the clock.

Was it true, Henry wondered? Could he still smell the scent of her, the perfume of lily of the valley, or was it the scent of this house, with its vast arrangements of hothouse flowers, sequences of contained rooms, of gorgeous tapestries and lowered drapes, the perfume clinging to them? He wanted to search every corner of the room to check whether there was any trace of her, whether there were even crumbs on the floor or a dropped teaspoon. But no: everything, and everyone, had gone.

For a brief moment he wondered if their encounter had been imaginary, a pleasant afternoon dream from which he would wake in a jolting carriage. He knew that people – like his parents and sister – could be gone in a moment, and never return. The thought twisted, serpent-like, waking the grief again in his brain. Peregrine was still talking manfully, clearly noticing that his friend was distracted. But when the venerable brown and gold clock in the corner began to chime, Henry came to: nothing was a dream. He walked to the case, and examined the dial.

'Ah, that clock,' said Ashton. 'You've spotted it. It's Boulle. Did you recognize it?'

CHAPTER TWENTY

1940

Entrance Hall, the Mirrormakers' Club

In the darkness of a winter evening a few days after Christmas, Christian rang the front doorbell of the Mirrormakers' Club and heard it echo through the building. Huddled into his coat, his hat low over his brow, he stood poised and tense until he heard Peggy's slow footsteps. Only then did his shoulders begin to drop.

Her eyes were bright when she opened the door and ushered him quickly in, closing the door so that no light would escape.

'Hello, Peggy,' he said. 'Is Livy here?' He couldn't help saying it; he had vowed to be calm, not to mention her, and yet it was the first thing he said.

She read his discomposure in his face, and smiled a

comforting smile. 'She is. We wondered when you'd come back to us, Mr Taylor.'

'Did you miss me?' he said, trying to sound playful, following her through the Entrance Hall in the sweep of her torchlight. The Stair Hall was dark, the shadows dense and cold, without a hint of its daylight colour.

'We did,' she called behind her.

The scent of cigarette smoke drifted up to them as they walked down the stairs. They found Livy and Jonathan sitting in the vaults, cross-legged on the floor, gazing at three large sheets of paper. Christian leaned over and caught sight of plans of each floor of the building. 'Are these original?' he asked, noting the copperplate handwriting labelling each room. *Scullery. Kitchen. Confectionary.*

'Yes,' said Livy, smiling up at him. But Jonathan was already folding the papers closed, hurriedly and protectively. He folded one in the wrong direction, and Livy put her hand on his arm. He released it to her, and she folded it. He took it quickly from her. 'I'll put these in the Document Room,' he said.

Christian watched him go with raised eyebrows. He smiled at Livy, as Peggy all but manhandled his coat from his shoulders. 'Any closer to solving the mystery?'

She shook her head. 'We've searched the public rooms and the service rooms, even those that are closed off,' she said in a low voice. 'And there are no hints in the archive. There are lots of interesting things there, though – did you know they pulled a Roman goddess out of the earth when they dug the foundations?'

'I didn't,' he said. 'Wonderful London.'

'There's something else.' She paused, and he couldn't help but see the beginnings of a smile on her mouth, slight but perceptible. 'I think your architect, Henry, was in love. I think he loved Charlotte. I keep seeing her initials in his notebook. Again and again.'

'Really?' he said, with a smile.

'I keep asking the portrait of Charlotte,' said Livy playfully. 'But she won't tell me anything. I wanted to unwrap her, hang her down here with us. But Jonathan doesn't want to look at her.'

Jonathan was bustling back into the room, speaking to Peggy loudly and jovially.

'Stayed here for Christmas, did he?' murmured Christian to Livy.

'It's really up to him, what he does,' she said. 'Happy Christmas, by the way.'

'Happy Christmas, Miss Baker,' he said, and handed her a small, book-shaped package from his pocket.

She unwrapped it and exclaimed with delight: *Poirot Investigates*, a book of short stories by Agatha Christie.

'What a lovely present!' cried Peggy.

'All hail the conquering hero,' said Jonathan sarcastically, lighting a cigarette.

'You will have some tea?' Peggy said, looking at Christian with a barely suppressed sparkle in her eye. 'Bill's just finishing his pipe, then we'll have one.'

Tea was served, and they all sat in an awkward silence

191

as Peggy presented one jam sandwich, cut into quarters and with a scraping of butter and jam. 'No need for me to have any,' she said, with a smile. 'I had so many of the liqueur chocolates Mr Whitewood bought for us, I'll be an inch wider by now I'm sure.'

'You deserved all of them,' said Jonathan. He glanced competitively at Christian. 'Mrs Holliday's mock turkey was a miracle.'

'I don't doubt it. Please, do have a piece of jam sandwich, Peggy,' said Christian.

'Aren't you at St Paul's tonight?' said Jonathan rattily.

Christian smiled. 'No, not tonight, old chap. Sorry about that.'

'Who's on the roof, Bill?' asked Livy.

'Barry Thomas and Louie Robinson,' said Bill, picking up the cup in both hands, without recourse to the handle. 'Went up half an hour since. Has been another quiet one for the day spotters, thank God.'

The words were barely out of his mouth when the air-raid siren began its melancholy wail. 'Christ,' he muttered under his breath, and received an elbow in the ribs from Peggy. 'I knew the Christmas lull was too good to be true.'

The alert was a little late. Almost at the moment it sounded, the thud of bombs began. Bill frowned, closed his eyes, and rubbed his temples, as though he were in danger of losing his temper with the bombers themselves. 'I'll turn off the gas and electricity,' he said. Peggy lit an oil lamp, and when Bill returned the group shuffled into the shelter section of the basement, Peggy carrying the quarter of jam sandwich which no one would touch.

Bang-bang-bang. Someone was hammering on the blast-proof doors of the basement. Bill went up the steps, swearing under his breath, and opened them.

It was Barry Thomas. He was wearing his tin helmet, and boiler suit, and his face was red and sweaty.

'We need all hands on the roof,' he said. 'Or the place will burn, I promise you.' He was not normally a man for drama. At his words, Peggy and Bill looked at each other with alarm.

A long line of detonations shook the building to its core. The ground seemed to shift beneath Livy's feet. She felt it: the falling away of life, and of time. Thought of how Henry's building had begun with the London clay, with foundations dug out of the earth, and had a vision of it, razed to the ground again.

'There'll be fire all around in no time,' shouted Barry, as he turned and began to run back in the direction of the stairs.

'You don't need to go, Livy, love,' said Peggy, touching her hand. She turned to Christian. 'She was injured in the past. A firebomb.'

'It's fine, I'll come. Of course I will.'

They went up the quickest way: the basement stairs, then the main staircase in the Stair Hall to the first floor, then the backstairs, up four flights, snatching up red fire buckets filled with sand on the way, and an extra stirrup pump too, the noise and vibrations of the planes and the bombs getting louder all the time. The door opened to the roof. Bill went first up the narrow steps, Livy behind him.

'Bloody hellfire.' His voice was low and yet audible, deadened with despair. Sweating, she pulled herself up, out onto the roof, and took a few steps forwards, aware that others were following her, and wanting to give them space. She did not know what she said when she saw it.

There were fires all around them. She caught Barry's eye as he passed her with a bucket of water. 'I told you,' he said.

Around them, the fires were starting, as far as they could see. It was obscenely beautiful: the gold, the red, the black outlines of buildings and people. The grey-smoked dome of St Paul's still stood, but for how long, it seemed foolish to bet. The sky was bright with the chandelier flares let loose by the enemy to light the planes' way to the cathedral. Livy exclaimed at the beauty of it: the red and yellow lights in the sky.

In the air, there was the smoke of a thousand fires. Before them, more were flaring into life under their eyes. There was no point in trying to count. The sky was filled with the angry drone of planes.

They all stood there: Jonathan, Livy, Christian, Bill and Peggy, stunned by what they were looking at.

An explosion blew them off their feet.

Thomas and Robinson were running towards them, their lips moving soundlessly. Livy felt someone's hand on her wrist, pulling her to her feet. Beside them, the dome of the Stair Hall, where the watchers sheltered during quiet times, stood with its door open. Her eyes focused on the cigarette ends left by the door. Built of wood and lead, it looked pitifully small, covered in its jacket of wire netting to protect it from the blasts. An optical illusion, Livy thought, that is all it is. She thought, strangely, of Henry, his drawings and plans, his letters. He surely would never have dreamt of this. It seemed so vulnerable in the midst of the raid. A fierce instinct to protect his creation rose in her.

She heard Christian shout out. He was staring at St Paul's: at the bombs glancing off the surface of the dome, and the showers of sparks pocking its surface. 'I should go there,' he said.

Livy shook her head. 'It's too late,' she said. 'There are others there. Stay here.' He read the words on her lips rather than hearing them, her voice drowned out by the noise of the planes and the bombs.

Soon, an order was established: the men worked with their buckets of sand, and the stirrup pumps, quenching incendiaries, sometimes even shovelling them off onto the street below. They covered the roof and the walls with water, with special attention to the woodwork, alongside the automatic sprinklers which had been activated. The women ran up and down the stairs with the buckets, filling them from the tanks on the lower floor. As evening drew on to night, there was no let-up in the bombing. With the electricity off, and no lift, Livy and Peggy used torches to negotiate the stairs.

Each time they reached the roof, it seemed worse to Livy. The fire grew in intensity, until it seemed that they, and only they, were not on fire, an island in the midst of flames. The City blazed around them, a forest of fire, the smoke in their eyes and their lungs. The men without overalls had their jackets off, they worked with a mechanical intensity which was exhausting to see, but Livy knew she did the same, and Peggy too, so that she wondered at their strength: all temporarily made strong by adrenaline. Still, on the horizon, the dome of St Paul's remained, and now and then Livy caught Christian glancing over to it, as they all did, as though touching a relic for blessing. The hours burned on. St Paul's still stood, and so did their Club.

Still the planes came; and still the bombs fell, blowing them all from their feet more than once. Living only in each moment, pushing through each pain and fall and detonation. And the women dragged the grey water for the stirrup pump, and the men sent it gushing over leadwork and wood; and they washed out and sanded out fire, all working together. As one, their thought was: *just one more moment.* Give me one more moment. Let the rain come, let the bombers leave, let the City stand.

More than once, one of them weakened, and turned away from the blizzard of fire. Robinson stood on the very edge of the roof, at dizzying height, and looked down on the burning street, and said, *it is close, Christ, it is close*, until Thomas pulled him away. They all fought the fire, as the flames revolved around them, like devils let up from a chasm in the earth. The fire was both beautiful and terrible. It seemed to have its own spirit, its own voice, its own hot breath. *One must not let the fire get into one's head*, Livy thought, as she heaved a bucket of water into Bill's arms. And she turned and gathered an empty bucket, and went down the ladder into the darkness, with the flames still dancing before her eyes.

Six hours passed before the single note of the all-clear sounded, high and unrelenting. Near to midnight. The fires raged. The noise now was no longer of the dreaded planes, but of distant sirens, whistles, and above all, of fire and its havoc: cracking, and creaking, and groaning, and collapse. Showers of sparks, and the sudden give of a building in flames. The women continued to run up and down, up and down, with their buckets of water, their arms aching and sore, their calves cramping, until the tanks were empty. The men fought the fires, and patrolled, and cast water over everything: this great, dripping, toasted building with the breath of fire upon it, even as the night hours passed into early morning, and dawn was near.

Gradually, so gradually, the intensity lessened. Stamping out a glowing ember, Livy turned and looked for the hundredth time: the dome of St Paul's still stood.

'The tanks are empty,' she said. Her throat was sore from the smoke.

'Do we stop?' said Barry.

The sky was still dark. They all stood: stinking and sodden. Limbs trembling from fatigue. Eyes running with tiredness and smoke. 'Yes,' said Bill. 'Time to call it quits now.' He looked at his watch. 'Five thirty,' he said. 'A nice round figure, at least.'

The day had brought fresh resources and crews: already the streets were full of overalled men and women with armbands, tin helmets, and eyes that had not seen last night's horror, joining exhausted comrades.

Christian turned, and caught sight of Livy. For the first time in hours, he gave her his full attention.

She was standing on the edge of the roof. The smoke around her rose like mist, lit by the still-burning City. At the precise angle she stood from him, light was haloing her – the palest seam of gold edging her face and hair. He stared at her bright, burning eyes, so vivid that it seemed her resources were being consumed by some inner fire. Completely independent of him, and of Jonathan; the Livy he remembered, with her own strange spirit. He had to force himself to take a breath. He had never seen anything so beautiful in his life. He stepped towards her.

'I saw it,' she said. 'The fire. Weeks ago, when you visited to see the Dining Hall. I was upstairs, and the hall door was open. I saw someone behind me, and I thought it were you. But it wasn't. The light changed. As though there were fire, outside the windows.' She could not say why or how it had had a quality of premonition. It was with the same sense that she had seen the doorknob turn on the door to the backstairs. Could a place hold energy? Hold on to suffering, and predict it?

She looked at his face: tired, but attentive. 'You do believe me, don't you?'

'Of course.' His voice shook.

'Are you all right?' she said. He nodded silently, and passed his hand over his eyes. She touched his arm, nodded, turned away. His hand caught a tear, and he did not know if it was from the smoke, or if he was weeping.

'I should have kept you with me,' he said. 'Last September.' But she was already walking away, and did not hear him.

They stood there, all of them, eyes glazed with fatigue, aware intensely of their survival. Thomas and Robinson came towards them all, their arms outstretched, and drew them all together, into a circle, which became a knot. Livy rested her head against Peggy's shoulder, and felt the warmth of Jonathan's breath on her hair.

'Thank God,' Bill said, his voice breaking.

'We are alive, aren't we?' Livy said, and her voice sounded small and hopeful.

'Sure we are, Miss Livy,' said Barry Thomas. 'Don't be so bloody daft.'

As they trooped down the staircase, Livy put her hand on Christian's arm.

'Do you think London will fall? Peggy said Mrs Billings at the butcher's has her suitcase packed.'

'Not a chance. Don't even think about it.' He saw her face soften, but the concern was still in her eyes, and in the line of her brow. 'You're too cooped up here. Why don't you come to St Paul's one day? I could show you behind the scenes, you could meet my chums. They are all older men – the original call was for men over forty and I had to do a lot of talking for them to let me join the watch. They're good chaps, and there are some women too. We have lectures, play dominoes, and keep ourselves snug in the crypt when we're not on patrol. They'd like you: you'd remind them of their daughters and granddaughters.'

'That's very kind of you. But – I prefer to stay here. Inside.'

'It's not healthy, you know.'

'I'll be going away soon. I should get my Land Army papers any day – and then I'll go. To the countryside. A fresh start. I may as well be useful in some kind of way.'

He shook his head. 'You should get well first.'

She gave him a mischievous smile. 'I have things to do here before I go. I should hurry. I need to know Charlotte more, and find the diamond.' She looked down, and he realized she was pushing the strap of her watch free from its catch. 'You said you could find someone to fix this,' she said, and her expression was evasive – almost shy. 'Would you mind dreadfully?'

'Of course not,' he said mechanically. And yet, as she placed it in his hand, he felt winded by it: an influx of hope. He glanced down the turn of the staircase, and his hand closed around the watch. The others had gone ahead, apart from Jonathan, who stood at the bottom, hands in pockets, looking up at them.

CHAPTER TWENTY-ONE

1940

COMMITTEE ROOM, THE MIRRORMAKERS' CLUB

Jonathan sat at the Committee Room table, staring at the piece of paper in front of him. At the first two words, addressing the director of the Club:

Dear Mayhew,
It was the Second Great Fire of London.

He was giddy with tiredness, still dressed in his grimy shirt-sleeves, his jacket cast aside in some other place, he could not remember where.

I write to tell you of the service your people have done here tonight.

He wrote an account of all that had happened, and he did it without any of his usual rhetorical flourishes, but with poor phrases, fumbling for words. When he closed the letter, he saw his black fingerprints, the marks on the white paper, and sighed. Mayhew would see them as a sign of emotion, perhaps even instability, he thought, and they would invalidate the contents. He had best rewrite the letter when he was clean and more in control of himself. But he doubted his ability to make real what had been gone through. He began to rethink how he would do it, and sure enough that raw emotion was being distilled out. *Some present should be made to them, in honour of their contribution.* He had separated the others from him. Already, in his mind, he had directed things, and they had worked for him. He put the letter in his pocket, and walked out, across the landing, and down the main staircase, through the green door, into the vaults.

He moved silently, and looked at the oblivious faces of Peggy, Bill and Livy, who had fallen asleep where they lay, on their pallet beds. Livy's hair was dark and tangled on the pillow. Her face: defenceless, and innocent, a grey smudge across her left cheekbone. Her glorious eyes were closed; he thought how pallid her face looked without them.

As the others slept, Christian had not yet reached his small flat, his gas ring, or his bed, only thought of these ordinary things with longing. He was still outside the Club on the road in the merciless morning light, inhaling the breath of the smoking City, having been attracted by a member of the rescue team who had just been assessing the remains of the building on the corner, and who recognized him from a previous visit. The man turned him around, and pointed out an area of damage to the Club. 'It will need scaffolding,' he said.

Christian swore under his breath. A bomb had made a half-hearted hole in the bottom corner of the Club. It was the exact place that he had leaned against, to catch his breath, when he had seen Livy again all those weeks ago. Christian and the man stood and peered down. It had taken the surface of the pavement up, and below was a passage, the height of a man, which, Christian presumed, had been dug around the building as a form of protection from damp. He crouched down and peered into the hole. 'Do you have a torch?'

It was produced. Kneeling, Christian shone it into the hole. 'It's not so bad.' He put a hand in, pushed aside some of the rubble. 'It's smaller than you think. Wait a minute.' He got down, heedless of his clothes, levered himself a little way down into the large crack, a blow from a pagan god. Livy's goddess, he thought, was annoyed at being disturbed.

'Be careful, sir.'

'Well, I'll be damned.'

'What's wrong?'

Christian turned off the torch carefully to conserve the battery, climbed out and got to his feet. He hardly knew how to describe what he had seen: the delicate white shapes, and their separation against the dense interrupted clay soil of London.

'There's a skeleton.'

'Not a body?'

'No, that is, not a new body. We don't need heavy rescue here. Whoever is there has been dead for a very long time.'

The man took his torch back and rolled his eyes. 'That's all we bloody need.'

By the time Christian had finished his conversation with the man, and had shone the torch several times into the pit so that he knew he was not mistaken, Peggy had risen from her bed and opened the doors to the Club. Christian had been standing, looking out at the ruined City landscape, when he heard the click and groan of the doors. Turned, and met her smile with his own.

'Still here?' she said, looking down at him on the pavement. 'I fell asleep, but only for a few minutes. And now I feel too tired to sleep.'

'I'm not sure I could sleep either.'

'I'll put the kettle on, if the water's on,' she said to him. He let her go without a word, and walked slowly up the steps in her wake. She had left the scent of cinders behind. The tiredness was beginning to catch up with him.

Peggy had descended into the vaults by the time he had reached the Stair Hall. He looked around at the building he had helped to save: at the walls lined by coloured marble, at the white marble staircase in its grandeur, and up at the dome. He saw dragons, and coats of arms, and the arms of the City of London. Although this building was special to him, he could think of a dozen similar. It was civic, he thought, it was impersonal. It was not a place that witnessed life and death, like a church or a register office. He heard the green door to the basement open and close.

'Christian?' Livy came out, rubbing one hand across her eyes. She was still dressed in the clothes she had worn the night before, and there was a smut on her face. He stopped himself from reaching out and rubbing it away. Behind her was Whitewood, with his tie on – *his tie on*, Christian thought – and he felt a sudden searing jealousy that the man had been down there, sleeping near Livy. He struggled to control it, not to let it show on his face.

'There's bones in the building,' he said, with an imitation of a smile. 'Like a Gothic novel.'

Livy blinked and frowned. 'What?'

Christian explained what he had found: Livy and Jonathan stared at him. 'I can only see part of it.'

'What can you see of the body?' Her voice was urgent; she looked even paler than the moment before.

'Not much. The top half. The top of the skull, some of the vertebrae, but some earth has fallen in.'

Jonathan had come up behind Livy, and put his hand on her shoulder. Christian stared at that hand, at that impression of ownership. The sudden anger he felt startled him. Dispassionately, he thought he might strike the man: knock him down. But it was the tiredness, he thought; he had to remember it was the tiredness.

'Show me.' Her voice was insistent, strong.

'Is that a good idea?' Jonathan, pulling her back.

205

Christian held out his hand. She walked towards him. And, just briefly, he brushed her elbow before he ushered her towards the front door.

As Livy walked through the Stair Hall and into the darkness of the Entrance Hall before that large rectangle of light, to step outside for the first time in many weeks, she felt the building retreat from her, felt it shrink away, so that her focus was on the light, and on reaching the bones which Christian had described to her. She walked without a glance at the beautiful walls, without a thought of their detail, without even thinking of the painting of Charlotte and its cool, contained beauty. She walked towards the anarchy of something. His words had broken through something, torn something open as easily as parachute silk. Her muscles were tired, but she was awake, and she knew she had given everything, and something had begun to stir inside her.

She went down the steps, blinking at the light, and let Christian pass her. He and Jonathan were speaking but she did not listen to them. She did not glance from left to right. They turned the corner.

A vast hole in the pavement: a darkness.

'I can't see anything,' she said.

'Crouch down,' said Christian. 'I'll shine the torch. Don't ruin your slacks.'

Jonathan murmured something: she heard the tone of disapproval. He took a few steps away from them, turned his back, and lit a cigarette.

Livy did as Christian said, narrowed her eyes: caught sight of something briefly in a wavering flash of torchlight as Christian swung it; rolled back onto her heels.

'The skull,' she said. Put her hands back on the London pavement, to support her weight. The icy dampness of the London stone travelled through her hands, her arms, and into her trunk. And she felt it, she really felt it. Felt it, she realized, in a way that these bones could not feel. And it struck her: Charlotte, in the painting, the golden light behind her, the white skin, the pinpoint of light in her eyes, and that smile, just beginning.

Charlotte was dead. Henry was dead. Ashton was dead. They lived in their letters, in the words, in the flat surface of canvas and paint as hard and bright as enamel, but these things were all just things, as dead as these bones, they were more dead than the London earth, for at least that was teeming with life. The thing that they had been was gone, burned out, released.

And they seemed to speak to her, these people, in unison. As though Henry had put down his pen and looked at her, as though Charlotte brushed her hair with the silver-mounted brush, and leaned to look in the mirror in her portrait, her face beside Livy's. And Ashton – oh, poor Ashton, never thinking of anyone but himself, never imagining he could ever die, just fighting death, and time, and imagining himself as permanent as a diamond. Christian said her name and touched her shoulder, and as she turned to look at Jonathan – insolent, proud, untouchable – Henry, Charlotte and Ashton turned to her, as though they sensed her presence in their world, a shadow in the corner of the room, there just for a moment.

They said it to her.

Life or death. Decide.

CHAPTER TWENTY-TWO

1839

Henry strode to the large windows in his room and flung them open. After the ordeal of tea, he required a smoke. But as he took his first breath of fresh air, and looked out at the hills, their outlines softening in the evening light, there was a knock at the door. The manservant apologetically informed him that Mr Kinsburg had requested to meet him on the lower landing. He suppressed the profanities which sprang to mind, and followed the man down, where he found Ashton and Peregrine.

Ashton announced that they were to have a tour. 'Before the light goes completely.'

The two men followed their host disconsolately. 'You look like you've been stunned for a kill,' murmured Peregrine.

'You're hardly at your best.'

'Better than you. Do buck up, Henry.'

They took in corridors, elaborate and pedestrian. Grand reception rooms and the cellar. Dead ends and wrong turns, so that Henry hardly knew where he was. From the rooms that Ashton had refurbished, including Charlotte's favourite salon, which Henry committed to memory, to the older rooms that Ashton despised – it seemed to Henry that he took them there merely to sneer at them. Henry sought to make Ashton be quieter in the chapel, the oldest part of the house, its stained glass bright in the light of the setting sun, but the man seemed anxious to be back in the other rooms of the house. 'I really wish to show you my best study,' he said, so they left the cool, damp air of the chapel, so different in character from the rest of the house, and went to the scarlet and yellow striped room, full of vitrines, jewels, and silver. A single moth fluttered in the darkened air.

Stepping back into the main corridor, and then through an anteroom, Henry caught sight of a painting in the shadows, and exclaimed. It was of Mrs Kinsburg, and it captured her entirely, but with extra spirit, it seemed: the slightly sardonic look in her eyes made Henry's heart beat faster. 'Why does this painting languish here, in a shadowy corner?' he said, turning to Ashton with a smile.

But Ashton did not smile in return.

'It requires alterations,' he said. 'I commissioned Mr Winterhalter to paint her. The paint is barely dry. You would not believe what it cost me to bring him here, and the time it took to persuade him. I am not sure he captured her.'

Henry opened his mouth to contradict him, but caught

Perry's warning glance. 'You can see the influence of Italy on his art,' he said. 'The soft light – the landscape beyond. I think it very handsome.'

'I am having it altered, in a few weeks,' said Ashton. 'I have acquired a great diamond,' his eyes brightened, 'and it must be included. Perhaps that will raise the portrait a little.'

Henry barely had time to change for dinner. 'It is at a late hour in your honour,' said Henry's manservant, a footman who had been charged with valeting for him, and who was gratifyingly loose-tongued. 'The routine is usually: dine at two; tea at five; supper at nine.'

'And what is your mistress like? Mrs Kinsburg?'

The man's face fell blank. 'I don't know what you mean, sir.'

Later, Henry hardly remembered dinner. The guests had gathered in one of the galleries: several couples, to whom he was introduced and uncharacteristically immediately forgot their names. There was wine, and more wine; his glass was endlessly full. More than once, he touched his pocket for his sketchbook – but of course, he had changed for dinner, and left it in his room. It was as well, for it would hardly be good manners to start drawing now, no matter how determined his host was to accommodate his eccentricity. He spoke to Nicholas about art, said he would be glad to make introductions in London.

Charlotte flitted around her husband and guests like a Brimstone butterfly in pale yellow satin. She did not speak to him, only granted him and Peregrine her brightest smile. At length, they processed into the dining room. Henry felt that he was lumbering, head down, and put his hand to his collar to check it was straight. Then he stood on the threshold of the ochre room, looking at the table, its mirror polish, loaded with silver-gilt epergnes and centrepieces; lines of cutlery; silver plates to hold porcelain plates in grand layers. Candelabra at two-foot intervals, lit with the finest and purest candles, and above the table a chandelier made of silver, suspended by a chain from the ceiling. Henry put his hand to his eyes.

'In heraldry terms, I'd say the dominant metal of this room is silver,' said Peregrine with a hiccup, as he passed Henry, still carrying a full glass and sounding as drunk as his friend. Henry laughed rather louder than he should have done and took a seat at the table. He felt the house pressing in on him: its colour, its assertion. He lessened the speed of his drinking, adjusting to his intoxicated state, letting the room, its noise and sensation, die down. And yet the evening passed in a blur. The dishes were elaborate, the conversation loud and unsettled. On his wrist, Henry felt the spot where Charlotte had touched him prickle in its coolness, building in significance like a sore. He pulled his cuff over it, as though worried someone might see it. Later, as he sobered up, he wondered at the balance of his mind.

After dinner, the ladies withdrew, but instead of taking port and cigars, Ashton drew his gentlemen guests through the house.

'Where are we going?' wondered Peregrine aloud.

'To the Bachelors' Wing!' cried an inebriated Ashton, plunging on through the dark corridors with a candle in his hand, with the same bluff aggressiveness as though he were leading a charge into the heart of a battle. They were followed by two footmen, fleet of foot, their antiquated wigs cast off earlier in the evening. 'Not that I have use of it anymore,' said Ashton, as they reached the threshold. 'But I may visit, may I not?' And he roared with laughter. Some of the other gentlemen guffawed politely.

The room, reasoned Henry, was as large as a great hall would have been in a medieval building. It was curtained with vast swathes of scarlet fabric, and the furniture was in the Gothic taste. He gazed at it: the dark wood, the soft-sheened fabric, spikily chased metal containers that resembled Catholic incense burners. He watched the footmen as they opened the pierced covers and lit aromatic tablets, placing the lids back down, so that sweet smoke spun and twirled from the holes. The room was partitioned by still more scarlet curtains, and Henry was informed there was a billiards table there, but he did not join some of the other men to play. Instead, he and Peregrine sank into one of the commodious sofas. He thought he might fall asleep. But then one of the footmen brought a silver tray, with an indecently large decanter; cigars were produced, and soon the sweet smoke was joined by the scent of cigars, their bitter strength mixing with the sweetness in a thick haze.

They talked nonsense, as men in clubs often did – talked

of horses, and women rather than wives, and laughed too loudly. Henry sat silent, his chin on his chest, and it was only when Ashton leaned forwards, and tapped him on the knee, that he came to.

'Stop dropping ash on my carpet,' said Ashton. And Peregrine laughed – again – too loudly.

'My apologies.'

'What do you think of my house?' said Ashton. 'Really?'

Henry did not pause. 'I think it a triumph.'

'I mean,' Ashton waggled his cigar in the air, and it too dropped a veil of ash, like a tree shedding autumn leaves, 'really.'

'I really think it is a triumph.' Henry raised his glass; it seemed to be the only thing he could do to emphasize the words, to try and create a kind of truth, when what he said was a lie. Ashton's eyes burned bright. 'To a triumph!'

Henry and Peregrine knocked back their glasses. Ashton stayed where he was. Then he put down his cigar, and rubbed his eyes.

He emitted a low wail, a kind of protest, so that Henry and Peregrine glanced at each other in alarm.

Ashton looked up and fastened his gaze on Henry. He had been so hale earlier, flushed with alcohol and good spirits. But now he was pale, intense, his black hair ruffled, his hands working, rolling over each other. 'I wanted the truth,' he said.

'I say, Kinsburg,' said Peregrine. 'He's telling the truth. It's a little late, old man. Probably had a bit too much of the . . .' He whistled.

Ashton nodded, but kept his eyes on Henry. 'It is late. I should go to my wife. She looked well tonight, did she not? That dress, I should have had her painted in it. Instead she chose black. Black! How I have indulged that lady.'

Henry looked down, a reflex he could not control.

'Am I right to have done so?'

Henry felt the man's eyes on him. Perry was silent; Henry sensed him struggling to find something to say.

'She is your wife. I would say it is right to care for her,' said Henry.

'How would you know? How would you know what a tie a wife is? What a burden?'

Henry drew his eyes to his host's face. He hardly knew what his own expression was, but he saw Ashton's reaction to it. 'I have said too much.' He put a hand to his head. 'I am two sheets to the wind. Forget it. You will forget it?'

'Of course we will.' Perry now, on firmer ground.

Ashton was delving into his pocket. Clumsily, he produced a brown leather box. Fumbling with the catch, he eventually opened it. Henry heard Perry murmur.

A diamond lay on a bed of blue velvet. What light there was, it caught and threw back at them.

'It's a beauty, isn't it?' Ashton was watching their faces.

'Quite extraordinary,' said Perry.

Ashton looked at Henry. 'Dale-Collingwood?'

'As my friend says, extraordinary.'

'A beauty for a beauty. Not that she cares.' He snapped the box shut, almost violently. Buried it in his pocket. 'I meant to show you it earlier.' He ran a hand through his hair. 'Not like this.'

'It's a privilege to see it.' Perry again, trying his best.

Ashton rose to his feet. 'I'll wish you both goodnight.'

He went, everyone calling their goodnights after him, laughing and waving. One of the footmen followed him. The other, who had been so impassive, lapsed into a tired, rather irritated expression the precise moment Ashton left the room.

The billiard party broke up. Only Henry and Peregrine remained, growing steadily more sober. Eventually they could not bear the darkling look of the last footman anymore, and rose to leave. 'Come back to my room for another cigar,' said Henry, going out of the door. Peregrine stayed behind, fishing for coins to tip the disgruntled servant.

Henry turned left, walked up to the leather-covered partition which had been pulled across the corridor to block the gentleman's noise from echoing down through the rest of the house. But its door had not been closed, and as he stood there, waiting for Peregrine, he saw her. She emerged, like a spectre, from the darkness of the far end of the corridor, a candle in her hand. He saw her upper body in the circle of light. Felt the jagged edge of grief, for a moment, still confused by the drink and the smoke, thinking it was his sister – his dear sister – and then realizing it was her. *Her.*

He stood rooted to the spot, as Charlotte walked the length of the corridor towards him. Opened his mouth to say her name, and then could not. She was still dressed in her yellow gown, but had removed her jewellery. Her face was open; her eyes softened. *No defences*, he thought.

She came to him. Reached out, and touched his face.

'I thought you were a spirit,' he said.

'I didn't wish to startle you,' she said. 'My husband said you had a terrible loss.'

He had not said a word about it, beyond the conventional. Never admitted anything, other than his wish to submit to God's grace, whatever burden that might bring. He turned his head, to bring it more in contact with her hand.

'Yes,' he said.

Her eyes were bright with tears. 'I am so sorry,' she said.

They heard Peregrine's voice, in the far room, bidding goodnight to the footman. Charlotte turned and went back into the darkness, turned right: some route that he did not know.

Peregrine appeared, the man at his side. 'As we didn't drop breadcrumbs,' he said, 'this kind person is going to show us the corridor where our rooms are situated. Henry?'

Henry turned. He was holding on to the partition. 'Yes?'

'You look as though you've seen a ghost.'

'No,' he said. 'It's just the port. Is there an outside route we can take? I would like some air.'

Sobered up, they smoked cigars out of the window in Henry's room. 'It's not as if anyone will smell them,' said Peregrine. 'The nearest bedroom from this is at least two miles away.' He lit Henry's cigar, and they perched companionably by the open window.

'It's almost morning,' said Henry. He had not mentioned seeing Charlotte. He did not wish to open that particular Pandora's box.

'Past two on one of the many clocks I glimpsed on my way here, but you're taking it like an old man,' said Peregrine.

'I feel like one,' said Henry. 'Do you not feel – Perry – something here. Like a suppression. Like the air is pressing down on your chest? And you cannot do anything for yourself, or make any decision of your own?'

'Yes,' said Peregrine shortly. 'And I'm afraid the fault all lies with our laudable Mr Kinsburg. He has every minute accounted for. I'm not surprised you felt so sorry for his wife. But don't go trying to be some kind of knight in shining armour.'

Henry stared at the lit end of his cigar, at its granular brightness against the blue-black of the open window. He looked up to see his friend watching him. They smoked on.

'Of course,' said Peregrine eventually, 'she is as much a creation of Kinsburg's as everything else here.'

Henry looked at him.

'He has taken everyday raw material – she is pretty, I give you that, fine-boned, and sweet eyes – but who does not have a housemaid with all of those things? Do you know where he found her, by the way? Gentle-bred, I'm sure; a younger daughter, though. He chose someone pliable, for I've seen many a broad and brisk young heiress who would have bettered her for wealth but not like to have their gowns chosen for them; they would like their own spheres. But Mrs

Kinsburg, I hazard, has no sphere. He has taken her, and he has created something. Her dresses – the man does adore colour, doesn't he? – her jewellery, in the eighteenth-century style. Do you think she chose all of those things?'

'She does not seem to give them much notice, from what I can see – that is, she is immune to vanity,' said Henry.

'It's a little too early to say that, even if she is a favourite of yours,' said Peregrine, giving him a look. 'But there is an air to her which indicates that she doesn't care for it all, overmuch. And yet how fastidiously she dresses – or is dressed. How she complements these rooms. She is a vision, created by him.'

Henry thought of the look Charlotte had borne, when he had glimpsed her in an unguarded moment during dinner. A fleeting, drained look, like one who had shed all her tears. 'She is overtaxed somehow,' he said. *But she feels it*, he thought, thinking of that touch. *There is something in her. Life, vividness, strength.*

'And who would not be taxed, living in such a place, with such a husband?' said Peregrine, delivering the stub of his cigar out of the window.

Henry gave him a look of disapproval. 'You show remarkable lack of breeding, sometimes.'

Peregrine grinned guiltily. 'I'm sure. Anyhow, he is a perfectly creditable husband. We must not play the tragedy here. There are thousands of women across England who would draw blood for such a husband. And he does not seem to harm her.'

'A man like that can do all the harm in the world,' said Henry. 'He moves through it like shadow, casting his darkness on everyone else.'

'This drama,' murmured Peregrine. 'It is not like you. My friend sees everything as a play for his own amusement. My friend would have made a hundred witty comments by now about the whole situation. On Monday morning we will leave these people with their problems, Henry. Do not become embroiled. You say she is overtaxed but, my dear friend – you are very tired.'

Henry decided to leave dangerous territory behind, though his mind was teeming with it. 'You see why I did not wish to have his opinion on the Club, or to have him too closely involved with decisions on it? Look at this place. He speaks as though it is innovative.'

'But it is just trying to be a little Versailles in a country manor.' Peregrine finished the sentiment, sitting forwards and rubbing his hands on his knees. 'Feeling the sting of the night air now. If I'm not too careful, it will wake me up completely. I'll take myself off to bed. I may get lost on the way. You perhaps will never see me again.' He rose to his feet, slightly unsteadily.

'And I thought you would stay here and encourage my bad manners of slandering our host,' said Henry. He was a little disappointed; he did not usually have the taste for malice, but now he wished to drain the poison of the day, and something was urging him to dwell on the events, like a thumb moving back to an embedded splinter in the forefinger.

'Sleep will do us both good,' said Peregrine, patting him on the shoulder, then moving off across the room. 'And Henry, my dear chap.'

'What?'

Peregrine looked at him with the brief, unnerving insight of the intoxicated. 'You may not like his ridiculous house, but he will triumph if he gets you to fall in love with his vision of a wife. "The perfect lady, by Mr Ashton Kinsburg", he who coats everything in gold and mirrors. He made her. Don't show your approval of it. She is as much a sham as every other bit of imported furniture in this place.'

Henry looked at his dearest friend with a sorrowful benevolence. 'You have it all wrong, Perry,' he said.

Peregrine raised his hand in farewell and toddled out, closing the door with remarkable softness. Henry heard no more from him as he made his way down the halls by the light of one candle. But he thought of him with a kind of paternal tenderness as he closed the window. Then he opened his bag, settled with his sketchbook, and began to draw. He fell asleep there, only waking when his man came to bring water in the early morning.

CHAPTER TWENTY-THREE

1940

DINING HALL, THE MIRRORMAKERS' CLUB

'What is disturbing you?'

Jonathan was standing in the doorway of the Dining Hall, and he turned at the sound of Livy's voice. He was watching Bill trying to put together the long mahogany table lying before him in twenty pieces. Livy had seen a design for it: a special table to be put out when the committee of the Club dined alone. Bill was standing with his hands on his hips, looking at it as though it were an immense jigsaw puzzle. The underside of the piece was rougher than the top: unvarnished, bare, imperfect wood.

Jonathan wore a faintly disgusted expression, as though he were looking at a maimed animal. 'I've only ever seen it complete, when I've dined on it,' he said. He wore the same look he had given to the section of bare wall in the hall, when its marble lining had cracked.

'You only want perfect things,' she said.

'I have standards, that's all.'

She saw that he had been trained to expect the best, in himself and others. His money and education made him well-groomed, gentlemanly. And yet, some underlying part of his character always seemed to be tugging at him – to make him slouch, rather than standing tall; to make him unkempt. Some deep shame underlay his disgust at the imperfect. She touched his arm.

'Perhaps you will see it again one day, in its splendour,' she said. 'There's been a delivery for you.'

Jonathan turned to look at Livy. 'What?'

'A trunk, from Redlands. Delivered by one of your servants. A Mr Simmons, Peggy said. I didn't see him.'

His steps quickened. 'Is he here? Has someone given him a cup of tea?'

'No. He went. She said he seemed keen to be gone.'

She turned away from the disappointment in his face, and went on ahead of him, walking briskly. Past the clock, its pendulum keeping time in stately fashion.

The battered trunk stood in the corner of the Document Room, where Peggy had directed the servant to leave it. There was an envelope tied to the handle, and Livy watched as Jonathan untied it and opened it, barely containing her impatience. His expression darkened as he read it.

'The papers are unsorted. My wife says she looked in the attic and found it, and she also emptied one of the bureaus into it. She says that she doesn't have time to look through it. We must do it. When she has time, she will go through the archived family papers and look for mentions of the diamond.'

'Please,' said Livy. 'Open it.'

He crouched down and unclipped the heavy brass latches.

The trunk opened silently, revealing piles of papers and ephemera. A small wooden box, decorated with flowers of inlaid ivory, lay in the centre. The scent the trunk released was musty and faintly floral. Completely unfamiliar to Livy. The scent of Redlands, she thought. Of Jonathan's other life. Even, at a stretch, of the world Charlotte had inhabited. She breathed it in: tried to pin the memory of the scent in her mind. In it, she felt the pull of them: Charlotte, Henry, Ashton, as though they were tugging her into their own orbit. *Be still*, she thought. *I will find out what you want me to know.* After a moment, the perfume faded to nothing, lost in the dusty, close scent of the Document Room.

Jonathan swore under his breath, and picked up the box which was nestled in the papers. As he removed it, papers fell inward into the indentation it had left behind. He put it carefully on the table. The key was in the lock. He turned it, and lifted the lid. Standing behind him, Livy caught a glimpse of necklaces and brooches. Jonathan lifted a small piece of white card from the top tray. Livy saw the message: written in bold black characters, the handwriting slanting forwards. His hand was trembling.

Jonathan. If it is as bad as you say, I suppose
you should sell these. It's not as if they really
mean anything. They are only so much metal and
stones. Stevie

He put it back, and shut the box with a thud. Turned the key, and put it in his pocket.

'You can put the box in the filing cabinet, if you want to keep it safe,' Livy said. He turned and looked at her as though he hadn't known she was there.

'Yes,' he said. He stared at the mixed-up papers. 'What a mess. It's as though she dropped everything in here from a great height.'

'We'll have it shipshape in no time,' Livy said briskly, trying to hide her impatience with efficiency. 'If we work at the desk, and sort by date.'

He put the jewellery box in the filing cabinet. They sat down. He smoked, and she worked.

'Some of these are recent,' said Livy, picking up a gilt-edged invitation to a ball at Redlands in July 1938, issued by Mr and Mrs Jonathan Whitewood.

He plucked it from her hand, his jaw flexing. 'She's put all kinds of things in here,' he said.

It was an hour before it happened. An hour of careful sorting, until Livy's patience was exhausted and she buried her hand deep into the trunk, pulling out a sheet of paper at random. As she pulled it out – a piece of music – another piece of paper fell away from it, and it was this she followed with her eyes. 'Henry Dale-Collingwood's handwriting,' she said. She glanced at it: just three lines.

'Good. Keep looking.' He held his hand out, and read the letter, then shook his head. 'Nothing. He's just replying to an invitation.' He put the letter down, clenched one fist, then released it.

'If there's one, there will be more.'

'I shall have to go home soon,' he said. 'I should never have stayed away for Christmas. It was the wrong thing to do. Dishonourable.' Then he looked at her as though something entirely different had occurred to him. 'Some of us don't have the luxury of beginning again,' he said.

'I don't call it a luxury,' she said. 'I have no obligations that I know of. Only ...' She let the sentence trail away; she thought he would leave it, but he didn't.

'What?'

'Only, I'd like to get this mystery solved,' she said. 'Jonathan. Do you think the bones Christian found are anything to do with this?'

'No. Don't be ridiculous.'

She nodded, but he had spoken too quickly and vehemently for her to believe him. He saw the doubt in her eyes, and put down his cigarette. 'Whatever ridiculous little mystery you're cooking up, don't go repeating it, all right? I don't want Peggy and Bill thinking my family was mixed up in some kind of sordid murder, or whatever it is those stories have put in your head.'

'I didn't realize you were so concerned with your

reputation,' she said, reaching for another letter. He caught at her wrist and held it tight. They stared at each other, and she did not know whether she wanted to slap him around the face or kiss him. He seemed to draw violent feelings from her; there was no calm way, with him. She gave a little pull of her wrist, and the tension withered in the air, dying like the perfume from the trunk. 'Shall we work?' she said. 'It's what we came here for, after all.'

He released her. She picked up and held out another letter with Henry's handwriting on it, suppressing her desire to read it, seeing the possessiveness in his eyes. He took it and put it on the pile. A thought occurred to Livy.

'I've never seen her handwriting,' she said. 'Charlotte's. All I know of her is in the portrait – the rest I've imagined. All the things we've read about, talked about – there's a space for her, but it's always other people writing, speaking. Never her.'

'There are gaps in this period,' he said. 'The family archives are in good order for the late nineteenth century. But you're right: all my evidence comes from others.' He passed a hand over his eyes. 'She may be an enigma, but as far as I know, Charlotte Kinsburg was the only person who ever handled the diamond apart from Ashton. In 1841, she came to London, to see a goldsmith about having the diamond set, which is when it was held in the safe here, according to the family lore the solicitor reported.'

'Where is the appointment recorded?'

'In a diary. There's only a few entries – times and

appointments. That is in her handwriting; the diary has her name written in the front. The entries stop soon after. I'm sorry I don't have it to show you. It's the only trace of her I've seen in our family archive. Unless Stevie can find anything else.'

'Don't you think – it's as though someone has tried to erase her?'

He looked down. 'Perhaps. I can't deny that, in the official part of the archive, there is nothing of her. No letters. Only the appointment diary, which somehow escaped the cull, and bills for items bought by Ashton for her, including for the diamond. I must find it, Livy. I must.'

'We'll keep looking, don't worry.'

'Yes. Don't touch that.'

Livy froze as her hand closed over a small box covered in ornate paper, cut to resemble lace. 'It looks Victorian,' she murmured, as he put his hand over hers, and removed it.

'It's not Victorian.' He stared at it in his hand. Untucked the small paper flap, and opened it. The scent of fruit cake: rich, spirit-soaked.

He looked at her puzzled face.

'It's a piece of my wedding cake,' he said, closing it up again. A faint tinge of red along his cheekbones. 'Why would she put that in there?' He closed his eyes for a moment. 'Please, just help me sort these letters.'

Livy went for the lowest layer again, knowing the earliest letters lay like sediment at the bottom of the trunk. Her own face was flushed now. She imagined Jonathan, this man she had kissed, this man she had desired, on his wedding day: staring at his wife's face with a complete devotion. It must have been unthinkable to that bride that his lips should ever rest on another woman's.

These thoughts had to be put away. She focused on the letter she pulled out, on the words. On Ashton Kinsburg's handwriting:

> *December 1841. I hereby gift to the Mirrormakers'*
> *Club a valuable painting by Herr Franz*
> *Winterhalter. Henceforth to be known as* Woman and
> Looking Glass.

Livy held it out to Jonathan. 'Charlotte has joined us,' she said.

CHAPTER TWENTY-FOUR

1839

Riding without pause in the morning light, Ashton leading the way on his bay thoroughbred, Henry glimpsed hills covered with trees, the sky above their outline slightly paler blue, fading into a darker shade. Even from a distance, each tree had its own shape and patina, texturing the landscape, the whole dense and varied. It looked ancient: a forest where one might be lost and find one's ancestors. There was the incipient promise of heat in the menacing brightness of the sky and the sharpness of the flickering shadows.

Hours later, the carriage ride to Henry's second excursion of the day was not a comfortable one for him. Separated from Peregrine, he travelled with Barbara and Nicholas, who had found new and mysterious things to bicker over. They seemed to exist in a kind of mutually acceptable hell. His conclusion was that they required occupations, and other company. 'Do you often have guests at Redlands?' he asked, purposefully interrupting them.

'Oh, yes,' said Nicholas. 'Politicians, musicians, writers, artists. Often my sister-in-law is not able to be present as much as she has been this time. She rests whenever possible. Her health is not good.'

'What rubbish you talk, husband,' said Barbara provocatively. 'She is strong. Do you not think so, Mr Dale-Collingwood?' She was wearing a pair of earrings mounted with hummingbird feathers, and they shivered alarmingly as she fluttered her head in disagreement.

Henry gave her what he hoped was a mildly puzzled smile. 'I am no judge of these things.'

'Ignore my wife, Dale-Collingwood,' said Nicholas. 'She has the gift of being able to destroy a perfectly civilized conversation.'

Henry kept the bland smile on his face and turned to the window. It was nearly midday, the promised heat had come, and the sky was now a furious white. Black starlings sat exhausted on the parched grass, stunned by the rising temperature. As the carriages passed, they flew into the shadow of the woods. Light dripped off the dark green leaf surfaces. Even the moving water in a brook they passed seemed dark and stagnant. Henry saw one field in the far distance, speckled intensely with red, and wondered if it held poppies. He turned to ask Nicholas, but saw that the feuding couple were now murmuring sweet nothings to each other, their heads

SOPHIA TOBIN

bowed close. He turned away again, with as much insouci-
ance as he could manage.

The two carriages drew up and let the visitors loose at
the top of the down, in the midst of a small copse of trees.
The effect, thought Henry, like everything else here, was
ornamental: as a group they walked through the light-flecked
darkness of the tree canopy's shade, and into the fullness of
the sunlight, looking down at the vast golden slope of the
down, the grass parched by the summer days. They all stood
there, foolishly, in a line, visitors and family alike. They
were meant to be alert and cool, especially the women in
their many-layered clothes, but he saw dull and stifled faces
masked by pretty smiles. Looking at Charlotte's face, he
wondered how a coating of white could really cool such a corseted body. Her gown was again decorated by a profusion of
flowers and plants, elaborate and busy. He felt Ashton's eyes
upon him. It was a familiar sensation now, being watched,
and for a moment he wondered whether he had become
extra-sensitive and was imagining it. So he looked. Sure
enough, the man was watching him. Henry swore lightly
under his breath.

'Are you bored yet?' It was Charlotte, speaking softly. Her
gift was a voice which was not easily heard. Even at dinner,
when she had meant to raise her voice, he had heard several
gentlemen ask her to speak up. No matter how hard she tried,
it seemed she could not make herself heard.

She was beside him. He glanced at her, her eyes fixed on
the horizon. He saw the slight shadows beneath her eyes, and

wondered if she had been wakeful after she had returned to bed. The long pink ribbon of her bonnet, tied beneath her chin, rippled in the breeze which now plundered the trees above and sent leaves floating down. He noted the effect, to draw later: the taut, rippling ribbon. Last night, he had paused to set things down: every detail he could remember of her, and of the rooms that held her.

'These trees are sick,' she said. 'Or so my gardener says.'

Without any sense or reason, he felt jealous of the man who had the ease to speak to her of trees, who had time at hand to look at her face. He heard the others, particularly Peregrine, remarking on the fineness of the view.

'To answer your question,' he said, 'how could I be bored? With such a charming companion, and in such an idyllic place?'

'You may dissemble if you wish,' she said. 'I do not speak of me. I speak of Redlands, and of my husband's desire to please you.'

He decided in that moment to set aside his manners. 'Of course I am bored,' he murmured. 'I'm also exhausted.'

At his words, she looked directly at him, and her eyes had such an effect on him that it was his turn to look away. It was the look which he had recognized in the portrait that Ashton so disliked: knowing, slightly sardonic, and full of life. 'You went riding with Ashton this morning,' she said. 'Did he show you his acres?'

'Every last one, madam,' murmured Henry, and, despite his painful disloyalty to his host, he observed her smile with joy.

He had been woken in his chair by his makeshift valet at first light with a basin of water and a note from Ashton, requesting him to ride with him in an hour. 'Why did he not ask me at dinner?' Henry had said, grumpy and half-asleep. The man only shrugged.

In truth, Henry was not that interested in agriculture, the home farm, land management, or the new workers' cottages that Ashton had built. 'We hope to keep revolution from our door, unlike our more unfortunate friends in France and Italy,' Ashton said. 'Redlands should be its own world, just and content; that is what I hope for.' Henry had nodded, and had done his best to seem interested as tenants came out onto their front steps to look actively grateful in a way that had made him shudder with embarrassment. He had paid many compliments, about the land and about the quality of the horse he had been given to ride. But he sensed, somehow, that no matter how gracious he was, he was somehow failing Ashton. The younger man wanted something from him which he was not able to give. His frustration showed itself in the way he turned his horse so sharply, and that was all.

On their return, Henry had only had time to eat a small breakfast before he was told that another excursion was planned. He had raced upstairs to find the valet waiting for him, with fresh water and a change of clothes. Even as he irritably tore his riding coat off, he had to admire the organization of Redlands. He had stayed at many grand country residences before, where it could be hard to find so much as a cup of tea at an irregular hour, so mechanistic was the machinery of keeping one hundred rooms going. But here, the routines and servants moved with every switch of the rein from Ashton, and thus his visitors all moved too. He wondered: how many times had Ashton had to hurt the mouth of this horse before it moved to obey him?

Beautifully choreographed, the visitors started forwards down the slope, and within moments Madam Barbara began to sneeze into her lace-edged handkerchief, barely gaining enough breath between each sneeze to apologize. Her husband silently took her parasol and held it over her head as she did so. 'She is always so, in summer,' he announced to the party.

Henry looked at Charlotte. She kept her delicate ivory parasol positioned at the exact angle to shade the entirety of her face from the blistering sun; her neck was protected by the small curtain at the back of her bonnet. She never looked at her feet, only moved forwards down the slope with measured steps, her chin up, her posture graceful. Peregrine was right: every gesture was deliberate.

'You are watching me, Mr Dale-Collingwood.'

'Do you mind?'

'Not at all. Would you tell me why?'

'I must keep making you speak, so that I know you are real.'

She frowned. He felt the disturbance of a missed step.

'What is wrong?'

'Nothing at all.'

'What is wrong?'

'I hoped we might talk of real things. I hoped you might converse with me, not just pay me compliments.'

'Look at me, then.'

She did so. At the contact of their gazes, he felt a tightness fold itself beneath his breastbone. He was breathless in the dry air. They both turned from what they saw in each other, and looked ahead as they walked.

'Am I as you remembered?' he said.

She smiled. 'Your spirit is the same. In your face, you look older than I remember.'

He laughed. 'I thank you. It is the building of the Club. I am tired.'

'Ashton talks of it often. Do not let the committee be too involved, if it is possible to drive them off. Ashton has his own world here, but he will not rest until everywhere is remade in his own vision. Your vision will be better. Resist him if you can.'

'I will do my best. Patrons often lose interest as time moves on.'

'He does not.'

Barbara sneezed three times in a row; Peregrine continued to converse loudly with Ashton, whose eyes were directed towards Henry, across the distance.

'I wish I could watch the building rise,' Charlotte said.

'I could send you drawings.' He hardly believed he was saying it. He knew then that he would go to great lengths simply to stay in some kind of contact with her, to know that her hand would touch something that he had touched, even if it was an architectural drawing.

'No.' She stopped for a moment, raising one gloved hand to the level of her eyes, as though seeking out a detail in the view. 'Do not do that. My husband reads my letters – every one I send and every one I receive. He asks that I read my correspondence to him when I open it. If you sent me drawings, it would encourage him to be even more involved, and he will never let it go.'

'Why must he read all your letters?'

'He does not like secrets. That is, he treasures openness.' He imagined, rather than saw, the spark in her eye.

'Are you well today? You look a little pale.'

'I drank too much champagne last night. My husband disapproved. And it made me queasy.'

'Why did you drink too much?'

'Because I missed you.' She tilted her head. 'Strange, is it not?'

He stopped on the spot, felt the mark where her words had hit him, subtle as the sharpest rapier. She looked warily at him as they began to walk again. 'Do you know my least favourite time of day? It is the evening, when my husband and I are alone. There are some lines from Tennyson, which I wept at, on first reading: he distilled it so completely.' And in a soft, low voice, she began to recite them.

'Mrs Kinsburg!' It was Ashton. 'Do not tire our visitor, my dear child. He has to make conversation at dinner.'

Charlotte inclined her head. 'An early dinner today, you will be glad to hear,' she said in a sing-song voice to Henry, and then she purposely increased her pace to leave him behind and join her husband, who had moved slightly ahead. Below, in a valley, there was an Elizabethan house of grey stone.

'The Birches,' said Ashton, over his shoulder. 'You will meet my good friends, the Halls.'

As Charlotte walked into The Birches, she paused in the sudden shade and coolness, and let her husband go ahead. She longed to be left alone in its shadows, and to lean against the wall, but instead she engaged herself in letting down her parasol, and folding its delicate span into the right shape so that it could be fastened. She turned away as Henry passed, talking to Peregrine.

'I must keep making you speak, so that I know you are real.' How disappointed she had felt at his words; how exhausted. It was always the externals. *What if I told him*, she thought, *that I sweat beneath these clothes? That I am hot, and stewing in it; that the wasps will soon attack my sugared hair. If I stumble – fall – if I shake off this grace which has been so hard won, which is absolutely a matter of discipline, will you still care for me? Will you still like me? Will you raise me from the ground as you raised me from the dirty squalor of a London street, in my despair?*

She had wanted to tell him that if he thought of her only as something perfect, then her husband had won.

'Ce-ce? Darling Ce-ce, are you quite well?' It was Barbara and Nicholas. Barbara sent Nicholas on ahead to the Halls, who were greeting the group in the dining room.

'I will look after you,' said Barbara. 'Was it the heat?' It was unclear what assistance she intended to offer; she neither took Charlotte's arm, nor sought a chair; she only stood and watched her. 'Perhaps a cold drink,' she said to a servant who offered assistance. The man went off, rather slowly. 'An old family retainer, evidently,' said Barbara, watching him go. 'With any luck, he will return within the hour.'

'I am quite able to go in,' said Charlotte. 'It was just the heat.'

'I feel it too.'

'I'm sure.'

'No, I really do, Ce-Ce. You see – I am. Expecting.'

Charlotte felt a falling away. All at once the world narrowed. Barbara's face swam before her in triumph. 'My dear, you look as though you really might faint this time! Do you not wish to congratulate me?'

'Of course, yes. I wish you every joy. I am very happy for you.' But she was not. She did not know why.

Barbara's gaze was steady, strong, unwavering. 'You see, dearest,' she said, 'circumstances do change.'

'Yes,' said Charlotte. 'You are right.' Unnervingly, Barbara had touched on the source of her distress. Everything had been the same for a decade. This one certainty had given her assurance. Now the world was set to crumble, its fragility revealed.

'Charlotte?' It was Ashton. 'What is wrong?'

She attempted a smile. 'I was a little faint from the heat – someone was fetching me a drink.'

'There are drinks in here – lemonade – if you care to take just ten steps forwards.' He was irritated. He did not come to her; instead he held out his hand. As she reached him, Charlotte saw the look of venom that Ashton cast at Barbara. 'Has she told you her news?' he said quietly, placing her hand on his arm.

'Yes.' She walked alongside him. 'You knew?'

'Of course. Nick told me yesterday.' He glanced at her. 'It changes nothing, of course. Other than that she will bore us with her triumph.'

The Halls were a family of twelve, well-known to Charlotte, so that she found a way to be absorbed into the group with little fuss: a few smiles and nods were enough. At dinner, Henry was seated at the furthest point of the room from her, and was entertained by the eldest daughter, a fine, bright girl. Charlotte watched him laughing and talking, and saw in his wilder moments of laughter the recklessness in him. He drank more than one glass of wine, and she saw it combine with the tiredness to make him louder and more boorish. She saw all of this, but she could not help her gaze from returning to him again and again, drawn by some magnetism which she could not explain. She tried not to catch his eye, and he evidently did the same for her. Only as the meal drew to a close did she see him grow more subdued. He talked less to his companion, who had turned to Peregrine on her other side, and gazed at his plate. He put his hand over his wine glass when he was offered more.

'Mrs Kinsburg?' said Mr Hall, the father of the family. 'I asked what you thought of the plans for Dower Coppice?'

'Forgive me,' said Charlotte. 'I am rather tired. Do tell me what the plans are.'

It was three o'clock when Ashton rose from the table. 'My dear infant of a wife is tired,' he announced. 'Luckily, I ordered the carriage for this time. We and our guests are so grateful for your hospitality.'

Farewells were said and promises of future engagements exchanged. As they passed down the grey stone hall towards the entrance, Henry manoeuvred himself to be near Charlotte. Even as she moved away, he took more steps to come close to her, as though they were engaged in a complex dance. She only wished to be alone, but in the end surrendered to him, and smiled.

'Did you enjoy dinner?' he said.

'Of course. I hope you were kind to your companion,' she said. Her disquiet created a flash of malice. 'She wished to marry my husband, you know, before he decided on me. She has been seeking someone comparable ever since.' She realized she had been jealous at lunch, that she clung to the fragments of their encounter in London, and that she did not wish to let go of it. 'You see, Mr Dale-Collingwood,' she said, 'I am the lucky one.'

Emboldened by jealousy, she felt wretched a moment later. But if he were to go so easily, then she wished to leave her scar.

CHAPTER TWENTY-FIVE

1941

<small>RED PARLOUR, THE MIRRORMAKERS' CLUB</small>

Livy sat, cross-legged, on the floor of the Red Parlour. In the midst of its shattered decoration, plaster and gilt, she had cleared a space on the deep red carpet and was reading through the letters she and Jonathan had gathered from the trunk. Beside her was an archive box containing architectural drawings she had not yet been through; she had decided to settle in for the afternoon. Refusing to sit on the floor, Jonathan had dragged in one of the heavy chairs from the Committee Room, and pulled it near to her.

Dear madam, I write because you promised me
an answer.

The letters from Henry which they had extracted from the trunk, buried amid hundreds of other pages, of receipts and ephemera, invitations and tickets, were all formal in their own strange way. They did not presume any intimacy, but were laced with mentions of public events. They were not letters of the boudoir.

I am late writing to thank you for your great hospitality. Nothing can excuse this – I am without any good reason. Other than the building work, which consumes me. I know you to have a generous heart. Forgive me.

Do you remember, Mrs Kinsburg, that day when we walked to The Birches, together with your husband, and your brother and sister-in-law, and my good friend Peregrine? If you remember, Mrs Kinsburg, the way the light fell on that day.

Your absence from London is felt acutely, dear madam. If you wish to inspect the works, on any given day, I will be at your disposal. One word is all that it would take.

Each one of the letters to Charlotte had been pierced in the top left corner, a small hole for a ribbon to pass through. Some still had traces of red, from the ribbon. At one time, the letters had all been tied together. Who had cut the ribbon, and scattered them free, to wherever Stevie had found them?

These brief, taut letters, were crazed with a brittle

politeness. Henry wrote as to a stranger, and yet in between each word, in each space, lay such suffused feeling that it made Livy's chest tight, as though the oxygen were being extracted from the air. Each letter began, *Dear madam*, or *Dear Mrs Kinsburg*, and was signed, *Your obedient servant, Henry Dale-Collingwood*. There was both nothing in them, and everything.

Jonathan looked back at her face. 'Read the last one,' he said. 'They are all the same tone, until that one.'

Dear Mrs Kinsburg,

Your husband tells me your diamond will be set in a tiara. Why do you need such a diamond? A jewel such as you.

Bring it here, and I will keep it safe.

But let me remind you. You are everything, already. You do not need jewels. You have your eyes, and your voice, and your sense. I beg you always to remember it.

Ever your devoted architect.
HDC.

Livy stared at the letter. The energy between the words reminded her of the portrait. The words, like the image, shimmered with it: the potential for action. The moment before stepping forwards. How had Charlotte read them, interpreted them? With that strange half-smile? Had she even seen them?

'What do you make of it?' said Jonathan, his voice flat and emotionless. 'They are strange letters. When he says "I will keep it safe", does he mean the stone? Or does he mean her?'

'I think they are concerned with the relationship rather than the stone,' Livy said, realizing that she felt rather protective of Henry. *Taceo*, she thought. *So you did not always keep silent.* 'Do you think Ashton ever saw them?'

'Undoubtedly. Even in old age, not a single piece of post came into the house that he did not see. He was not always an easy man to know or deal with, as I told you. My grandmother spoke of him sometimes – always with admiration, but not really with warmth.' He sighed. 'There is no evidence that Charlotte wrote back to Dale-Collingwood. Perhaps, if Dale-Collingwood was an obsessive kind of person, then her husband kept the letters as a precaution.'

'And at least he mentions the diamond in that last letter.' Livy handed the letters to him. 'Henry kept notebooks, dated by year. I'll go and get the 1840 one. There may be clues on second reading.'

'Do you think?' The hope on his face was almost painful to see, and she put her hand on his arm.

'I don't think anything. But let me check.'

She hurried downstairs and extracted it from the vault. When she returned, Jonathan was still sitting in the chair. Sitting as though he waited to be sentenced for a crime, his foot tapping. 'It's here,' he said. 'If I could only understand where.'

She sat down on the floor and began to read. He sat

watching her, smoking, until he could bear it no longer. 'Anything?'

Livy looked up at him. 'It's about the design of the Club. Nothing about the diamond, at least not yet. I'm sorry. Although some of it is uncanny. Less measured than his earlier notes and letters.' She showed him one page.

The coving of the Committee Room: the cherubs'
faces. High relief, as per my drawings. I have drawn
the face, and the modelling must capture at least
the ghost of its beauty, if only that. I do not expect
verisimilitude. I have given up hope of that.

'I'm going outside,' he said. 'I need some fresh air.'

She turned the page. A drawing of a chaise longue; a scrap of fabric, pinned to the page.

And the next, and the next.

More drawings: this time of cherubs' faces. Several angles, the same face, again, and again. Then, she froze.

A small note, in Henry's slanted, agitated hand. A note she had missed on first reading, but which she couldn't imagine missing.

And what of the child, Charlotte?

Livy pushed her chair back. She felt hot and nauseous. Looked back at the page: had she imagined those words? No. She had not.

246

And what of the child, Charlotte?

It was a phrase, she thought, written by a man who was no longer keeping silent about anything.

She heard the bang of a distant door in the building. Remembered the rattle of the backstairs door. The violence of it. What had he hidden here, she thought? What part of him had he left here? Just as she had left part of herself in a distant street, in a flattened, bombed-out building?

It was suddenly unbearable. She found herself fighting the urge to throw up, her body burning with a surge of heat. After a moment she struggled to her feet, and ran to the window. Bill had not boarded up one of the glassless panes, and as her face met the cold winter air she felt the relief as her temperature began to fall.

As she stood there, she remembered Charlotte's face in the portrait. She had looked at it so often now that it was as familiar as her own. But now the face seemed to shift in her mind, and she saw it in a different way, so that she knew she would have to go and look at it again. Could it be, it was mocking her? Amused, and withholding? Could it be that she had tormented Henry? Had tormented Ashton?

She thought of the diamond pinned to the black dress, and how painful it must be for Jonathan to see it; how he had gladly taken the painting down and covered it with wrappings. That diamond, worn not with pride, but as though it were just another trapping of a wealth too wide to be admitted. She thought of the landscape beyond Charlotte. The vast estate which was her home.

Those white shoulders, and those watchful, amused eyes. Sardonic, she thought. Perhaps, even, cruel.

And what of the child, Charlotte?

Livy felt the heat rising up her face. And all at once, the world fell away, the firm ground sucked from beneath her feet. A dark night, and a light burning as bright as a diamond. And Miss Hardaker, screaming. The world ending. A familiar feeling. And for a moment, it were as though a page was about to turn backwards; could she go backwards in time? Could she remember herself? As she struggled for control, a movement caught her eye in her peripheral vision, and a hand closed around her arm. She turned with a cry.

It was Peggy. 'Are you all right? Livy. Have you been crying?'

'No, I'm quite all right. Just felt a little unwell.'

'Mr Taylor's here.'

'Is he?' She looked around her, blindly. It was as though the room was suddenly narrow and dark – too dark to make out faces.

'Livy.' It was Christian. He came to her and put his hand to her forehead. Peggy was saying something – she heard the words 'shock' and 'unwell'. He took hold of her shoulders. 'Livy?'

She came to with a jump. Christian's face hovered before hers.

'I've said your name a dozen times,' he said. 'Can you hear me?'

She nodded. He nodded in reflection of her gesture; even in her perplexed state, she found that endearing. 'All right,' he said. 'Do you remember something?'

'I was on the roof, with Miss Hardaker. She was trying to put out a bomb. I didn't get there in time.'

'I know, my darling.'

She noticed the endearment, and did not protest. In some deep part of her, it comforted her.

'Do you remember anything else?'

'No.'

She saw the disappointment in his face: saw it even though he tried to hide it. But he smiled, and nodded, and it seemed to her in that moment that he was brave. She sensed it as one sensed things in people – happiness, sadness, solidity, flightiness. She sensed his courage.

'Did something upset you, though? Something now?'

She nodded.

'Did it?' Peggy hovered behind. 'Livy? Sweetheart? What's happened? Has Mr Whitewood done something?'

She saw them glance at each other: *they think he is dangerous*, she thought. And she wanted to laugh out loud, and say: *no, it is I who am dangerous to him. We could destroy everything together. My life, his life, and his marriage. He and I are loose cannons, set up for destruction, pointing at each other.*

'No,' she said. 'It's silly. It's just the archives. I was reading them, and there was mention of a child. Suddenly, out of nowhere. I can't think why it shook me so much – perhaps because I thought of Charlotte. Because I thought she might have had a child – and it shocked me a little. It made me realize how little I know – how little we all know – behind the façades of people. And I thought of all that happened behind that face, and I thought of the bones then. That must be why. I keep thinking about the bones. About death.'

'I see.' Christian was speaking carefully. He was frowning, a deep frown that made a ridge in his normally smooth forehead. 'Just sit down here. Take a breath.' He guided her to the chair, and watched her as she sat down.

'Mr Whitewood's been pushing you too much,' said Peggy quietly. 'He's so obsessed about that diamond.'

'He's not been pushing me,' Livy sighed, and brushed her hair away from her face. 'I want to know too.'

Peggy glanced between Livy and Christian, then quietly excused herself to go and begin the dinner. 'Bill's been working in the Committee Room all day tidying things up, and he says he's famished.'

Livy and Christian stayed together in silence.

'Did you just come to say hello?' she said eventually, when she was calmer.

'Yes.' There was more behind the words, she sensed it. 'I was on a site visit yesterday when the siren went. I spent the night in the underground. Do you remember that? Having to take shelter in the Tube?'

'No.'

He smiled, folded his arms. 'It's official now. Allowed. They have beds in Liverpool Street station. People buy tickets for a place. I don't like going into the Tube, really. I'd rather be in the open air, even with bombs falling. At eight o'clock, the ground shook, and there was a hot rush of air, and I knew something had happened.'

'What had?' Livy spent her evenings reading – some of the mysteries Christian had brought her, or the archives – she didn't like the news.

'They bombed Bank station,' he said, turning to look out of the window. And she saw him clench one fist and rest it against the wall, as though he were marking the spot for a punch.

'I'm so sorry,' she said.

He stood perfectly still. He was looking ahead of him, at something she could not see. 'I prefer to be at St Paul's,' he said. 'Not sitting somewhere, waiting. At least I'm doing something. I like to be so exhausted that I have to sleep – that there's no choice. I was always a poor sleeper.'

Unbidden, she imagined him, working his way through the many corridors of St Paul's – corridors he had described to her and Peggy over tea before – balancing on the beams during dome patrol, and she wondered if he looked different in the darkness and firelight, in his tin helmet and blue uniform.

It was then they heard Jonathan. Heard, rather than saw him. It was the sound of him dragging Bill's ladder across the Committee Room that alerted them. From the Red Parlour, they saw across the small anteroom into the Committee Room, where he was haphazardly leaning the ladder against the panelling.

Livy and Christian stared at each other in astonishment, before Livy got to her feet and walked quickly if shakily towards the Committee Room.

'Jonathan?' she said. He had put one foot on the bottom of the ladder. The scent of brandy fumes sank through the air, diluting the clear winter air with its sweet, dangerous taint. When he looked at her, his gaze was hazy. She realized with a slight shock that he was drunk. Had he gone upstairs to the members' rooms and knocked back a whole decanter?

She walked towards him, then stopped. He had a hammer in his hand.

'What are you doing?' she said faintly. Christian had approached and was standing behind her.

'It's in here,' said Jonathan. 'The diamond.'

Hope rose in her, then fell; a slight sense of being cheated, as though he had finished a cryptic crossword puzzle she had set out to do. 'How do you know?'

'The thing you showed me earlier. The cherub in the Committee Room. That it had to capture the ghost of its beauty – don't you see? The ghost of it? It must be the diamond. I've been thinking about it. Ghost diamond. It must be the diamond.'

'I don't know about that,' she said doubtfully. 'Really, I don't.'

He laughed and took a few steps up; on the third rung, he wavered, as though his balance might be lost; his weight sank into his heels and for a moment it seemed as though he might fall backwards. Christian went to the ladder and put his hands on it to keep it steady. 'Mr Whitewood,' he said. 'I think you should come down. We can look into this later.'

Jonathan looked down at Christian. Despite his befogged gaze Livy could see the fury in him. Silently, he turned back and began to climb upwards.

'No,' she said. 'Please don't. Please don't destroy anything. Mr Whitewood. Jonathan!'

Her cry of distress was too late. He was within reach of the coving. He reached out and hit the cherub's face with a hammer. Once, twice, three times. Livy stood back as lumps of plaster and gilding fell. Christian dropped his head forwards; in a moment his head was white with the dust. He did not let go of the ladder.

Jonathan hit it again, and again, and once more.

He hit it until he knew there was no diamond there. That he had simply destroyed a face of carved plaster. A face carved according to Henry's drawing, to capture the beauty he had seen in a child's face. It had been safe for a hundred years, thought Livy, as she stared at the smashed coving, and at the back of Jonathan's head as he looked at what he had done. She turned away and covered her face. Henry had recorded something for posterity, so that a reminder, an echo of what had been would remain when he was long gone.

'Livy,' said Jonathan.

'What have you done?' she said.

CHAPTER TWENTY-SIX

1839

In the quiet hours of early evening, Henry stood in the *salon de printemps* and watched Charlotte walk slowly in the garden on the arm of her sister-in-law. He had spent the past hour drawing her son, as per Ashton's direction, capturing the light on the babe's chubby face. It should have soothed him, but he had found his agitation increasing. He was to go on the morrow, and he felt only the desire to speak to Charlotte before he left this gilded, fantastical house, its gardens and hills and copses, and her. He sat down and drew, watched by a single servant, a maid. No one could be alone in this house, he had discovered.

He drew the things he had seen that day: horses and trees. A frieze, he thought. A frieze in one of the rooms at the Mirrormakers' Club. Why not place things there, from life?

The door opened and Charlotte entered. She untied her

bonnet – that tangled pink ribbon, which at this very moment Henry was sketching – and handed it to the maid.

'Will you take this, please?' she said. 'And once you have delivered it to Miss Besson, please go and check on Madam Barbara. She has gone to lie down, and may need refreshment. And, Janet – there is no need to come back here.' She looked at the maid with an air of command, as though she were trying to imprint the words on her mind. The woman left without so much as a word.

Charlotte turned and looked at Henry.

'Are you well now?' he said. 'Madam Barbara said you were close to fainting.'

She smiled scornfully. The expression did not suit her. 'I am perfectly well. I was not ill. But I could not say what was wrong, and illness meant I was excused from speaking overmuch when I preferred to be left alone.' She sent a fiery glance his way. 'Yes, sir, the claim of illness serves me, sometimes. And it works well for others too.' She touched the back of a chair absentmindedly. 'Where is my husband?'

'He is showing Peregrine his gun cabinet at my insistence.'

'Consider yourself released, then,' she said, turning away, her back to him as she surveyed the garden she had just left. 'I would take the opportunity to rest now, before my husband returns and thinks of another occupation for you. Our next appointment will be at supper; you are at liberty until then.'

'Have I offended you?' he said. 'We have been on good terms, until now.'

'On far too intimate terms,' she said. 'Forgive me. I have

255

been reckless in the way that I have spoken to you. I do not speak to other gentlemen as I speak to you – I fear the compliment is not returned.' For all her wretchedness, saying it was a release.

'Do you think I spoke to my dinner companion in the way I spoke to you?' He frowned, sought her gaze, and won it. 'Tell me. We do not have the time for politeness.'

'Yes.'

He came over to her in two hasty steps, pushing the sketchbook and pencil into his pocket. 'Then you mistake me. I did not.' He laughed rather desperately. 'Do you think me some kind of Lothario?'

Close to, he saw the turmoil in her eyes. That face, which was usually so controlled, with its mask of beauty and elegance: now he saw the breaches in it, the slight movement in her expression, which betrayed her.

'Why do you doubt me?' he said. 'Do not doubt me. I have thought of nothing but you these last few days – these last few months, if I am truthful.' The words tumbled out: he felt shaken.

'I doubt you because I can hardly believe what happened,' she said. 'That day, the carriage accident. The world seemed changed, after that. Was it the violence of it? You seemed imbued with it – some special magic,' she laughed. 'Like something a girl asks for in her prayers, when she is young and foolish. But then, the world continued, and I thought I had dreamt it all, with my jolted mind – but it really had changed. The world had changed.'

She had been thinking as she walked in the garden, with Barbara talking on and on about the new baby. And she had realized, and hoped that Henry knew, all those months ago, that as he had leaned over her, taken her hands, and pulled her to her feet in the middle of the road, she loved him. From that moment. She had known it then in some inner place, though she had hidden the knowledge from herself.

'Yes,' he said. 'Things changed for me also. Which is why I have stayed away.'

She nodded. 'It was the right thing. I am sorry he brought you here. I am sorry he has put us through it.'

'Does he know?'

'Ashton?' Her face was the picture of amazement. 'No. He is preoccupied with you, but that is because he admires you. He would not suspect anything of me.'

'And you have given him no reason to suspect you. Your behaviour has been entirely proper.'

She laughed bitterly. 'Until last night, when I walked through the corridors just to catch a glimpse of you. I could not help myself. I must see you. I am myself again when I am with you, the self I was years ago. I feel that I am that person again – a person I thought lost. I thought myself unfinished then, but it is who I was. I have been a wife, a true wife, and yet, I feel no loyalty to my husband, to my role as his wife. Yet, I feel loyalty to you. Why is that? Why do I feel loyalty to you? When you are a stranger to me?'

'Because I am not a stranger,' he said. 'I don't know how,

or why, but I am not a stranger.' He did not advance towards her any further. What he felt was dangerous.

She did not advance either. She wrung her hands, and looked at him. All the words that came to her mind, she discarded. There was only one thing which she needed to say.

'I love you.'

He looked at her with astonishment: her dark hair, elaborately plaited, her pale face, still with the line of the bonnet across her brow, and those full eyes. 'And I, you,' he said. 'But I cannot ruin your marriage. I cannot injure you in that way – I cannot injure your husband, either.'

Charlotte felt her lacings then; knew she was short of breath. 'Of course,' she said. She turned frantically; he had not seen her move so before. 'You will leave, and your life will continue. The building of the Club, I suppose, is more important than this. That building is your mistress, as the diamond is my husband's.'

'Do not say such a thing.'

She shook her head, and walked to the window. He could see she was trying to regain her composure. 'It is not a slight. I have been too indolent, all these years. This has overexercised my sluggish brain. You are free. You have other things to turn to. More than one place, more than one role.' She wrapped her arms around herself.

'Even so,' Henry said, 'I have imagined our life together. What it would have been.'

When she turned, she saw that his eyes were full of tears. And at the sight, her bitterness dissolved. 'My dear,' she said.

He covered his eyes with one hand. She saw then that he too required her to be strong; that he would be strong if she would. She thought carefully, in that silence, the only sound the ticking of the clock.

'You say you wish to make me happy,' she said after a moment. 'The truth is, my happiness is dependent on yours. If I can know that you are happy in London, building the Club, thinking of the future, then I will be content. But I will have you make the choice for yourself alone. Do not speak of injuring my husband. My loss would mean nothing to him – not in his heart. Husband and wife – what does that even mean, in a moment such as this? What lies between me and Ashton is complicated and difficult, but at no point does it involve the kind of warmth I feel for you.'

'He must love you. How could he do anything else?'

'He is a good man, of sorts. He believes in charity, yes, he believes in civic society and helping those he does not see. But as for the secrets of the individual's heart – of my heart – he knows nothing of them. They are indecipherable to him. When my first child died, he stopped me from taking so much as a lock of hair from her head. He said I had an unhealthy attachment to her. So do nothing for his sake. If you go, and never return, then let it be because that is the best course for your happiness.'

Henry stared at her, sweat on his brow in the infernal heat. He wiped the warm tears from his eyes with the back of his hand, hoping she had not seen them. 'I have wronged you,' he said. 'I should never have come.'

259

'You have made everything real,' Charlotte said. 'But now it must return to being a dream.' She walked to him, swiftly, put her hands on his chest, and kissed him. He breathed the scent of her: the lily of the valley. He did not release her from the kiss; it maddened him. He kissed her back, and pushed her against the bureau, one hand at her waist, and one in her hair, the shape of her head against his hand. She did not struggle; she pulled him closer. Leaned back, and – intentionally, he was sure of it – swept the contents of one of the small tables onto the floor: a small wooden figure, and a porcelain figurine which shattered against the stone.

The door opened.

They released each other in that moment, and Henry saw that although Ashton led the way, he was turned back, talking to Peregrine. But Peregrine had seen everything, the blood draining from his face. Ashton read something there, and turned.

They all stood, staring at each other.

Then Charlotte stepped forwards. 'Mr Kinsburg,' she said. 'The commedia dell'arte figure is broken. Forgive me, I thought I was going to faint, and I knocked it. Mr Dale-Collingwood caught me.'

Ashton blinked. He stared at the fragments on the floor for a long moment. Henry turned away, trying to gather his composure. 'Beyond saving,' Ashton said. 'Ring the bell for a servant to clear it. And why is there no servant in here? Charlotte?'

'Janet was in here,' said Charlotte. 'I sent her to Barbara.'

Peregrine yanked on the bell pull. Charlotte sat down, visibly trembling. When the door opened, it was Janet.

'Clear that up.' Ashton spoke with a new harshness. 'And where have you been?'

Henry held his breath as the girl looked at her mistress. 'I'm sorry, sir,' she said eventually. 'I was asked to attend to something. I only meant to be a minute.'

'Very well,' said Ashton, turning away from the debris. 'Just clear it up. Clear it up now.'

Peregrine came to Henry's side. Henry saw the fury in his eyes, the doubt and displeasure. *What on earth?* said his gaze.

'Save it for the journey,' Henry said, under his breath. And he turned to look at the gardens again, in their untouchable perfection, as Ashton walked to his wife, and dropped a kiss onto her dark head.

CHAPTER TWENTY-SEVEN

1941

<small>COMMITTEE ROOM, THE MIRRORMAKERS' CLUB</small>

'And I thought I was the mad one,' Livy said.

She, Christian and Peggy stood, drinking tea, staring at the fragments of plaster on the floor, all that remained of the cherub's face. It was Christian who had taken the hammer from Jonathan's hands, as Livy called for Peggy. It was Christian who had guided him down the ladder. Jonathan had walked away without another word; they had heard the door to the backstairs bang.

'If he finds the diamond, he'd better pay for the moulding to be repaired,' said Peggy. Her servitude had slipped fully from her, thought Livy: the building was what counted now.

'It can't be repaired,' said Christian. 'Not as it was.'

He had brought the archive box in from the Red Parlour, and was looking through it. He unfolded a piece of paper onto the Committee Room table. Scored deep with its folds, it was a plan of the basement as Henry had drawn it. He heard the chink of a cup in its saucer, and looked up to see Livy approaching him. As she leaned over his shoulder to look at it, he took a breath.

'We haven't been able to search that part because of the bomb damage,' she said. 'But Mr Whitewood didn't think the diamond would be stowed away in that part of the building anyway.'

'Where does he expect it to be?' said Christian. 'In a golden box in full view, under a shaft of light?' He traced the plan with his finger. 'The skeleton is in this area.' He pointed. 'There's a passageway running around the building in the basement. Henry labelled it as the moat. It's an early form of damp-proof course. I took another look today, on my way in, and noticed something. The bones are in a coffin: you can just see the outline of it. The bombing sheered the end off it, which is why we saw the skull.'

Livy stared at him. 'What does that mean? I just assumed it was a body that had been buried hastily.'

'As did I,' he said. 'But apparently not.'

'But if the moat runs around the building, surely the coffin would have been seen a long time ago?' said Livy. 'That area must be checked regularly.'

'Exactly,' said Christian. 'Some alteration must have been

made in order to create a space for the coffin. It must have been intentionally hidden in some way.'

Bill appeared. He was carrying a large cauliflower. 'What's going on?'

'Mr Whitewood took a hammer to the cherub,' said Peggy, pointing up. Her husband glanced over his shoulder and raised his eyebrows. Gently, he placed the cauliflower on the Committee Room table.

'That's a fine vegetable, Bill,' said Christian.

'Louie Robinson gave it to me. He's grown a few in his garden. All above board.'

'Of course – I didn't mean to imply you were in possession of a clandestine cauliflower.'

Bill gave a little smile and a nod; Livy wasn't sure she'd ever seen him so cheerful. 'We're talking about the body, Bill,' she said. 'The skeleton in the foundations. Have you been out and about talking to people? How will they investigate?'

Bill shrugged, in familiar fashion. 'I hardly know they will. We have higher priorities. It's more imperative that they put the scaffolding up,' he said. Livy got the sense he rather liked the word *imperative*. 'Whatever's happened down there – and I'm not saying it isn't creepy – we have to care about the living.'

'Yes and no,' said Christian. He smiled again, brightly. 'Let's say we care about both, but the living most of all.' Carefully, he folded up the plan again, and put it back in the box.

'Hello?' It was Jonathan. He had padded up silently, and was standing in the doorway of the Committee Room, holding something. Livy recognized the jewellery box he had unpacked from the trunk.

'Mr Whitewood!' said Peggy, as Bill choked on the cup of tea he was pouring down his neck. 'Would you like some tea? I made it specially for you.'

'No, thank you,' he said. His eyes sought out Livy, who was standing towards the back of the room, next to Christian.

'I'm so sorry,' he said. 'I'm so sorry for vandalizing the place like that. I don't know what came over me. May I have a word with Miss Baker?'

Reluctantly, Livy put her teacup down and went to him, walking past the plaster pieces with a wince, without looking at the others. She followed him a few steps out into the anteroom. They only went a short way: the rooms were so big they swallowed up sound.

'How can I help?' She found that she couldn't look at him, and the coldness of her own voice surprised her. He swallowed hard, and opened the box outwards. Inside, there was a jumble of jewellery of different vintages. She stopped herself from reaching in and rooting through.

'I don't suppose you've found the diamond there,' she said.

Jonathan shook his head. 'I have to sell the contents,' he said.

'I'm very sorry for you,' she said.

She saw the tightening of his expression. 'I have to go to Bond Street. Will you come with me?'

She looked into his eyes with surprise; into that cool face, which had remained so stealthy even as he had apologized. Her expression was enough to show her surprise and misgiving.

'It would be a favour to me,' he said. 'I don't feel quite myself. Tomorrow, I will go. Please, come with me.'

Livy hadn't left the Club for weeks, other than to view the skeleton. To think of even going past the end of the road seemed impossible. She could manage while she stayed here. But beyond the end of the road, the world was continuing, and she could not bear to face it.

'Let us see how you feel in the morning,' she said. 'You don't need me. I'd be a hindrance, if anything.'

'Please,' he said. 'Please, Livy.'

Christian watched Livy walk back into the room. He had been barely listening to Bill and Peggy as they had discussed how to eke out the cheese ration, and the bare minimum needed to bring cauliflower cheese up to scratch. Beyond the doorway, he caught sight of Whitewood slipping away, his head bowed in a way that was uncharacteristic. He knew Livy to be kind; he knew her kindness would put her in danger with such a man; and he also knew that what felt like his certain knowledge of her being in danger was based on his own jealousy. That he had to let her be free, when he had never wanted to hold onto her as tightly as he did now.

She came near to Christian, whispered to him as Bill and Peggy continued to talk.

'He wants me to go to Bond Street with him on an errand. He looks unwell.'

Christian stared into the final mouthful of tea in his cup; a trace of leaves. He swilled it around, and knocked it back.

'I think you should go with him,' he said.

CHAPTER TWENTY-EIGHT

1941

BASEMENT VAULTS, THE MIRRORMAKERS' CLUB

Like a voyager to unknown shores, Livy prepared for her
journey with misgiving. She put on her fuchsia rayon day
dress, the one chosen months ago by Miss Hardaker for its
brightness. Its vivid colour suited her pale skin. Her coat was
of the same vintage, the one she had walked to the Club in:
a grey woollen swagger coat, its line falling outwards from
her shoulders, giving her a broader silhouette. It had holes
under the arms that she had mended in the days when she was
orderly, and this evidence of her past efficiency cheered her.
She brushed her hair, powdered her face, put lipstick on, and
squandered more perfume than she would normally wear in
a week. After lunch, she put her grey hat on, and borrowed a
small brooch from Peggy, pinning it to her coat.

It turned out to be surprisingly easy for her to leave the Club. In the end, all one had to do was put one foot in front of the other. At the end of the road she had the uneven medieval street plan to thank for the fact that when she turned back, she could not see the Club. It had already dissolved into the London landscape.

Her anxiety sat in the pit of her stomach, so that she jumped at loud noises, but other than that she was proud to think that she looked quite normal. They took two buses, both of which were on diversion, and then they walked. On Bond Street they passed cracked windows and what seemed to be an eruption in the pavement – Livy wondered if it was a gas main. They walked with a distance between them; once, passing close by another couple, they were forced together, and Jonathan took her elbow to steer her.

He smoked continuously, and she realized that he was nervous. The fingers that held the cigarette seemed suddenly frail and fidgety. Every now and then he patted the breast pocket of his jacket, a regular checking pattern. She supposed he thought he was subtle about it, but his agitation was obvious.

She knew she looked for Hamptons constantly, her eyes darting here and there, her shoulders straight but tense. A fine pair they must have made, the pair of them, she thought, in their agitation, giving out whole constellations of movements and gestures, bright signals of anxiety.

For, goodness, how long this road seemed. Far less picturesque than its illustrious name might have suggested. Had people trod for centuries all this dirt, and rush, to seek a little glitter, to buy a jewel from the right shop? Was this what stood for glamour and luxury? She had thought remnants of it might remain here. But she realized she was longing for clean air. To be standing on the roof of the Club, looking at a sky free of planes.

'Are you worried?' he said suddenly.

'Not as worried as you.' She had meant to make him smile, but he caught her arm and spun her to him.

'I say, if you don't want to – that is – I have delicate business here.'

She sighed. 'You asked me to come. I won't be an embarrassment.'

He reddened; a touch of grace. 'I'm sorry. I don't mean to be . . .'

'None of us means to be.'

'It's just, they're the most powerful antique dealers in London.' He was tired, and she saw the strain in the shadows beneath his eyes.

'Don't worry.'

'Forgive me,' he said, at length: said it to the air in front of him, without turning to her. She let her hand brush his, and he gave her a small, worried smile.

Hamptons looked as though it had stood in the mid-point of Old Bond Street for time immemorial, when really it had just been a hundred years and fifteen more. There were gold letters on its glass windows, and a fine wire mesh had been put over the irregular old glass to protect it from bomb damage. There was not much in the window, as though they thought it vulgar to display too much in wartime: that was how they played it, at least. Jonathan thought that they were more afraid of theft than of accusations of extravagance, the latter being the cornerstone of their reputation.

'I'm not sure I want to go in,' said Livy, as they paused on the chessboard tiles outside the curtained door, a heavy in a bowler hat peering over.

'Just smile,' said Jonathan, and nodded sharply and imperiously at the doorman.

The door swung open with a violent jangle of the bell. Walking ahead of Jonathan, Livy found herself in a different world: hushed, deeply carpeted, surrounded by reflections from precious things, and eyes watching her. A long mahogany-framed glazed counter stretched the length of the first room. The walls facing it held cabinets with shelves, and the room was dotted with vitrines. The pieces within – jewellery, enamelled boxes – were not, it seemed at first glance, arranged by theme. Colours clashed, small jewels lay in boxes next to vast, trembling, diamond-set corsages. When she moved closer, though, Livy caught sight of a tiny slice of white card with the words 'eighteenth century' written on it in beautiful black handwriting.

Livy turned around and saw that behind the counter there were four men dressed in suits; men with neatly cut hair and one with a finely trimmed moustache. To her left there was a green velvet curtain, swept back to reveal a further showroom, and an office beyond, its occupant's name, Mr Hampton, gilded on the glass.

'Good afternoon, sir,' the moustached man said to Jonathan, and Livy was surprised to hear that his voice was deeply unpleasant. He spoke with a self-conscious precision, but there was an unidentifiable twang to his voice which she couldn't pin down, and which was the more unpleasant for the fact that he did not own it, but tried to chase the twang away with the force of his enunciation.

Standing beside Jonathan, she realized that the man had automatically assumed a certain relationship between them and was playing to it. Unleashing a ghastly smile, he unlocked the counter and drew out a sapphire brooch, rather old-fashioned, bordered with diamonds in a swirling gold mount and with a pearl drop. The kind of thing, she thought, which would have been in fashion when Jonathan was young: and it was not a serious thing, such as an engagement ring, but an expensive trifle for a mistress. Older man, younger mistress, he wants a nostalgic present for her. The girl would want something angular, deco, diamond-set; the man would waver, but come back to this thing, which suited his fond memories rather than his troubled present.

She tried to hide the revulsion she felt. Proffered the brooch, she smiled. 'How beautiful.'

'I'm not here to buy, Terry,' said Jonathan. 'Ask Mr Hampton if he is free to speak to me. This young lady is an employee of the Mirrormakers' Club – may she wait here for me?'

'Of course, Mr Whitewood.' The young man withdrew the brooch sharply, shut the case with a bang and locked it with a flourish. 'Michael! Go and see if Mr Whitewood can go in to Mr Hampton.' A smaller man hurried off.

And you even knew Jonathan's name, thought Livy. *Yet you thought I was a tart, so called him sir.* Salacious, obsequious discretion. Her eyes met Terry's and he sneered, openly, in front of her. It was an expression he had evidently practised many times and revelled in. When the other man returned, and ushered Jonathan to Mr Hampton's office, she turned away to gaze in one of the cabinets. Examining a paste brooch, she found Terry behind her.

'Eighteenth-century Portuguese, going for a song these days.' His voice and phrasing was less polished and polite now; the effort had gone out of him. He was examining her closely and she sensed he was cataloguing faults: beneath his eyes, she sensed, a woman would always be found wanting.

'What do the letters mean?' She pointed at a series of letters in tiny script, four of them underlined.

He raised an eyebrow, and clearly calculated that she would never be buying anything on her own behalf. 'The first four are the cost price in code. The underlined ones next to it are the lowest we'll take – that's the number that counts.'

'Oh.' The underlined ones, she thought. *That's what counts.* And something clicked in her mind. Henry's letters, so many words underlined.

Terry looked rather intrigued by the expression on her face. He pointed at the small gilt brooch Peggy had lent her,

273

in the form of an ivy leaf. 'Ivy for fidelity,' he said, and tilted his head, his expression softening a little.

'Thank you,' she said.

'Didn't say I liked it.' There was that smile again.

Livy turned back to the case. 'I don't need any help here, thank you.'

He took a step away, and gave a half-bow. 'Yes, madam,' he said mockingly. 'Of course, madam.' And he made his way back to his place behind the counter.

Livy stood, staring at the pink Portuguese paste. She felt someone's eyes upon her. She turned. It was not Terry. He had turned himself to torturing a fellow employee. Her eyes travelled up the panelling behind the counter. At the top, there was a ledge, where the secretaries sat. All-seeing, a security measure, perhaps.

One of the secretaries stood, the top half of her body just visible to Livy. Tight blonde curls, pale powdered skin, red lips. The perfect bow of them – painted or natural, she couldn't tell. They stared at each other. The woman's hair and skin seemed to have a kind of radiance to it which shone out on this room with its dense carpet and dark wood. A spotlight seemed to be permanently turned on her. She reached for a piece of paper, and the gesture was in the manner of a performance. Then her mouth twitched into a slight smile; no, it was a sneer. A sneer based on past knowledge. How many women had Jonathan brought here, in the past? Livy wondered. It was disconcerting to be one of so many.

The woman sat down, and disappeared from view. Livy

was left staring, bereft, at the space where she had been. She turned back to the damned paste brooch. Stared at its every detail: at the dust which had gathered on one part of it, at a smudge on one of the stones.

It was with relief that she heard a door open and male voices in the far room. Jonathan came to her. He was flushed and she could see the relief on his face – things, perhaps for the first time in a long time, had gone well for him. He saw the opposite in her. 'What's wrong?' he said. She shook her head. Her eyes went to the balcony, where a tube containing a rolled note had been sent on a wire.

'It will be only a moment, Mr Whitewood,' said the smiling man Livy took to be Mr Hampton, with a half-bow to Livy – he must have trained Terry, she thought. 'Our girls are most efficient.' Above, the hard mechanical tap-tap of a typewriter began, and Livy wondered whether it was the blonde woman's fingers, her nails lacquered red, which struck the keys so hard and fast.

Jonathan cleared his throat. 'Just a little paperwork,' he said to Livy.

The doorbell was shaken into life. A man came in with his hat on and collar up, with a confidential air. Terry sold him a brooch and he left again, maintaining his obtrusive air of secrecy. Terry only referred to him as 'sir', and the recipient of the gift as 'the lady'.

Livy turned to her wall-cabinet again. 'Anything you like?' said Jonathan, but his too-cheerful smile wilted under the look that Livy gave him. Then his attention was caught by movement above and he looked up. She saw what he saw – fragments of the woman in her peripheral vision – pale gold, red and white, and she saw also the instinctive flicker of desire in his own gaze, the beginning of that unconscious half-smile. She glanced, and saw that Jonathan's eyes had met those of the woman.

'I should awfully like to leave,' she said, in a low voice. 'The air feels rather thin in here.'

'In a moment. The paperwork has to be done. Can you really not bear it? Wait outside if you wish.'

She went without another word, the door pulled open by the doorman with what seemed to be his customary violence.

On the street, she felt immediately better. Standing outside the door, she saw the eyes of the doorman appear over the once-white pleated curtain which covered the door glass panel almost to the top.

It took such a long time for Jonathan to come to her that she took to counting the moments. When at last he emerged from the jangling door she started off without waiting for him any longer – anything to be beyond the reach of the doorman's steady, inquisitive gaze. It was the unashamed quality of their looking – his and Terry's – which had made her wriggle inside her clothes. She supposed she deserved it. The closeness between her and Jonathan had felt different within the walls of the Mirrormakers' Club. It had not felt impure, or morally wrong, to desire him, to let him put his hand on her leg. But in the real world, it did not stand up to inspection: it was just another tawdry liaison.

She heard Jonathan calling to her to stop, and in the end he reached for her arm and drew her back against a shuttered shop front.

'What on earth is the matter?' he said. 'You seemed eager to come and then you darted out of there like a scalded cat. I've never seen you like this.'

'It's nothing,' she said. 'We'd best get back. There's something I want to check in Henry's letters.'

'Wait. Tell me what's wrong.' His concern for her filtered over his face.

'They thought I was your mistress,' she said.

She saw all the emotions: his realization, the shame, the desolation. Saw them pass over those usually cold green eyes like fast-moving weather. 'Did they?' he said. 'I see.'

'You must have known they would.'

'Why? I didn't know they would remember me.'

'Of course they remember you. They all know your name. They've seen scores of women go through there on your arm. Did you not want to lose face? Did you want to show them your unlimited capacity for getting women?'

'Stop.'

She stared at him in stubborn fury. She realized how angry she was. Anger pure and clean and bright as a flame that one waves a knife through. She felt the world shift a little, as it had when she had seen the bones in the London earth.

'You must believe me.' His impassive face, that slight

flush building near his cheekbones, the immense beauty of the angles of his face. Such a man, she knew, would only have to look at someone to gain their interest. 'I didn't take you there as some kind of trophy. What kind of man would that make me?'

She shrugged. Knew Miss Hardaker would tick her off for such a thing. *Words, Miss Baker, are the doorway to respect. Choose your words carefully, speak clearly, do not fumble with gestures and slang.*

'Livy. I took you there for moral support. I needed company and I wanted that company to be you. You have been my companion in all of this. You give me strength, you give me the interest to put one foot in front of the other. That's why I asked you.'

She looked at him disbelievingly.

'I mean it,' he said. 'You are not like – the other women. No, listen. Do you think I would have shown this part of me to another woman? My weakness, my hopelessness? I feel truly dreadful. To have sold my wife's jewels. Can you imagine what that means to me, and to her? That I have not been able to provide for her. And now that they seem to mean so little to her that she throws them in a box and sends them to me?'

'Yes,' she said. 'I can imagine, I think, what that must feel like.'

'Yes, you can.' He looked around them, at the pale, washed-out landscape littered with rubble. 'I do love her, you know. As much as I love anyone. When I think of her now I feel sorry, and wretched. But when I think of you, I feel that I am still a person. A man. That there is still some life in me. I know it was selfish to take you. But I am a selfish creature, you see. I don't think I've ever pretended otherwise.'

'Let us just go home,' she said. *Home.* The Mirrormakers' Club. She desperately wanted to be sitting in the basement vaults, listening to the wireless with Peggy, wondering which part of the archive to look in next. Ignoring the fact that the past was vacant, and empty, in her mind; and so was the future.

They began to walk, both of them tired and slow, visualizing a broken journey of buses on diversion past bomb sites and eradicated buildings. She thought of Redlands, serene in its estate, bordered by hills and trees, and realized she had no vision of it at all: Jonathan had no talent for description. She had conjured her own house out of the landscape. It was all her imagination.

'Will the money be enough?' she said. 'For Redlands? You talked of saving it.'

He glanced at her. 'To shore up the house? Yes. We have damp – but I won't bore you with the details.'

'You said you didn't have the luxury to begin again,' she said. 'But the diamond will give you that, won't it? That's what you want.'

'Yes,' he said.

'Only you will begin again with the same things – you will stay at Redlands, you will stay with your wife?'

He looked puzzled. 'Yes, of course.'

'It's a wonderful thing, then, isn't it?' she said, stopping and turning to him. 'Not to want life to be different. Just to want to improve it a little. It's not as if you really want to destroy everything. Not like me.'

As he reached out to take her shoulders, the air-raid siren began to wail.

CHAPTER TWENTY-NINE

1941

On Regent Street, Livy had been walking for ten minutes, stumbling along in the darkness, Jonathan at her heels.

'Livy, the raid,' Jonathan said, taking her arm and pulling her to a stop. 'We have to take shelter.'

'Leave me if you want,' she said. 'I don't want to go underground.' She thought of Christian. *I'd rather be in the open air, even with bombs falling.*

In one hand he held his hat; his other hand curled and uncurled, the only sign of agitation – except that his grey winter coat was undone, where he had fled after her. The flush in his face, against his pale skin and dark hair, made him look older and a little feverish. His uncertainty woke her affection for him. 'Don't worry about me,' she said.

'Come with me,' he said, and he took her hand. She was

about to protest when she realized that he was leading her away from the Tube. They walked for five minutes before he led her down a side alley to a metal door. He banged on it. No one came. He swore under his breath and putting his hand into his coat pocket, fished for and pulled out a bunch of keys. He struggled to find the right one, but at length he unlocked the door, and they went in together.

There was post on a small table with a telephone, and an ancient staircase. Livy followed Jonathan up one flight, then two flights more. Another key produced entrance to an office, which was in an ornamental turret of the building.

'We'll go to James's office,' said Jonathan, as if she would know who that was. 'It's the most comfortable.'

James's office had a vast desk, a small bookcase, and a leather buttoned sofa against the furthest wall from the window. There was also a drinks trolley. Jonathan poured them each a glass of whisky. 'I'm sorry there's no ice,' he said. 'It's cold enough. Perhaps we don't need it.'

Up here, there was no wire mesh on the windows, and the blackout paper applied to the panes had been torn. 'We won't turn the lights on,' said Jonathan, as though to himself. Livy took a gulp of the whisky, and nodded. Jonathan turned from the window and came to sit by her on the sofa.

'Why do you have the keys?' she said, and took another mouthful, as though it were medicine.

'Stevie's family has a controlling interest in the business,' he said. 'Not that it's worth much, these days. I used to work here one day a week. I'm a working man too, you see.'

She looked at him, and couldn't suppress a smile. 'Hardly.' She drained her whisky glass and put it down.

He gazed into her face in the shadows; at the uncompromising shine of her eyes. 'You're an innocent,' he said. 'You talk about your darkness, your urge to destroy. I don't buy it, Livy. There are some types of innocence which can never be destroyed, or driven away. They are not a matter of decision; they are in the very grain of you.'

He thought of Stevie then, walking in her garden. He thought of her with a twinge of guilt, at the jewellery he had just despatched to an antique dealer. On her white shape, he could pin purity, but not innocence. No matter how hard he tried. He thought of the empty doorway at Redlands, as he trundled away to London.

He needed to forget. He put his glass down. Then he reached towards Livy, and raked his fingers through her hair; held the back of her head in his hands as one would a precious thing, then leaned forwards and pressed his face to the side of her neck.

The gesture changed everything. The pure relief of his physical touch took her breath. She drew back, and saw it in his eyes, saw the choice in that moment, although it had the quality of the inevitable about it. The danger. The edge of the roof, the light shining on bones in the earth. All these things pulled her towards them, had their own magnetism, as he did – as he had, from the first moment she had seen him. She closed her eyes, and kissed him.

When she opened her eyes she saw that in his face was that

mixture of tiredness, and honesty, and perplexity, that chink of openness, which unlocked her desire for him. One kiss led to another, and another, a seamless process set in motion. They could only both yield to it, in its immensity. A silent agreement not to think about the past, or the future. Equal in desire, they lived in the moment. One touch for another, an exchange, equal and opposite. Through the moments, through the hours; through the crisis, the ragged peak of pleasure, and then another.

The night poured in through the windows. A darkness as dense as the London earth in the moat.

They woke at the same moment, as a bomb passed the open office door, down the stairway, rattling its way through the building like a rat in a drainpipe. Jonathan's eyes widened in shock, and he silently folded his body around Livy's. She pressed her face to his shoulder, pale and clammy in the moonlight.

The explosion rocked the building, but, though they waited, curled around each other, the ceiling did not fall. Broken glass glittered on the floor. They lay there for several minutes, as though hesitant about whether they still lived.

Jonathan sat up, and turned, groped for his shoes in the darkness so that he could navigate the room. He walked across the room with their glasses, rinsed them out with soda to rid them of any fragments or dust, and filled them with whisky again. As he stood doing it, Livy sat up too, and reached for his jacket to cover her nakedness. She looked at his pale back in the moonlight, his shoulders slightly hunched. She felt stiff, a little sore, the impression of his fingers on her back, where he had gripped her. She stared ahead of her, at the shapes in the darkness. There were so many different shades of darkness.

She took the glass from him, and drank. He looked at her, without drinking.

'I didn't hurt you?'

She shook her head, but didn't meet his gaze with her own. The moment of deepest pleasure had traded one memory for another. Lit the fuse. She could not speak: she could not say what was unfurling in her mind. Memories, page after page of them, as though she flicked through a book.

One minute per page. Speed reading. As she had in the architect's office.

He smiled like a boy. She watched him drink. She felt strangely detached from him, as though their love-making had delivered her from his spell. His power was gone. For a man who was meant to be important, he was strangely unobtrusive. He wished both to be benevolent and to impose his will on the world. It was impossible, she thought, to live such a contradiction with any clarity or real happiness.

'You're shaking,' she said. She had noticed it before, on long evenings in the shelter, but never spoken of it.

The smile faded. 'Yes. Can't help it sometimes. All of this. Reminds me of the past. Not that the last war wasn't great fun, obviously.'

'Obviously.'

'Why are you not afraid? Not visibly afraid, anyway.'

'The whisky, mainly.' She looked at him, finally took a sip, and gave a sigh of surrender. 'I am afraid.'

'Who taught you how to take pleasure like that?' he said. She said nothing.

He kissed her passionately, until she pulled away and told him that she was exhausted. He nodded. 'Lie down then, and we'll get some rest.'

They lay entwined, and covered by his jacket. It was strange to her, how he stroked her, as though he could not keep from touching her; this taciturn man.

'Am I your first?' he said.

She knew then what he expected: to be flattered. As the other women who had gained brooches had perhaps flattered him.

'No.'

He stopped stroking her, took a breath. 'I suppose I deserved that.'

'I didn't say it to wound you. It's simply the truth.'

He nodded. He no longer stroked her, but nor did he remove his arm.

'What do you want? After this?'

She turned her head, and looked up at him. 'Peace, of course. And tea and buttered crumpets with lots of jam.' Her voice wavered. 'And a strong shoulder to lie my head upon.'

He thought of Redlands and its empty nursery. 'What about children?'

She shook her head. 'Go to sleep, while we have the chance.'

But he hardly slept, shifting in the darkness, stirring, and waking every so often. As Livy lay, one hand behind her head, staring at the ceiling, her eyes wide open.

CHAPTER THIRTY

1840

Letters, thought Henry. *So many letters, every day.* And he kept all of them. Evidence for the committee, of expenditure, of time spent, of his great labour.

> *I know you are very much annoyed with me, sir.*
> *Please understand, sir, this kind of thing has never*
> *happened on any other job before.*
> *The glass has blown six times on some pieces.*
> *We beg leave, sir, to say that ...*
> *We crave your indulgence ...*
> *If you could explain to the committee that ...*

Henry closed his eyes, and brushed away the thoughts of work. He checked the knot in his white muslin cravat in the looking glass, put on his tailcoat, then walked up and down his dressing room, the bare boards squeaking underfoot. In the distance he heard the retreating footsteps of his new valet, who walked at a slow and dignified pace. He had hired the man on the basis of his airs; he enjoyed them. He knew the man was, at this moment, taking the front stairs rather than the back, for there was no one to see him in this grand but half-empty house, for all its many branches of candles.

Ten months had passed since his visit to Redlands. He had moved in to the Russell Square house when it was in far from a finished state, for he wished it to look completely different from the family home he had left. The painters and paperers had been efficient. Many of the rooms were empty; lacking, Henry thought with a sardonic smile, 'a woman's touch'. But there were enough conveniences for him to move in, and to engage servants. At the moment, so involved in the Club was he that he had no spare energy to design the furnishings for his own home. Peregrine had appeared on his doorstep with a drawing for a ridiculously elaborate boudoir, which Henry had threatened to despatch to the flames.

In his own rooms he had a bed, chairs, bookcases and several candelabra, because he could not bear the darkness. He needed light for reading and work. He had brought back some of his parents' furnishings, but not all, and he could not bear to have the rooms arranged in the way they were when his family was alive. So many things he left in store in a distant warehouse, and even with many candles lit, and a fire built to a rage in the huge drawing-room fireplace, there was an air of sparseness which he could not seem to vanquish. Thin, temporary drapes had been hung in the windows, for he hated the idea of others seeing in at night, but they already looked grubby with London smoke, and he had instructed for them to be washed every week, to his housekeeper's irritation.

Perhaps he had lived too long in his club room, he thought. Perhaps he had grown comfortable with small spaces. Here, in the darkest hours of the night, he would lock the front door himself, and walk around the rooms, closing the shutters, as his father had once done. He had thought he would find comfort in resurrecting this paternal routine but in fact he found it unnerving and time-consuming, yet another tax on his resources after a day on site. Sometimes, as he walked, he would find himself musing on the Club and its decorative schemes, and pass a succession of windows without closing and fixing the catch on the shutters. Retracing his steps took time, and irritated him into a kind of anxiety. Having witnessed this, Peregrine arrived one day bearing a sleek terrier puppy in his arms, which he handed over to Henry. 'For company,' he had said, and resolutely refused to bear the thing away again, announcing halfway through dinner that she was to be known as Polly.

She was here now, curled up on the chaise longue – his mother's old chaise longue – despite the fact that Henry had told her a hundred times to get down. She was there, watching him with her large eyes as he adjusted his cravat, and paced the creaking floorboards. When he looked at her and said 'what?' her tail wagged.

He picked her up – she still fitted in the crook of one

arm – took a candle, and went out of his room and down the stairs to the front hall. His butler sat there, and rose when he saw his master.

'Is the carriage here yet?' asked Henry.

'No, sir,' said Marks.

Henry put Polly gently on the floor, and checked his watch. It would not do to be late for Ashton Kinsburg's ball, especially not when it was ostensibly being thrown in his honour. Still, the committee member who had said he would send his carriage was not late yet, and who knew what obstructions were out on the London streets.

He replaced his watch and picked up Polly again. Gratifyingly, she nestled against him. 'Would you like her for the evening?' he said. The man shook his head fervently.

'Not me, sir, can't be doing with her. Give her to Mrs Smits. Loves the little—' He paused, and thought twice about finishing the sentence. 'Shall I take her to her, sir? Before she ruins your apparel?'

Henry smiled. 'If you would.' The man was right. Polly had a penchant for pissing on him, it seemed, as though she thought it was the sure-fire way of keeping her master only to herself. She gave a little whimper as he handed her over. The man took her carefully, with distaste, and set off with quick steps.

Henry looked out of the rippled pane of glass by his door. He saw draw up from the vehicles outside, a carriage, a fine and luxurious town coach, its lamps lit and glowing. His throat felt thick, as it had with the summer pollen over the months in this city. He swallowed once, twice, before the rap on the door. The obstruction would not clear. He must bear it.

The Kinsburgs' London house was in Mayfair. Situated behind high walls, it glowed pale in the blue-black night, its windows sending out the glow of candlelight. To Henry, it seemed almost to pulsate with light, and noise. The house was crammed with people: he could see them at every window, bright and unruly, the women in gowns with pearls and diamonds at their throats and ears. He might not even need to converse with Charlotte. So many people would dilute everything. He climbed out of the carriage last, and felt the coolness of the night with relief; it cleared his head and brought him back to himself.

They were announced, and passed into the throng of people. He passed below an enormous Roman sculpture, three times his height. As he did so he took a glass of champagne from a silver-gilt tray, proffered by a stern-looking footman dressed in a silver coat, whose expression indicated that he was less than happy with his role. Henry drank the champagne rather quickly: cold and fizzy, it cleared his throat and added to his bonhomie. But as he looked about him, suddenly exhilarated, he saw all of the servants had the same look of the footman, who had by now long passed into the throng: the tightness of anxiety, of dulled annoyance. This, he thought – even a touch drunk already, for he had not eaten since the evening before – *this* was not a happy house.

'Dale-Collingwood!' It was Ashton. Weaving his way

through his guests where the servants had had to fight their way through. Only for him did space open up around him: his way was perfectly smooth. Henry could not see Charlotte anywhere.

'My dear sir.' Ashton had reached him too quickly, and had seized his hand and his elbow. Was close to him, smelling of a sweet musky scent. Carefully dressed, in black slim trousers, tailcoat, shirt and velvet waistcoat. Henry extracted his hand, and bowed, in a manner which showed his submission. He could not see whether Ashton liked this or not. 'No such formality,' the man murmured, 'we are such friends – one might almost say brothers.'

One might not say that, thought Henry, the only comfort being the thought of Peregrine's face when he reported this night's work back to him. Not that Peregrine had much humour about the Kinsburgs. He had lectured Henry endlessly on their journey back to London from Redlands – the shock, the dishonour, *another man's wife, Henry ... Thank God it was an age ago*, thought Henry. *Thank God I have been honourable since then.*

'But come with me,' said Ashton. 'Mrs Kinsburg most wished to see you.'

Swallowing back the words of protest which rose to his lips, Henry followed him dully through the joyful, chattering crowds, trailing in Ashton's wake, through one gorgeous room after another. The London house was less lavish than Redlands – of course it was, a place could hardly be more lavish – and at first the dominant shades were white and gold, giving a kind of cold purity which could hardly be softened by the candles, the fires, and the men and women in their velvets and coloured silks. Like Redlands it, too, was not a home: it was more of a show house, a demonstration of something. Henry passed through one room of conversation, and one of dancing. 'This is not the main ballroom,' called Ashton as they moved through it, its marquetry floor depicting flowers in different coloured woods. Here were the reds and the blues. *Of course not,* he thought, *of course this is not the main ballroom.*

They found Charlotte taking refreshment, or poised to do so, holding a glass. She was surrounded by other women. Henry never saw her drink from it, as they approached from the far side of the room. She was dressed in a pale blue silk dress, which lay off her white shoulders and plunged to a deep V. Around her neck was a chain, from which was suspended a large, pear-shaped diamond set in a silver frame mounted with smaller diamonds. Henry recognized the jewel, and found his eyes drawn to it, resting on her white skin. She wore it self-consciously, like a badge of office; it reminded Henry of the new ceremonial chain worn by the director of the Club. Official jewels, he thought. Her brown hair was smooth and low, braids looping over her ears. A diamond necklace had been threaded through her hair as an ornament, and it twinkled in the candlelight, so he noticed every movement of her dark head as he crossed the room.

'Mrs Kinsburg,' said Ashton. 'Our most honoured guest has arrived.'

Without hesitation, her gaze cool, Charlotte held out one

hand. Her gown had short, tight sleeves, and her white kid gloves ended only a small way above her wrists. On her arm she wore several bracelets. Henry stared at her white arms, the expanse of them. He took her gloved hand and bowed over it.

'Thank you for coming this evening,' she said. Her voice was soft and childlike, and puzzled him. He remembered her voice being deeper. He supposed she played her role again.

'I must thank *you*, Mrs Kinsburg,' he said, 'for inviting me to this splendid occasion. A triumph.' And suddenly he could think of nothing else to say. He rose from the bow, and just for a moment, their eyes met cleanly. He felt the impact of the contact move through him. He saw no such tremor in her. She stared at him, unblinking. As he rose from his bow he tried to keep his face still and emotionless.

'Let me take you to the ballroom, Dale-Collingwood,' Ashton was saying, drawing him away. 'A bachelor such as you will be tempted by the many beauties here tonight.'

They walked away, Ashton's hand on Henry's arm, and Henry allowed himself a glance back at Charlotte. There she was, sitting straight and upright, her dress spread in waves around her. She was not looking at him. He saw her, as though unaware, reach up and touch the diamonds in her hair, as though to be sure they were secure. Then a young man approached her, bowed low, and said something in her ear. He saw her laugh, and he felt as though a metal crank – brutal, like something one might find on his building site – had opened a chasm in his chest.

*

The sides of the ballroom were three-deep with the press of beautiful people. He saw some look at him, with recognition. 'We have already toasted you, before the dancing began,' said Ashton, as though it were an afterthought. Henry murmured his apologies, without blaming the person who had brought him: talked of the London traffic, and of skittish horses. Only the briefest nod showed that Ashton had heard.

A waltz was beginning, and as though by design a woman resolved out of the crowd. She was put into Henry's arms. He danced well, correctly, though without spirit. She asked him questions, and laughed at his answers, but without being indelicate. When the dance was finished, Ashton led him to another lady, introduced them, and begged them to dance. It was, Henry thought, barely within the bounds of decency. But each time the music ceased, another lady was brought to his side; a well-connected lady, as dark as the other had been fair, as tall as the other had been short, as quiet as the other had been lively. Was Ashton trying to tempt him? He would have been offended, but the women were all well-bred and seemingly undisturbed by Ashton's arrangements. He did not do all of it; his brother, Nicholas, took his turn too, making introductions.

Henry was dancing when he saw Charlotte. She was walking along the edge of the room, her eyes fixed on the dancers, moving gracefully through her guests. When she saw him, she stopped, and raised her fan to cool her face in the heat of the ballroom. The dance necessitated a bow, and a turn. With each rotation he saw her again, and saw that she saw him. The conversation between him and his partner had died. Even when she spoke, he did not answer, moving only mechanically to the music. Charlotte closed her fan, and he saw her put her hand out, and grasp a chair. The handsome young man he had seen earlier approached her; she put her hand on his arm, and smiled up into his face. Henry released his partner's hands, and she murmured. One more turn; and he saw that Charlotte was walking away, nodding at something the youth said. He longed her to look at him one more time, but as the dance wound down, she did not.

He was breathless. At the close of the dance he bowed, apologized, and began to fight his way towards the entrance. Ashton moved to intercept him, but Henry brushed him off. 'I must have a drink,' he said. His host acquiesced.

Cold champagne was what he sought, and found, at the mountainous refreshment tables. Acres of glasses, the light falling and flickering through them, so that he took one glass, and then another, anything to dull his feelings, before his well-wrought professional discipline kicked in, and the Mirrormakers' Club loomed in his mind. He could not let the building down. He took a plate, forked a slice of cold ham onto it, and was looking for something else to take when Ashton joined him.

'You must try the terrine,' Ashton said. 'My cook keeps the recipe under lock and key.'

Henry said nothing. There was no way, it seemed, to bat this man away. All the time he sought to divert himself from searching the crowds for Charlotte. Kinsburg too seemed to be looking for something. 'I had thought of a better time,' he said. 'But you are so hard to pin down. And it seems not right to trouble you when you are working at Mirrormakers'.'

'Speak now, then,' said Henry, trying to sound bluff and good-tempered rather than plain rude.

Ashton smiled, brightly and broadly. 'I have a commission for you, my dear Dale-Collingwood, when the Club is finished. I should like you to design my mausoleum at Redlands.' He paused, and looked at Henry's untouched plate of food. 'A place for Charlotte and I to rest together. *When the hurly-burly's done, when the battle's lost and won.*' The smile did not leave his face, but it had not quite penetrated his eyes.

Henry said nothing. The room seemed suddenly cold, and he would not have been surprised to see his breath misting in the air. He opened his mouth to speak, but Ashton made a gesture to stop him.

'Do not answer now. Think on it. I would like it to be the greatest tomb in England.'

Your house is already that, thought Henry, but Ashton was saying he would leave him to enjoy some repast, and would go and socialize with other members of the committee. As he left, Henry's attention was caught by a small knot of ladies. They were clearly gossiping with each other, and looking at Ashton with evident admiration. He supposed that in the end, Ashton was a handsome man, a rich man.

He put his plate down with a clatter. A passing footman enquired of him and for a moment he yearned for the freedom of his half-furnished empty house. 'Coffee,' he said. It was brought to him on a silver tray. He poured cream into the coffee until it was pale; gazing at the yellowish cells of fat on the surface, he drank it back, rich and luxurious.

It had no effect on his clarity, but it gave him space to breathe, and to be alone in the midst of the party. He spoke to a few members of the Club, but the effort was surprisingly tiring. He decided to stay in perpetual motion, moving through the rooms. As he walked towards the dancing, he saw Charlotte going up the stairs, purposefully and quickly. He turned away, as though to press on, but then changed his mind. He waited until she was out of sight, and then went to the foot of the stairs. There was no possibility of following her; the guests might be full of their own concerns, but the servants were watching. He looked at the place her feet had passed on the stairs; he wondered whether he might catch the scent of lily of the valley, but did not: there was only the faintly stale smell of alcohol, of pomades and perfumes, shot through with sweat; the roaring babble of voices, and cutlery on china; the faint struggle of the music to break through it all.

He put his hand to the smooth bannister. When he saw her reappear at the top of the stairs he did not know where to look, and settled on the dancers in a far room, their movement at the end of an enfilade of rooms, hoping that she would see him. She paused beside him, on the bottom step. Her gloved hand rested on the bannister an inch from his.

'Mr Dale-Collingwood,' she said. He turned his eyes on her.

'It does not do to stay away from the party,' she said. 'I have been sent down again.'

'By whom?'

She smiled. 'My sister-in-law,' she said. 'Her baby daughter means she has a reason to rest, but I do not. And I am the hostess.' She looked around. He saw it. Servants, duty, the fear pervading this household and making everyone step to Ashton's direction. 'It is quiet enough in my husband's study. I will go there in half an hour or so. Past the dancing; through the red and blue salon, and the white.' And she went, smiling at the other guests she passed.

CHAPTER THIRTY-ONE

1840

He went early to the study. He walked in the opposite direction to his hostess, who was taking the salutation of her visitors. On the way, he paused and watched a quadrille being danced in one of the subsidiary rooms, but he could not stay there long. He had to keep moving.

The study was dark, lit mainly by the healthy fire burning in the grate. A couple of large ormolu candelabra, taller than Henry, were also lit, but their flames struggled to alleviate the darkness. They were decorated with putti, and Henry wondered at Ashton's obsession with miniature cherubs and Cupid, as though he knew something of it, when they seemed the very opposite of Ashton's inclination. Two men sat in buttoned leather seats beside the fire, discussing bonds and stocks. Henry did not know them. With confidence, he went to the decanter at the back of the room and noisily poured

SOPHIA TOBIN

himself a brandy, putting the decanter down heavily onto
the tray and clearing his throat with gusto. Disconcerted,
the men left, glancing at each other as they did so in silent
agreement at his ill manners.

He drank the glass back and, as he put it down, saw that his
hand was slightly unsteady. He thought of Charlotte, looking
into the face of her young admirer. He poured another drink.

For a moment, he glimpsed the man he had once been,
free from the storm of his emotions, sensible and rational,
unrushed and unhurried. Or perhaps he had never been any
of these things. The sting of the brandy opened a brief gap in
the clouds, a brief gap in the static that filled his head like a
headache. What was he doing? How did he think this would
end? Without reaching any kind of decision, he put the glass
down and walked towards the door. But at that moment,
Charlotte opened it, and came in.

She closed the door behind her, and leaned upon it as
much as the circle of her dress allowed her to. 'Mr Dale-
Collingwood,' she said, as though she were surprised to see
him there.

He came to her, still half with the intention of leaving.
But as her face resolved out of the darkness, he saw the light
shining off her blue eyes, blue as lapis. She was a jewel,
Ashton's perfect construction, and his desire cooled. Then
she put her gloved hands out, and placed them flat against his
chest. She breathed out, gave him that sardonic, half-amused
look, and was flesh. 'I am so glad to see you,' she said. 'To
see a friend.'

In that moment, all thoughts of leaving were banished. Henry reached past her, and turned the key in the lock. She turned her head towards it, as the mechanism clicked. 'We should not,' she said.

He took a step away from her. 'Unlock it yourself, then,' he said. He went back to the decanter. 'If you prefer to go back to your young admirer.'

She watched him pour another drink. 'What is wrong?' she said. There was uncertainty in her voice now.

He knocked it back. 'Forgive me. Do I seem unkind? I am not being unkind to you?'

'Of course not,' she said.

'I would not have come to this house.' He tried not to make his voice sad, but when he heard it, it seemed neither masculine, nor confident, only weary. 'But your husband invited me in such a way – I could not refuse.'

'I understand,' she said. 'You do not wish to be here, and I have now brought you in here. Please do go, now. Forgive me, Henry.' The sound of his name in her mouth blotted everything else out. She walked over to a wall of shelves, as though seeking a book, in the midst of a ball. Turned her back on him, so he could leave.

He slammed his glass down and went to her, but she did not turn, even when he put his hands on her bare shoulders. He did not dare to lean against her, to drop his lips to the place where her neck met her shoulders, to feel the roughness of the diamond upon the softness of her skin. He stared at the stone, cold and rough. 'What a wretched thing,' he said.

'He had it set so I could wear it,' she said. 'But his intention is that it should be set permanently in a tiara, once a design has been agreed. I can't bear it.'

He felt her move, and then he saw that she had unbuttoned one of her gloves, and pulled it from her arm and fingers as she turned towards him. Her left hand was bare, and he saw that she was not wearing her wedding ring. And she reached up, and raked her hand through his hair, until her hand lay fast and warm against the back of his head. He lowered his head and kissed her.

He had never kissed a woman of his own class in such a way. This was not a chaste kiss, or hurried, as their first had been. It had its own rhythm, in which one gave and the other took, so that when they drew apart they laughed, breathlessly, at their synchronicity. Henry's hands had found her waist; he was frustrated at the hard, corseted shape of her, she seemed so like an object, a doll. He lifted her clean off the floor, and held her against him, and his mouth found the base of her neck. She clung to him; buried her face in his hair, and inhaled the scent of him.

The fire let out a sequence of crackles, and the moment of shock broke their reverie. Holding her against him, he clung to her, savouring her warm breath against his face. After a moment, he put her gently down. She held his face in her hands, one gloved, one bare.

'Who was that man?' he said hoarsely. 'The one forever at your side in the ballroom?'

'A mere child – I am a friend of his mother.'

'Don't try and fool me. He is in love with you.'

'He is not.' She looked at him, and he saw watchfulness there. 'I was not sure – if you would still love me, after all this time.'

In answer, he kissed her again.

'You sent watercolour sketches to Barbara. You sent a note explaining them.'

He held her away from him. 'You cannot think that a sign of my regard for her? I had promised her those things. I had to send them. Who is that boy? Who is he? You must promise me—'

'I have told you who he is. I wondered if you would notice it, if I smiled at him.'

He gripped her arms. 'Notice it?'

She searched his face with her eyes, and kissed him briefly. 'I am sorry to have doubted you. I cannot stay here too long. I will go.' She made to pass him, and he seized her wrist. 'I must go,' she murmured, and this time he let her. She went to a servants' door in the wall, opened it, and went out.

Henry knew he could not drink another brandy without making himself as sick as a dog. He crossed the room in three strides and unlocked the door.

He walked numbly through the dancing, through conversation, through drinking men, all the time the ache in his head building. The music seemed tuneless, the guests' frivolity jarring, almost crazed in its pitch. He collected his cloak and hat, and went out into the darkness, down the front steps, through the gates, and then out onto the street. He shook off the attempt of servants to aid him: he would travel without help of any kind from Ashton Kinsburg.

On the street, he hailed a hackney cab and directed it to Pall Mall. He could not go home tonight.

The doorman of his gentlemen's club greeted him with only slightly raised eyebrows, and directed his usual suite to be prepared. Henry thought of sending a note to Russell Square, but decided against it. He barely spoke to the man who showed him to his room and lit the lamps. He was consumed with thoughts of Charlotte.

He had admired women of his own class before, but not in this way. In the past he had admired from an emotional distance, as one admired a painting, or a view. In their clean, icy, uncorrupted beauty they were sculpture as much as flesh and blood. More than that, he had never examined his skills as a lover and found himself wanting. He had assumed he would marry; that the duty of procreation would lead to the pleasure, the normal pleasure he had only found in women of a lower class until now. And of those women, he had never thought of giving them anything, of asking them anything: the act itself was enough, he had assumed. Now he wished to question it. He had known that he loved her, but now – if they could, just once, be together, as they might have been as husband and wife. As he had kissed Charlotte, they had enacted a kind of game; he knew she had chosen to yield one moment, and to seek the next. It had been a conversation in touch which needed to be continued, as intoxicating as it was dangerous. But he must give her satisfaction.

There was a knock at his door, and when he called out, Foi came in, bearing a decanter and glass.

Henry groaned. 'For God's sake, Foi, do you ever sleep?'

She was not as neatly dressed as normal; there was no white cap on her head, only a long, mousy-coloured plait of hair down her back. Her mouth had its same pertness, and she leaned close to him as she put the tray down. 'I shall now,' she said. 'Wishing you a good evening, sir.' Then, with her usual lingering look, she curtseyed and turned.

'Wait.'

She looked back at him. Did she see it, he thought? Did she sense the fire in his blood? Was there proof of it in his face? *How base men are*, he thought. He poured a drink, and threw it down. The moment had a quality either of revelation, or terrible mistake.

'Do you require anything of me, sir?'

Choose, he thought.

'Yes.'

It was enough. Glancing behind her, she closed the door. She came to him, leaned over him, a few inches from his face. 'Sir?'

He put his hands to her waist, held her back from him, for a moment. The alcohol sang through his blood. She was not wearing her stays beneath her black gown. He felt the rise and fall of her sides as she breathed. She was so unlike his Charlotte that he could have laughed out loud. Oblivion rushed towards him.

307

'Sir?'

He saw, beneath her brazenness, a slight uncertainty, almost a fear.

'I want you to teach me, Foi,' he said.

She frowned.

'Pleasure,' he said. 'How to give pleasure.'

He filled the glass again, and pushed it towards her.

CHAPTER THIRTY-TWO

1840

Charlotte walked amid the ruins of the party in the plainest morning dress she had. Katie, sleepy and quiet, had helped her dress before Charlotte sent her back to doze in the adjoining dressing room. When she came downstairs the entrance hall was full of light. The servants had risen early, of course, and opened several windows, but the smell of alcohol, food and sweat still lingered in the air. The chairs were still arranged as they had been; the tables still covered in their white cloths, stained with red and white wines, with sauces and food. She walked gingerly around the remnants of a glass, left shattered on the stone floor of the entrance hall.

There was the sound of servants gossiping as they worked in the white salon, and someone was whistling in a distant room. Of course, no one expected her or Ashton to be up before ten. They thought them asleep, high above, in their separate rooms. So she walked quietly, remembering the sounds of the night before, savouring her aloneness. Especially in the ballroom, where so many beauties had twirled in Henry's arms. Yet all that was left was debris: feathers on the floor from so many headdresses and shawls, crumbs and spills, a piece of torn lace.

A maid came scuttling out of one of the rooms, bearing a tray of wine glasses, and skidded to an absolute halt at the sight of her mistress.

'Mrs Kinsburg,' she cried, and attempted to curtsey. 'You'll be wanting breakfast.' There was a slight resentment to her discomposure, a sense that Charlotte was breaking a well-known rule by being up before her time, while the servants claimed the house as their own.

'I will wait until Mr Kinsburg is up before breakfasting,' said Charlotte. 'He will come down at ten, as usual. I will go and sit in his study. If you could ask someone to set a fire there.'

She walked through the rooms slowly, the other servants falling silent as she did so. She smiled at them. One of the footmen rushed into the study after her, and began to make the fire with many apologies. She asked him to open the shutters once the fledgling flames were climbing into life.

She walked around the room, looking at the spines of the books. She couldn't help but think of them as witnesses of what had passed between her and Henry. She couldn't help but think of this room as infused with love, somehow. Then, near one of the occasional tables, she paused.

Pinioned beneath the empty decanter and glasses was a

sheaf of papers. She came closer and examined them. They were architectural sketches of a domed room, with a plinth in the middle, a wavy outline upon it. She saw the note, in Ashton's handwriting: *Kinsburg tomb*. She closed her eyes. So he had continued with the plan. He had even been discussing it with his acquaintances: another huge project, this time to record the details of his life, to leave his heavy-footed trace upon the world. And now she realized what those wavy lines in the centre of the drawing represented: Ashton and her. Beside each other for eternity.

She thought of the diamond, cold and heavy on its chain. How he had undone the necklace the night before, and replaced the stone tenderly in its box. Would it, too, have its place in their mausoleum?

She looked around the study. Ashton was there, as Ashton was everywhere. There was no escaping him. Henry's kiss seemed like something imagined. What was real was this room, with her husband's prints all over it; what was real was this cold morning light, this insubordinate fire which did not catch properly, and the drawing of a tomb weighted down by empty brandy glasses.

This place would always be his. But she could find other places.

Henry woke with Foi sleeping beside him. His head throbbed and his mouth was dry. He moved, slowly, and sat upright on the edge of the bed, naked. It was only when he pulled a sheet towards him, to cover himself, that she woke.

He could not meet her eyes. It was the quietest he had ever known her, as she slowly dressed and plaited her hair at his looking glass. He pulled his trousers on, and his shirt, then found his wallet. He stood back from her as she put her shoes on. Then he handed her the money.

It was far too much, but she did not protest, despite looking hard at him. There was no pertness about her today, no smart remarks, but no desolation either. He could not pick a single emotion from her inert expression. She went from the room without a word.

He waited for a decent interval before ringing and asking for hot water. The young man who served him was not self-conscious, even though Henry looked for it. He sent the man away, and left himself unshaven. He could not seem to wash the smell of Foi from his skin, from his hands. He went out into the Sunday morning light still feeling rank, and went to church.

Henry took communion, then went home to Russell Square, where he greeted his rather shaken servants with an apology. Polly leapt into his arms and tried to lick his face, and it was only this which made him smile, at last, and think that life might return to normal. The housekeeper told him that Polly had slept outside his room, whimpering, and had refused to leave his door or come down to Mrs Smits' room. He cradled the dog affectionately and petted her.

He was not hungry, and gave everyone the afternoon off – most, but not all, had been due to take the afternoon anyway. He washed, and re-dressed, dousing himself with cologne, but still could not raise enough hunger to eat even a hunk of bread and cheese. He left his discarded clothes on the bed and the soapy water in its basin to be collected later. He drank some cold coffee which had been made for him before the servants had gone out, but only because his body needed something, and the headache had returned.

He went out onto the squares and streets, where Londoners walked in their Sunday best. He felt that people looked at him, even as he walked, well-dressed, his top hat on and with him swinging his cane in an impression of energy and jauntiness. He simply kept walking, hoping that he might become more inconspicuous, to himself and to others.

He had been walking for an hour or so when he recovered his hunger at the scent of food from a chophouse. He went in, ordered, and was swiftly brought a dish of stew, which he ate hungrily. Warmed, and full, he felt the tension leave his body, a strange kind of security dull his feelings. The night could be forgotten; in the morning he would go to the office, and direct the building work, and answer his letters, and be himself again.

He tipped the cook and went out onto the streets once more. The shops he passed were closed, but he glanced in the windows cheerfully. At a bookseller's window he scanned the shelves, looking for diversion. At the sight of *Poems Chiefly Lyrical* by Lord Tennyson he swallowed down his dull shock. He had not expected to see it; nor had he expected to feel his cheerful mood shift and fall sharply. Charlotte had loved the book, and she had quoted lines from 'Mariana' to him once: telling how she dreaded the evenings, sitting with Ashton.

But most she loathed the hour
When the thick-moted sunbeam lay
Athwart the chambers, and the day
Was sloping towards his western bower.

He hurried home through the twilight, past churches and shops, couples and families. A light was lit within his house. He went in to find the servants returned, and him expected to dine. The book spine hovered in his mind, gold on blue. He went up the stairs, Polly at his heels, and into his room, where he put his cane down with a clatter and handed his hat to his valet. The man brought him hot water so that he could wash the London grime from his face. Henry watched him go, and sat on the edge of the bed, as he had sat on the edge of another bed, that morning, and watched Foi plait her muddy-blonde hair.

The dinner gong sounded. It was only then, with Polly looking up at him in concern, her tail wagging, that something crumbled within him. Last night had not been a dream: he had lived it, and there was no going back now, and no erasing it with the most fervent of prayers. The clock on his mantelpiece chimed the hour, and he felt the house thick with the ghosts of his family, and his regrets. As Polly leapt onto his lap, he covered his face with his hands.

CHAPTER THIRTY-THREE

1941

Jonathan and Livy parted at eight, going out into the grey morning dishevelled and bruised, still brushing dust and glass from their clothes. Things looked different in the light, clearer, and colder. Jonathan told her he needed to call on an acquaintance, and asked her if she minded going back alone. She shook her head. She had lain awake, seen things run across the shadowed ceiling as the dawn filtered in through the torn blackout.

As she turned away, fastening the top button of her coat, he caught at her wrist, but she smiled and said goodbye, kindly. She knew that regret was written across her brow – there was no use hiding it. He was, of course, unreadable, his green eyes steady and distant as he put on his hat and strode towards Piccadilly.

She caught a bus, and found herself praying that the

Mirrormakers' Club would be there when she got back. She couldn't shake the prayer from her lips; for variation, she began the Our Father, which brought memories of school assemblies and distant Sundays. Her memory was suddenly clear. Perfectly restored and, like the morning light, too bright. It crowded upon her: the smell of lamb and mint sauce on the table on Sunday. The dull prickle of cold in a train carriage with all its windows open. The touch of a lover. The shipwrecked things she had forgotten raised out of the water of memory, glittering in the morning light. She fretted the handle of her handbag through her hands rhythmically, like a rosary, as though she were counting her prayers, but they were indiscriminate.

The landscape of Cheapside had shifted overnight; she walked past another shop gone, blown like a faulty light bulb, leaving its socket behind, and she felt the thud of the alarm in her stomach, in her chest. When she turned the corner and saw the Club still standing, she almost bent double and wept, but her discipline – newly remembered – kept her upright. As she approached the familiar façade, she noted new scars. Some men were cheerfully and efficiently putting scaffolding up to support the south-west corner, and they called to her.

'Hello, lovely.'

She nodded at them, but did not say anything.

'Pretty girl like you, give us a smile.'

'Morning, morning. Been a naughty girl, have you?'

Tight-lipped, she hammered on the front door. The men laughed, and she could feel a blush rising traitorously in her face. She put a hand to her lips, wondering if any trace of her lipstick remained and if it was smeared. She had not so much as glanced in a mirror.

The door opened. It was Peggy. As she looked at Livy's appearance, her face set in some new and disturbing expression.

'Hello there,' said Livy.

'No Mr Whitewood?'

Livy felt everything stop. Felt Peggy's knowledge enter into the gap of the night. How foolish she had been to think the other woman would assume something innocent. 'No.'

'You'd best come in.' Peggy opened the door, let her pass, and then shut it hard and locked it. 'The water's off but I saved you a tiny bit from the tank if you want to wash. Your young man was here early this morning. He's been looking in the archives and charging around the depths of the Club. Bill gave him the keys.'

Livy stopped rubbing her eyes. 'Mr Taylor?'

'Who else?' Peggy held her gaze for a moment. 'He's arranging a proper burial for that body. But I said to him it's probably a Roman or something. They're always digging up all kinds of things around here. Anyway, he's still around here somewhere. I lose track of him. I wanted to ask Mr Whitewood's opinion about it all.' She paused. 'Will he be coming back today?'

'I expect so.' Livy kept her head down, and slowly followed Peggy across the Stair Hall, and down the stairs into the vaults.

'I'll draw you some water,' said Peggy. 'Do you want a little vinegar? It's for the best, if you need to wash ...' She lowered her eyes, and blushed. 'There. What kind of world is this to bring a little one into?'

Livy felt unsteady, but knew that the truth was the only way forwards. 'A little vinegar would be helpful, thank you,' she said.

'I'll go and get it. Then I'll make us a cup of tea.'

Washing helped Livy to wake up, but she still felt as though her head were full of cotton wool when she went out to have the tea.

Peggy looked at her for a long moment. Then she went to a drawer in the far corner of the room, opened it and took out a scarf. Gently, she put it around Livy's neck. 'There's a mark,' she said. 'Best keep it covered.' She poured the tea.

Livy wiped away a stray tear with the heel of her hand, and sniffed. 'Where's Bill?'

Peggy looked hard at her. 'He's working. I need to talk to you.'

Livy began to cry then. 'No. Please, Peggy, no. Don't be harsh to me. It's too much.'

'I'm not being harsh. I've been young too. We were at war when I was young, and I did just what you have done.' A rosy colour infused her cheeks. 'And you're not to speak to Bill of this, by the way.'

'Of course I won't.' Livy took a gulp of the scalding tea.

'So I know in principle why this has happened. And I saw the way Mr Whitewood looked at you. But I didn't think you would fall for it, a clever girl like you. And I cannot see why you have. He is married, Livy. It is just plain wrong.'

Livy began to sob. Peggy stared in astonishment at her, doubled over in that bright dress. Her dark hair dusty. Her skin so pale. And how she wept. As though her heart were breaking. Peggy had never seen her like this; she had not seen her broken open. 'Sweetheart,' she said. And then saw the glitter on her. 'Is that glass on your hair?' She reached out.

'Don't cut yourself.' Livy caught her hand, and squeezed it. 'I'll get it out later. I should have picked it out when I washed, but I couldn't face it.' She looked up at the housekeeper, choking on a sob. 'Please forgive me. Please say you don't think badly of me. Please.' Her voice rose in volume.

'Calm down, now. I've said too much. Hush, hush, I will leave you alone.' She reached out, put her hand gently onto Livy's back. 'I'm sorry. I didn't mean to upset you.'

Livy wrapped her arms around Peggy, and buried her face in her shoulder. Smelt the soft, talc-floral scent of her. Peggy was someone who always smelt the same; who always knew how to fold a jumper correctly, and to cook a sauce. Only now, when she felt the slight tremor in Peggy's arms, did Livy wonder how much effort it must have taken the woman to be so strong.

'Why do I not know the things you know?' said Livy, looking up at her. 'I should know these things, and yet I can never do them as you can. I tangle things.'

Peggy cradled her, let her cry, and stroked her hair, glass and all. 'There, there,' she said. 'Give it time. Do not worry. One day you will be a comfortable old housewife just like me.'

'I don't think so,' said Livy. 'I can't see it. I will always live in chaos and uncertainty. I am bad. It's in my nature. I know that now.'

'No, no, no,' said Peggy. And she held Livy in her arms as though she were the most precious thing in the world. She rarely held anyone in that way, for she had never had her own child, and she and Bill were not affectionate. The warmth of Livy in her arms unlocked something; the mercy seemed to flow from her. All the accumulated years of patience, and suppression, and devotion, and duty. Peggy felt more like herself in that moment than she ever had. 'When I speak to you of this,' she said carefully, trying to keep her tone prosaic, as though speaking of household accounts or the price of potatoes, 'please believe that I am trying to protect you.'

Livy nodded, and drew a tremulous breath. Peggy took Livy's face in her hands, and wiped the just-fallen tears with her large thumbs. 'You look different,' she said. 'I don't know how. But your face has changed. And for the better. A good cry helps things sometimes. Now, chin up.' Livy blew her nose on her handkerchief, and smiled. 'Good. Things aren't lost yet, my sweetheart. Now go and find your Mr Taylor, who is tearing around this place unchecked. Now he is a nice young man. If I were twenty years younger . . .'

'Can't I go and sleep?' said Livy. She wasn't sure if she could face Christian.

'No. You cannot.'

'I don't have the strength.'

'Yes, you do. You spoke to him a day or two ago. You can speak to him today.'

'You don't understand. I remember. I remember everything.'

Peggy stared into Livy's hazel eyes: wide and vivid, the iris ringed with a colour that looked like fire. And just as she had all those months before, when Livy had come to the front door, Peggy ran out of words.

In the Stair Hall, a layer of dust floated through the air like a shade, catching what light there was. Livy watched it fall and dissolve, then began to climb the staircase and took the left branch. She went to the Hide, that room which had been used by Miss Hardaker before the war. She thought, for a moment, she could smell her perfume in the locked-off air, and stroked the bright length of the day dress she had chosen for her. Livy looked at the room as though she had never seen it before: the Victorian desk, the shelving and cabinets, the two tall windows which looked out onto bombed London.

She left it quietly, and returning to the landing, glanced into the Dining Hall, the lower parts of the windows with their stained glass now covered by boarding. Bill had been busy. There were no echoes of music or dancing, the large space deadened, something absent. There was no sign of the light she had once seen there. It was empty. She turned right and walked down the landing to the anteroom between the Committee Room and Red Parlour, and stood there: to her right, through the doorway, she glimpsed the white patch where Jonathan had smashed the face of the cherub. To her left, the shredded Red Parlour. She walked into the Red Parlour, and turned a full circle. As she stared at it, it gave away a breath of plaster from the ceiling. Then she heard footsteps: distant, in the Stair Hall, echoing off the marble.

A quadrille, she thought. A man in pursuit of a woman. She thought of the words Henry had written in his notebook.

I propose the Red Parlour to be a more feminine space, for here is where any ladies will take tea after balls and entertainments, having withdrawn from the gentlemen. I propose that the space be not as robust as the decoration in, for example, the Dining Hall.

It is to be delicate, floral, with shells – in short, a French style which, though I know may not be popular with the membership, is nevertheless more appropriate for ladies and their delicate sensibilities.

Christian appeared in the doorway, and Livy realized the distant footsteps must have been his. His hands were in his pockets. His outline was suddenly familiar to her: the ruffled hair, and the broad shoulders. The quiet voice, every inflection known to her.

'Morning! I've been looking at some records.' He spoke hurriedly, nervously, and did not wait for her to respond. 'Bill let me in and gave me the keys. I suspect he's rather glad that I've taken that body off his hands, so to speak. I've spoken to the vicar of St Anne's and he will come and say some words over the hole. With the building as it is, it would be dangerous to start disturbing things.'

She nodded. It was good to talk of normal things. 'You're just going to leave it there?'

'For now, yes.' He wouldn't look at her properly. 'There are rather more pressing problems to face. When the war is over, when the Club is properly shored up and rebuilt, the body can be moved then. For now, the resources are needed for the people who are living and dying today, tonight. You should see the bomb damage maps. Bill was right. We need to care about the living.' He paused, and when he spoke it was clear that he was saying something which he had bound himself not to say. 'Where were you last night? With Whitewood, I gather. Peggy's face was a picture, when I asked where you were this morning.'

'I'd rather not talk about it.'

A half-smile of disappointment. 'I see.'

'No, you don't. It didn't matter at all.' She felt rather desperate. 'Will you show me the moat? We talked about it before.'

He frowned. 'If you wish.'

She thought of the Hide; its tall windows and dark shelves, its light and its darkness. *Chiaroscuro*, she believed Caravaggio had called it, that contrast between bright light and shadow. She and Christian had looked at one of his paintings in the National Gallery, before the war. She remembered that now. *Light, dark*. She wanted to speak to Christian about it, but for the first time in months she saw that he was not open to her, and did not wish to talk. She sensed that he was closing himself off, as they had closed up the service rooms in the Club, one by one. It rather frightened her: the laying of dust sheets, the turning off of the lights.

She tried to stay bright and businesslike. 'If you've looked on the plans, do you know what that room off the landing was, originally? The Hide?'

'The Surveyor's Room. It's the one Dale-Collingwood intended for himself.' He glanced at her. 'You know that Bill doesn't like going in there?'

'No? Why?'

'He says he saw Miss Hardaker in there, the day after the accident. He said she was sitting in the chair, and that she turned and gave him a terrible smile. That's what he said: terrible.' He took in the look on her face. 'Yes,' he said, and his voice had an edge. 'You're not the only person who sees ghosts, you know. Who's been broken by this whole bloody business.'

He went past her, wordlessly. Onwards. As she followed him, Livy glanced back at the Red Parlour, its *feminine* white and gold blown to pieces. In the Hide, Henry had planned the last details of the building. And now it was being taken apart piece by piece, like the people who lived within it.

Livy followed Christian through the kitchens at the back of the Dining Hall. Left unused and in darkness since the beginning of the war, it was a part of the building she had hardly ever visited, and at its unfamiliarity she was reminded of its scale, its many hiding places. They went down an unfamiliar set of backstairs and into the very depths of the building, then through a door which he unlocked. Down a corridor she had never seen before, through a bathroom and then out through a small hatch in the wall. He paid no mind as she scrambled through. In the earthy darkness, she kept her eyes fixed on the shape of his back. As they turned the corner they saw light, and the bars of the scaffolding.

'This is the moat,' said Christian, putting his arm out to halt her. 'Do you remember? We saw it on the plans. Early form of damp-proofing; separating the sodden earth from the building. Only on the plans it was meant to run the whole way round, at the same width, but it narrows here. Strange. And then – the bombing happened, and part of the moat, at the narrowed section, collapsed. It's best if we stay back here.'

He turned on a torch and she saw, from a distance, a white shape.

'Remember that?' he said.

She swallowed hard. 'The skull.'

His voice was bereft of emotion. 'Exactly. The explosion sheered off the end of the coffin. I'm not an expert of course, but I'd say from the size it's probably the skull of a woman. Although, I suppose, men were smaller in the past too. I went a little closer before and saw the arm bone. There's a delicacy to it.'

'Did you tell the City Police?'

'Of course. They say they'll send someone round at some

point, but they're not that interested in someone who's so long dead.'

'Peggy thinks they might be Roman.'

He smiled; in the past, she thought, he would have laughed. 'No, no. Not here, not in this part. It's highly irregular. Someone put her here. A mystery. We might have to look in the archive a little more – see if they mention when the moat outline was changed.'

Livy felt short of breath, her throat tightening in the darkness. 'Can we go back up now? I don't want to stay down here.'

He helped her out of the hatch this time, holding out his hand to her as she stepped out, but releasing it immediately afterwards. She felt both his closeness and the distance between them, as they went upstairs. He took her a different route, so they came out into the Stair Hall, emerging from the ring of service rooms. He had left his hat and coat tucked into the V-shape of the carved marble bannister at its terminal, and now he put them on, his back to her.

Livy's sense of helplessness intensified. 'Are you going?'

He settled his hat on his head; still he could not look her in the eyes. 'Yes.' His movement, his tone of voice, was too final.

'You will come back?'

Finally, he looked at her: those dark eyes, whose emotions she could read so easily in the past, now walled up to her. 'I don't know.'

'But I have things to say to you.'

'I don't think you do. I have waited—'

'Yes, you have, and I am grateful—'

'But perhaps you're right. You wanted a new life, and I keep trying to drag you back to the old one. It seems to me you made a choice, last night.'

'No. I didn't.'

'I'm not blaming you. It's not as if you even know . . .'

'I didn't make a choice.'

He put out his hands: the wounded and the whole. A 'stop' motion. 'Please, Livy. I don't have the strength.'

She watched him turn. Took a breath. 'Last night, I remembered.'

He was already two steps away from her, but he halted at her words. Halted, and did not move.

Livy thought of the things she could say. Thought of the explanations she could produce. Tried to form sentences that would make things better. And then realized: the sand had slipped through the hourglass. And there was only one thing which he really needed to know, and which she really needed to tell him.

'Christian.'

He half-turned, and looked towards her. And his eyes seemed truly haunted, and fearful. Livy felt it: the turn in the air, like gears. The reverse magnetism which had kept them from touching each other beginning to uncoil itself.

'Yes?'

'I'm your wife. Aren't I?'

CHAPTER THIRTY-FOUR

1840

Henry pushed aside the drawing of a basket of flowers which he had prepared for the plaster carvers.

On his desk, he sought, and saw, the expected letter which had come by hand; the dear, untidy writing. He remembered the first time he had received this daily note. *I have found a way to write to you. I had to find a way to write to you.*

He had folded away the night with Foi, put it away in his mind. He had not stayed at his West End club again.

The letters were brought to the Mirrormakers' Club each day by Katie, Charlotte's maid – for the building was now secure enough that Henry had his own surveyor's office, one of the first rooms to be finished. Charlotte had taken the maid into her confidence, bribed not just by affection but with money too. It was the first crack in her grand edifice, thought Henry. His own trusted ally was the housekeeper at the Club, whose warm-hearted, incurious nature meant he simply trusted her, without a word, or any money. He knew better than to try and tell her what the letters were, respecting both her intelligence and his own lack of talent at lying.

They had been helped by the fact that Ashton had returned to Redlands, having engaged Peregrine to design his tomb. Henry had dissuaded him on his many visits to the Mirrormakers' site, saying again and again how Gothic-friendly Peregrine was and more suited to the task than Henry. Yet, he had still been astonished when Ashton had one day suddenly agreed, as though some well-defended citadel had fallen.

He wished me to return with him, but I said I was too unwell to travel, Charlotte had written. *He agrees that the best doctors are here.* She would not tell him what her illness was, or whether it was feigned. But he suspected that she had had a miscarriage. And the thought that she might have been carrying another child of Ashton's, even on the night when he had kissed her at the ball, made Henry so miserable that it silenced him. The thought returned to the surface of his mind, again and again, hideously and repetitively buoyant, but he would not admit it to the light by asking her, for her sake as well as his own.

He did not want the Charlotte that Ashton presented to the world.

He wanted the traces that he saw of her, the real Charlotte, to coalesce and become real. There was an austerity he saw in her, and an intensity, which matched his own. Oh, it was buried, of course: wrapped and scented in manners and artifice. But some deep kindling had brought them together.

Or is it just the flesh, he thought? The strange alchemy of desire. It was the touch of hers that had wakened him to her. The way their gazes met and sparked off each other. And yet, he did not want her smooth, pale, plump flesh. He wanted her brown after days walking through wheatfields with him, in the sun. He wanted her to pull her bonnet back, and let the sun freckle and blemish her marble face. With the edifice taken down, he would show her how he still loved her. He would draw not just a smile from that watchful face: he wanted to hear her laugh.

These visions were dense and vivid. He imagined drinking a cup of tea in the evening, her sitting beside him, and think how comfortable it would be to see her lift the pot in her capable hands – hands that could be capable, if she were released from her director – and pour the tea, the room warmed by the flames in the grate. Or her, eating her eggs across from him in the morning, the way in which she would lift her cup to her lips and what they would speak of: a book she had read, or an idea he had had, or even his vagabond workmen. The visions were comfortable, and domestic. They had the materiality not of wishes or fantasies, but of things that would come to pass.

He had grown to depend upon the letters. He would wake each day feeling relaxed, but then the tension would gradually rise in him, until two, when he would come into his office and find the letter lying there, amid business correspondence.

And then, released from his purgatory, reassured, he would put it in his pocket and wait until the evening to read it, at home in Russell Square, when he would write a reply which would be collected by Katie the following day from the housekeeper at Mirrormakers', when she delivered Charlotte's latest note. Their letters crossed each other, and a thousand coloured threads of delayed answers and reassurances wove their story.

Henry had never realized how closely he was watched until he fell in love with Charlotte. It seemed impossible that they might meet, alone. Once, she had come to the Mirrormakers' Club herself, ostensibly to see how the building work was going on. She had confessed to the whole room of people, labourers and craftsmen alike, that she intended to surprise Ashton with a written account of how things were progressing. But during that whole visit they had been surrounded, not one word unheard by others. They barely looked at each other. It had caused, if anything, a breach between them which could only be healed by the following day's letter. He had taken a risk: he had written it when he should have been supervising the plastering of the Red Parlour. He had taken it to the Kinsburg townhouse himself, and asked that it should be put into the mistress's hand, as it pertained to urgent business. *Did I seem cold, my darling?* he had written. *Do not think it, do not. I seek only to protect you.*

He did not trust his own words which were, he thought, sometimes over-fevered, sometimes pompous with convention, for how was he to express what he felt for her, truly?

There were not words for such things. He asked her to tell him the meat and bones of her life. He wished to know of her as a real being, not an angel or a goddess. What she ate, what she wore, how her clothes felt against her skin. These brief sentences of intimacy unlocked what he truly sought. *I am bleeding today*, she wrote once, and her trust pinioned him, a sharp needle of both privilege and intimacy. He saw her breath on the page. He wished to know her hurts and her pleasures; the things she thought of in the moments before sleep. Only in this way did he know that he knew her better than her husband. Once or twice she wrote briefly, and politely, and the convention of it maddened him so much he thought about bringing the world down about their ears. Publish it in *The Times*, he thought, and let us be ruined. But the day was coming when they would be together, if only briefly. Ashton could not be held off for ever, and had forced them to decisiveness. Barbara had written to Charlotte and told her it was her duty to return, ill or not. It was nearly winter, Barbara wrote: surely Charlotte had healed now?

It was a Monday, and Henry had given his servants the evening off. It had all been arranged and yet, when he heard the door knocker, he broke out into a sweat. A part of him had thought it would never happen, and that she would never come. There were so many hurdles to all parts of their relationship that seeing her again, touching her, seemed impossible. He felt their love to be a healing force, but the waiting sickened him.

He ran down to the kitchen, to the servants' entrance. In came Charlotte and Katie, both cloaked and bonneted. He looked at one, and then the other. Katie seemed cheerful enough, more cheerful than Charlotte, who was pale.

'I have madeira for you, and eat as much cake as you wish,' Henry said to the maid, who took her seat eagerly by the fire. He scooped up the over-excited Polly, and Katie stroked her and cooed over her. Then he went silently from the kitchen, with Charlotte behind him, so quiet that he looked back more than once to check that she was there.

In his room, they stared at each other with what seemed like misery, until he finally smiled at her, and she at him.

'It is strange, but I feel shy of you,' she said.

'It is only natural,' he said, but he did not think it was. He was nervous of her, but also eager, although he did not wish to frighten her. As though newlyweds, as though embarrassed, he helped her to undress, a long and difficult process; and when at length he undid his shirt, he could only think that, of course, she had seen a man naked before: she had seen her husband, and that chilled him. Then he reached out, and ran his hands through her long hair, which she had just released from its pins. He kissed her, and as her mouth opened beneath his, it was as though he were in the study on a long-ago ball night, with the music and the chatter fading from his mind.

Charlotte knew she could be free with him: he had demanded it of her, in his letters, and she had decided to take the chance. If he was disgusted with her, this night would remain a secret and she would return to what Ashton had shaped her to be, cool and calm and obedient. But for this moment, she grasped at life, at pleasure; and Henry both followed her and led her. Each moment was as passionate as she had hoped; but she had not been prepared for the moments of delicacy, as exquisite as a feather turning as it is carried by the currents of air to the floor. When the moment of deepest pleasure came she found herself weeping at it, the moment when everything met in a place as tiny as the point of a feather's quill. Wept for the brevity of it, the torturous brevity of the deepest pleasure she had ever known.

But she also wept because she had been proved right. She knew now what she had been reaching for, with Ashton. But it was something that her husband could not understand and, even if he had understood, he would never have granted it to her. It was strange, she thought, how he had defined her. Even in another man's bed, her thoughts were full of Ashton.

Henry tried to wipe her tears away but she smiled and shook her head, and kissed him again, and held him close to her, the perspiration cooling on their skin. She tried to commit to memory the feeling of his skin beneath her hands. The line of muscle in his upper arms, and the coarseness of the dark hair on his chest. 'You know this cannot happen again,' she said to him.

'Be patient. We have managed it now, so why not in the future?'

She shook her head.

'Believe it, Charlotte.'

She said nothing. If he wished to dream, if it made him happy, then she would not seek to erode it. It was such a gift.

They held each other for a few moments, moments that seemed both long and short; and then she told him to go and fetch her maid. He put on his coat, which he had left on his chair, and went downstairs. She heard his little dog yapping in the distance, and then Katie came, and helped to dress her, her fingers nimble, not saying a word. They went downstairs again, and Charlotte saw the half-eaten cake and crumbs on the table, the madeira all gone and sweet on her maid's breath. She stood on her tiptoes and whispered in Henry's ear. 'I will not wash tonight. I will sleep with the scent of you on me.' And she kissed the side of his neck, and put her hood up over her bonnet, and was gone. Afterwards, he realized she had not worn her lily of the valley scent; there was no trace of her left behind, in the air.

He slept late the next day, and missed a committee meeting. When he came to the Club he looked for her letter on his desk, as he always did, but it was not there. He did not hear what his assistants asked of him, and they had to repeat themselves several times before they got an answer. His clerk of works asked what was wrong, and he said he thought he might be sickening. At the end of the day he threw his own letter to Charlotte into the fire, worried that someone might find it. He walked home from the Mirrormakers' Club to Russell Square, and there was no letter there either.

He wrote again, that evening, a more innocent and

straightforward letter which could be read by anyone without danger, but Katie did not come. He slept fitfully, and when he woke it was five in the morning, and he had slept with his fists clenched, so that his finger joints ached with it.

There was no letter the next day, and that evening he walked to the Kinsburg house to leave his card, to see if there might be someone at the window, looking for him, thinking that the maid might be sick, and had not managed to deliver. Whatever happened, he knew that he and Charlotte would find a way to communicate with each other. But the servant who answered the door said that Mrs Kinsburg had gone to the country, and that she was not expected to return for some time. The covers were being put on in the house. That she had left no message, and that she had said, distinctly, that she did not expect any callers, now or in the future.

He wrote strained letters after that, to Redlands. Odd, he knew, but respectable in their language. Asking her to come. Asking her to visit the Club. Strange letters, with words underlined so that she might see what was in his heart.

He received no answer.

CHAPTER THIRTY-FIVE

1941

<small>BASEMENT VAULTS, THE MIRRORMAKERS' CLUB</small>

'What's going on here?'

Jonathan stood, faintly flushed, in the doorway of the Document Room. He was dressed in a grey sweater and trousers, and the colour cast his gauntness into relief, painting the hollows beneath his cheeks with shadow.

He looked between them: Livy and Christian, seated alongside each other at the table in the yellow light, books and documents spread out before them. His mouth set in a hard line.

'Have you seen Peggy?' said Livy.

'No. Bill let me in. What are you doing?'

'Looking at the evidence,' said Christian. 'I've been doing some research in your absence.'

'What it has to do with you, I have no idea.' Jonathan looked at Christian's arm, resting along the back of Livy's chair. He put his hand to his pocket, and realized he had left his cigarettes upstairs when he had washed and changed.

'Thank you would be a more appropriate response,' said Christian. 'But never mind.'

'Henry's letters,' Livy said. 'There were words underlined. Do you remember?'

'And?'

'And I think he was trying to say something. Now you're here, we can open the trunk. I didn't want to do it without you.'

Jonathan felt obscurely touched by the gesture. In a moment, Livy scrambled up, and heaved the trunk open. No perfume now: the contents belonged to the Club's air, as if they had always been there. Henry's letters, where Jonathan had left them, newly tied in string, on the top. 'I'll say the words, you write them down,' she said, to Christian. To Jonathan's intense annoyance, he saw the man already had his notebook out.

My dear Mrs Kinsburg, <u>I am</u> late writing to thank you for your great hospitality. <u>Nothing</u> can excuse this – I am <u>without</u> any good reason. Other than the building work, which consumes me. I know <u>you</u> to have a generous heart. Forgive me.

But in the end he did not need to write anything, because as she said them out loud, they all made sense. Clear, precise, and with no code to break.

I am
Nothing
without
you.

'How conventional,' said Jonathan, and Livy thought she saw the beginnings of a sneer on his face.

She turned the next letter and began the process again; then the next, and the next.

Do you remember that day
One word
I beg you.

Livy's face was flushed as she stopped speaking. Her eyes were bright. 'It's so sad,' she murmured.

'Don't get overwrought,' said Jonathan. 'It just confirms what we thought – that there was a relationship.'

'And there are other mysteries too,' said Christian. He patted the leather-bound book on the table in front of him. 'This morning, I read the building committee minutes. And I found something in 1841. The Club had been opened. Dale-Collingwood was just stationed here to oversee the last details. He was the building surveyor, so kept an office here afterwards too.'

'You read several years' worth of minutes in one morning?'

'I can speed read, didn't you know?' he said. 'One of my many talents.'

He opened the book and pointed at a line of script, crossed through.

~~Miss de la Fointaine called at the Club to make a complaint about Mr Dale-Collingwood.~~

'I'm sorry, what?' said Jonathan. 'What does it say?'

~~Mr Dale-Collingwood was not present at this meeting of the committee, owing to an illness which had taken him to the country. Mr Kinsburg oversaw the questioning of Miss de la Fointaine and found her accusations to be utterly unfounded and malicious.~~

'Scoring through doesn't quite fulfil its purpose, does it?' said Christian. 'Draws the eye somewhat.'

'I haven't seen that name – Miss de la Fointaine – mentioned anywhere else,' said Livy. 'Do you have any idea who she was?'

'None whatsoever,' said Jonathan, frowning.

'And I hate to seem unbearably smug,' said Christian, 'but I found something else too. Livy told me that Dale-Collingwood's last notebook was missing. It's not. It's out of sequence. I found it in the box for the 1870s. Just having a rifle through.'

Jonathan glanced at Livy irritatedly. 'Why didn't *you* find that?'

She raised an eyebrow. 'We were concentrating on when the Club was built, if you recall.'

He looked back at Christian. The wretch still had his arm draped over the back of Livy's chair. 'What does it say?'

Christian leaned forwards, and opened an ivory leather-coloured notebook from the back. There were several folded pieces of paper there.

'See for yourself,' he said.

Jonathan glanced at Livy. 'Have you read them?'

'Yes. Christian just showed them to me.'

'Letters?'

'Drafts of letters.'

He took the first one and began to unfold it. As he did so, he saw Livy open the front of the notebook. For a moment, her finger traced over the writing there. The familiar inscription.

Henry Dale-Collingwood.
Architect and surveyor. 1841.

He turned his eyes to the handwriting. So often, Livy had read the letters out to him, so that it seemed strange to engage, man to man, with this person – this ghost.

My love, your last letter filled my mind and my
senses, so that it was not possible, not possible,
for me to continue talking of glass and marble

and gilded bronze, but I could only think of you,
of the light gilding your pale shoulder, of your
perfection, of that look in your eye. Half-amusement,
half-challenge.

I need your presence here, I need it. I need to hear
your voice, I need your hand to pour the wine into our
glasses, I need you, all of you.

Within the draft was a bill for a book: a volume of poetry by Tennyson.

Livy watched Jonathan steadily as he read the letter.

'I meant to say before,' she said. 'Is there any suggestion that Charlotte had a child by Henry?'

'What?' Jonathan looked irritated; more than irritated. He looked as though she were insulting him. 'No. Don't be ridiculous. This is not a sensation novel, Miss Baker.'

Livy looked at him, steely-eyed. And opened the last piece of paper.

Again, it was a draft of a letter, not stamped or sealed, so it had never been sent. It was written with a perfect hand, neat and controlled, from Henry Dale-Collingwood, dated September 1841, a full year after the others.

My dear Mr Kinsburg,
Please accept my sincerest condolences on the
death of your wife.

Mrs Kinsburg was an example of the perfection of
womanhood.

*I pray that she has found her place in heaven, for
she gave us all a glimpse of heaven on earth.*

It recalls to mind Proverbs:

*'Who can find a virtuous woman? for her price
is far above rubies. Strength and honour are her
clothing; and she shall rejoice in time to come.'*

Your obedient servant,

Henry Dale-Collingwood.

'It's so strange,' said Jonathan. 'I wonder – he mentions rubies – not a diamond.'

'Is that all you can say?' said Livy. He looked up, and saw light in her eyes, and he realized that it came from unshed tears.

'I suppose you want me to become sentimental,' he said. 'Like you. But I am not a fantasist. These people have been dead a long time. What matters is now.'

'How did Charlotte die?' It was Christian now. He had removed his arm from the chair, and was sitting forwards. Livy paced up and down, but turned to look at Jonathan when Christian asked the question.

'I don't know how.' Jonathan's voice was tight. 'An illness. That's what I've always been told. Ashton was grief-stricken, I believe, which explains why he did not keep her letters or papers.'

Just an absence, thought Livy: *just a space in the record.* 'You should have told me when she died, at the beginning. That she died in 1841.'

'What difference would it have made?' he said. 'You knew she was dead. Why does it matter when?'

Livy tried to keep her voice steady. 'Because she means something to me. I've returned to that picture, again and again.'

'Don't be ridiculous. It's just a painting.'

'No, it's *not*,' Livy said.

'Where was she buried?' Christian again. That calm, curious voice. Jonathan felt as though he itched all over: the irritation flooded over him.

'It's nothing to do with you,' he said. Christian shrugged.

'Where was she buried?' Livy spoke now. She had stopped pacing and was standing, shoulders back, staring at him. She had not changed from the day dress of the night before: she had washed her face, brushed her hair. The fuchsia dress was so vivid against her pale skin and dark hair. And in that moment she was the same vivid presence he had reached out for in the darkness. It won honesty from him.

'I don't know,' he said. 'There's no record of it. Ashton said she was buried in the church near to Redlands, but there is no record, no stone, and nothing in our private chapel, either.'

'So you think she's in the foundations?' Christian again.

Livy turned, and stared at Christian. Jonathan had not thought she could get any paler, but she did.

'I don't know,' he said.

'You think it's her, don't you?' Christian said. 'I can see it on your face.'

'Possibly. There's enough evidence. We should think about excavating the body.'

'We're leaving that coffin where it is. I've asked a clergyman to bless it. The scaffolding's going up as we speak. There are more urgent things to work on. And you won't be able to tell if it's her – she's just bones now.' Christian looked back at the table; at the papers and boxes.

'You don't understand.' Livy's voice was calm and clear. 'He wants to see if the diamond is there. Don't you?'

Silence fell. Jonathan patted his pocket again. No cigarettes. 'If you must know, yes,' he said. 'I want to see if the diamond is there.'

She had picked up the last letter written by Henry. She stared at it. 'You shouldn't be trusted with these,' she said. 'You're nothing but a grave-robber.'

'Don't be ridiculous.' He snatched the letter from her.

'And what about Charlotte?' She reached for the letter; he held it away from her, at arm's length.

'What about her?' He stared at her. His perfect face, bleached white with anger. 'I don't care about just another faithless woman and her sordid affairs.'

'That's enough.' Christian stood up, the chair legs scraping against the floor.

Jonathan turned to him with a sneer. 'I'm sorry? What?'

'You know what. Don't stand over her with that look on your face. I've had enough of your superiority. Take that look off your face and treat her with respect.'

'I've always treated her with respect.'

'No, you haven't.'

Jonathan glanced at Livy. His coolness disintegrated just a little. With astonishment, he saw Livy reach out, and place her hand briefly on Christian's chest.

'Please,' she said softly.

'Just stay out of it,' snapped Jonathan.

'No, old chap. Not possible, I'm afraid. Give that letter back to Livy. Or don't. I'm itching for an excuse to knock you down.'

Jonathan laughed. 'A knight in shining armour, are you?'

'I mean it.'

'For God's sake, Livy, why did you let him in here? Tell him to go.' But Livy's face was set, her eyes fixed on the floor.

Christian met his gaze, level and unwavering. 'She won't. And I've a perfect right to stay.'

It took effort for Jonathan to rouse his best commanding-officer sneer. 'And why is that, Taylor?'

Christian answered him with a smile that was almost seraphic in its quality.

'I'll tell you why, Whitewood. Because she's my wife.'

Jonathan stared at him. Even as he felt himself crumbling, he drew on every part of his coldness, that ice in the blood which he had inherited. Felt the strength of it in him: the Kinsburg backbone.

'You're welcome to her,' he said. 'She's keen enough, but no breeding.'

Livy turned and looked at him. He looked for the sense of betrayal in her eyes; he looked for some sense that he wounded her, in the way that she had wounded him, for he felt as though he had been hit with a cannon ball. As though he were bleeding inwardly, and that he would never be quite right again, his life force draining away. But he saw only, in her eyes, an anger to answer his own. She stood up, and walked towards him. It felt as though it took her minutes to get to him, but it was only moments.

She hit him so hard across the face that he felt the force in his neck, and, a moment later, the warmth of blood trickling from his nose.

CHAPTER THIRTY-SIX

1941

BASEMENT VAULTS, THE MIRRORMAKERS' CLUB

Peggy found Livy sitting with the painting of Charlotte, its wrappings pushed back. She stood over her silently, and reached out to touch her hair. 'There's still some glass there,' she said. She handed her a glass of brandy. 'There was a drop left from Christmas,' she said. 'Medicinal.'

Livy knocked it back. 'Has Christian gone?' she said.

'Yes. For today. He said to tell you he'd be back.'

'I should help with dinner,' said Livy.

Peggy put her hand on her shoulder. 'I suppose you should,' she said. 'But there's no need. It's just sandwiches tonight, and yesterday's soup, and Bill can say what he likes.' Carefully, Peggy eased herself down onto the floor beside Livy, complaining about her bones as she did so.

Livy rested her chin in her hands, and stared at Charlotte's face. 'Her skin is perfect,' she said. 'White, like moonlight. Does anyone really have skin that colour?'

'It's funny,' said Peggy. 'I never liked the painting much. She's a little too perfect, the lady. Miss Hardaker liked it for a long time. Years ago, she said the face reminded her of Mr Whitewood. Then she used to criticize it. Say the diamond was vulgar. There was a disappointment in her.'

Livy glanced sharply at her.

'Yes,' said Peggy. 'Mr Whitewood always did leave a trail of broken hearts behind him.'

Livy closed her eyes. 'Is he going to dig the coffin up?'

'He's talking about it. Bill's not convinced and neither is your Mr Taylor. I don't think they'll let him – they don't want things disturbed. The building is getting enough of a battering as it is. He can do it with his bare hands if he wants, but none of us will help him.'

Livy shook her head.

'He said a lot of wild things,' Peggy said cautiously. 'Is it true? Are you really married to Mr Taylor?'

Livy nodded.

'Why didn't he say anything?'

'He said he was trying to protect me.' She glanced at Peggy. 'We weren't even happy. We were separated. All that I remembered originally was that I worked with him in the architect's office of the LCC. I was in the typing pool. I remember I was happy then. Last night, I remembered the rest of it. It came back, Peggy. It came back in the darkness.

All of it, piece by piece. We were friends at first.' When she thought of the times she spent with Christian, she thought of them out in the open air, walking in the squares of London, pointing out architectural features to each other. He had taught her the names, and tested her.

Egg and dart. Vermiculation. Greek key pattern.

Did he remember that? she thought. Those same streets, onto which he now mapped the damage of war. Did he pause and say: there, we were happy? When he looked at them, did each street raise a memory in him, leaving its scratches and scars, as the façade of this great building was pitted and scarred?

'The thing between us grew – until it wasn't just friendship anymore. We were so happy, and it was so simple. He asked me to marry him. I wanted to carry on working, so we kept it a secret.' They lived in a little flat, one gas ring, one small speckled mirror, their sheets mended but clean. She hardly ever wore the slim nine-carat gold wedding ring.

'But you weren't with him when you worked here?' said Peggy.

Livy swallowed hard. 'No,' she said. 'I came here after we separated. I lost a baby. It was an early miscarriage. Five months, at most. But I blamed myself. For staying at work, for tiring myself too much. I was angry, you see. Angry that I had fallen pregnant. I wasn't ready. Everyone tells you it is what you're meant to do, but I wasn't ready. And then – when I lost the baby. It was early on – but. Suddenly, it was as though the world fell away from me. Christian was kind to me, but I could sense that I had wounded him, by not wanting the child.

Loving me, it was an effort for him, after that. It ruined things between us. I should have stayed. Waited. But I couldn't bear to be with him – to be with anyone. So I left, one day. I just left. I found a place in a lodging with other girls, on Woodville Street. And I applied for the job at the Club.

'I began again. And tried to be another person, instead. But the fight had gone out of me, somehow. I told myself: give yourself a year and a day. And I did. The day my lodgings were bombed, you remember, I said I had something to do?'

Peggy nodded.

'I was going to go to the LCC. I was going to see if I could find Christian. Speak to him again.' She wiped a tear away roughly. 'I just wanted to see his face.'

Leaving Christian.

When she had decided, it was all Livy could do to pack a bag with some clothes. She left the breakfast things on the table: a crust, and crumbs on a plate, and the tea cooling grey. A note, scrawled on the back of a bill. *I don't know when I will come back. I'm sorry.* She did it quickly, knowing that if she paused, and thought of her husband, she would never go. How unfair she had been, she thought later.

The day had that autumn light which poets and painters wait for, which seems divine in some way. It dipped the blue-grey streets of London in gold. She brought a paper, and telephoned a place at random. Her shadow was long on the pavement, as she walked. Woodville Street was the first place she saw, and she took it. A bedroom with a sink, and a shared bathroom, the upper floors dense with the scent of young women: perfume, and cigarette smoke.

She had put aside the sense she had of the past. She put aside the silence of the flat when Christian opened the door, and found her gone. These things were too unbearable to be thought of. She sat at the window of her new room, and smoked a cigarette, and one of her housemates – a literary girl – laughingly quoted poetry to her.

> *But most she loathed the hour*
> *When the thick-moted sunbeam lay*
> *Athwart the chambers, and the day*
> *Was sloping towards his western bower.*

Peggy put her hand over Livy's and squeezed. They sat there for a few minutes in the silence, looking at Charlotte Kinsburg's portrait. It seemed so far removed from the dust and damage of their lives. In the half-light, the face almost seemed to have agency; but it was an agency in her own world, a world of country houses and balls, which had been lost long ago.

'What about Mr Whitewood?' said Peggy.

Livy glanced at her. 'I did want him, Peggy. He made me feel. It was a basic thing.' She wanted to say: it was his beauty. It was the scent of him. But it had been something else, too. 'He was strong, and certain, but he was also weak. I thought I might help him, and he might help me. But I don't love him. And I don't want him now.'

She remembered the look on his face when he had spoken of excavating the body, and marvelled at how cleanly it had severed any feeling she had for him.

Peggy got to her feet. 'Come out when you're ready,' she said. 'Mr Whitewood said he would dine out this evening. Things will be all right, lovey.' She tried, but she could not keep the uncertainty from her voice, and Livy heard it.

'Go on without me,' she said. 'I'll be there soon.'

As Peggy walked away Livy sat, hugging her knees, lost in the past. But not Charlotte's past now: her own. When, eventually, she got to her feet, she went and found Bill and Peggy in the makeshift sitting room in the vault. As Peggy dished up the soup, Bill came to her, put his arms around her, and gave her a paternal squeeze.

'I've always wanted to clobber him,' he said.

That night, beneath burning skies, the Mirrormakers' Club sighed, and buried the hopes of Jonathan Whitewood. The floor of the News Room gave way, falling through the empty south-west corner of the building, and the reverberations concertinaed downwards. In the morning, peering at it, the workmen called it a slight collapse, though Livy wondered how a collapse could ever have been thought of as slight. In the bomb shelter, they had thought the building was coming down on top of them. But it was just some masonry, and then some earth, flooding the cavity.

It buried the skeleton all over again, but without the blessing that Christian had promised it.

CHAPTER THIRTY-SEVEN

1841

Henry stood in the darkness of the Surveyor's Room at the Mirrormakers' Club. It was a warm summer night, and the London heat felt like grime on his skin. One light illuminated his room: a small lamp, turned down low. Beyond, he could hear the sound of voices building in the Stair Hall. Many voices echoing off the marble, for the first time. Outside, the sound of carriages arriving, of people stepping onto the pavement, and looking up at what he had created. The great and good of London society: dukes, even a prince. Men, of course; no women. It was not a ball. It was a banquet. And he would be the toast of it. *Thank God,* he thought: *no dancing.*

He had already given a feast for the labourers, though it had been far less expensive than this, of course, and held in the new and pristine Servants' Hall. Those who had painted, plastered and gilded had been given bonuses, but the feast was a small gesture to the lowest paid, who had clawed the building's foundations out of the earth, and built it up again. And he was sure that none of them liked him, now; they thought him sharp of voice, high-handed, changeable, unreasonable. He had been guilty of all of these things over the past three years. Not from grief, but because such qualities were necessary in order to bring a building such as the Mirrormakers' Club to its completion. With each hitch in each task, though, he had found real anger to access. He did not regret showing it; he did not regret cursing, and shouting, and writing down in his large, heavy hand the icy rage that he felt. Had he been a superstitious man, he would have thought it likely that he left some of his anguish in the place, engrained in the stones of the building.

His men would remember it, but he knew some would remember other things too. He wagered Harry remembered lifting the Roman goddess out of the earth, and the joy they had all shared in seeing it, their eyes meeting beneath a blue sky with clouds racing above them. It did not soften the affectedly blank look Harry had worn at the feast. As the men looked around at the clean white spaces of the Servants' Hall, Henry knew they were thinking of the Dining Hall, where the glassmakers were still putting the chandeliers in place, and how they had built it, but could not eat there.

Henry went to that feast only for a few minutes. He had raised a glass with them, and seen them reflect back at him all that had happened. They spoke of leaving the building, the old girl as they called her, in her violent colours, glittering with glass and gilt, like a woman too made-up for the dance she had turned up for. 'After today,' Dylan said, as Harry was draining the dregs of his cup, 'we will never be let in here again. We will only be able to pass outside, on the street, and say "I did that".'

'My wife will never see my work,' said another. 'It's not likely she'll ever set foot in here. And for all that I've described it to her, it hardly does it justice.'

'Bring her here today, or tomorrow,' said Henry. 'She may see it.'

The men looked at him, and said nothing.

As everyone turned back to their meal, their voices growing louder in the afternoon light, tiredness overcame Henry, tiredness as potent as strong drink. 'I'll wish you good day,' he said, rising to his feet. No one turned to bid him farewell. He said it again, more loudly this time, and when no one turned again he realized that it was deliberate. Their work was done, they had been paid, and he was master no longer. In this small way, in this silence, they showed their contempt for him, and he felt his own anger rise towards them. *We have done this thing together,* he thought, and he felt it was a cold thing that they did. He had done his duty; he could not question himself further, or examine their lives further. *I have given you this feast*, he thought, when really it was the least he could have done. But he could not admit that to himself, not yet.

After he had gone, they drank a toast to him. They did not hate him, not really.

*

As he stood in the Surveyor's Room on opening night, he thought of the times he had heard his men shout across the rooms. Conveying information, their voices hard, sometimes urgent. Sometimes followed by a crash, sending him darting across the building. *I was this building's midwife,* he thought; *I was its nurse.* He remembered standing at the committee table in the lodge. He remembered unrolling his plans: first the ground plan, so functional, so handsome, so balanced. Then, the decorative plans, proof of his study of classical architecture, proof of his education and his worth. The other things, the things that meant something, were added towards the end: he had encrusted the building with them. But he would not think of that now. Beauty out of nothing, made by other men's hands, but drawn by him.

He only thought how young he had felt when the building had first been proposed, unrolling those plans on that old committee table, which now lay in splinters in some layer of London, or stood in some man's dining room. How he had placed small sandbag weights on each corner, and was proud to let the committee lean over the drawings and examine them. Content to stand back, and let them say their piece, knowing he could answer every question. He had felt so young then, so proud, so relaxed, his hands folded neatly before him – he fancied, yes he fancied, he had dressed better then, too, paid more heed to fashion, in a gentlemanly way. Had Ashton Kinsburg stood there, then? Henry closed his eyes, and frowned, and tried to remember, but he could not see Ashton; he did not know where the man had stood in that moment, and it pained him. He should be able to remember someone who had become so important to him.

Four years had passed from that moment to this. Nearly three years since a carriage accident had sent him blundering down from his cab onto uncertain ground. His house in Russell Square was finished, as finished as a house could be without a mistress: a showpiece for clients. It was no longer his childhood home, aired of all its ghosts.

Professionally, his practice had expanded, and he stood now in this grand building, that would, he hoped, outlast him. A building that he had imagined and calculated into existence and bought with many hours and the hours of his fellow creatures: hours that he had bullied, and bargained for, and cajoled, and asked, and paid for, and sometimes even stolen. And the gathering noise from the crush of people below was the peak of that journey. Below him, encased in marble, the gathering noise of approval – of self-congratulation and approval – oh, he could hear the notes of it, like a symphony. He had had trials and obstacles: clocks unmade, glass that had blown, arguments over silks, arguments over colour – colour, he hoped never to see red and blue and gold again – but he had triumphed, and what he had put on the page with his watercolours he had made into reality. His will alone. He had willed this building into being.

He waited for it: the sense of accomplishment. It would come, he had assured himself, Peregrine had assured him, it would come tonight. With the great and good waiting to see him, and the committee gathered and what passed for smiles on their reddened faces, and the best silver on the table, and the best port ready to be passed: it would come. The pain would fall away, and he would feel honest and unfettered pride.

He heard the first chime of six from the clock on the landing: the great mahogany clock, its case designed by him, made by the best clockmaker in London, hauled here on a cart from Bond Street and placed, and petted, and wound and adjusted as though it were some mythical creature that wanted teasing into life. He had seen the first sweep of the pendulum, the awakening of it, the measuring of time in this place: his time, his place. He stood, erect as he had as a young man, and he heard the chimes ease their way into life, definite, insistent, and he admitted that the pride had withered in him. He didn't know when it had died; if it had been sudden, or if it had been eroded. If it had crept away in the night like a club maid he had paid to fuck him, or if it had slammed the door when his workmen turned their backs on him. But it was gone, and the only time he could remember having it completely was on the day that he had unrolled his plans on the table at a committee meeting of the Mirrormakers' Club, and Ashton Kinsburg was nowhere in sight. The journey had been all; and this, his arrival, was nothing.

They would be waiting for him. He heard a whimper, and saw the shine of Polly's eyes where she lay beneath the table. He crouched down, and stroked her sleek head, then rose and adjusted his cravat. 'Stay there,' he said. And he went out of the Surveyor's Room, down the short corridor onto the north landing, softly and quickly down the first flight of stairs. And Polly, her head raised, heard the masculine voices rise and bubble, and then the great thunder of applause, of stamping feet, and the shout, 'The architect! The architect!'

To the porter's amusement, Henry slept at his desk, his head thick with port fumes, not trusting himself to even climb into a cab, or to accept another's carriage without belching or saying something untoward. He had gone further into the land of drunkenness than he ever had before, so far that he knew he was no longer in control of himself. The toasts had lasted so long – toasts to the queen, to the prince consort, to the royal family, to the committee – they had streamed long into the evening as the meat grew cold and the sauces congealed. His own toast was lost among the others, even as they were saluting him with the words inscribed on Sir Christopher Wren's tomb in St Paul's. *If you seek his monument look around you* he heard them pronounce, but they said it in their prep school Latin, all of those voices as bluff as his, rowdy as his, slurred as his: and he had stood upright, even if he had swayed as he took the toast and proposed the next. Who gave a damn, anyway? This was not a holy ceremony, the only god present was Bacchus, and he believed he had said the same to the fellow sitting next to him. All evening he had received compliments from the worthies with the same expression on his face: a smile he had constructed in the looking glass, earlier that day. He had even received Ashton's embrace, smelt the scent of his hair pomade, felt the man's hands on his wrists, and thought *thank God you do not smell of her – I could not have stomached that*. It was that which had made him empty every glass that was put in front of him, thinking even as he did so: *I have drunk much for a long time now. I am not the man I was.*

It was in the midst of sweet fumes that he left, as others were staggering to their carriages – and he slipped back through the low-lit passage to the Surveyor's Room, where he greeted Polly, sat down on his chair, and fell asleep with his head lying on his letters.

He woke suddenly in the depths of the night when Polly whimpered at him, and he opened the door so that the little dog could hurtle down the stairs to the porter below, with his lantern. Henry stood at the top of the stairs, in the marble Stair Hall, and watched her race, her large eyes using the little light there was from the demi-lunes and the moon.

'All right there, sir?' called the man. 'You were spark out when I came on my round: I was scared the light would wake you.'

'Let her out, will you?' called Henry. He felt the vastness of the space now, in the night, with it empty and the revellers all gone. The place already seemed to have its ghosts. He was glad when he saw Polly bounding up the steps again; he had felt curiously alone, waiting for her at the top of the stairs. They went back into his room, and he drank a jug of water which had sat on his desk all afternoon. He even put a splash of it into a discarded saucer, which had held his empty teacup. Polly lapped it up, then leapt onto his lap. He put her back down. The porter had closed the shutters during the evening, and he was sad for it. He wanted to look out at the London night, to see if there was any life on the streets at this time.

There was nothing to do but sleep again, to try and escape the dull pitch-and-roll of his port-filled head, and his parched tongue.

He did not dream of Charlotte: he never had. But he did, even tonight, dream his customary dream. It was of small strong hands, gripping his shoulders from behind. The hands were childlike but vastly strong, and they gripped him so suddenly that always he would panic in that first moment, until he said to himself: *it is a dream. Be calm, it is a dream: it will end.* He did not remember when first he had dreamt it, but it had not been long – a year or two. So childish, he thought, for a man to dream with such intensity.

Henry went to the porter's apartments the next day to wash and dress – he had learned to keep clothes in his office, and a small press had been provided for that purpose. The Club's director's room, and the members' rooms on the upper floors, had not yet been finished: that was for the coming weeks. But the housekeeper had her apartments and she cooked Henry scrambled eggs, before the porter brought him the day's newspapers. He turned to the art pages and the social pages and noticed, dully, that the reception had been reported respectfully. The building in the 'classical taste' was declared a triumph.

His assistant arrived at nine, bearing duplicate newspapers, his face falling when he saw that Henry already had them. 'Tomorrow's wrappings and rubbish,' Henry said, 'but if you could cut out each article, and paste them onto card, I will show them to the committee, and then they will be archived.'

'Did you stay the night here, sir?'

'Yes, I was perfectly happy here in my Hide.'

'Yes, sir. Oh, and you have an appointment, sir, at three.'

Henry frowned at him. Even that small movement made him feel nauseous. 'With whom?'

'A lady, connected to the committee. Mrs Kinsburg.'

Henry spun around. 'Not possible,' he said. His assistant looked at him, open-mouthed.

'You can take her around the public rooms,' said Henry. 'It doesn't need me, surely? I have the director's furnishings to attend to.'

'I think, sir, you will want to. I did not think—'

'You did not think it worth checking with me whether I have the time to take some fine lady around this place, talking of pretty things and furniture, and whether I can get her a scrap of fabric for her own chaise longue?'

'The director said you would not mind, he gave this, to give you, I—'

Henry snatched the envelope from his hand, and opened it. The letter was dated that morning.

*My dear Dale-Collingwood, forgive these few hurried
lines, I had intended to speak to you yesternight, but
events rather took precedence. Mr Kinsburg's wife
is in London and she wishes very much to attend the
Club and see it, having visited during its infancy.
Kinsburg fancied it would not be possible, and did not
trouble himself to make the arrangements, and he is
taken up with urgent business, and so she begged that
I would arrange it, and so please I ask you to make
yourself available at three this afternoon for a brief
time to show her the place, I know you will grant me
this small favour, yours etc.*

It was signed by the director of the Mirrormakers' Club, and
for good measure he had affixed the seal, the same seal which
had been used in conducting legal affairs for the business of
the build.

Henry looked at his pale assistant. 'Very well,' he said. He
patted the poor boy on the shoulder. 'I am sorry if I troubled
you, Charles. I drank a little too much port last night and I am
in a foul mood as a result. Will you take Polly to the kitchen,
and ask Sarah if she can find something for her to eat?'

CHAPTER THIRTY-EIGHT

1841

Henry let her wait. The porter came up to tell him that Mrs Kinsburg waited for him below, and he left her there. He wondered whether she would ask again, or whether she would remain standing beneath the dome decorated with the chequerboard pattern, with her eyes upturned, looking for him.

He had sent Charles off with Polly on some useless errand. He wanted neither of them seeing this. As he set off down the stairs, having waited long minutes, there was a moment when, on the wide staircase of white marble, carpeted in scarlet, he thought he might fall, he felt unsteady. He turned the corner, and paused on one of the flights, and there she was. The porter had left her alone. Just there, where he thought she would be: dead centre, looking up, her hands gloved, her gown of amethyst-coloured shot silk, which changed to pink when she moved, like a gemstone in the light. She looked different; of course she would, even his fervent memory could not be faithful to her. She looked smaller, paler, and thinner. Her skin was no longer the sheer white of girlish purity, but the dead white of inferior marble. He thought this with a sneer; he fancied it even affected the line of his mouth, and he stood a little straighter.

'Mrs Kinsburg,' he said, and bowed, two steps above her.

'Mr Dale-Collingwood.' Her voice was that low alto and it pierced him in a way that seeing her there had not. His sneer fell from him like broken armour. He did not want to hear that voice. It was a voice which turned back time. And it was her true voice; not that girlish concoction which she had used on that ball night long ago.

'It is an honour to welcome you here. But where is your maid? She should not feel intimidated, you know. She is welcome to view the Club too.'

She coloured. 'She is in my carriage. She feels unwell today.'

'But Katie was always such a strong girl.'

'It is not Katie. Not any longer.'

He paused, on the brink of further enquiry. Curiosity ravaged him, and he suddenly realized how thirsty he was for information of her. This past year repressed questions about her had run like lines of scripture behind his thoughts. 'Very well. Please, do follow me.' He did not offer her his arm. He did not dare to.

'I will not look up as we walk. The dome made me dizzy.' There was a hint of a smile on her face.

366

'It is an optical illusion. Very small, really; it looks much larger than it is.' He never told anyone this. Not a single person present on the opening night knew it. Apart from Ashton of course, who had consulted every detail of the plans.

'Oh.' She looked disappointed. She kept a yard between them, as they walked up the stairs.

'I am astonished you have found the time to visit the Club. I did not think you visited London anymore.'

'I had an appointment with a goldsmith. Do you remember the diamond?'

'I do not,' he lied. 'Forgive me. But look at this.' He made an expansive gesture as they reached the top of the stairs, towards the balustrade. 'These columns and pilasters are made of the finest scagliola, painted in imitation of marble, but the Stair Hall itself is clad in slabs of marble from European mines.' They stood alongside each other. She gripped the balustrade with her small kid-gloved hands, and looked over it. He kept his hands folded before him.

'I could climb over and jump,' she said. A faint smile played over her face. 'A height of this kind tempts one, in a strange way.'

'Don't do that.'

She looked at him. 'Would you care?'

He could not help the sneer again. 'I'd care about the distress you'd cause the porter. I'd care about the mess they would have to clean up. And what would we tell your husband?'

'Would it cause you distress?'

367

'I am beyond distress.'

Her smile broadened, but he saw its frozen quality, as deliberate as his own expression the night before. 'The Club has hardened you; you are battle-scarred, like an old soldier.' She moved away. 'Is this the Dining Hall?'

He could have taken her by the shoulders and shaken her. 'Yes.'

'My husband has told me to look carefully at the stained glass.'

He let her look; he took her compliments. He pointed out the chandeliers and their glass lustres: seventy-two candles in the central ones, forty-eight in each of the corner chandeliers. He had watched them flare the night before, the light transforming the room, and bringing it to life. And it had tortured him, seeing his creation live, while he felt so dead inside. He did not say that to her, of course. They moved through the public rooms, talking with the same forced, affected air. He sauntered, hands behind his back, but his eyes caught every detail of her hair, her face, her eyes. She removed her gloves, and he saw a new ring on her finger, the large red-domed stone, framed with diamonds, a gift from her husband he presumed. He did not point out the mirrors, the infinity he had designed.

They walked to the Red Parlour. 'Designed for the ladies,' he said, trying to keep the sarcasm out of his voice, 'in a more delicate, feminine style – French rococo.'

She looked around, as though some mistake had been made. 'But this is a copy.'

'Of your private salon at Redlands?' He walked ahead of her, so she could not see his face. He felt a mingled sense of triumph and desolation. 'Yes.'

'Did my husband order this?'

'No. He allowed me my head on this room.'

She frowned, openly puzzled, but he did not address it. Then she went to the window and looked out.

'So, you have seen the main rooms,' he said. 'The News Room is undergoing some final decoration. Don't allow me to keep you, Mrs Kinsburg. I'm sure you have many important affairs to attend to.'

She spoke without turning towards him. 'I'm not sure I've seen the real building at all. I'm sure it has many things you haven't shown me.'

'I've shown you the public rooms, the rooms which ladies wish to see.'

'Do you hate me, Henry?'

He could have struck her; his breath caught in his throat, and he suddenly felt the tension in his neck and shoulders, he was as stiff as a guard on parade. The truth fell from him without effort or judgement. 'Yes,' he said.

She turned and looked at him, unblinking. He saw her strength, he saw that he had not created it, and he hated it.

'You want to see the real building?' he said. And he seized her wrist and pulled her through the Red Parlour and out onto the north landing, talking all the time. He named the amount he paid for the excavators; how the Club was built on a plinth of granite from quarries in Derbyshire; of concealed lamps, and plasterwork. He took her through the back of the Dining Hall, through the kitchens, and he talked of the range, the stewing stoves, the boiler for vegetables, the fittings of the confectionary. He took her into one of the service lifts, and pulled the iron grille across. She followed him without a word, although he felt the weight of her as he dragged her, and it satisfied him. He was a gentle man, and yet, perversely, he hoped he was hurting her.

Out of the lift, he took her through a privy, to a small wooden door, which he unlocked and pulled her through. 'Keep your head down,' he said. She did, but struggled to fit her dress through, and he held her close to him and half-lifted her down.

He closed the door behind them, and released her wrist. They stood in near-darkness, in a passageway which stretched on around the perimeter of the building. Further down, light streamed through a glazed grille.

'What is this place?' she said.

'It's called the moat.'

She smiled, and looked around her. 'What is it for?'

'It's a passage dug to protect the building from damp,' he said impatiently. 'Did I hurt you?'

'What do you mean, Mr Dale-Collingwood? When, exactly?'

'Oh, for God's sake, Charlotte!' he cried. He turned, and rubbed his eyes. 'I didn't mean to hurt you. Your wrist. Dragging you down here.'

'You didn't hurt me,' she said, her voice soft and low.

The things he had wanted to say to her crowded in upon him. 'Was there a child?' he said. 'That has haunted me. The idea that there was a child.'

He saw her lips part, the shock in her eyes. 'Oh, Henry,' she said. 'No. There was no child.'

But I have felt its hands on my shoulders in my sleep, he thought. *I have felt the knowledge of it pulling me back.* Now that he knew it was his imagination only, he did not know whether to weep or be glad. His body sagged. They stood, listening to the sound of feet on the pavements above, and watching the way the light changed as people walked over the glazed grille. The moat smelt of earth, of damp and ruin.

'I have missed you,' he said. 'I have loved you all this time. And you have taken everything from me, even my pride.'

'Do not say such a thing,' she said. She did not take a step towards him, and yet he saw the sorrow in her face, and heard it in her voice. 'This is not you speaking, Henry. I know who you are. I know you to be strong, and good, and made, yes, *made*, to be content. I left to give you that, to allow you to be free of me, and to let you have a happy life. I came here today to celebrate your achievement, not to grieve you.'

'I don't believe that you know why you came here,' he said. 'I fancy it is to see whether you still have power over me. And now I have given you your answer.'

She shook her head. He turned away, and rubbed his eyes again, eyes that were red and sore.

'I did not think you would still feel things so deeply,' she said.

371

'Why? In God's name, after everything, why would you think that?'

'I have thought it for a long time. Ever since I left London,' she said. 'The day after I spent the evening with you, at your house, someone visited me, a maid called Foi. She was desperate. She had already visited the Club site, when the committee were meeting. You did not attend that day – you were unwell, I believe.'

He felt fear then, a terrible realization. 'I did not wish to be there. I slept late, that day. I did not wish to be with anyone – only to remember that night with you.'

'In any event, they had turned her away.'

He rubbed his eyes. He had seen Foi a handful of times after their night together. And she had always been the same: cheeky, but slightly distant. No hint of deeper thought or action. Then she had gone, to another post, he had been told.

'How did she find you? Or even know you?'

'Henry, dear, our servants know everything. Surely you've noticed that.' She said it sadly.

'What did she say to you?' he said. The words came out only with effort.

'That you had spent the night together. That you were kind to her. That she thought she might be expecting a child – no, do not worry, she did not have a child, not in the end. Of course, I was angry. I wept. But after she had gone, I sat, and thought, and I realized how unfair I was being.'

'No,' he said.

'I already knew that we could never be together. I saw then

that you already had a life, not the kind of half-life I lived, but a life with possibility, and action, and a hundred different characters within it. I saw that I was one small part of the richest of lives. And instead of causing you unhappiness, or poisoning it, I could just let you live it. I hoped you would understand. It was wrong of me, perhaps, not to leave a letter or an explanation, but I admit I was stung too. It was spiteful of me. I could justify it to myself a hundred times, but it was wrong.'

'It *was* wrong,' he said. 'If you had only trusted me, just a little – I wish I could have told you what that night with her was really about. I am sorry, so sorry, that you had to hear it from her. It seems impossible to explain now.'

'Then do not.'

'How could you have left, without a word?'

'I reasoned. It was the accident that brought us together, Henry. The accident – your grief. Without them, you would not have loved me. I kept your letters, though. I could not bring myself to destroy them.'

'And I yours. But now – I will give them back to you, if you will accept them.'

She gave a brief nod.

He leaned against the wall. They looked at each other, the only noise the footsteps above, the sound of the city's continuing life.

'Why did you bring me here?' she said, after some moments. When he looked back he saw that she was trying to smile. 'Is this your favourite part of the building? Some plain and useful part that you would like me to see?'

'No. I prefer the public rooms.'

'Oh.' He saw her mystification. It seemed to her, he saw, that they still did not know each other. That a thing she had thought was certain, was not: absence did that, allowing the lover to spin threads into the gaps, but one thread off meant that the picture was not perfect, always uncorrected, a small fault growing into a large misunderstanding or misrepresentation. 'And why do you like the public rooms so much? Is it the glitter, the splendour? Are you more gaudy than I thought, Mr Dale-Collingwood?'

He breathed the thin air in the earthy darkness. 'No. How little you know me, Mrs Kinsburg. You see nothing.'

She sighed. 'I am trying to be your friend. We were always friends, were we not? But if you wish to insult me, I must go. My carriage is waiting.'

'I like the public rooms because they remind me of you. The scagliola columns in the Stair Hall, for example: the blue is matched to the colour of your eyes, captured by my watercolours. The yellow colour, to the dress you wore on my first day at Redlands. To put it in more romantic language, for you, madam: this building is my tribute to you. My heart, and every mark you made upon it.'

He saw the shock on her face. 'But the design was set, long before you met me, I believed.'

'The basic design, yes, but I had freedom with the details. Great men on committees do not concern themselves with details – apart from your husband, of course. But I continued on. Did you see the central coat of arms, in the Dining Hall?

They allowed me some freedom with it. The motto ribbon is the shade of your bonnet ribbon, and billows just as your ribbon did, on the day we walked to The Birches. The flowers above the pier-glasses, either side, are those in your bouquet on the first day; the exact arrangement. And the graceful lady surmounting the frame – perhaps you noticed her?'

'I did not.'

'You and everyone else, it seems. Her face is yours, carved of gilt gesso. The craftsman did not quite capture you, I think, from my sketch, but still a trace of you is there. The lover's knots. Did you not see them? I expect the crowd to notice only the general effect, but you, when it is done for you, I thought you might see those knots. They are everywhere, Charlotte. The building is smothered in them. The faces in the Committee Room, gilded on a bronze ground, those faces—'

'The faces are half-turned away. You showed them to me, just now – I did not like them.'

'You did not look at them properly.' His frustration showed in his voice. 'Your son's face. Do you remember I sketched him? And the mottoes—'

'Henry—'

'There are many members of the Club who have coats of arms, you know. But I selected the mottoes which were used. Mostly they are chosen only for you. Do you know my favourite? *Ad finem spero.*'

'I don't know what that means, Henry. Ladies are not taught Latin. Surely you know that.' Her voice was higher, a little unsteady.

375

'You would have been a fine scholar. *I hope to the last.* Or I did, Charlotte. I did. You began all of this. And now,' he turned about him, in the dark corridor, the light level low, '*completur.* Surely you know what that means?' He looked at her face, stubborn, ungiving, in the shadows, and smiled sarcastically.

'I can guess.'

'Allow me to translate. *It is finished.*'

She stared at him. He felt something shift between them. For the first time, he saw anger in her face. 'Do you think you are the only one who has known suffering?' she said. 'Do you think I am so easily pinned down, like a butterfly with a pin through my heart? You are like Ashton. Creating a beautiful illusion. He chose me because he saw something other in me. He saw that I was strong, that there was something in me which he did not have, which he wanted to own – to pin down, as you have tried to do. But he has never truly owned me. And neither do you.'

The maid in Charlotte's carriage grumbled after ten minutes; moaned after half an hour, sticking her head out of the window to chide the driver; and was incandescent after an hour and a quarter. It was then that she went to the porter of the Mirrormakers' Club and asked what was keeping her mistress. But a preliminary search of the public rooms found no mistress, and no architect either.

'Don't worry, miss,' said the porter. 'It's a huge place, they'll be rattling around like two dried peas in a jar, but there's no way they've been lost. I'll turn the night-glass over and set off to look for them. If I'm not back by the time the sand's gone through, feel free to write to the director, and ask him to send a search party.' And he chuckled, and set off up the staircase, with Polly at his heels.

The housekeeper came forwards, smiling soothingly. 'Can I get you a cup of tea? Miss?'

'Fointaine. Miss de la Fointaine. And yes, you can.'

CHAPTER THIRTY-NINE

1941

Livy and Christian walked through the London streets. Past ruin and rubble, their coats buttoned up tight, Livy's hat on a slant, low over her eyes. Now and then Christian glanced at her profile and her long hair. Once, he touched a strand of it as it fluttered in the air, holding it just for a moment between the tip of his thumb and forefinger.

'Will you cut it, before you leave?'

'Yes.'

The letter from the Land Army was folded tight in her pocket. A farm in Bedfordshire, the following Wednesday.

They reached the station. 'You go on,' he said. 'I'll wait here.'

Peggy had told Livy the train Jonathan was catching. But even as she stepped into the station she half-believed she wouldn't find him; that it would be a relief to miss him.

She saw him on the concourse. In his coat and hat, holding his brown leather case, his gas mask in its carrier, over his shoulder. He was buying a newspaper. She ran down the steps, onto the concourse. Something stopped her from calling his name. Instead, she walked up behind him, and put her hand on his arm.

He turned, and his gaze was as cool as ever, as hard and impenetrable. She noted the small mark on his face, where she had caught him.

'Miss Baker,' he said.

'Mr Whitewood.' She lifted her chin, looked him in the eyes. 'I wanted to say goodbye. You've been avoiding me, I think.'

He looked at the newspaper in his hand, rolled it up tight. 'I thought it was for the best.'

'I'm sorry that we didn't find your diamond.' She meant it. She searched his face for any further clues or information, as though suddenly everything might be resolved. As though he could tell her what had happened to Charlotte.

Finally, he met her eyes properly. 'And I'm sorry, for saying such a vicious thing to you, that day,' he said. 'I was nettled, that's all. A little jealous, I admit. And I'm sorry if I hurt you in any way.' He too was searching for something in her face. 'But I don't think I did. I don't think I matter that much.'

She nodded. 'No.' She glanced behind her. At Christian, standing on the upper level, his hands holding the rail. She squeezed Jonathan's arm. 'Thank you,' she said. 'I hope we part as friends. I didn't want to leave things as they were.'

'We do,' he said. 'Good luck.'

'Oh,' she said. 'Good luck to you, too.' She smiled, nodded, and turned. He watched her walk away from him, threading her way through the people. She did not look back, but he waited there, until she was gone from his sight.

Livy and Christian walked to the South Bank side by side. Now and then she reached out, and took his hand. The County Hall sat long on the bank, faced by Portland stone like the Mirrormakers' Club. It hovered above the water, the rippling, dense green-brown of the Thames. The mint-green frames of its upper windows were the colour of weathered copper. Too many windows, she thought: remembering how in awe she had felt when she had first come here, feeling herself be swallowed up by city life. She put her hand on Christian's arm before they turned onto the waterfront.

'Will they let me in?'

He smiled that bright, youthful smile. 'Of course. They might even remember you. Oh – I meant to give this to you.' He took something from his pocket, and put it in her hand. It was her watch: the glass fixed. Livy lifted it to her ear, heard its gentle ticking. She kissed him on the cheek to thank him.

'Come on,' he said, a gruffness in his tone. But he waited for her to buckle the watch onto her wrist before he led her into the building.

First, he showed her the library of new materials they were compiling, the empty shelves ready to be filled with samples. He watched her calm down and adjust to being back there. On walking in, she had looked stricken, murmuring that the smell of the building was the same: antiseptic and wood polish.

He saw her gaze brighten as she looked at the samples, at the neat efficiency of the library. 'Once the war has been won, we will build a new London. We shall have a new city, nestling within the old. Bold statements. I have no idea if I'll be part of it. I'm still torn, you see. Between the old and the new: I don't know what to focus on. One must make a decision, and follow it completely, but I'm no good at that. I've only done it once.'

She looked at his hand; she did this all the time. His sleeve folded around the hand which had once worn a wedding ring.

He led her on, to a room like any other, but with its central space cleared of the usual office cabinets and desks. Instead there were large tables, over which were spread maps of the city. The one Livy stopped by was for the Metropolitan Borough of Paddington. She braced herself.

'You must remember,' he said. 'It's a tool, to help people. To help us find housing, to rebuild and renew, to make people's lives better. It's a memorial, to what everyone has suffered. We will use it to rebuild London, when the war is over.'

She stared at the bruised streets of her city, at the blocks marked with damage. The colours: shades of orange, yellow, green, purple, red. She remembered something, then: how much she had always loved London.

'What does the black mean? On the buildings?'

'Total destruction,' he said.

381

Each symbol, the symbol of something greater. Her mind juddered with it: ruined houses. The cries of the injured. The clouds of dust in the air. The terrible randomness of it. A house concertinaed to wood and rubble. A single survivor, standing outside, staring.

A fragment of red satin, fluttering in the breeze.

How had it happened in her lodgings? she wondered. Were the girls upstairs, preparing for an evening out, laughing? Painting their nails, and putting on stockings? Or had they taken shelter, under the kitchen table?

It was the former, she knew. Remembered Jenny's reckless laugh. *If I go, I go*, she had said. *At least I've had fun. It's just sex, Livy. You'll get over him. Have some fun.*

She remembered the loneliness of it: standing in the night air, staring at the house, the sky light from the dock fires.

She turned and looked at her husband.

'Are you all right?' he said.

She nodded. 'Are you?'

'Yes,' he said. He brushed her face with his hand. 'When I saw you again, that morning, after the Club was bombed, and you didn't remember anything. I thought I should probably let you go. But I found I couldn't.'

'I'm glad,' she said.

He looked into her eyes. 'I was changed, and so were you. I wondered if we could find our way back to each other. We are surrounded by so much force. So much violence. I wanted you to choose.'

She took his hand, and put her head against his shoulder.

Together, they looked down at the map. She was glad it was not her borough; glad that her eyes were not drawn, inexorably, to Woodville Street, to a small square coloured black.

'I suppose it's rather beautiful,' she said, 'for such a terrible thing. But I don't want to look at it anymore.'

'One more,' he said.

He showed her a map of a section of the City of London. So many black sites, but the Mirrormakers' Club coloured a light red. She felt obscurely proud of it, thinking of that night in December on the roof: their hours of labour, their camaraderie. She looked up and met his smile with one of her own.

'If we keep fighting,' he said, 'we win, sometimes.'

She nodded. It was a kind of assent to something. They were wary of speaking plainly to each other. They treated each other carefully, like tender and bruised things which needed time to heal.

'I've realized something about the Mirrormakers' Club,' he said, taking her arm, and leading her away, with a nod to one of his colleagues.

'Yes?'

'I think it was about her. Charlotte Kinsburg. I was blinded when I came to it – everywhere I looked, all I could see was *you*, and try and work out what you thought of it. But the truth is, the building was about love. Outside, for example – the configuration of the columns in the façade was meant to depict that of the temple of Mars Ultor in Rome, but he changed them, without permission as far as I can see – to those of the temple of Venus and Roma.

'I think he was memorializing something to do with Charlotte. That's my hunch. You said he drew flowers, tiny details like ribbons, children's faces. These things are taken from life. And I knew I'd seen the Red Parlour before. It's a replica, of one of the rooms at Redlands. When I was a patient there, my bed was in that room. It gave me a start, seeing it – I didn't recognize it at first. It just seemed nightmarish, in some distant way. Would she have seen that message?'

'Perhaps.'

'Perhaps, perhaps not. He was fevered with it. There is no unity to it, no resolution.' He nudged her. 'Like us.'

She looked at him sadly. 'Yes,' she said.

'I read through the building committee minutes, to see when the moat was changed,' he said. 'There's a small note about "a change" in the 1880s, but that's so long after everything we've been reading about. Oh – and – well, maybe you'll like this, maybe you won't – but the surveyor at that time was Dale-Collingwood's son.' Livy's eyes widened, and he nodded. 'Yes, Henry had a ward. He adopted him as his own child.'

And what of the child? she thought, remembering Henry's note. But she could not think anymore on it, she knew: otherwise she would spend her life trying to find out answers from the dead.

'I found something else in the building committee minutes,' he said. 'A note about *Woman and Looking Glass.* That they accepted it from Kinsburg, but that he gave it on condition that the plate on the frame bearing his wife's name was removed and that it was given a new name.'

Livy nodded. 'I didn't know her name was on it originally – but Jonathan had a letter, stating that it was to be known as *Woman and Looking Glass*.'

'And he specified that it hang on the far side of the Stair Hall, in a dark corner by the door leading to the basement. The minutes are polite, of course, but it was obviously most irregular.'

When she had returned to the Mirrormakers' Club, Livy went back to the Document Room, turned on her lamp, and fetched a box from the shelves: 1880–85. She took her place at the table. It was strange working there alone. She had the sense that Jonathan might walk in at any moment, or that Miss Hardaker might come and take her to task for some typing she had done.

Her eyes skimmed over various papers and bills. And then: another notebook, this one covered in ox-blood leather. She opened it, and started at the name.

James Dale-Collingwood. Surveyor.
The Mirrormakers' Club.

It was a harder hand than Henry's, the characters more laboured, more self-conscious in style. As she read through it, Livy sensed that every word was deliberate; there was no rush or hurry. But, she supposed, the Club had been built by then, and his job as surveyor was not so pressurized.

Her eyes caught the phrase.

... an irregular matter. In this I was commanded by Mr Kinsburg. As the financier of the building it was not in my power to refuse.

She glanced at the point marked in the minutes by Christian. *A small change in the moat structure was also approved at the recommendation of the surveyor.*

After she had put the boxes away, and exhausted her attention for the afternoon, Livy went to the storeroom to see the painting of Charlotte. She uncovered the face and looked at every detail. The painting seemed a quieter thing, now: the image did not thrill before her eyes, or pulsate like a heart on its last beat. Livy thought of the colours on the bomb map, and of the green hills of Bedfordshire where she would go and plough the land, and of Christian's brown eyes. 'Goodbye,' she said. Her voice sounded strange in the empty room. She leaned forwards, her face inches from Charlotte's, and then pulled the sheets back over the painting so their faces were separated by the white cloth. She wondered if she would ever look at that face again.

A moment later, the detonation.

The walls around her shifted sickeningly. She got to her feet, and found she was shaking. She ran out of the storeroom and into the area of the vaults where they had their living space. Peggy was standing there, frozen to the spot.

'Where's Bill?' Livy cried, her breath catching in her throat.

'He's gone out,' said Peggy. 'Maybe, if we just stay here—'

'We have to get out,' Livy shouted, and she ran forwards and took Peggy's hand, pulling her towards the stairs. They ran, and it felt as though they were running on the spot, on an ever-revolving staircase, until, finally, Livy reached forwards and pushed open the green door to the Stair Hall. A vast slab of coloured marble had fallen from the opposite wall. It lay at a diagonal over the door, a small margin of triangular space left at the side. Livy shuffled through the space, then held a hand out to Peggy. Peggy came through.

They did not look up. They ran towards the doorway to the Entrance Hall. A door that was already in flames, like the panelling of the room beyond. But there was only one thing to do, and that was to go forwards, hand in hand, to reach the door. So that is what they did: the simplest thing. As the building screamed and groaned above them, they ran, holding onto each other, until they found themselves in the midst of the light, and the fury, and the flames.

CHAPTER FORTY

1941

Redlands in the evening light was a benign place, its downstairs shutters shut tight against the approaching night. As Jonathan walked up the driveway, he caught the scent of cigarette smoke on the breeze, and saw a soldier smoking at an open window. He had sent no word. He wanted to happen upon the house like a stranger. Walking, taking it in slowly, he saw how strange it was, with its classical centre and its long wings. Ashton's son had added Gothic dressings to it, and it seemed a sad mish-mash, but grand still, and aloof.

He came through the front door, past nurses and patients, unacknowledged like a ghost. Up to his wing of the house, where he knocked on their sitting-room door. It had once been a guest bedroom, and he wondered for a moment whether Henry Dale-Collingwood had slept there, and looked out of its windows.

Stevie opened the door. 'Jonathan,' she said, as though he had been gone for hours rather than weeks. She kissed him on the cheek. 'You're in time for tea.'

She went and got the extra cup and saucer herself, and he asked her where the maid was. 'I sent her home this week,' she said. 'Her brother was killed in France.'

He sat down on the sofa with its faded floral textile, and looked around at the familiar room. A small fire was already burning in the grate with Stevie's old Labrador, Mitten, dozing before it. He looked at the same silver and enamel photograph frames containing pictures of them as a couple over many years. He felt himself sink into the sofa, and he watched with tenderness as Stevie poured tea into a white and gold cup. She was dressed in an emerald-coloured housecoat; the cut nipped in her waist and broadened her shoulders. He remembered it from before the war, and it gave her a certain glamour.

'Did you find what you were looking for, in London?' she said, in that same calm tone. Mitten got up and went to her, nosed at her hand, and settled at her feet.

Jonathan looked at her. He felt nothing so much as a desire to weep, which he pushed down.

'No,' he said.

'You should have telephoned more often,' she said. 'I heard every morning of the bombing of London, but nothing of you, apart from the occasional telephone call about that wretched diamond, and your note about Christmas.' Her eyes focused on him at last. 'It was cruel of you.'

'I am sorry.' He put his tea down, leaned forwards, and clasped his hands. His signet ring caught the light; she saw the sheen of white on the red carnelian. 'I am sorry, Stevie, I am so very sorry.'

'I suppose you had other things to think of, in London,' she said, as though to the room in general. 'Was it – Bunty?'

'Bunty?'

Then he realized: the couple he had dined with, their friends, Bunty and Edmund. And Stevie thought, that is, she implied—

'No!' he said.

She exhaled. 'That's a relief, at least. I couldn't have borne it, for her to triumph over me. She always wanted you, you know.'

Her openness alarmed him. She had never spoken of such things before. 'Please, Stevie, my dear. How are you?'

'Well enough. Not much energy. Dr Lamb is very good, and calls every day. But Jonathan – how are you?'

'I looked for more information on the diamond, in the archives of the Mirrormakers' Club.'

'Oh, that funny place,' she said. She had been there once. 'I still remember that dinner – when I had to wash my hands in the rosewater dish – they made such a fuss.'

'Yes.' He swallowed. 'There was a girl there.'

She looked at him again, her eyes sharpened. 'Please, Jonathan. Don't say any more. Everyone is allowed a *crise*, I think? And if we are truthful, I suppose you have not been right for some time.' She put her cup down carefully, and offered him a piece of bread and butter. 'I remember talking about marriage once, with one of our patients. A young soldier. He said he was ready to forgive his wife anything.' She flexed her hand. 'The occasional infidelity is only to be expected. We are all just human beings, after all.'

As Jonathan looked at her, her words sinking in, she seemed to change before his eyes, from victim to something else.

She saw the look on his face, and raised an eyebrow. 'Let sleeping dogs lie.' She smiled down at Mitten, who had risen and was wagging her tail. 'Not you, silly doggy.'

Jonathan picked up his cup, and stared into his tea, wretchedly.

'My poor Jonathan,' said Stevie. 'You are like a moth in the spider's web I saw one day in the glasshouse. One evening, we go to sleep, and our life is perfect. Then, in the night, you are caught, and you turn and thrash wildly and blindly, and when we wake our life is full of holes. When I had taken such care, to make sure things went well.'

He frowned. It was true: they had always got on so well together. It was so strange that something so small had tipped them off balance. Perhaps that was their problem: they had never cried, never fought, never had any differences. How perfect they had seemed, and yet it could be wrecked, just like that, their contentment nothing but a thin silken tissue, easily torn.

'Everything has always been about you, hasn't it, Jonathan?' she said.

He looked at her questioningly. She leaned forwards, and put her hand on his knee. 'But that's all right.'

'I missed you,' he said. He only realized how much with her sitting there in front of him. Looking at her now, he could still see a hint of the girl she had once been: that girl who had played tennis in white, careless of her brown muscled limbs and her freckled face, free from any kind of make-up, her face and her body shaped by the air and the sunshine. He remembered how he had adored everything about her: her physical strength, her ease and jollity, her good sense, without neurosis of any kind. Stevie saw his sudden watchfulness. Her mouth tilted upwards, with a knowing, dark humour.

'I remembered something else, after I sent you the letters,' she said. 'I think you'll be pleased.'

'My love?'

'I'd forgotten about it. When I was a bride, your mother took me aside and gave me the key to a small safe, in the wall of the lady's closet, behind the panelling. "The grey box", she called it. She said it had been handed down through the women of the family. Can you imagine? It was such a lark. I almost told you at the time, my darling. But she swore me to secrecy – and she was so fierce.'

'She always was rather fierce,' admitted Jonathan.

'Of course, she always said the house had to be kept the same – that it really was a kind of museum to the Kinsburgs, even the lady's closet, where I write my correspondence – and I have kept it the same, haven't I? That's why I turned my attention to the garden, and did not think of anything else other than preserving – that is what your mother said, "preserve, Stephanie, preserve!"'

'My poor Stevie.' He was puzzled. 'And you never said anything to me.'

'It hardly mattered.' She gazed at him. 'I had you. Then, at least – I had you. The house did not matter to me.'

'You still have me.'

'It seems so. However did I manage it?' She petted Mitten. 'The safe. I looked through it, of course. And the truth is, it is just a poor collection of things – rather pitiful. A few letters, yes, but other little things that make no sense. Knick-knacks and the like, which were collected by Charlotte's daughter – your grandmother – and kept. Poor old Isabel. She must have missed her mother a great deal. I put it away, and never really thought of it, until you rang. I looked again, of course, but it still made no sense to me. And there's nothing to do with the diamond.' She rose, with her customary grace, and walked into the next room. He knew that he was expected to follow her, and did so with a growing sense of anticipation. The next room was used as their bedroom, and a crude box he had never seen before lay on her table, so unlike the other refined objects of Redlands. Badly made, as though by an amateur, and dirty, with a grey wash of paint as thin as watercolour.

Stevie picked it up, opened it, and emptied the box out onto the bed. Newspaper clippings fluttered onto it, carried by musky-smelling letters, heavy and folded, yellow, large black handwriting, some beads and other small objects. A slight aroma: a little stale, but just detectable.

Lily of the valley.

CHAPTER FORTY-ONE

1841

REDLANDS

The evening began quietly enough for Ashton. His wife had just returned from London, arriving early enough in the day to order a good dinner, which he had enjoyed. Nicholas and Barbara were away with their daughter, and he had been relishing their absence and the serenity it provided, for his wife always understood when he wished to be left alone. After supper had been cleared, he had taken his place at his desk in the *salon bleu*, to look over some mineral samples he had recently acquired. He heard the door open and close behind him, and the shift of his wife's skirts as she walked across the room. But instead of going to sit in her usual chair, Charlotte came to his side, and stood there until he looked up at her.

When he did, she put a leather-covered box down on the

desk in front of him. He recognized it, and looked at her questioningly.

'I thought you had better put it in the safe,' she said.

He couldn't help it; he flicked open the box to look at the diamond. Just to see, for a moment, the light shift and quiver in its depths as it lay on its blue velvet bedding. 'What did the goldsmith say?' he murmured, as he looked at it.

'We couldn't agree on the correct setting for the tiara.' She turned to the footman. 'Michael, would you leave us, please? And send Miss de la Fontaine in. She is waiting outside.'

Ashton shut the box, and looked at her properly then. He saw that she had changed her dress. 'My dear?' he said. The footman had gone, and in came her new maid, her face set, carrying a bonnet and a cloak, and wearing her own.

Something softened in his wife's face as she looked at his puzzled expression. She pulled a small upholstered stool over and sat opposite him, in the pool of candlelight. She took his hands. And she began to speak. She spoke in a low voice, soothing, and all on one note, as though she were telling a story to one of their children. She said that her trunk was packed. She said that she was leaving Redlands, and that she planned never to return. She said that she was unhappy, that she had been unhappy for a long time, and that she wished to go.

'I will go tonight,' she said. 'I thought about not telling you, but that seemed unfair.'

He could not speak; he only shook his head.

She agreed to sever any claim: to Redlands, to his fortune,

to his children. To separate, and to disappear – as much as one could, in the modern world.

'Send the maid away,' he said. 'I will not speak in front of her.'

But she put her hand out, and motioned for the girl to stay.

'Why will you not speak to me alone?' he said.

She stared at the closed box, which held the diamond. 'Because I am a little afraid of you,' she said.

'Do not talk of leaving. It is a ridiculous thing. I will never agree to it.'

'I have taken a lover,' she said. And all at once, the world changed. He saw that she saw it, in his face.

'So you see,' she said. 'You can divorce me. I know there will be a scandal. I know it will be expensive. But they will blame me. You can begin again.'

'No.'

It was a comfort, to see the surprise on her delicate face. He stared at her gown. She was dressed in that purple shot silk, so different from the hard bright colours he loved. Why had he ever had her painted in black, with that strange look on her face? But in the end, she had just been a setting for a diamond. When it had been added to the portrait, it had shone out so brightly from the painting that it rivalled Charlotte's face and eyes, claiming every viewer.

As he stared at the pale oval of his wife's face, the thoughts raced through Ashton's mind, chief among them the fact that he had already lost her, perhaps long ago. He stared at the subtle change of colours in the gown, and wondered when she had ordered it – wondered how, in degrees, he had lost her without even noticing it.

'No divorce,' he said. 'How can you even suggest it? To have our names dragged into parliament? Our marriage mocked, and gossiped about?'

She let go of his hands, and rose to her feet, the layers of her gown sighing into place. 'I will go,' she said. 'I will not come back. As long as my father and brothers live, they will not allow me to starve.'

'You are mad.' He tried to stand, and found his legs did not work. He fought to find words. She began to walk away.

'You have always been a burden to me,' he said, as she walked into the half-shadow, and took her bonnet from her maid.

She placed it on her head. Tied the ribbon below her chin. 'And you to me,' she said.

'Charlotte,' he said, as the door closed behind her. 'Charlotte.' He reached out to her, his hand grasping the darkness. He had never really known her, never understood her. But she was a burden he wanted.

He stayed, sitting at that desk. He did not raise the alarm. He toured the house that night, with his servant, as though nothing had happened. As though a trunk had not been packed into a hired carriage and set off at a pace into the night.

Alone in his room, he had vomited. Crawled onto his bed, where he lay without undressing. Where he spent the night shivering, as though in a fever. Shivering, and thinking.

At dawn, he rang for fresh water, and fresh clothes. He sent the house scrambling into action. A fire was lit in the *salon bleu*; he came down. It was best to face the scene of betrayal, he thought: *face it now, and you never need worry about it again.* He set to work with ink and paper. A letter to his lawyer was the first that was sealed and sent; the second was to Nicholas.

He would create his own truth. Let the gossips whisper. The image would be so complete that they would be silenced, sooner or later. In a day or so he would address the servants. But he must straighten the details in his mind first.

He opened his drawer, drew out his journal, straightened his writing implements, and dipped his pen.

Then he began to write.

The death of my wife, in August 1841, was most regrettable.

CHAPTER FORTY-TWO

1941

Dear Mrs Taylor, Livy,

    I hope this letter reaches you. I did try to telephone but the line is down, and I am going away, with my wife, to Scotland.

    I am writing because I discovered something, and I know you would want to know it. A small cache of love letters, from Charlotte to Henry Dale-Collingwood, had been kept with some other mementoes of her by her daughter, and passed down through the family.

    Whether Charlotte asked for them back, or whether Dale-Collingwood sent them back of his own volition, I do not know.

    They are passionate letters. They prove beyond doubt that the pair were lovers.

There were newspaper clippings telling of Charlotte's death. That she suffered a swift decline and died here, at Redlands, and that there was no public funeral, but that she had been buried privately here. But, as I told you, there is no stone for her here, and no record of her burial.

The other things I can make no sense of. There is a carte de visite *for a Miss Emily Granger – neither I nor my wife have ever heard of such a name; a paper fan, with a child's drawings on; and a bracelet of blue stones – Stevie says they are lapis lazuli. They do not resolve the mystery. Nothing about a diamond. And – I almost forgot – a riddle, in Ashton's handwriting, which I write down here, as I know you will wish to know it.*

My love lies in a gilded cage
A jewel box built for her apart
The proof lies heavy on my chest
Turned on the tablet of my heart.

I am dreadful at riddles, being rather a straightforward man, and my wife says it seems Ashton was rather dreadful at them too. It is rather a horrible thing, do you not think? Of course, there is the idea of the jewel box. It does not matter now. My wife has decided that the diamond does not matter, and I follow her good sense in everything.

I write partly to recompense you – to tell of what I have found, because I know you will want to know – because I should never have so entangled you in it all. My wife has told me how wrong I have been, how it has all been a kind of madness. I write also to apologize to you, for any confusion or damage which I caused you. I should have said sorry a hundred times to you for all that happened.

I wish you much happiness in the future.

Yours,

Jonathan Whitewood.

CHAPTER FORTY-THREE

1884

On a cold night in February 1884, eight men gathered at a suburban graveyard. They had two lanterns between them, which was agreed to be a paltry amount of light.

'Bit creepy, this.'

'I'm not sure about it.'

'Fuck off then, I'll have your share.'

It was amazing what money could buy.

The roses on the grave had only just started to turn. There was no stone, nor was there expected to be, Miss Granger had said. She had given the location exactly. The fresh grave, on row seven, between the Elton grave and the Hunter grave.

Their lanterns on the ground, the men began to dig.

*

Ashton Kinsburg was not at the graveside. He waited in a carriage at the perimeter of the graveyard. He huddled into the leather seat, his eyes on the pinpoints of the light he could see from the window. He was in evening dress from a ball he had attended, his fur-trimmed cloak pulled up around his shoulders, his top hat on. Alone.

The carriage door was pulled roughly open. His steward, Watson, got in. 'Shouldn't be too long,' he said. 'The transport is already at the west gate.'

'It is definitely her, isn't it?' said Ashton. He had asked the same question six times that evening.

Watson sighed. He often thought he was paid well, but not well enough. 'Yes, Mr Kinsburg,' he said. *You wretched old man*, he added silently.

One of the digging party fled into the night, claiming that it was godless work. They all knew that already, so the rest continued, slightly gleeful at the thought of keeping his share. Still, they swore at each other extravagantly, the number of curses increasing the lower they got.

The coffin was not too far down. It was difficult to lift the thing out, but the men were strong, fearless and muddy, three of them scrambling down into the grave.

'There's one below.'

'It's the top one we want.'

Foi had been buried below, eleven years before.

Once it had been heaved out, six men raised the coffin onto their shoulders, and carried it – haphazardly, it had to be admitted, and with less dignity than it deserved – to the hearse carriage waiting at the west gate, its panels veiled.

One man stayed behind, to fill in the grave again.

It was past one when the hearse carriage, followed by another, pulled up at the back of the Mirrormakers' Club. There was no one in residence apart from the housekeeper and porter, and Ashton had told them he would not return until late. As director, the ceremonial head of the Club, and still its main financier, he had lodgings at the top of the building. The building had been the centre of his life for over forty years.

As the coffin was unloaded in the narrow lane, beneath the windows of the Dining Hall, the double doors swung open and cast a dim square of light. Climbing down from the carriage, Ashton saw with relief the features of James Dale-Collingwood, the company surveyor. An adopted son, whom Henry had claimed to be a distant cousin, he nevertheless looked so similar to Henry that Ashton presumed him to be a by-blow. Sometimes Ashton caught the similarity with a sharpness that drew him up; even more so now that Henry was in the ground himself.

Tonight, James looked as though he would rather be anywhere else than here. He said nothing; having opened the doors, he stood aside, and let the coffin pass.

'Thank you,' said Ashton. He leaned on his stick. His breath was a little short.

'You know the way,' said James, without ceremony. 'I have left the moat door open, and you may direct things. I have had the niche prepared. Once it is placed inside, come out, lock the door, and give me the key. I will arrange for it to be bricked up, as agreed. It is,' he murmured sullenly, the scent of brandy on his breath, 'most irregular.'

'You have been paid well enough,' said Ashton.

It had been his motto.

They achieved it. The coffin was placed. Ashton sent the men away, grumbling, through the dark tunnel. He directed Watson to go with them, to settle up, and to threaten them satisfactorily, so they would remain silent.

He stood with one lantern, staring at it. He had not so much as touched the coffin.

'Goodbye, Charlotte,' he said. But despite his expectations, the words sounded stilted, and false. He had expected so much: a surge of feeling, perhaps, a sense even of vengeance followed by peace. But he felt the same as he always had, as he had since that evening she had come silently into the *salon bleu* at Redlands, her maid beside her.

He had not really believed her. His plan to announce her death was a kind of reflex, a striking out, an immediate revenge. He did not believe she had gone for good. But she had, and only through agents and lawyers did he learn of her after that. She had not a single penny from him; he ached for the day when she would return and beg for his money, for his mercy. He was a disciplined man, but there were still days when he was possessed by it: when he spent hours locked in a one-sided conversation with his absent wife.

As the weeks passed, then months, he had done everything he could to convince the world she was dead. How far he had succeeded, he wasn't sure, even now. He did not wish to marry again. But always, her empty room haunted him. He had missed her. The shadows between their profiles as they lay, face-to-face, in the bed. The vision of her, her dark hair spread over the pillow, the diamond lying just above her head. She had looked like an angel.

He had wanted to ask them to open the coffin, so that he could see the old woman she had become, but he knew they would refuse.

After a year or so, he had sent agents to look for her. They found her, living without her jewels and rich dresses, with one servant, in a suburban villa, under an assumed name. An annuity from her father kept her barely comfortable. He knew that much. Now and then, he employed an agent to check on her, to check that she was still at the same address. What he really wanted was proof of her unhappiness. But he had never sought it. Because he knew that if he found the opposite, he could not have borne it. Once, his agent had mentioned how a man had come to visit her: coyly, his face monitoring Ashton's expression. Every week, the same man, carrying a gift; he had seen them through the window, their heads together, talking, laughing. But what the agent had seen in Ashton's face had obviously frightened him, because he had never mentioned it again.

Once, at a dinner at the Mirrormakers' Club, Ashton had sought out the painting which he had given to be hung there.

Gone to its dark shadows to look at her face again, now only described as a 'woman', not even a 'lady'. A beautiful face, for every man's delectation. He could hear the banquet in full swing above him, the roar and babble of men eating and drinking. And he had thrown a full glass of white wine into her face.

But there she was still, poised in dry amusement, even as the rivulets of wine ran down her face. He had always disliked that expression. The black dress. The diamond she had never liked.

This building towered above him, already full of memories, and gathered whispers, whispers which strengthened in his mind. He felt sure people knew, and spoke of him, said things of him: this wealthy collector, who had made the Mirrormakers' Club his life, after his wife's death.

This place had meant everything to him. Looking at the carvings, at the coloured marble walls, at its grandeur, gave him a feeling close to happiness.

And yet Miss Granger, on her last visit, to tell him of Charlotte's death – Charlotte had never known her last companion was a spy – had mentioned, in passing, in that over-refined, sing-song voice of hers:

'She said the architect built it for her, you know. The Mirrormakers' Club. Everything in it referred to her in some way.'

Of course, the wretched woman was not to know. She had cared for Charlotte only during her last six months. The words had spread like an ink blot in Ashton's mind. Who was that man his agent had described; the weekly visits, the talking, the laughing?

It was Henry, he thought.

And Henry had a ward who looked like him. Who stood outside, even now, waiting to wall up this coffin. His voice, familiar in some terrible way. Could Charlotte have borne a child, in her exile? A child adopted by its natural father?

'No,' he said, to the cold and damp darkness. He stared at the coffin in its niche. He clutched the key in his hand. Ashton thought of his own son. Thomas had been a sad disappointment: spending money wildly, refusing to make a suitable marriage. How many times had Thomas asked him about that diamond, when Ashton knew all the boy really cared about was the money it was worth? His mouth set in a hard line when he thought about the steps he had taken to keep the gemstone safe from his children. He was determined that, even after he was gone, they would search for it in vain: in his papers they would find only gaps, riddles and misdirection.

For Ashton's daughter was also a disappointment to him. Isabel was the same as her mother: disobedient, secretive, hiding things from him. Once, he had caught her, turning over an unfamiliar bead necklace in her hand, and as she turned, surprised, she looked so much like Charlotte he had wanted to strike her. He had never been able to erase Charlotte from her mind, even as he had instructed everyone not to speak of her, and destroyed any trace of her in his papers. Isabel remembered, he knew. She knew it was her mother in the painting; she remembered the scent of her. She would hand the knowledge down: in whispers, in things said between sips of tea. The power women had, he knew, was in never forgetting.

He realized then that this great effort he had gone to had brought him no peace. That what he wanted was not Charlotte's corpse in a box, buried where he wished. He wanted her to rise again. To stand before him in their rooms at Redlands. To wake from the last forty years, as though it had been a terrible dream.

Leaning against the wall, James Dale-Collingwood looked wretchedly at Watson. 'He's taking for ever,' he said. 'Can you not get him to move along?' He drummed his fingertips against the wall. 'It doesn't sit well with me,' he said. 'My father died last year. If I had even an inkling that his body was moved, I would bring the sky down on that person's head.'

'He has the money,' said Watson sharply. 'He can do what he wants.'

'Whatever you say,' muttered Dale-Collingwood.

But he did take too long. So, at length, Watson opened the door, and dipped his head into the darkness of the moat for a moment, before he closed it again. 'Oh, dear,' he said.

'What?' said the surveyor.

'I believe the old man's crying.'

Above in the Club the picture hung, newly conserved and cleaned. She reached out to observers with her steady gaze, the outward expression of a mind unfettered and uncontained.

Through time, she would continue to say it, again and again, with her eyes. As she had tried to say it to her husband, as he stood behind the painter, looking critically on. *I was never yours. I belong only to me. Do you see, really see, me now?*

EPILOGUE

1966

THE STAIR HALL, THE MIRRORMAKERS' CLUB

It was so strange, coming back to The Mirrormakers' Club.

They were late to the party – a reunion for old staff – and their lateness made Livy even more nervous. She and her husband lived in the country – *once a land girl, always a land girl!* as they said so cheerfully – and the clamour of the city felt foreign, long-forgotten. No longer was the building she looked for a lone survivor among bomb sites. She had told herself it would seem smaller, drained of its power in the modern city, with the Barbican estate rising just a few moments' walk away. It would seem unfamiliar and strange to her.

But she was wrong. It was utterly familiar, as though it had waited at the back of her mind all this time, bedded into the layers of her memory, to be raised whole and complete

411

in every detail. She stared at it as one would at the ghost of a loved one or a darkest enemy. The years fell away, and she was young again.

She had peeled off her white gloves in the heat, and her husband held her hand, as London continued around them in its obliviousness. The Club stood in the twilight, a spectre from another time, faced with pale Portland stone and set on a plinth of storm-coloured granite. Above each of the upper-storey windows were decorations darkened by pollution: overflowing cornucopia, a flaming torch crossed with a sheaf of arrows – the trophies of a former age, their messages meaningless to an age of concrete and glass. Its large windows were bright with electric light.

They crossed the road, and went closer still. Livy walked up to it: put her hand to the wall. The building towered above her. Closer, she saw its scars; stared up its flank, pitted and blackened in patches. It bore its imperfections triumphantly, as though they were of no consequence. She saw no broken windows, no fluttering drapes, no signs of major damage. Its bruises sympathetically restored, it stood as firm as a fortress. The front doors were thrown open and from its entrance came the sound of laughter and voices echoing off the marble-clad walls of the Stair Hall.

'Are you sure you want to go in?' her husband said.

'Yes.'

There was no Bill. No Peggy. She looked for them, but saw only unfamiliar faces. So much had changed in the meantime – whole lives been lived, children been born, but the interior was uncannily the same: perfectly restored after the bombing, even the Entrance Hall with its panelling. She remembered how she and Peggy had emerged from the fire, gasping, into the London air, astonished to be alive. There was the same dome, spinning away from her. And *Woman and Looking Glass*, reinstated to its pre-war position, so that she exclaimed out loud, her breath catching on a sob, and her husband seized a glass of wine from a passing tray and put it gently in her hand.

As she drank it, she looked around. No Jonathan. And she hadn't thought of him for years; could barely remember his face. They had gone to Redlands, once. The house thrown open to visitors, a museum of a lost world. No sign of the family. The land rolled on for ever. She hadn't known how responsible Jonathan must have felt for it all, how vast and rich it was, how ungovernable. She and her husband and children had picnicked on the front lawn.

Her eyes focused on the painting as she took her last mouthful of wine, and her husband took the glass to find a refill. *How we lived through that time, I do not know. You and I, Charlotte, how we survived.* How strange: it was just a painting now. Familiar, yes, but not freighted with that intensity which she remembered.

'Very fine painting. I've always liked it.' She turned to see a man she did not recognize. He introduced himself as the current director of the Club, and Livy put her white gloves on again, to shake his hand. He wore a ceremonial jewelled badge tied on a ribbon round his neck.

'That's a beautiful thing,' she said, the drink giving her courage. 'I don't remember seeing it before. I was here in the 1940s.'

'It was put away with the treasures during the war, so I'm told,' the man said. 'It's Victorian, and was designed by some past director. It has a crystal behind the coat of arms. I have no idea why. He was rather a strange chap.' He pulled a face. 'Eccentric. It makes it so heavy.' Laughing, he flipped it over, and back again. And she stared at it, this irregular, pear-shaped crystal.

'Can I see it again?' she said. And the second glance confirmed it as much as a glance ever could. 'You should have it valued,' she said. 'As a piece of jewellery. It looks like a diamond to me.' She was amazed at how calm she felt, saying the words.

'I don't think so.' His face was still jovial, but doubtful.

They talked over other things, until, laughing, the director moved on. And Livy closed her eyes for a moment. It made sense, she supposed, that Ashton should put the diamond into something related to the Club. The place which had been the centre of his life after Charlotte's departure. *The proof lies heavy on my chest.* The Kinsburg Diamond. How hard it must be, she thought, to think you are powerful, and yet have the one thing you want always slip through your fingers. But though she pitied him, she could not forgive him leaving the fake stone for his descendants to find, sending the echo of that bitter disappointment and disillusionment down the generations. Had he really wanted his children, or his children's children, to feel the shock of that fall in the heart, as he had? She thought of Jonathan, of his struggles, and she thought she might weep.

'Here you are.' It was her husband, bearing more wine, his face bright and slightly flushed. 'How are you feeling?'

'Well, thank you.'

'You put so much more feeling into your thanks when I bring you wine.'

She laughed. 'You should have some too.'

'Don't you worry about that, I certainly will.'

'Odd, isn't it?'

'Beyond odd.'

'And to see the painting.'

'What does it feel like, being here?' She saw the concern in his face, the slightest hint of insecurity. 'Any ghosts?'

'No.' She turned away from the painting, towards the growing party, voices rising cheerfully in the echoing marble hall. A grand building: a place built for dining, and celebration; a place built to outlast generations. 'No ghosts at all.'

And at those words of reassurance Christian Taylor smiled, and kissed her on the forehead.

AUTHOR'S NOTE

The Mirrormakers' Club is a fictional club. The first gentlemen's club in the City of London was the City of London Club, founded in 1832, and designed by architect Philip Hardwick, who also built the nearby Goldsmiths' Hall (1829–35). Hardwick's correspondence in the Goldsmiths' Company's archives was of immense value when creating Henry Dale-Collingwood. To Hardwick, Henry also owes his house in Russell Square.

In appearance, the Kinsburg Diamond is based on the Beau Sancy diamond.

For Livy's amnesia and associated fugue states I am indebted to Daniel L. Schacter's book *Searching For Memory.*

The records of the Architect's Department of London County Council, held at the London Metropolitan Archives, were central to my research, as were the works of many fine authors and historians of the Second World War. All errors are my own. I am particularly indebted to *The London County Council Bomb Damage Maps, 1939–1945* edited by Laurence Ward, and *Recording Ruin* by A. S. G. Butler. I am also indebted to the witness account of the Second Great Fire of London recorded in the Goldsmiths' Company court minutes of 1940. The PhD of Bethan Bide (*Austerity Fashion 1945–1951*) meant that Livy was clothed in colour rather than the drab clothes I had originally pictured her in.

The two main firewatchers in the book are affectionately named for Barry Thomas and Louie Robinson. I hope they both enjoy seeing their names in print.

ACKNOWLEDGEMENTS

I am grateful for the dedication of my editor, Joanne Dickinson at Simon & Schuster, whose guidance and advice greatly improved this book. My thanks to editorial assistant Alice Rodgers, publicist Jess Barratt, copy editor Susan Opie and proofreader Clare Hubbard.

Gratitude as always to my wonderful agent Jane Finigan, and to the fantastic team at Lutyens & Rubinstein, especially Juliet Mahony, Fran Davies and Hana Grisenthwaite.

I am indebted to the staff of the London Library and the London Metropolitan Archives for their assistance. Nigel Israel alerted me to the existence of the City of London Club, for which I am truly grateful.

Grateful thanks to my colleagues at the Goldsmiths' Company, including (but not limited to) faithful book-buyers Chan Allen, David Beasley, Eleni Bide, Caitlin Brannan, Clare Breen, Ciorsdan Brown, Mairi Dunn, Jake Emmett,

Teresa Hassett, Liane Owen, Deborah Roberts and Stephanie Souroujon.

For their moral support, and so much more besides, I am grateful to: Lucy Adams, Sophie Carp, Emily Kidson, Sian Robinson, Gill Sampson, Ruth Seward, Amanda Wright and Samantha Woodward.

During the writing process Kate Mayfield talked me off many a literary ledge and I am immensely grateful to her. I am also indebted to Sophie Hardach, Jason Hewitt, Antonia Hodgson and Mel Backe-Hansen who were supportive of the book. Thanks also to the many other writers who have offered camaraderie and friendship.

I am grateful to my family, near and far, including my sister Angela and her family. As always, my love and thanks to my parents, my sister Lisa and her sons Samuel and Harrison for their steadfast faith and affection.

My husband Aelred makes everything possible with his love and support.

This book is dedicated to Miss Kilmartin (whose first name I never knew) and Dr Robert Hume, two influential teachers whose love of English and History respectively has shaped the lives of hundreds of schoolchildren, including me.

The Silversmith's Wife

Sophia Tobin

'A self-assured, page-turning debut which leaves you guessing until the last – a great read' *Daily Mail*

The year is 1792 and it's winter in Berkeley Square. As the city sleeps, the night-watchman keeps a cautious eye over the streets and another eye in the back doors of the great and the good. Then one fateful night he comes across the body of Pierre Renard, the local silversmith, lying dead, his throat cut and his valuables missing. It could be common theft, committed by one of the many villains who stalk the square, but as news of the murder spreads, it soon becomes clear that Renard had more than a few enemies, all with their own secrets to hide.

At the centre of this web is Mary, the silversmith's wife. Ostensibly theirs was an excellent pairing, but behind closed doors their relationship was a dark and at times sadistic one and when we meet her, Mary is withdrawn and weak, haunted by her past and near-mad with guilt. Will she attain the redemption she seeks and what, exactly, does she need redemption for . . . ?

Rich, intricate and beautifully told, this is a story of murder, love and buried secrets.

Available now in print, eBook and eAudio

SIMON &
SCHUSTER

The Widow's Confession

Sophia Tobin

Broadstairs, Kent, 1851. Once a sleepy fishing village, now a select sea-bathing resort, this is a place where people come to take the air, and where they come to hide.

Delphine and her cousin Julia have come to the seaside with a secret, one they have been running from for years. The clean air and quiet outlook of Broadstairs appeal to them and they think this is a place they can hide from the darkness for just a little longer. Even so, they find themselves increasingly involved in the intrigues and relationships of other visitors to the town.

But this is a place with its own secrets, and a dark past. And when the body of a young girl is found washed up on the beach, a mysterious message scrawled on the sand beside her, the past returns to haunt Broadstairs and its inhabitants. As the incomers are drawn into the mystery and each others' lives, they realize they cannot escape what happened here years before . . .

A compelling story of secrets, lies and lost innocence . . .

Available now in print, eBook and eAudio

SIMON & SCHUSTER

The Vanishing

Sophia Tobin

'Think *Wuthering Heights* or *Jane Eyre*, but ten times darker ...
One to curl up by the fire with on a windy night' *Stylist*

On top of the Yorkshire Moors, in an isolated spot carved out
of a barren landscape, lies White Windows, a house of shadows
and secrets. Here lives Marcus Twentyman, a hard-drinking
but sensitive man, and his sister, the brisk widow, Hester.

When runaway Annaleigh first meets the Twentymans, their
offer of employment and lodgings seems a blessing. Only
later does she discover the truth. But by then she is already
in the middle of a web of darkness and intrigue, where
murder seems the only possible means of escape ...

'Undeniably page-turning' *Mail on Sunday*

Available now in print, eBook and eAudio

SIMON &
SCHUSTER